Satan's Eyes

Satan's Eyes

Vincent Havelund

iUniverse, Inc.
New York   Bloomington

This is a work of fiction. All of the characters, names, incidents, organizations, and dialogue in this novel are either the products of the author's imagination or are used fictitiously.

iUniverse books may be ordered through booksellers or by contacting:

iUniverse
1663 Liberty Drive
Bloomington, IN 47403
www.iuniverse.com
1-800-Authors (1-800-288-4677)

Because of the dynamic nature of the Internet, any Web addresses or links contained in this book may have changed since publication and may no longer be valid. The views expressed in this work are solely those of the author and do not necessarily reflect the views of the publisher, and the publisher hereby disclaims any responsibility for them.

ISBN: 978-1-4401-6187-2 (sc)
ISBN: 978-1-4401-6188-9 (ebook)

Printed in the United States of America

iUniverse rev. date: 09/02/2009

Author's Profile:

The Author is New Zealand born but has lived in Australia since 1970, including quite a long period in America and Europe. A lot of his travel has been as a financial Missionary in America and the Philippine's. His work has been mainly as a financier for an Australian Developer, but he has always had a yen to write books. Now in retirement he has authored five books that he has now had published, and ready to be sold. 'He has six adult off spring and a growing team of Grandchildren'.

Introduction:

A successful business man becomes enmeshed with a Drug Gang when one of the company executives is found to have stolen the companies' identity to import 100 kgs of cocaine from Mexico into Australia. Then several other executives are found in the same gang and the company has obviously become infested with corrupt officials. Several are killed and the businessman narrowly escapes when a car bomb misfires and he escapes, but is badly injured.

He makes a decision to sell out all of his company shares, and sets up a new business specifically to attempt to get revenge on the leaders of the Drug Gang, but finds the structure is really controlled by the Mafia in Chicago. They are going to attempt to buy out his old company in an attempt to import drugs through New Zealand for re export to Australia and America.

His new business is successful beyond his wildest dreams, and he finds he has unlimited resources to set up a counter gang to battle the Mafia. Because he has no knowledge of what he is trying to do, he has to set up a total new management structure, but finds he is getting out of his depth, and that money and revenge isn't really to his taste. After he finds the Mafia have executed several of their own people because of his gang's subversive activities his negative feelings strengthen, and he again moves to sell his new business. He sets up a new structure with the intent to continue battling the Mafia Drug Lords, but without the direct responsibility being his alone.

CHAPTER 1

The early years.

Jason Andrews had led a charmed business life, everything he had done in his business had been successful. His success has made him an attraction to the media and he is constantly being featured in all media outlets, printed and electronic. He was again in the middle of a corporate takeover bid and once again it seemed his calculations were correct, and he was going to succeed. The run of success was soon to end, and he had some difficult situations in the near future with Cocaine imported in his name, but this was in the future for now another takeover success was near. Although he had made his name as a businessman his life was to change dramatically and he finds himself fighting the Mafia in Chicago who decide they want to take over his company. Unfortunately he finds himself in a dramatic fight to the death, after his assassination is ordered from Chicago and he barely escapes with his life, but only after eight months in hospital under an assumed name, 'The Mafia thinks he is dead and their attempt to kill him had been successful'.

For the present the media was in full attack mode, Jason Andrews they stormed on T/V and in the print, will lose this time! He has gone too far and he will suffer, he is going to lose a fortune of hard earned Cooperate Developments Ltd Investments money? It was the years end for 1998 and Jason Andrews was in the news headlines again, and for his Shareholders it was going to be all bad according to the Australian media! His company Cooperate Developments Ltd had moved again to take over another company, the iconic National Airline; and the media was attacking their most successful company takeover specialist, once again with all of the venom they could produce. Cooperate Developments Ltd was a firm they loved to attack, even though their business analysts knew what they often accused, the Company and Jason Andrew's of doing was all not fully understandable to them and was therefore often unfair in content.

Jason Andrews had been successful for many years, and now he was reaching the pinnacle of his career, but he wasn't really happy. He hated the media and their constant haranguing of everything he did, he had nicknamed them Satan's Eyes, and he was constant in his dislike of all sections of the media. He had amassed a fortune, but he freely admitted that it was more good luck than skill, he said he just seemed to know when he was doing the right things, and he had had very few setbacks in his career. He had always donated every year a lot of money to several charities, but when he was congratulated on his good works he just smiled and said, "Yes well that's all tax deductible!"

The Cartoonist at the Australian News had had a field day, he in particular loved to ridicule Cooperate Developments Ltd and its leader, but then that's what cartoonists do isn't it? He had pictured Cooperate Developments Ltd as a pirate boat, that in the middle of one of its voyage's had sprung a huge leak, and was sinking fast. There was the captain with the proverbial patch over one eye, ready to jump overboard with a huge bundle of money in his arms singing, goodbye "Me Hearties," to bad but there is only room for me in the dinghy, so its time I left you all. Jason looked at the cartoon and let out a big laugh, in only hours metaphorically speaking, he would be able to spit in that mugs face when he had won again, and the shareholders would earn good bonuses with their dividends, at the end of the year once again? This would be the fifth year straight that Cooperate Developments Ltd would pay increased dividends to their shareholders, plus there would be a big jump in the share values!

The Media claimed Jason was a womanizer of the most rotten caliber the media all hinted, but since he wasn't married maybe there was a reason they all wandered nastily, maybe he didn't like girls after all? Maybe the many women he squired around the night spots, was just a front? It was all so interesting, what were his preferences they asked Cooperate Developments Ltd had some pretty boys on the staff, and who really did the hiring around at Cooperate Developments Ltd it was all as nasty as the media could be without leaving themselves open to court slander charges?

Cooperate Developments Ltd and its flamboyant Managing Director Jason Andrews; were always hot news! They all believed that this time Jason was going to fail and fall flat on his pretty face; the media was busy forecasting and enjoying the fall, which they were certain this time would happen. This time they all chorused in delight; Jason Andrews will cost his shareholders a lot of money! His offer they shouted; was just too low and therefore arrogant rubbish which was so typical of Cooperate Developments Ltd; and Andrew's attitude to their corporate victims. This was typical Aussie style of knocking down the tall poppies, and Andrews and his company Cooperate Developments Ltd; were certainly tall poppies, they in return referred to the media as Satan's Eyes, mainly because Jason Andrews hated the media with a vengeance. Jason had started from humble beginnings in Blacktown, one of the outer western suburbs of Sydney NSW, and had over the years established himself as an expert on company takeovers, and then stripping off the parts that his company didn't want and selling them, normally for very large profits. He had often been criticized by the media for his very clever strategies, and they were always predicting he would fail for reasons best worked out by their own experts.

But time and again Jason Andrews had been successful, and had made huge profits for the investors! The value of the broken parts of companies he had bought was worth far more than the whole. In every break up case he had provided big profits for his shareholders and himself. He laughed at the so called experts that was what Cooperate Developments Ltd paid him big fees to do, make profits and the bigger the better, the only ones who disagreed was the media and to hell with them they didn't know what they were talking or writing about anyhow? Jason had become so used to the media continually baying for his blood to flow in a failed takeover, that he often said that it was because he had Satan's Eyes watching, that he got inspiration and that was what made him successful.

Jason as he sat and waited for the acceptances to start flowing in felt just so pleased anticipating those news papers critics, who would have to retract their silly lead comments in tomorrow's morning's headlines. As for those foppish T/V news readers male and female, they didn't have a brain between the lot of them, who cared what they had to say actions not bulldust words, were what mattered, and Cooperate Developments Ltd; and Andrews created plenty of action.

Jason Andrew's only aim it was claimed; was profits for himself; he found this very funny, if in the process of making money for himself others made money too, what he asked could be the problem? Cooperate Developments Ltd; shares had been rising from the time of the first float when he had sold over 25 million by $1.00 shares at $1.00. the price of those shares were trading at $5.00 within 12 months and having since issued another 475 million ordinary shares since then, they were selling at $12.50 to $14.00 and rising.

The evening news channels were having a field day; this time they trumpeted Andrews will fail, his offer price is way too low, and anyhow the company he was after this time was too good for him and his low life associates, at Cooperate Developments Ltd; Investments. How they asked could such low life company run Australia's National Airline, this was an iconic company a National Treasure etc. All this in spite of Cooperate Developments Ltd; now owning huge assets accumulated over the last 25 years, and never having missed paying dividends and for the past ten years record dividends, getting bigger every year.

As the market's and the media seethed with anticipation of the outcome of the offer, Jason Andrews was the epitome of confidence. He had cheekily put out a news flash that Cooperate Developments Ltd; would be winning a good investment for a holding asset, and that the airline would fit in well with the company's management methods this win, he suggested would make Cooperate Developments Ltd, an Iconic company it must do since it would own an Icon. This further outraged the media and the analysts, as they as always did their utmost to ridicule Jason Andrews. He was the Managing Director and the Chief Executive Officer of the Cooperate Developments Ltd group of companies, but he was also the company's founder and still owned 25% of the issued shareholding. There was another four Directors, but they only ever endorsed what Jason was doing, he was the one who made the company big chunks of money, so why would they ever question him they had no intention to attack their money making machine. The company had built up an excellent administration to run its conglomerate, Jason wasn't involved with that side of the business he was the takeover expert and that work was left to him and his PA with help when needed from the executive team. As long as Jason kept making so much money for them why would they question him, leave him to do his job they thought was their best policy, and the share holders agreed.

The results had now come through and there was going to be a big celebration at the companies head office (Corporate Developments Ltd -CDL) in Sydney Australia. The bid was successful, the offer for the Australian Major Airline, (The Offshore Kangaroo Ltd (OKL) had been accepted by a majority of the airlines share holders. The Managing Director of Jason Cooperate Developments Ltd Andrews (JA) was being feted as a financial Guru. Against all media predictions, the Cooperate Developments Ltd offer had been accepted by 80% of the OKL shareholders. In a few days when the contracts were signed, Cooperate Developments Ltd would own an airline, in fact Australia's major airline. Everyone in the company was elated, this would be a great boost to the Cooperate Developments Ltd Investments every one of the executives were so excited.

Trading in both stocks on market had been suspended for three days, but now the suspension would be lifted and trading would restart. What the media had not factored into their intense speculation; was that Cooperate Developments Ltd was a far better managed company than the airline, so Cooperate Developments Ltd had won. Cooperate Developments Ltd also had a very large loan from an American Insurance company, and had lots of money to spend; some had been used to buy the Airline, but even so the leverage was only about 45% which could be dangerous on market, but there were built in insurance measures that JA had set up and the local traders knew Cooperate Developments Ltd shares were dangerous to play with.

Cooperate Developments Ltd had grown steadily over the previous twenty five years, and was now quite a major company on the Australian Stock Market. They had acquired over many years, a lot of property and looked set to keep buying, there was no end of their appetite for growth, and their retail division was now very large specializing in food, child care and general merchandise.

The acquisition of an airline was a prestigious one for the company, and would lift their profile in the words of Jason Andrews, very nicely! This would be such a drama now as the media kept trying to make Cooperate Developments Ltd; look bad but their attacks were useless this Investment company; was a very well managed one. It would be claimed that Cooperate Developments Ltd; and its Managing Director JA as unsuitable to own the Australian National Airline, but only the media believed that, or at least pretended they believed. Not enough skill to run our National Airline they would shout, Pirates at the helm others would say! But who cared certainly not JA and his company they had won again and to hell with the media, most of all who talked but had little knowledge. What Jason found the most upsetting was the silly comments on the electronic media, when young men and women tried to sound so knowledgeable, yet the more they commented the sillier they sounded, the print media when the comments were from the financial reporters, was usually quite sound but some of the comments printed and electronic, by others with no knowledge often sounded just so silly?

Jason Andrews was feeling terrific, he had withstood all of the flack that had been dredged up, on the stock market as well as the media, and still won by a huge margin he was the darling of his shareholders, they were the important ones not the critics?

It was almost twenty five years, since the chairman of Cooperate Developments Ltd, JA had started out with nothing, and it was a credit to his hard work, that he had grown the company as he had done with integrity and learned knowledge. He often said that his success was 90% luck and 10% knowledge, that was fine all his shareholders really knew, especially those who had been in Cooperate Developments Ltd; from the start was he had made them a lot of money, luck or knowledge they didn't care.

Jason from the start had had a burning desire to succeed not so much for the money; but for what he felt money could do, he had wanted to succeed so he could help others who had been born in the low class areas, such as he had done himself. He had for years watched in the newspapers as huge sums of money had been made and wondered if those monies made the owners, great happiness mainly because he couldn't imagine it would. He had started off with no money no knowledge but a lot of luck.

His first purchase was when he had bought a general store on the basis of a promissory note, for which he was due to, have to pay for in 12 months. He had known what a promissory note was, and he felt he could do well, if he got a chance but was very surprised when his offer was accepted, gosh they must have been real desperate was his only thought back then. He was right the shop was losing money, and the owners were very happy to have off loaded their liability. Their thoughts had been simple if this young bloke wins we will get some money for our shop, if he fails we have lost nothing because we had nothing but losses anyhow.

Jason had immediately borrowed against that first store, and bought another four stores for which he had again issued a promissory for the agreed price. He figured he had found a formula that worked so why not keep pushing his luck, when it worked again he was so happy he felt like a business Titan already. He was doing well now he had five shops that lost money, but he didn't even know that was the case all he understood was that he now owned five shops. He had a lot of money going through his cash registers, but because he hadn't paid for the shops he seemed to have money to spare, he was just lucky he had no accountant, to point out he was actually losing.

He then valued his now five shops in his own mind as a group and they were by now worth far than they were originally or so he thought; in fact they were a pretty motally group. When he had bought them because of how he had bought them with no money. Then he had paid for his first promissory note, by borrowing against the four new shops he had bought, he thought it was great using other people's money to keep growing, so he thought why not do it again, as far as he was concerned so far he had five shops and they had cost him nothing. By forecasting his cash flow over twelve months, twice as high as he really should, because he had the cash flowing in for five shops, not just the one he had paid for his business and things looked fantastic.

He immediately bought another ten stores! Again he had issued a third promissory note on the ten new shops and paid of the second promissory note which he had issued on the four stores. He now had the cash from fifteen stores but only owned five, total daily sales went into his company, and he now had a sound cash flow, he was riding the crest of a business wave. Because all of the shops were all stocked up when he bought them, in reality he was losing more money than ever now, but it didn't show because the cash flow masked the losses. The big problem was really that he hadn't paid even a deposit on most of his stores, and he wasn't allowing for the time when he had to pay? His bankers didn't know he had a debt on ten stores, and that he had only paid for five stores the other ten were still owned as a debt still to be paid for, now he had 15 stores but only five in his company, and ten in his own name. Now he was taking his daily cash from the 15 stores, he had paid of the first five, so the business was now looking very good, the cash flow as far as the banks were concerned were impressive, but he wasn't borrowing of them anyhow, he was privately funded. All the banks were seeing was a strong cash flow from what they thought was five stores, not fifteen the bank manager only thought he was an up and coming Tycoon which he was?

Finally he bought another 20 stores and issued the fourth promissory note using the same strategy again, he had simply rolled the same system over again this made it four times and, further bluffed his banks. He appeared to have bought 15 stores but his income was very impressive. He had now paid for 15 stores had a promissory note out on another 20 stores, and the cash flowing into his company account for 35 stores, but this move bought his ratios down he now had less than two to one store, whereas before he bought the twenty stores the ratio had been 3 to one, suddenly his cash flow as a ratio of stores was moving backward so he needed to sell out and if he didn't sell real quick his losses were going to catch up to him. Jason had suddenly realized he wasn't as smart as he thought and that he was on the way to big trouble.

This was the background in later years, for which the media justified their constant harassment of Cooperate Developments Ltd and Jason Andrews. But that was in the future after he had become a wealthy man, by then the media was just a joke, and Jason enjoyed nothing more than reading what a rogue he was? He also loved reading the financial pages; and seeing Cooperate Developments Ltd Investments often listed as the top performing company, for the day's trading. He loved that because he knew so many of his rivals hated to see Cooperate Developments Ltd way up on top of the charts. But now back to the start up!

Having now achieved an apparently sound business, but himself realizing the flow was now reversed he offered for sale the 35 shops, on which he had one unpaid promissory note for the 20 shops. He wined and dined would be buyers, but to no effect the result was always the same, they all had accountants who told them those shops are a disaster? Thanks for the opportunity but not interested! The next six months were most frustrating as he wined, dined, cajoled; and tried every idea he could think of as a way to sell his loss making shops, it was the worst time of his new business career.

The shops appeared as if were making quite a good profit on the money he had spent. But since he had put in none of his own money because he had none he was not earning very much, in the sense that he was really leveraged all of the way, even though as a group the value had doubled, he thought, that didn't create cash in his pocket. For a while he was flummoxed what was he to do with the shops that he couldn't sell? He now understood such a small group of shops were hard to make viable, at least 100 were needed to be able to bulk buy and get the best discounts; and without those discounts his retail prices were too high and his real position was continuing losses?

Then one day he got a bright idea! In one of the daily papers he had seen that a national retail chain was up for sale, it was quite a large company and had over 200 retail stores division nationwide, they wanted to sell privately or as a group with the buyer taking over the division and acquiring the tax losses, which were substantial?

He quickly set up a new public company and issued an offer prospectus, he then sold that company his 35 shops, and in other words he had sold his 35 shops to himself! He had meanwhile arranged to buy the 200 shops which he had optioned; and then sold them plus his 35 shops a total of 235 shops to the new public company he had just formed Cooperate Developments Ltd?

His offer was very fair and reasonable and again he had twelve months to pay for the 200 shops, which he was sure he would be able to achieve, by way of the public issue.

With the now 235 stores which he valued as he was entitled to at their true new value, which was double what he had paid for them. With the volume he was buying now he was sound making profits at last, but it had been pure luck, he had no idea what he had been doing? He then spent a lot of money to publicize the name of his company Cooperate Developments Ltd Investments of which he still owned 100%? Jason now poised himself and the company to sell off the shops as Franchised Agreements, with Cooperate Developments Ltd being the franchisor, the key here was that Jason was still the single shareholder, and the profits all accrued to himself.

A new Franchise company was set up fully owned by Cooperate Developments Ltd and the franchises were offered for sale by Jason privately through his company Cooperate Developments Ltd which had made very big profits. After he had all of his plans in place he now followed through with the prospectus offer and sold off 75% of the share capital issued at $1.00 each and waited to see what happened. The price rose first to top out at $4.00 and kept rising until it was just under $8.00 and that was within a month of the shares being offered. Those who had bought at $1.00 right from the issue start had made big profits, which they could cash out if they wished; the original issue had been well over subscribed. In simple terms Jason had made a double killing first the 235 shops had doubled in value, then the Franchise offer had bought in another large profit, which he had sold out a 75% share and still he owned 25% of the company, but he had a lot of cash which he had received from selling his 75%. That cash he could work with and he could if he wanted borrow a lot off his bank but only if he wanted that type of loans

Jason then decided to take a break he was then 30 YOA and recently married, so he and his new wife Jean left Australia and spent six months traveling, on their Honey Moon around the world. He also wanted to learn how to carry his company to greater heights of prosperity, using the art of the American style business, which included sophisticated financial manipulation? But when he had had time to look at the American methods closely, he decided their type of company manipulation would not work in Australia, so he settled down and was satisfied to work using the system he understood, which was Australian style conservatism? A visit to London taught him how to work with currencies, and earn an income just from currency trading and margin borrowing It was all a wonderful new world of mirrors, what you see is not always true. JA was a very good student and learned quickly, he returned with his Wife to Australia knowing how easy it was to use the mirrors of deceit to make lots of money! And he was determined to use his knowledge to the full advantage for himself. In the meantime Cooperate Developments Ltd had been buying and franchising off all of the general merchandise stores they could find. They now owned over 800 stores, accumulated within the last two years all franchised, and they were aiming for a total of 2,000. All of this had been achieved by a business man who had shown he had the Midas touch but had little or no knowledge right from the start.

On returning to Australia JA decided he needed an avenue of foreign cash flow, what better he thought than a couple of export meat companies, so he immediately set out looking for targets he could buy. This proved to be a lot harder than buying retail stores; even the small meat companies were very profitable and therefore hard to buy in Australia. He had a look at the NZ meat companies, but found them even harder to buy. As far as shareholding was concerned in NZ it seemed to be Aussie keep out, so he withdrew and didn't bother with NZ in his search for takeover targets. Jason had spent a lot of time learning the idiosyncrasies of the meat industry, and was certain there was big money to be made if he got Cooperate Developments Ltd; to invest at a proper level, which meant at least $10 million.

He made an offer for two quite large meat companies; which was way over their true value, but from which he could make very good profits. There followed many complaints from those customers which had been buying of his newly acquired meat businesses, so Cooperate Developments Ltd; offered them the same meat orders as before but at cheaper prices. He then arranged to write and sign contracts, with New York based agents at higher prices! This increase was meant to show an increased net profit; to the new owners which were now Cooperate Developments Ltd; Investments. Jason Andrews had spent a lot of time and money on the meat company livestock; and the meat industry in general, it was a very successful blend into the retail franchise group Cooperate Developments Ltd; now owned. But in this case there was no retail it was all export, with a local wholesale division, selling only to hotels and restaurants. The amount of money that had been used to purchase, and then to finance the meat export sales was very large, and it was now necessary to borrow heavily! This was done with a large loan from an American Insurance company; that had to be repaid in five years? The cash flow generated by the export meat business showed a net profit on sales of 25% so that even though the loan repayment times, that is usual with exported products were long, the profits to redeem the bond was available within three years! Instead of paying back the loan Cooperate Developments Ltd; had bought another two meat export companies! This meant that Cooperate Developments Ltd was now a major meat exporter, but not yet involved in processing, that would come later.

All those years ago when Jason had started up as a trader none including himself, would have dreamed he would achieve what he did, but whenever someone expressed admiration his answer was, yes and the harder I work than smarter I become. A friend one day said he should write his memoirs for posterity so he decided he would, and did so more as a way to keep him occupied. It would he thought be fun to give some misleading answers to some of the sillier members of the media, who had always insisted he was a disgrace to his profession as a businessman. No major businessman had ever come from Blacktown the outer west of Sydney and been as successful as he was becoming, but he knew he had a long way to go before he could claim his place as a top level business man in the eyes of all around him, most still thought of him as that Blacktown guy?

The pet hate in Jason's life had become media analysts, most of who seemed to think they knew more about his business activities, than he did himself and yet they understood very little. Jason knew well he could be completely honest in his memoirs, and the media would still read deception, into everything he said because they were determined, no one from Blacktown could be so successful without cheating? And so irregardless of everything he could do to show it was all genuine good business, he was still considered to be some type of smart Alec crook. The few that did support him could never be heard above the clamor of those who were determined, that he had to be stopped the trouble was they didn't know how to do this, which made them even louder in their condemnation. When he had finished his biography he decided to publish it, more as an answer to his critics than anything else. The uproar the book caused was worth the effort to him, because he achieved record sales which meant a lot of people had read his point of view, and with that he was content, the public could choose. Even his most ardent detractors in the media, were silenced at least for a while which couldn't last, because people like Jason created interest and therefore sold news. He was actually a real asset to the media because the ordinary people loved him and wanted to know what he was doing, he might have come from Blacktown but the ordinary folk loved him.

CHAPTER 2

Starting Work.

Jason had been born into a family of laborers, his father had been a brickies laborer and his mother had been a waitress in a full service restaurant, both had been employed in this way for years. They had both worked long hours for many years, but had never been able to accumulate any money; all if any extra money they earned had been spent on cigarettes and booze, which they both enjoyed immensely but whatever their mistakes they had created an extremely loving family. They had a Govt; commission home which they had never wanted to buy, with the back yard heaped high with liquor and beer bottles! Throughout Jason's young life, there had been constant weekend parties at his home, and all of the siblings had loved their happy go lucky lifestyle. They had all been boisterous and very keen on the constant parties at home as they were growing up, and now most were married they all lived the same way. They partied saved no money but they sure as hell enjoyed life, and they were all proud of their parents, after a life spent working hard the Andrews were a terrific family, the love generated among them when they were all together was tangible and real.

There had been four children and all except Jason had been the same as their parents, smoking and boozing laborers. In spite of; or maybe because of their common interests, they were a very close family unit; Jason's preference for a different style of life made no difference to his inclusion in family gatherings etc; the entire Andrews family was a unit of one.

Jason was the youngest of the four but not spoiled, it was obvious from his early years he was going to be the odd one out in his family. At school he was an A grade student and his grades in Math's was always very high, but he excelled in all areas of his schooling. But was only average at sport, and never made the college team in any sport, even though he tried hard because he had wanted to be one of the in crowd of the sports clique, but that was only motivated by the girls, who hung around the sport stars of the time? Jason showed an early taste for beautiful women, and they showed a reciprocal liking for him, his looks they said would be his fortune, they were wrong his mental acuity would be his future success? Jason was never aware of his natural good appearance, he could always be seen with his nose in a book of some type he seemed to read so fast that others would chide him that he didn't really read, just browsed through, but if asked what a book was all about he could always quote accurately what he had just read. He was an attractive young man, just over 1.8 meters tall, an athletic build, blond hair and startling blue eyes, as well as well as a nicely shaped mouth, around which a ready smile always seemed to lurk, and from which often burst forth spontaneously a wholesome smile. It was early obvious that Jason had a gift for business, but he wasn't to going be the hard working hands on type, from the start he was obviously more inclined towards financial gymnastics, at which he became sp good! He knew his near future could only be on the basis of working for others, so he went looking for menial work until he could find a way through to becoming an employer entrepreneur. He had heard that Mc Donald's restaurants had great training programs for Youths, so his first job at the age of 16 had been for them. The work was easy and the training was good, he worked at a company operated store; which were not as strict as the franchised stores, but still working to Mc Donald's rules. He really loved his two years at McDonald's because there were lots of girls his own age, and it was true he did learn a lot about how to work properly in a team environment, much of what he learned stayed with him for the rest of his life. . From the start the, as was company policy, they all received training about how to work properly, and It was while employed at McDonald's he had his first love encounter? She was a gorgeous girl of his own age and he soon fell deeply in love! He could neither sleep nor eat, he was at seventeen YOA having his first real love experience, and he was in heaven, asleep or awake all he could think of was this female vision, but It took him two months to become brave enough to ask her for a date, and he was elated when she agreed! He took her out for dinner then to the movies it was all so wonderful, then he was very surprised when he got her back to her home. Her name was Glenda and when they got back to her home she suggested he could climb into her bedroom through the window, her parents wouldn't know he was there, but she would lock her bedroom door anyhow. With his knees trembling he found it was as she had told him, really easy to get through the window and into her room, and there was no reaction from the rest of the house. He couldn't believe his luck his girl loved him, that was why she had invited him into her bed, or so his inexperienced mind thought. Jason had been a virgin so he had to be led, but his girl was an expert; she took him to such heights of delight that he had never imagined possible, but as in all things Jason was a quick learner he learned to return the art of sexual achievement quickly, so that his partner also achieved an orgasm to their mutual delight.

When after two hour of delights and exploration of the female anatomy, he climbed out of the bedroom and went home, he was floating on air. He couldn't wait to get to work the next day, but was very sad when he found she was rostered off work for that day. It was going to be several days before they were both on a work shift together, he felt so dejected even to the extent of actually feeling sick. Then the next day he was at work feeling sorry for himself when Glenda walked in, and came to greet him with a big smile. Jason try as he might couldn't conceal his delight, it was all he could do to restrain himself from taking her in his arms; and passionately kissing her, immediately. Over the next two weeks he took Glenda out to the movies several times, and it was becoming just natural, to climb through that window when they arrived at her house? He told Glenda he loved her every day, but was disappointed when she never responded the same way! In the end she was at least honest, and told him she just enjoyed the sex she had never, she told him loved any of her boyfriends. Jason was really shattered, but when she told him a week later it was all over, and it was time to move on he was at least prepared. Belatedly he had found to his disappointment that Glenda had an appetite for sex; that included encounters with any male, at any time, her dalliance with Jason was just another adventure to Glenda, and it was time to find another partner. It had been good but hey there were a lot of males out there, and she wanted to sample as many as possible and as quickly as she could? This disappointment slowed down his hitherto constant search for a steady girlfriend, but it was in his nature to keep trying? After his experiences with Glenda he had a steady flow of short term experiences; he became far more cautious in future before professing his love to any girl, he kept his first impressions very much to himself and found that his girlfriends were quite prone to talking about love. He now just smiled and kept his own feelings private, he felt more secure that way, and was not always worrying about how his date of the moment felt?

He now realized that an easy sexual encounter wasn't an indication of emotional love, it was a mere adventure and he needed to understand that simple fact of life and go on from there, he now knew that just as many females were as promiscuous as the male gender were, it was just that normally but not always the male of the species was the aggressor. He soon found that quite often the art of the female was to make it look as if she was being pursued, until the chase was over then the truth became obvious; when the male suddenly found himself caught?

At 18 YOA he had enrolled in the military, he wanted to get any possible national military commitment over and done with, so that he knew he was free to go and do anything he wanted, without wandering if the military was going to reach out and claim him unexpectedly. Jason had enrolled in the army; and much to his surprise found he loved the experience, even if it took him a while to get used to making his own bed, polishing his boots etc. For a short time he even considered re enlisting for a second term, but he quickly decided this would not satisfy his desire for the excitements of life, which he had now discovered he liked.

At no stage had he ever turned his back on his family, the major experience he had had with them, was a closeness and love all from one to the other. His parent's one brother and two sisters were very close! In spite of Jason being different than the rest of the family, when they were all together they were as one. Togetherness had always been central to their existence, and if anything Jason's difference was admired by the Andrews family, they had always encouraged him and were very proud of their baby brother who was so different, all of them knew instinctively that Jason would be very successful at whatever he chose to do with his life, but they never dreamed he would reach the heights of success that he did?

After he left the army Jason had an assortment of short time jobs, not because he couldn't keep a job; his constant changing was his desire to get as much different work experience's as possible. He even for a short time worked as a line worker at the Melbourne, Ford Motor plant! All told over a period of fourteen years until the age of 30, he had been employed in over twenty industries. This had been deliberate; he looked on this period as his apprenticeship, for what he really wanted to do in his career, but he had no idea what it was he really wanted to do with his life? The purchase of that first shop and what followed wasn't planned or premeditated in any way; it all just seemed to happen in spite of him and not because of him. It seemed to him he just did everything automatically, but whatever he did it was very successful and he was a self made multi millionaire before he really knew what he had done, by the age of thirty five.

CHAPTER 3

Expansion.

After the setting up of the retail shops into an effective group, it had been easy to keep adding to the Cooperate Developments Ltd; retail franchises the system was now firmly in place and all the company managers had to do was to keep buying up shops as they were put up for sale, anywhere in Australia. Within another two years after Jason had returned from overseas, the retail shops under the Cooperative Developments Ltd; umbrella had been increased to over 2,000 franchised units nationwide, just by judicious buying and then selling off the franchise. Some owners of shops just wanted to buy a franchise so as to become a part of the group chain, and get the buying advantages there from. The export meat business was also flourishing, and very profitable, with sales growing exponentially faster than the retail division with a far higher net profit, those two businesses alone made Cooperate Developments Ltd; a sound company. The franchised shops was as good a business as could be found Cooperate Developments Ltd; carried no risk and reaped all of the big profits while the capital asset grew, just as quickly as the cash flow.

Jason had set up secret accounts to hide profits, because he wanted to safeguard himself and the company, but also to delay taxes that would be due once declared. He was well aware that there could be future aggressive takeover by transferring profits so he was setting up a cash asset into a separate company? This company was owned by the Cooperate Developments Ltd; Investment group but it didn't show as an asset. This was a policy he continued to follow, and over the years these secret accounts grew steadily, until there were many hundreds of millions of dollars hidden in that account, which of course had to be held off shore in a tax haven? This transfer of profits was quite easy he had learned that little secret when he was learning all about currency while he was in London; he had also learned a lot about tax havens and how to use them? This was his policy of building up a reserve of money which in the end saved Cooperate Developments Ltd and gave his shareholders a windfall profit. Years later when he needed a slush fund for self protection it was there and was to be used to counter attack, he had cause to be very happy that umbrella account was there and could be used, much to the chagrin of his business enemies. That little safety investment allowed the door to be opened to self protection, but unfortunately also several bizarre murders, which all had to be revenged and took him years of hard work to redress, but to which he in the end triumphed?

Cooperate Developments Ltd; Investments next moved to expand the export meat part of the asset port folio which was proving more profitable than expected; and they acquired in the process another three meat export businesses. Cooperate Developments Ltd had recently bought a full processing plant which James the new CEO had managed to manipulate. Jason had not been involved in creating these last four takeover's he had retired from the CEO; position and was now acting as a self employed consultant, who was just another shareholder in Cooperate Developments Ltd; Investments. Cooperate Developments Ltd; had now become involved in the killing and processing of animals, beef, sheep and pigs as well as boning and the export of the meat. This meant they now had a full range of abattoirs products, such as bone meal, casings wool skins and hides (sausage skins) etc; they then created a local sale for many of their abattoir products and now had a faster cash flow, which made it so they needed far less loan money and of course meant the business was now cheaper and easier to finance.

Jason was in no hurry and while he was waiting for another target to chase, he simply watched the stock exchange, for any company that was foolish enough to accumulate assets that were not performing at full potential. The usual type of company that Cooperate Developments Ltd; wanted to buy was one that was short on cash in the bank, but had a lot of assets this was the typical type of company that was in danger of takeover, and then being broken up. Often this type of company had started life as a family company and had grown well under the founder, but once the founder passed on or retired the new management lacked the original drive, but the founder's family normally still owned the majority share holding.

After 12 months of patient watching; a target came up, a big group that had become too big and hard to manage, a typical formerly private family company gone public many years earlier. This company THDL Developments was wallowing in its own cumbersome management systems! The company's main business; was as the owner of land to subdivide and sell, and it had been in the business for over 100 years. Since becoming public owned several years earlier the company had changed, first it had begun building houses and office blocks, and then it started building and owning high rise tenements, which was where the problems were now developing. When out of the blue Cooperate Developments Ltd; made a quick attack and bought up 10% of the shares, then announced a full bid the Media woke up to another of the Cooperate Developments Ltd; aggressive takeover attempts, and the war with the media was instantly in full swing.

The return on the huge amounts of money tied up in the THDL assets were yielding very poorly which was based on the books valued the company at, but the true return as Jason could see was even worse, this was a takeover dream for a company like Cooperate Developments Ltd; and big commissions for the architect Jason Andrews.

The media analysts had a field day again; they labeled Jason with every corporate misdemeanor they could think of, he was labeled as a modern day rogue. None allowed that he had pulled the original THDL shareholders out of a poor performing company and had made everybody including them a healthy profit, all they could see was the millions Jason; and Cooperate Developments Ltd; Investments had made from another strategic corporate move?

The cartoonists were at it again! Now they had Jason as a great big fat man, with dollar signs all over his paunch, saying "hell I should go on a diet all of this money is giving me heart burn" that was in The Australian. The Sydney Morning Herald was a big shark swimming around a with lot of little sharks, the big Shark is saying "hmm wonder which one will taste the best, its feeding time"

Cooperate Developments Ltd; had captured acceptances for almost 90% of the issued shares, the founders family being one of the first to accept the offer, there were several none performing subsidiaries to sell off but the major parts of the new acquisition was going to be kept, and a new Cooperate Developments Ltd; division created. It was only a week after that very successful company raid that a new Personal Assistant was hired to look after Jason's affairs, her name was Jean Brown, and in Jason's eyes she was really gorgeous. Jason feigned a lack of interest for over a week, but then couldn't help himself he started to talk to her, while still trying to conceal his interest in her. At first Jean was polite, but made it obvious she wasn't interested in her boss! Gradually over the following months, whenever he came into his office, which wasn't very often, Jason was always very courteous to Jean, never pushy even if he did look at her surreptitiously, whenever he got the chance.

Gradually Jean began to realize that he wouldn't try to take advantage of his position, so she started to loosen up towards him. One afternoon when he had come in after a business lunch, he had drunk a couple of glasses of wine and was feeling a little brave, with no hesitation he asked Jean out for Dinner and perhaps a Movie, she declined but did so with a big smile which encouraged him to try again. He asked again a week later, this time she accepted again with a big smile, and he was highly elated, but remembering the past he was very careful Jason had already decided this girl was special, and she would possibly be wife material. Jason had decided it was time to get married, but he had been unable to find someone to whom he could see a lifetime together, this one his new PA seemed to be just the type he was looking for, but she was several years younger than him?

CHAPTER 4

Marriage by Jean.

When Jason picked me up from my parents home, he did so in a small car so that neither his corporate position; nor wealth was showing, although of course I was aware of his true position. We had a great night out together; and we discovered that we were both from a simple family's? Mine was a strict Catholic family, while Jason's parents were agnostic, this I knew was going to be a problem in the future if our relationship should blossom out, my parents and siblings would be strongly against him. Jason had never thought of what religious beliefs he might have himself, but as we talked he quickly realized he definitely wasn't of the Catholic faith. This was much to my disappointment, but it made no difference at the start it was only a casual date now and again, we waited for some time, but began to realize we were falling in love with each other. The fact he wasn't a Catholic was a problem but a risk we had decided to take, I had spoken to my priest and he had warned me it was the wrong thing to do, but I decided it was my life not the priests, nor anyone else it was just me and Jason, assuming of course our relationship was to develop.

Jason definitely wasn't like the media made him out to be, he was a warm gentle person and constantly aware of the needs of those around him, since I was his personal assistant none were in a better position to get to know him than me. I had been out with several different men over the years, but witout exception they were mainly utter bores, most were totally absorbed with themselves. Jason was just so different he never tried to take advantage of his position as head of the company, and he was so delightfully respectful he was all most well bought up Catholic girls could hope for in a man of our own Faith. Sadly there was no one I could talk to about Jason, my own mother was horrified that I was going out with a man that to her was an atheist, and my father was violently opposed.

Regardless of their opposition I found that it was such a pleasure now to go to work, and on the days he was there it was always a great happy day. Jason was an extremely handsome man, probably a little over one hundred and eighty five centimeters tall quite well built, but didn't look as if he was a ball of muscle such as some men who train at a gym are. He was fair haired and had a ready smile that lit up his face in a friendly manner, whenever he does smile which is often. The most noticeable thing about Jason is how quickly he understands what is going on around him. Because it was my job to attend business meetings with him in the Board Room, and take notes, I was constantly amazed at how quickly he picked up the threads of any discussion and how rarely he really needed my notes.

Before long I began to look forward to our evenings out together and his slightest touch began to resonate through me, so that it was exciting just to be with him. Neither of us were great dancers, but I think it was just the electricity that seemed to engulf as we held each other, and created such intense feelings that meant we loved to dance. Jason wasn't a great talker he seemed to be happy just to sit and enjoy the moment, as we got closer it was me who created the chatter between us, but once he was started off he was great company.

Slowly but surely I began to realize I was falling in love with Jason, and I as a woman will knew he was falling on love with me to, but he tried hard not to be to forward with me, he treated me as if I could fall apart at any time which was nice but sometimes frustrating. We had some wonderful times together, we went out to a winery in the Hunter Valley one Sunday and had a wonderful time, first there was just strolling around some of the vineyards then, the wine tasting after which Jason bought 12 bottles of mixed types of wine. Then there was a wonderful meal served in the small but intimate restaurant attached to the winery. Jason was the epitome of good manners none would have ever guessed we had both grown up in the Blacktown area, myself in Doonside and Jason in Blacktown.

The following Sunday we went for a day trip on the Sydney Harbor and then up the Hawkesbury River, one doesn't know the beauty of Sydney unless one takes that trip just once. Neither of us had taken the trip before and Jason's enthusiasm was just so infectious, so that we both had a wonderful day During the entire day he was so solicitous trying to be sure I had just as much fun as he was having that it turned out to be an even better day than our trip into the Hunter Valley the previous weekend.

I had noticed that Jason was never ostentatious even though he could buy anything he wanted he never did; he seemed to always want to be sure we didn't stand out in any way in a crowd, and it was so nice. On the other hand in private he was just so generous, for example he would give large amounts of money to all and any well known Charity Group who was collecting money.

I was at first a little overwhelmed by his innate manners, he would always walk around and open my door when I was getting out of the car, then he would take my arm ever so gently and help me out. His touch was like electricity to me and whenever we touched even in little ways, I felt a sort of excitement surge through my entire body. His table manners were also impeccable I guessed he had learned these at his many business dinners, for a while it was a little hard to get used to eating out together, but with practice it became easy. Never once while I was in the learning phase did Jason make any comments, instead he politely guided me through until I was quite comfortable in company.

After we had been going out for three months Jason finally plucked up the courage to take my hand as we were walking, and for me it was such a joy, of course I never let him know all of these innermost joys, those were our delightful days of courting.

Neither of us are particularly sporting types, but we both loved to watch the sports channel on T/V whenever we could, Jason favored Rugby and Rugby League, whereas I favor Basketball and Swimming all sports we had played at school. The excitement wasn't in the sports it was the closeness as we sat side by side eating sweats and cheering for our chosen teams. We would just snuggle together and it was so warm and cozy at Jason's unit, more especially on the weekends we would spend hours in the evening enjoying ourselves. During all our times of courting and until we became engaged Jason never asked me to stay over, in fact I never did until after we were married. I must admit though Jason did make a few hints after we were engaged which I pretended not to hear and he never pursued.

I knew the special night had arrived and when he proposed it was without any hesitation that I had accepted him because after all it was no surprise, I had known he was going to do so for some time, in the very near future.

My family were against my marriage to Jason, my father warned me it would be very difficult; living with a man whose family, as well as himself were, soulless do nothing agnostic's Both of my parent's warned me that Jason might object to the children being bought up as Catholic's, and he would certainly not accept the family priest. They even almost panicked, at the thought that any children we would have, he might refuse that the priest, should christen the children in our church.

My family kicked up a real big fuss when I told them we were getting married in the little Salvation Army Church in Blacktown, both my Mother and Father were so upset and passed their annoyance on to my Siblings. They wanted to know quite naturally if the children would be bought up Catholic or not, then one night they had the family priest around and then there was a real upset. My entire family had come that evening and I knew it was going to be very difficult, when the Priest arrived as well obviously there was going to be an all out attempt to make us marry in the church. This I had decided I wouldn't ask Jason to do, not that I thought he would refuse, but because I felt we would be better making up our own minds and not being pushed by my family. I had found that Jason and his entire family were very close, all agnostic and all party types, so I felt there would be resistance from them all to Catholics and in time it was confirmed that my intuition was right.

We were courting for over six months, before he even kissed me; because he knew I was special he wanted to do things right, but he himself was certainly no longer a virginal innocent? In his position Jason had any amount of ambitious girlfriends, but none could possibly love him as much as I did, if he lost all of his money today for me it would make no difference, I will love him until the day I die, no matter what his position in life could be. I was delighted with Jason's self restraint; there was no doubt of his manliness, so I respected his not wanting to jump into the nearest bed. There was no doubt he could afford to do anything he wanted, he had the wealth to buy anything, but he made no sexual advances whatsoever.

After all objections had been beaten back and my Father especially had had his temper tantrum, my Mother must have calmed him down, because our marriage went off without a hitch. It was just a very quiet affair Jason was almost terrified the media would find out and spoil the day, but the day was beautiful and sunny, the ceremony was nice and simple, then the reception afterwards was terrific, and we left without any noise except a few balloons on the bridal car.

CHAPTER 5

The honeymoon:

It was obvious that they were getting closer daily, the only problem was Jean's religion, there would be a problem with Jeans parents and her five siblings; they would find it hard to have an agnostic in the family. It was for this reason only, that Jason had not proposed. Finally his mother who could see her son was in love with Jean, told him to stop playing around, propose she had told Jason one night when they were alone, even when he explained the problem, she was adamant propose now, it' time she insisted? If Jean really does love you she will marry you, if she hesitates it means her priest is more important than you, if this is the case best find out now, and walk away?

The next time they were out Jason proposed and Jean without any hesitation accepted, that was the first time he had even kissed her, he was so determined not to make a silly mistake, he still remembered Glenda and how exciting her sexual lessons had been to him at the time? He had had many partners for sex after that! Jean was the first girl with whom he had tried to do nothing, and had been sure she was the one with whom he wanted to build a family, he didn't tell her he would love to have six children.

He was never going to forget the experience with Glenda; he wanted his wife to be his alone; not someone he had to share with the entire neighborhood males. He knew when he proposed Jean would marry him for himself, not for his money or his position, but strictly for himself. Jason knew instinctively Jean was going to marry him for the same reason he wanted to marry her, they loved each other. They were married in a Salvation Army Church within a month, and they then left for that prolonged six month honeymoon immediately.

There had been two days in Holland! The sight of the hundreds of small farm holdings, and the far harder methods of animal care was quickly evident, to Jason and his Wife; it was all so different than the large land holdings in Australia and even NZ. The farm lands looked so beautiful as they passed by and those huge windmills with their sails revolving endlessly looked so awesome. The boat rides around Amsterdam was nice, and the sight of the house; on one of the main roads that was only one and a half metres wide was amusing. All of the tourists on the boat loudly wondered, how the owners could live in what appeared to be such a cramped house. The skipper of the boat assured them all, the house was indeed lived in and wasn't just a tourist gimmick. Some of the churches in Holland they found uniquely interesting, and they spent time in Rotterdam the country's main port connecting to the North Sea.

They had travelled from Paris to Holland by train so as to see the countryside in a leisurely fashion. This had proved to be a good decision because they had the chance to see the farms; and the drainage system in first class comfort. All of the farm lands were well set up with drains, but the water level in every paddock was obviously very high. There was no need for fences as we know them down under, because the paddocks were all marked out by water drains, which were full of water up to about 8 inches below the paddock levels. There had been an amusing interlude with a German elderly man, who spoke a little English and Jason who spoke a little German. Between the two of them they had just managed to have a conversation much to Jean's amusement. The other thing they noticed was the area next to the railway tracks, were all set up into small gardens. All of these small plots of land were well kept and all planted with vegetables; the plants were all growing well and carefully tended. There was not bit of land wasted that Jason and his wife could see, during their total tour of Holland. (The Netherlands) There appeared to be some opportunities in Holland for the purchase of a listed company, Jason had played with the idea of making a bid, not for a serious attempt just for training purposes, but then decided against the idea it would be silly to win a company, then have to spend time in Holland which was so far away from Australia?

On the way back to Paris the Andrews had stopped off for two nights in Belgium, and during the evening they had gone for a walk. Jason had been interested when he happened to notice a team of council workers working on road repairs. He had commented much to his Wife's amusement, those fellows need to be careful, the Australian Union will come and tell them they are working way too hard; they had better slow down! Whats more if they don't slow down the Union will call for a strike, and have them black balled as scabs for working too hard. The next morning when leaving the hotel, the footpath was heavily covered with dog shit all over the place. Gosh we had better be careful here said Jason the council will come and close this street down, dog shit is not allowed, in fact no dogs allowed at all in George St Sydney. These Belgium's had better be careful, we will complain to the council when we get home, and we Aussies wont visit anymore.

From Belgium they flew to Greece and spent a week there, that included a boat trip around the Greek Islands, a trip Jean said she would always remember? The waters of the Mediterranean are so clear, compared to the Pacific; they both gazed in awe at the beauty of the Mediterranean, and the white homes so prevalent and easy to see from the boat. The couple gazed in wonder, as they found the water seemed to be so clear, that they could both seemed to be able to see right to the bottom of the ocean. There also seemed to be such calm, without the rough waves that one experiences all of the time, when sailing on the Pacific around the shores of Australia. They had a wonderful week and went to several islands, they had only heard about in books. There was a moment of surprise on the Island of Rhodes, which seemed to be a haven for deliberate sexual foolery! Both found it rather amusing, but frankly silly. There was a stop in Turkey, which seemed so much cleaner than anywhere in Greece, and the fashions they bought at the local bazaar was great fun. Jean in particular enjoyed the atmosphere of bargaining, and to Jason's amusement bought a lot of leather clothes just for fun. Most of what she bought was off a Turk, who spoke perfect Australian English, he was he claimed an Australian Turkish resident but was working for his family, for a while, he was just on holiday and would be glad to go home to Melbourne, it was now so boring in Turkey for himself and his wife and three children. They had visited the island of Ephesus and seen the ruins and the small stadium where the Apostle Paul had preached. It was also where the local residents had chased him away, because of their Goddess Diane! When the local trade's people found the sales of their statuettes declining and they blamed Paul. They had also visited the isle of Patmos where John had written the book of Revelation, Jean had been fascinated by the small cave and the tiny alter at which John had worshipped while in exile. Their arrival back in Athens and the subsequent tour of the Parthenon was an anti climax to their Grecian visit, that city seemed to be so dirty, but it was probably because there was a Garbo's strike in full swing and rubbish was piled up everywhere. Jason was highly amused his comment had been that while their city was suffering from uncollected garbage all the Greeks could do was stand around and argue loudly; in a manner that appeared to tourists as angrily.

They then flew to Rome and again had a great time, for another two days! They visited the ruins of the Coliseum and were both fascinated to see many of the historic areas! The ground they had stood on was where the Gladiators waited for their turn to go out and fight, as well, they could see where the wild animals had been kept, also ready to go out and fight. In the case of the carnivores lions etc; they were kept hungry so they would eat their victims. Their guide also pointed out where Nero had sat and fiddled while Rome burnt, or that's how history remembers him. The guide also pointed out that Nero had been the father of inflation in the Roman Empire in that he had reduced the value of the minerals in his coins by 5% and thus started Rome on the way to hyper inflation, as successive Emperors did the same? At the end of the Roman Empire the currency had been defaced by 95% and was worth only 5% of the original value, this the guide claimed was the real cause of the collapse of the Roman Empire both West and East? Jean commented on the many small cars and the noises of Rome. If one driver honked his car horn that would set off a barrage of car horns honking like crazy for about 15 minutes. Jason who loved pizza's pronounced the ones he had eaten in Rome as the worst in the world, just a little worse than the pizza's in the USA.

CHAPTER 6

Marriage problems.

Anyhow it was time to go home, and on his arrival the work for them both had stacked up, much to Jason's annoyance, there seemed to be so much for him to do. Why he asked James the new CEO, "has this work been left for me, you have been employed to deal with this is no longer my job it's yours."

The Executive was embarrassed but not fazed, "you he said are the expert on this type of work, and if I could do that work I would have your job, and I would be wealthy like you I am not, and never could be creative like you, that work isn't part of the job specification I signed when I joined up with Cooperate Developments Ltd."

Jason reluctantly agreed he had been hasty but still didn't want to do the work that had been left for him, until he found that what James had said was true there was no one but Jason that knew how to do those particular chores. The work was directly involved with the investigation of a proposal, to attempt a takeover of another company, and only Jason could approve the work already done by the scouts who had made the presentation, in the hope of earning a commission. Their hopes were dashed when Jason had turned their proposal down!

The new CEO had been appointed by the board when Jason had resigned the position, but he hadn't been hired to attempt takeovers that was a position all recognized as Jason's area of expertise and nobody wanted to take that from him, but Jason was getting tired of the strain that type of work created, and he had mistakenly thought James was taking over his complete job.

Dave the Cooperate Developments Ltd; general manager had met Jason as soon as the couple deplaned, and drove them home! He had a list of company targets for possible takeover and break up, looking at the list Jason had felt there was a target among the list, but more as an addition to the Cooperate Developments Ltd; stable of companies than as a break up situation. In this business the company Superior Homes Ltd was a public listed one and the share trading was sporadic. Cooperate Developments Ltd under the guidance of Jason; was used to take this new company over as a wholly owned subsidiary. Superior Homes Ltd was perfect fit to the current Cooperate Developments Ltd; group and the administration had no problem adding this work to their daily routine. A new management was put in place, and they were sold 35% of the shares at purchase cost, and as usual left completely to run the company, but Superior Home Ltd was now a company controlled by and administered by Cooperate Developments Ltd; and would in future be in a different type of business. All Jason cared about was that he had engineered another big profit for himself and the company. This job had taken the Cooperate Developments Ltd; team and Jason six months to complete! Jason had been working seven days a week sixteen hrs a day, by the time the contracts were completed he was due for a break.

Without notice Union trouble broke out within the Cooperate Developments Ltd; group engineered by the AWU which was trying to become the only union representing all of the workers. There was at that time six different unions representing different subsidiaries controlled within the group. This included the CWU at Cooperate Developments Ltd; head office, and the meat workers union at the meat businesses. The workers themselves rejected the one union concept, therefore under the threat of a Union black list a total blackout of all Cooperate Developments Ltd; businesses was put in place.

Suddenly there was a total shutdown and the future looked bleak, as the union was unable to negotiate with the company only the workers were involved, this wasn't a strike it was a lockout, but one created by the union not the company. Now the unions started to fight between themselves as the six individual unions defied the AWU, and the lockout continued. After two weeks of no work there was no apparent intention by any of the unions to back down, and the company appeared to be on the verge of collapse.

The Franchises were privately owned and could work with family running the businesses, but then there was no administration being done, and the shops were only part staffed. The child care centers were in even worse condition, because their staff had to be registered and parents were in trouble with their own jobs, it was a serious situation. Then the meat companies started to have refrigeration breakdowns, with now no staff to service them, and all unfrozen stock had to be destroyed. These were all problems for James the CEO, but when he called a Directors meeting Jason as Managing Director became involved? All of the Directors agreed there was nothing the company could do, so Jason and James were authorized to approach the minister of industry to ask him to intervene urgently? The minister arranged a meeting with all of the union leaders, and James to represent Cooperate Developments Ltd; for two days time.

It was a total fiasco AUW; claimed there were members of their union in every branch of Cooperate Developments Ltd; and as such they were the only union that could cover all of the workers in every subsidiary of that group of companies. All of the other unions sat back and insisted it was just a power grab by AUW; who wanted to sign up all of the 100,000 workers involved, and they weren't about to sit back and let this happen. The minister of labor at this stage wasn't prepared to do anything, theirs was a labor Govt and the voter back lash could be considerable, and the elections was only nine months away. It was a gridlock the unions were intransigent among themselves, the Govt; was too scared to act, and the company could do nothing. James as the CEO of the company announced he was going to shut the company down, because they were losing over $2 million per day, and the union lock out was to blame. He further announced the company was going to sue the leaders of the AWU individually, as well as the union and all of its members for losses suffered by the company. The company claim was a simple lock out by the AWU and its leaders, and he would be claiming $2 million per day plus interest until paid, and so far the claim was close to $50 million, plus bank interest. In the face of this the union now tried to negotiate a settlement with James to go back to work, if he withdrew the class action against the AWU.

James refused the offer but agreed to a return to work, and to allow the courts to set the penalty payable by the union, plus interest from the date of agreement to settlement of all monies payable. The union had made a mistake and was caught, they had no choice but to accept and the lock out was lifted immediately.

The union finally settled out of court they agreed to pay $30 million plus 5% interest for six months, a total of $37.5 million. The union had to take a collection off its members to allow them to be able to pay, and at the next election all of the main leaders were defeated, and forced to retire.

Now there was trouble on the way in the export meat business, but that period was still a short way in the future, the cost for this problem threatened to be far harder to fix than the union's had been?

Jason now had a break while he waited for his wife to give birth to their first child, these problems at Cooperate Developments Ltd; were to be handled by the CEO not him. He stayed home every day and even took the phone of the hook! When challenged by his associates he replied, if they want me enough they can send a person from the office; to pick me up and take me in, but if they pick me up for something trivial there will be a cost, I am a consultant not an employee anymore!

Jason had never forgotten his family and his success had been enjoyed by the entire Andrews extended family. There were now five nephews and three nieces, and as ever all were very close, the grandparents were eagerly waiting for Jason's first child to be born. Jason had supplied his family with new homes and furniture and his Mother no longer worked as a waitress. His Father still worked, but now had a position with one of the Cooperative Development Ltd; subsidiary companies as did his siblings. The only odd ball out in the family was Jason's wife, who seemed to resent the gifting of homes to the Andrew's family, Jason deeply involved with looking for takeover targets, never noticed the problem until it was too late?

She constantly complained about his family, and it was becoming a source of dissension between them! The Andrews family that had never been in arguments before, but now there was constant little niggles, Jean made it plain she didn't want that bunch of smoking drunks, hanging around their home; after the baby was born. Jason was just as determined; his family could come and go as they pleased, and if Jean didn't like it well she was welcome to leave via the front door.

This meant if she ever left she wouldn't be coming back, further since the entire Jason Andrew's fortune was owned in a family trust and he had nothing in his own name, she would get nothing. His estate had been well protected against marital mischief; by his accountants and lawyers. Jason wanted to be sure he was safe, he wasn't about to be blackmailed by a spouse; who objected to his laboring class family. Jason was proud of his family, but he had known that any wife may not be so happy with them, his instincts had proved to be right again; Jean didn't like any of his clan.

Jean for her part, felt that once the baby was born Jason would do as she wanted; and exclude his family, but it seemed as Jason's wife; she had obviously learned little about her husband. Jason had been coerced by the best in the country, no girl who was from the laboring classes herself, was going to be able to manipulate him. Even if she had the most beautiful; baby in the world, he wouldn't allow his family to be put down in any way. Jason was really close to his Mother so that especially applied to her. The Andrews were just too close and unless or until she accepted that, Jean had a major problem. Jason for his part was just staggered, that Jean; whose background was almost exactly the same as his, should suddenly as he bluntly put it; have her nose stuck up her arse.

The closer to birthing her time became the more difficult she was, but Jason didn't have a problem with that; he knew she was anxious because of the baby. He hoped deeply that her attitude to his family was also because of her pregnancy, in that thought he was wrong. She was really unknown to herself, angry that the Andrews family had been treated so well, but her own family had received nothing.

Jean's family was very different than the Andrews, her parents were both practicing Catholics, and had six children including Jean; who were always fighting and arguing among themselves. They had done this since they were children, much to the disappointment of their parents, who as a result were both unhappy; which of course meant they were an unhappy family. Jason wasn't a Catholic, so unfortunately wasn't a happy addition to the family. All of Jean's siblings were practicing Catholics, as Jean had been until she had married Jason; her marriage to him without the blessings of their church, to them wasn't a real marriage? The family had never asked for nor wanted anything from Jason; the problem was that in Jean's jealousy on her family's behalf, she was causing her own unhappiness. But to be honest Jason could have easily done a little for his In Laws, in the same way Jean didn't like his family, he was just as sincere in his dislike of her family, so there was a very real problem that would need to be dealt with.

Jason was to be with Jean at the birth, but she went into labor prematurely while he was away on business so that he almost missed being in the delivery ward on time? When he was finally found and told she was already in labor, Jason was caught unaware, by that time; Jean was already on her way to the hospital, so he decided to go to the hospital direct, and arrived just after Jean was admitted. She was experiencing contraction pains every ten minutes when he arrived, and was already in the delivery ward. Jean's arranged team of medical doctors and nurses; were gathered around her when Jason was admitted. They pointed him to his position standing beside his wife, and holding her hand. Jason had arrived just in time, his first Son was born only ten minutes after, he had got into his place. With a lusty cry the baby announced his presence, to the delight of both of his parents; and murmured approval of the medico's, who were immune to new baby's because they helped deliver so many every day.

All was going fine until suddenly Jason's parents arrived, and Jean's attitude changed immediately, she went quiet and ignored their congratulations, as if they had no right to be there in this her moment of triumph, so they left with obvious disappointment.

Jason walked to the exit with them both; and really felt sad for his Mother, who was in tears as they left?

Composing himself he went back into the room, and sat quietly as Jean was crooning over their new born Son, and admiring him as any mother would. After Jason had sat down she offered the baby to him to hold, he took the baby in his arms and sat admiring the little chap, but his mind was racing as the memory of his mother came to his thoughts. How he wandered was he supposed to react when Jeans family arrived, as they would and very shortly? He was twelve years older than Jean, and was determined not to be influenced; by her ignorance towards his parents.

As he expected Jean's family arrived en masse about thirty minutes later, and just as he had promised himself, Jason was the epitome of hospitality to them all. As he watched Jean make a fuss over her family, anger simmered deep inside his being, how can she do this he wandered it's as if my family are alien beings, and not to be welcome into my own child's presence. Yet here is Jean's family all of them a bunch of morons, who are very welcome and celebrating, as mine should have been able to do and just as easily? His anger mounted as he sat looking as if unperturbed, but in reality seething with anger against his wife and her kin, deep inside of himself. Jason had always been like that; he was able to conceal his feelings at all times, and now he was using this skill to the full. For the next hour as Jean laughed and joked with her kin, he just sat and joined in the happiness; if and when they included him, which wasn't very often.

After the crowd had left Jason excused himself, and above the protests of his wife, made a quiet exit, Jean in her pride in the new baby; didn't notice the ominous stand offish attitude of her husband, if she had she might not have been so happy. Jason immediately went to his parent's home, and spent several hours with his Father, his Mother had gone to bed with a headache, the usual sign that she was deeply upset.

Jason sat with his Dad just sitting, talking and having a few beers, but his thoughts were not on the beer he was so angry, he barely tasted what he was drinking.

His siblings joined them after work that day and when his Mother recovered they all celebrated with the new father, but all felt a sadness that wasn't usual with the Andrews clan. The next day when Jason went to visit Jean, she asked what he had done the previous day when he had left her, when he told her he had celebrated with his family she protested, why then didn't you stay with me and our baby, she asked with some anger showing? Jason didn't even bother to answer how he wandered can she be so bloody stupid, but he said nothing just smiled, and pretended to be a bit thick himself.

Jason had a situation now, one he didn't know how to handle for one of the few times in his life he felt helpless, this served to inflame his anger with his wife, and as a result he missed some visiting days. Back when Jason Jnr; was born it was usual for mother and child to stay in hospital for 14 days. During that time Jason only visited four times, much to Jean's anger and his own indifference. To top that off, two days before Jean was due out of hospital; he announced he was goin away on a business trip for two weeks. Jean was furious, but when she challenged him he merely smiled and said; well get your mother to help out! Jean was totally confused, what had happened she wandered; to her usually so very caring husband, he was doing the opposite to what she had expected.

Jason knew he was wrong but he didn't care, as far as he was concerned, no women was going to be so unkind to his mother, he was quite prepared to see his marriage dissolved if necessary Jean as far as he was concerned was way too cruel, and if it weren't for the child he would see her no more. In his confused thoughts marriage to him wasn't what he really cared about, all he wanted was some company, and sex was just a duty he performed, but could do without hell he could have a different women every night if that had been all he wanted, no sex wasn't the problem his wife's attitude to his mother was. There were so many accommodating females he didn't need a wife, and just at present he didn't really want one especially Jean.

For the second time Jason was suddenly facing real problems within his business activities, the meats divisions had suddenly gone crazy. The group now had 500,000 tonnes of meat processed and waiting for shipment to the USA. There was a herd of 100,000 head of cattle ready for kill and processed, all had been going well. Suddenly word was received from America that their agriculture dept; had succeeded in having a 25% tariff imposed on all meat from Australia and New Zealand, this was a major blow to all in the meat export industry, and huge losses would be common for quite some time to come. The U.S. Congress had just voted on the tariff request that had been lobbied in the house, now for several months? It was being pushed by the farm states such as Ohio on behalf of their ranchers, Jason had missed the implications the mistake was totally his? Now in the Senate it had also been passed, this was just hours before Jason had been advised. There was no chance the American President wouldn't sign the bill into law, within a few days? Cooperate Developments Ltd; was looking at a disaster, at quick estimate it was a loss of a very large sum of money. This would be the situation unless the orders could be rescheduled for sales outside the USA; without any consequences.

A quick call to the US clients confirmed that if Cooperate Developments Ltd; didn't deliver as per contract, the Americans would sue for losses caused by none delivery. Further Cooperate Developments Ltd; would never receive orders from those clients again, and would be blacklisted in the industry as none performers. Such a blacklist would last into perpetuity! James was struck dumb, for the first time he called the full Board of Directors together, to see if he could get some advice that would ease the problem, but he got nothing from them? There was no need to book the losses until; the meat transfers had been made, so with a successful deal the losses could be cancelled out Jason hoped. The media were on the attack the next day, how much they screamed had Cooperative Developments Ltd Investments lost in Jason's mad dreams. Again Jason thought it was funny, how often had he proved himself, yet here it was again the Australian's Cartoonist did it again. This time he had Jason drowning while a caricature of America's Uncle Sam waved goodbye, saying thanks Aussie for your contribution to our struggling ranchers! The Sydney Morning Herald had Cooperate Developments Ltd; in a coffin with Jason crammed in as well, and a big fat American with dollar signs on his stomach, waving their flag singing Australia's National Anthem.

The next day Cooperate Developments Ltd; had an advt in both papers with Jason in dark glasses, looking like the Mafia; waving happily to the media dressed up as dingoes. Jason was merrily saying, where the hell would Cooperate Developments Ltd; be without all of the free advt; these mugs give us. Crikey if we had to pay it would cost millions, God bless them all well we at Cooperate Developments Ltd; do anyhow?

Jason then went home for a month, in the hope that there would be an improvement in the situation with his wife, but they were both intractable they hardly spoke to each other night or day, when the ice seemed to be never ending, he simply announced he was going to America for at least 6 months, and if Jean wanted anything she should speak to their personal accountant. Jean objected vigorously, but Jason simply said neither he nor his parents were welcome so he was off. If she needed help she should go to her own family, because his were not good enough. To his amazement Jean agreed, that yes his parents were not good enough to even enter her home. And yes her own mother would help, but she would have to be paid a wage! She Jean couldn't be expected to do housework as well as look after a baby that would be stupid! Jean also demanded to know why she was not going this time, "do you," she asked, "have a girl friend you are taking?" Jason didn't bother to answer, he just walked out and never came back for eight months until his mother asked him too.

The Cooperative Developments Ltd office was growing now as they added new divisions, plus the shop franchises to administrate, there were now over 2,000 franchises which was the biggest job. But the administration of the other businesses was demanding attention, the office staff was now over 450 by number. There were two accountants, an in house lawyer, office manager and senior lady administrators. Jason had resigned from the position of CEO and just stayed on as a consultant to the group on a commission basis. The new CEO James had now signed his contract offer; he had formerly been employed by an American Company! There was a small sales team and the manager was a Latino who was formerly an insurance salesman.

Jason had changed his mind about going to America, he felt he needed to do another company stripping job, so he started to look for a suitable poorly performing conglomerate, but he wanted one for a full strip (break up) but It wasn't so easy any longer as soon as Cooperate Developments Ltd; appeared on any companies' share ledger, the share price would soar on expectations that an aggressive takeover was near, with or without compliant Directors. To achieve the latter it had to be a good deal for all concerned, what was needed was a purchase; very much like the retail division with all of its franchises. Jason put the Cooperate Developments Ltd; scouts on the job and after a month they came back with Child Care Centre's, a large group of over 800 was getting close to bankruptcy. At the same time a group of aged care centres came up and it was hard to decide which one to go with. Cooperate Developments Ltd; Directors had decided the Child Care Centers were the ones they wanted to buy so an offer had been made and accepted by the owners, their relief at having sold out was obvious? The management of the child care centers, had handed over control as soon as they legally could, they were delighted to have sold out? Jason was delighted, but it wasn't a stripping job. The company now set about getting ready to sell the franchises off for each of the Child Care Centers to any who were interested to buy. They were pleasantly surprised the nationwide advertising bought together buyers very quickly, and the 800 centers had been sold off within two months. Cooperate Developments Ltd; had made substantial profits from the sales, and had added to their cash flow and net income from commissions.

Jason now embarked on a new business venture, and deliberately forgot his problems at home? His wife's attitude was one he just didn't know how to deal with, so rather than creating more trouble he was refusing to face the problems. He was very unhappy, but could not bring himself to accept how Jean had treated his Mother. Jean had now started to ring him daily, but he refused to take her calls, finally in desperation Jean had rung Jason's Mother, and asked her to intervene on my behalf. Please she had cried I don't know whats wrong, even if you can just find that out at least I would know. Jason's mother had a fair idea what was wrong, but said nothing and immediately rang Jason, what are you doing within your marriage she asked? Jean is desolated, she has just rung me crying, you have got to ring her; she is after all the mother of your Son? And you are my mother Jason retorted, and nobody treats my mother like she did, not while I am alive!

Son she replied you have to talk to your wife there must be a problem that can be solved, but it never will be if you don't talk to her!

Look Jason had replied, give me a few hours to think; and I will come home tonight and we can talk, you are my mother, I will listen to you just as I did when I was a small boy, I. love you Mum he finished.

And I will always love you Son she replied, but you are a married man and father now, that is your main responsibility.

That night when he arrived at home, his father was there as well; so he knew he was going to get a lecture they came straight to the point, much as they loved him; he had no choice but to put his own family first. We will always be here they declared, but Jean has the first call on your time, and Jason Jnr; was at home now; and was entitled to have his father there too. His siblings they declared understood, Jean didn't like them so that was it, and they had to keep out of the way.

Jason couldn't agree; there was no way he said he could accept his wife being so unfair. His family's love he said was what had kept him going, he just couldn't, no he wouldn't live without knowing they were there; whenever he needed them!

His parents were surprised at the deep feelings he had expressed, you are so wrong his mother said she is your wife, and right or wrong there is now your own son to think about!

I am so sorry said Jason but if my parents and siblings aren't welcome, then there is no place for me either, Jean he declared had her nose up her arse, and he wasn't about to put up with her and her families Catholic shit, and no priest was going to be snooping around his home, either him or the priest had to leave and it sure as hell seemed there was no place for him?

His parents could only shut up they had no idea such a deep problem could exist, they had never been religious and were now tongue tied, what the hell do we do now they asked each other later that night in bed? Neither of them had an answer, it was way beyond their understanding!

The next day at work when Jean rang he took the call, Jean asked, " what is happening now your mother won't talk to me; tell me please what I have done that I deserve to be treated like this?"

"I am not surprised my mother won't talk to you, not after the way you treated her when Jason Jnr; was born. Then the last time I was there, you had the cheek to tell me my family isn't good enough to be in our home,

I hope that when some day Jason Jnr; has a wife she doesn't treat you the way you treated my parents?" he said very quietly into the phone.

"Does this mean that your family is more important to you than I am?" Jean asked.

"Yes it does if that's the way you want to see it, I tend to see it as that we all aren't good enough for you, all of us and that includes me, so why should I listen to your rubbish?" he replied.

Jean started to cry into the phone, "this is so unfair you knew we were Catholics when we married, now you want me to be like you just agnostics believing in nothing, I cannot do it and our son won't be able to do it either?" She wailed loudly.

"And why is that?" Jason asked in surprise.

"Well he will be bought up as a Catholic as I have been what did you expect?" Jean asked.

"I have never thought about it, why is it so important anyhow, he is still just a baby?" Jason sighed.

"Well said Jean, he is due to be christened in a week, are you coming to that or will you ignore that to?"

"I guess not but I don't know what the fuss is all about, can't you let him grow up and make up his own mind?" Jason asked in surprise.

"No we can't do that," wailed Jean! "He is going to be a good Catholic; I am beginning to realize now what it means to marry a heathen such as you, It's wrong my parents told me but I wouldn't listen now you are penalizing me?"

Jason was stumped he didn't know what to say, but he knew he wouldn't live being controlled by some priest. The priest had to go or he would, no mere man was going to tell him he had no rights to see his own family in his home!

He finally said; "let me think I will ring you back, all I know is I won't accept my family being so badly treated, by you or anyone else. When is this christening going to be? I suppose I will have to come! But to be very honest I don't like the idea at all! Jason Jnr is too young, children shouldn't be tied up to something before they are old enough to decide for themselves, but if that's what Catholics do I will respect that. But I won't accept my family isn't good enough to come into my home. If that's what you insist then there is no point, I won't accept that even for you and my son. Anyhow give me time to think about your decisions, I will ring you tomorrow about the christening, but let me say what you are doing leaves me cold. I see my Son having to answer to some bloke with a cassock on telling him what to do, that may be fine by you, but I don't like it, not one little bit as far as I am concerned the only father in my home is me, and if that's not the way it is to be then it cannot be my home?" Jason said softly.

The next day in the morning he rang Jean, and told her he didn't like the christening; so he wouldn't be coming. He also told her if his family wasn't welcome then neither was he, so he wouldn't be coming even to visit, until that problem was fixed.

Jean broke into a tremendous bout of crying, "You she declared are in the wrong not me, and I told you I was a Catholic now you are treating me like a heathen. It's you who is the heathen not me, I have spoken to the priest and he agrees, I must pay the penalty for being stupid. But surely for the sake of our son you must reconsider, we aren't married in the Catholic Church so you aren't bound to me for life. But for Jason Jnr; its different he is ours you can't change that, nor should you want to unless you are completely unbalanced?"

"No that's true he is ours, but it's hard to understand all of this Christening stuff for me! What is this all about, I suppose we do need to get together, so you can explain what it's all about, ok when can we meet and where?"

Jean replied, "it needs to be soon because the event; is in just over ten days time."

"Well that is up up to you, just tell me a place and I will be there,"

"Can't you come here and see Jnr at the same time," asked Jean?

"Yes I suppose so, when shall I come and at what time?"

"What about tonight for dinner; and I will keep Jnr awake for you at 7.00 pm." Said Jean.

"That's fine said Jason, but just be sure none of your family is around, I have no interest in dallying with your family now or ever, let us just accept there is no common ground as far as our mutual families are concerned." replied Jason.

'Yes" replied Jean, "no one will be here except me and Jnr; I am quite capable to cook a meal and look after our Son myself you know?"

They both laughed and rung off, but neither thought it was at all funny.

That evening when Jason left to see his family he wandered if he should take Jean some flowers as he had always done in the past, but he decided not to she might that as a sign of a weakening in his resolve against a priest having too much say in their lives'. The evening started off very stiff, both of them were uncomfortable, and it took a while to say much, Jean bought out Jnr; for Jason and he enjoyed an interlude with his Son. Then Jean started to dish up dinner and they both began to loosen up if only a wee bit, after dinner was finished and the kitchen cleaned up, they both sat in the lounge room and started to talk.

Jean started by explaining what the christening was all about; and how important it was to practicing Catholics. When she had finished Jason was a bit more aware of his wife's church not that he agreed; but at least he understood a little. They finally got around to talking about their family problems, and why Jean had been so rude to the Andrews clan, she made no excuses just expressed what she thought was the problem, and that was the fact she had married outside her church.

He asked, "Why do you think your priest, can have so much to say in our affairs, that to me is wrong I have been checking the catholic faith out a little, and I know for example these men have never been married, so what makes them so wise without any experience in life, frankly for me he said it's a great pile of rubbish?"

"Well because he is my spiritual guide, he is my intermediary with God, what should I do if there was no one to intercede on my behalf, to whom could we confess our sins and be forgiven?" she replied defensively.

This really puzzled Jason, but he said nothing just listened!

Jean went on to explain that to all of her family, only Catholics were the true Christians, and they did not believe in mixed marriage, when she had married Jason her parents had warned her she would rue the day, but she had refused to listen? The truth had been; that she herself couldn't understand the possible problems, only when she realized how different the two families were, could she see that there was going to be problems ahead. But she continued with the marriage, she loved Jason and thought the so called problems was a load of old church rubbish, now she realized she had been wrong. She stressed she had no problem with the Andrew's, except their agnostic life style, or lack of religious commitment only after Jnr; was born she stressed did she see just how big a gap, there was between the two families.

Jason had sat and listened all that Jean had said, but finally spoke up with his own thoughts. Jean was he said, unhappy with what he had done for his family, without helping hers, this he understood and they could deal with, but to treat his Mother badly was just too much, and there was no way he would ever accept that. Then he described how his Mother had been crying, on the evening they had visited after Jnr; was born. He went on to describe how Jean's family had been welcomed with great fanfare, and how for him that had been just too much, and he had left knowing that in all probability their marriage was over.

Jean had protested that her intent had not been vicious, but admitted she had been wrong. For a start Jean denied the jealousy charge, over what had been done for the Andrew's family, but finally admitted Jason was possibly right? She insisted that she had no ill intent, but she was a young wife, who had been over influenced by her priest, but she reminded him it had been how she had lived her entire life, and it was difficult to change just like that, what was she to do tell the priest he was no longer welcome, no she couldn't do that and she shouldn't be expected to ever do such a thing!

They were both fighting for their marriage, but for the first time Jason could see the look of loss in Jeans eyes, but conversely Jean could see that Jason was lost, and really didn't know what to do!

Suddenly they were in each other's arms, and each one of them was trying to apologize both at once, it was a bitter sweet reunion, their marriage was probably better for having weathered such a storm. Jason moved back home that night, but both agreed they needed marriage counseling, because without it their marriage would not survive

Jason wanted to know more about the Catholic Church! This before he would agree to Jnr; being christened as a Catholic, it was he said too important for him to agree without knowing more?

CHAPTER 7

Drugs Galore:

Jean and Jason, for the first time since Jnrs; birth were together but both knew this may be the only chance they would have, to heal the damage to their marriage? Jean knew that Jason may be called away at any time; and he would have to go, in her mind she wandered if there was any chance of a true reconciliation; even though there had been no split up declared at this point their situation was still very sensitive.

Jason also knew he wanted to reconcile, but the two issues family and church was keeping them apart? They had stayed together on the previous night, but slept in separate rooms; they had longed to be together but he just couldn't and wouldn't overlook the problems, that idea of a Priest intervening in his private affairs, were just too much for Jason to accept. The more he thought of a mere unmarried man telling them how to live, the more unacceptable the idea became, Jason felt some degree of horror at just the thought of a priest hanging around his home, and he objected to an unmarried man counseling his wife.

Jason was totally confused, how he wandered could Jean place such a high importance on what a damned priest had to say, the man wasn't even married yet he was supposed to give advice on children and marriage. How was it possible to put a mere man before the most important person in his life his mother, in fact all of his family, the idea that his wife should look down on his family because they were agnostics, was to Jason unthinkable.

Jean was also lost in thought! How she wandered could Jason not see the need for God in their lives, and how ridiculous not to care whether their Son was Christened or not. Jean loved her husband dearly, and she wanted him back in their bed, she missed his warmth and they had had a great sex life. What was she to do she wanted her husband back, but she had been raised to believe none Catholics were abhorrent and not to be trusted. She had married outside of her faith, but had been warned she would pay the price for such foolishness was this now coming true or was Jason right, she knew instinctively he was partially right?

In the morning early before breakfast, Jason had received a call from the office, there was real trouble ahead, and he needed to be on hand to check personally on what was going on. A serious problem had been found in the business and he was needed urgently, he left immediately, but told Jean that unless he was forced to stay late at the office, he would be back that evening. They kissed in a friendly, but not intimate embrace and he drove off!

As soon as he had parked his car in his reserved space at the office, he sensed real trouble but his mind was a blur; what could possibly be wrong? As soon as he walked into his office the lady who was now his Personal Assistant (Rita), having taken over Jean's job when she had become married to the boss, came to speak to him in private. The Aussie Feds have been looking for you all morning she said, they are very concerned and you must contact them as soon as you come in. They wouldn't tell me more, except that the situation is very serious, and is about building materials we have had imported, from Mexico eighteen months ago. They have called about six times this morning already, the caller's name is Inspector Juan Chase, and he works in the drug squad, but he wouldn't tell me anymore than that. He wanted your private mobile number, but I wouldn't give it to him I told him the only person that had that number was me, and I wasn't about to pass that onto him. He accepted that but has kept ringing ever since!

Well could you get them on the phone for me now; let's find out what this is all about, Jason replied? He sat back in his office chair and waited, the connect call came through soon enough, and Jason was through to the Inspector as Rita had described him to be!

What can we do for you Inspector asked Jason politely?

I don't think what we are after should be discussed on an open line; Mr. Andrew's was the reply, our need to meet with you is very important for you and your company! Perhaps it would be best to meet me somewhere in private, you are a high profile man; and we don't want the media to get a hold of this problem from us. If and when you release it, it needs to come from your own handlers, because what we have is a Federal problem, and it is a very serious one, leading to a possible serious charge against somebody in the Cooperate Developments Ltd; organization.

It is a bit hard for me to get privacy that's true, probably its best if I come to your office, which will be as private as possible for me, said Jason who by now was quite alarmed!

That's fine Mr. Andrew's come into the Central Aussie Feds office and asks for Inspector Juan Chase! We will get a private office to talk in and I will explain what has happened; that will affect your company very badly.

As soon as Jason had been ushered into an office at the Police station, Inspector Chase walked in, and the interview was started.

We understand your publicly owned company Cooperate Developments Ltd; Investments owns a construction company; that imports building materials from overseas Mr. Andrew's the Inspector started.

First Jason replied can we just cut the formalities call me Jason, and I will call you Juan is that OK? Now to answer the question, yes we import from China, Mexico and Ecuador, so how can we help you and what is these serious problems tell me the innuendos I am hearing are really upsetting?

Let me come straight to the point Juan replied! The Aussie Feds have been able to prove that a company owned by Cooperate Developments Ltd; Investments, 18 months ago bought into the port in Sydney forty tonnes of inside wall tiles from Mexico, can you confirm that please?

Not without my office confirming for me, shall I ask my PA to confirm all details for you, and ring you back personally Jason had asked?

That will be fine Jason; Juan said if you could just make the call now please?

This problem, said Jason will need to go to the full Cooperate Developments Ltd; board I don't know the people in charge of imports for the group. Our Directors will need to be advised, so will the various managers, this is a big job for us, geez it's a big problem that's for sure? We are used to problems, but this is a totally new experience for us, let me arrange the meetings? My PA; will arrange another meeting between us two for this afternoon, just as soon as I can down load this mess to the others. Jason rang his PA; immediately and gave her the instructions, to set up the meetings urgently, starting with the Directors. This was done in Juan's hearing, so he could be assured; Jason would and could move quickly!

Now let me tell you what the whole problem is said Juan! In the last shipment of wall tiles that came in for your group; there was concealed in them 100kgs of Cocaine. We have now traced the source, and we know the shipment came to, and was picked up by an officer of your company. We have been monitoring your group for at least 18 months, and now need to investigate them more closely. Do you have a problem with us speaking to all of your staff?

Well yes I do actually Jason replied! We have over 450 people at this office, and another 10,000 at that particular subsidiary company, so a full staff interrogation will be difficult. The media will give us all hell; the damage will be terrible, and possibly irreparable! Drugs are of no interest to me, our last corporate raid gave us a very large profit, and so what the hell is 100 kgs of Cocaine to me, nothing?

Yes it's a shame, but unfortunately the drugs were imported by your company, and we have to follow that lead there is no choice. We can and will be discreet, but with that number on the staff it's going to get around! But tell me how many people in the Cooperate Developments Ltd; organization, would know what is being imported and from where? I suggest no more than half a dozen people, would be that close to the company! What may be the case; is the company identity has been stolen, that's a strong possibility. We have seen this before where one of the managers of a firm, is used by a drug cartel to import a large shipment of drugs. This case is unusual in that the drugs actually got through, and has mostly been sold! We estimate the volume would have fetched $25 million dollars on the street prices, they are charging $200 -$400 dollars for 1 gram, just work it out and it's a huge sum of money. This is big time Jason believe me, there isn't many if any drug teams in Australia that could afford to bring this amount in with one shipment.

Jason then left the Aussie Feds offices and returned to the Cooperate Developments Ltd; head office where the Directors were all in the Boardroom anxiously waiting for him, as soon as he arrived? They were all mystified, about why they had been called together so suddenly! This was not usual Jason never panicked and they were all curious, whats happening; they asked as soon as he entered?

When Jason started to explain there was a gasp of surprise, Cocaine what the hell was the main response, it seems more likely that probably our identity has been stolen, Jason said! But to do that, someone on our staff has given away information, about our shipping procedures so the culprit has to be found and quick, before we all go to bloody jail!

"Well we can get our import manager in this afternoon, and quiz him before the Aussie Feds do, the sales manager may have information also, so we can bring them in as well?" Dave the general manager was quick to take control of following through, with the senior staff.

To Jason's surprise the new CEO was a little slow to react, because this problem was at top level; Jason had expected him to be immediate in his response, but he was very slow Jason tucked that away in the back of his memory, for future reference.

The police have asked me to go back to their central station, to see the Aussie Feds again later today, so I want your verbal reports by 3.00 pm today in my office please, we need to give them as much as we can as quickly as possible.

Jason then went back to his own office and put a call through to Juan, I will be back in your office by 4.00 pm today, let's hope my managers have some answers for us by then, he told Juan?

That's fine replied Juan; let's hope we can clean this up quickly, but we have to be honest it's a tricky looking deal, there are some big criminals involved in this drug importation; my pick is you have a lot of trouble coming? I am so sorry but there is nothing we can do to avoid implicating you and Cooperate Developments Ltd; because legally the company; are the importers, even though they have no knowledge of this whole drug deal.

By 3.00 pm he had had reports back from Dave about the two divisions, Imports and Sales!

The GM had come in, and said he had had no luck so far, but he had some ideas he needed to inquire around and check on. The imports people he said are as clean as can be; they definitely have nothing to hide! Sales however could spring some leaks through the manager, a Latino, there was nothing for real yet, but he Dave (The GM) was going to follow through that evening and meet with the sales manager again?

Jason arrived back at Aussie Feds headquarters; and sat down in the same interview room! He had waited only a few minutes; when Inspector Juan Chase entered and sat down. Well Juan asked do you have any good news so far for us Jason.

Well no I didn't think I would have, if you have been checking us out for eighteen months, it's not likely we will find the culprits in hours now is it? Jason said in a rather preemptory manner! I said I would come back immediately, out of concern for our situation, which isn't a good one to be in is it? Our General Manager; is convinced there is no leak in our Import division, but needs more time to check out our sales manager, who is a Latino and speaks the Mexican language. "I have told him to report back to me in the morning; and to move as quickly, but as cautiously as possible. I don't need to tell you, just how sensitive this is for us and especially me! The media is going to crucify me and Cooperate Developments Ltd; anyhow if they even think that we are passing the blame on, hell I can just imagine what the impact will be. Bloody hell I will have to go into hiding, there will be riots on the streets in Sydney town, believe me the media is going to love this?"

"No don't take me wrongly; we are aware how sensitive this is, if we make a mistake with a company and a person like you, we are in real trouble. Canberra will hang me out to dry; and the bloody Pollies will be like flies walking on my carcass. You are not the only one who has to be very careful! I could get the sack without notice; and for me that would be a catastrophe, I have a family to feed too you aren't alone in this investigation? This is a sensitive job for all of us believe me Jason! We aren't looking to investigate you that just wouldn't make sense; you in your work quite reasonably would see this as small time, but its big time criminals we are dealing with here, take my word for it they play by their own hard rules?" Juan hastened to assure Jason of Aussie Feds intent.

That evening back with Jean and Jnr; Jason was so morose and unhappy, Jean couldn't help but ask what the problem was?

After Jason started to explain, Jean began to lose her composure too! "That is terrible," she said! "My God there will be those media parasites, running around here everywhere? Even our Son will get photographed in the scrum; it won't be safe here for any of us!"

"To be honest I don't know what to say or do, but we will all be crucified for sure we had better go into hiding, for the first time in my life; I just don't know what to do?" Jason said ruefully.

Later that night, while Jason and Jean where still talking, Jason's mobile rang! A deep voice on the other end of the line asked, "Is this Jason Andrews I am talking to?"

"Yes it is, now how can I help you?" Jason asked in surprise; this wasn't a voice he recognized.

"Never mind that have you been talking to the police Aussie Feds today?" asked the voice.

"What the hell has that got to do with you?" asked Jason in some anger.

"Just be careful what you say and do Andrew's, we know where your home is. We also know where your family and you're in laws live. Say the wrong things and we will take somebody out; and we will do it very quickly?" snarled the voice.

"What?" asked Jason in shock!

"You heard me Andrews, let me repeat the message! Say the wrong thing and somebody related to you, in some way will die within 24 hours," then click went the phone as the voice hung up.

Jason just staggered from the phone, Jean who had been watching his reactions, as he was answering the call was startled?

When she heard what Jason had been told by the voice, from the phone call he had just had and was reacting to; she went as white as death.

"My God!" she almost screamed; when she after a few moments could again speak, "what are we to do, this is your and my families' our Son and us; can we all hide?"

Jason was so shocked himself he couldn't speak, suddenly the enormity of it all was sinking in, what Juan had said that afternoon had suddenly become real! There are some big criminals in on this he had said; now he knew what Juan had meant, that voice hadn't even told him not to tell the Aussie Feds. Obviously they didn't care about them, Jason felt a twinge of fear, run down his spine? This was beyond him, to hell with the money, how was he to protect the families that were now under threat, because of him and his bloody money. For once he wished that money would all vanish, so far he wasn't finding any happiness with it, none at all.

There was little sleep that night for either Jean or Jason, they sat up almost all night and talked! The only good thing that was happening from the shock; was they were talking freely. Their personal problems were being forgotten, and the more important one of family safety was being discussed. As they sat and talked their former closeness returned, common danger drew them back together to the husband and wife bond they had so recently shared? Their main thoughts were first for their son, then the families, and finally for themselves. But the fear of the unknown is all pervasive, as they sat all through that night and talked, all they could really do was sink into a feeling of and being overtaken by fear. They finally sank into deep sleep, late in the night, right where they had been talking, on the lounge! They had barely fallen asleep, when they were awake again both hoping they had been dreaming, but the light of day banished that hope?

Jason could hardly swallow the very nice breakfast that Jean had prepared for him, it was no use he just wasn't hungry, fear and nerves had deprived him of his appetite! This goliath of the business world, was after all just a man in fear for his families, he must act but how, he realized the most important thing was to not lose his nerve; he had to appear confident just as he did in business. He had to project strength to all around him it was the same now! This was no different than a 'business face off' he was thinking bravely, but in his heart he was scared. He knew this was life and death, not just a money program and it was beyond as yet, his skill to deal with, all he could do was struggle on and search for a path back to decency, the criminal mind he just didn't understand, and he was scared for everybody not just family?

He left Jean to go to his office, both of them smiling bravely, but the last thing he said to her was, now don't tell anyone in the families, I will see the Aussie Feds this morning; and ask them what we must do let them point the way, and then we will make up our own minds tonight, after we have thought about what they have said? Jean had smiled bravely and agreed with what she had heard him say, but she was numb with worry all she could think about was Jnr; what could happen to him? He would be the one most at risk, as she kept thinking she suddenly felt faint and exposed to danger gradually without knowing it she passed into a faint, and crumpled to the floor. Even when Jnr; started to cry she heard nothing, she was lost to this world Jnr; calmed his cry to a whimper, even he seemed to sense his mother was in a feint.

As soon as Jason had reached the Office, he asked his PA to get Inspector Juan on the phone as quickly as possible. When Juan came on the phone he didn't hesitate, but described the previous night's happenings in full. Gone was the self assured multi billionaire! Jason Andrew's was totally shaken; and now lost in a new world, one that is full of everything he hated most? At the other end of the line, Juan had been quietly listening, but when Jason finished he provided no encouragement!

CHAPTER 8

Security.

When Jason finished talking Juan said, "yes this is what I thought may be the case, someone has led you into a hornet's nest, and you and yours are in real danger. There is contempt for the Aussie Feds here that is deliberate! They have let you and us know they don't care a fig for what we; or you with all of your money does, they don't care in the least and it's a challenge to us, they see us as nothing in fact to them we are just a joke?"

"So what do I do you are the experts now we need your help, obviously my Son is at extreme risk so is my Wife, don't worry about me, but what do we do for them?" Jason asked.

"Yes you are right that's where the main risks are, it's easy to give them sanctuary, but what of all the others, they can and would without hesitation attack your families, executive staff and their families, and anyone who gives you any sanctuary. What must happen now is that we leave you alone! Only when we know; we have got the leaders can we act, we have to be careful sorry but that's how it is, you will have to act alone, can you do that without getting into a panic?" asked Juan with little or no emotion in his voice.

Jason was awakening to reality, he needed to act to protect his own, he would follow through with his GM, to find out if there was any news from the meeting the previous night? But first he would ring Jean to check if she was OK he would ring now, now he rang off from Juan so he could ring Jean! The home phone was ringing and there was no answer, so Jason rang Jeans mobile, still no answer! Now Jason was in a real funk, he rang Juan and asked for two of his men to go quickly to his home, to find if his wife was ok; he explained there was no answer to the phones, and he was deeply worried! He told Juan he was on the way himself, but the Aussie Feds could get there far more quickly? As soon as he had dropped his phone, Jason ran for his car, when he finally got the car underway his whole body was shaking, he was terrified for his Son and Wife. When he arrived at his home the Aussie Feds were already trying to get in, but the house was securely locked up? Jason had been shaking before, but now he was really in a mess, suddenly he could hear Jnr; crying, what he wondered has happened? When he finally got the door open, the first thing he could see was Jean lying on the floor and now Jnr; was screaming he had heard his father's voice?

The Aussie Feds helped Jason to resuscitate Jean, who as soon as she opened her eyes, started to scream, what happened to me she was screaming, where is my baby?

Jason and the two men were totally perplexed; yes they wandered, what had happened to her? Finally after Jason had managed to quiet her down, he went to pick up, and bring the screaming baby to his Mother!

Jason explained to the two Aussie Feds it was a mistake, they would all be ok now and he thanked them for coming so quickly, we are in the middle of discussions with their head office he told them and they have to protect us from criminals. He explained his Wife had been under pressure and the lack of sleep, so she must have feinted. They were only a uniformed patrol team so they wouldn't be privy to the problems, they left saying they hoped everything was ok, and if needed they could come back quickly.

Jean by this time was fully awake and suckling Jnr; who seemed to be rather indignant, at having had to call for his meal so loudly and long? Where the hell have you been, he seemed to demanding an answer from his mother? If things had not been so serious; both Jean and Jason would have burst out laughing, instead both could only manage small smiles.

Jason prepared coffee for them both and then sat explaining to Jean what had happened; and how he had panicked, when she hadn't answered either phone. He then told her what the Aussie Feds had to say, but he watered the discussion down! There was no use alarming his Wife anymore than she was at present, he would for the moment; keep the extent of the problem quiet. Thinking he may stay home, Jason checked in with his PA; she had been asked by the GM; to transfer any call from Jason to him as soon as he rang, so she did?

How are you getting on Dave, Jason asked as the phone was answered?

Quite well Jason replied Dave, I think we may have the culprit; you need to come in, so we can talk and let me explain. Ok replied Jason let my

PA confirm my arrival; and you need to come straight to my office we will talk in private I will be there within the hour!

Dave was in Jason's office within minutes of Jason arriving, he had a very solemn look on his face. I think he said, without any preamble the Latino in sales may be mixed up in this damned Cocaine mess. We went out for coffee last night, he's Mexican not Latino! When he started for us; he was in the export division, for three months! He could talk his way in and out of hell, a real smooth talker that's for sure, but he almost choked when I casually asked him, if he took the occasional line or two of Cocaine. He admitted he did, and offered to get me some top quality product real cheap, if it was needed! We just kidded around he asked if I wanted to sniff a line, but I declined we don't want him to know we are trying to find a rat in the team, just yet do we? But personally I think he is the culprit he is just too smooth one of those types that I don't like.

No Dave Jason said pensively just keep all of this between you and me for a while, "what help have you had from James, our CEO has he helped you at all?"

"He has been very quiet, actually he hasn't been around got a personal problem I think," replied Dave with a smile.

"OK that's all for now, ask James to come in when you see him please, and thanks for the good work Dave, it won't be forgotten?" said Jason.

Next Jason asked his PA; to arrange a meeting with Juan, for as soon as he was available. Suddenly James was at the door, so Jason invited him in!

"Have you, had any thoughts on our Cocaine incident as yet? It's been pretty hectic here, so I have stalled the Aussie Feds at present, but they are pretty persistent and starting to get on my nerves?" said Jason.

Frankly I have been caught up one of these scams before, and I prefer to deal with it pretty quietly. Stealing the identity of large firms like Cooperate Developments Ltd; isn't new and the Aussie Feds know that? But they like to make a big fuss; and get the victims in this case Cooperate Developments Ltd; to do all of the work and then they step in and claim all of the credit. The time when I was with a firm in a similar position, the crook was in the firm's team and he was soon found, but the whole thing was hushed up for various reasons? I have no doubt this one is similar! But for example; I can tell you that Dave was out for a coffee with our sales manager last night. They sat for maybe a half an hour and then Dave left! As soon as he left our Mexican Salesman, was on his mobile talking very animatedly for fifteen minutes, all of which the police were probably listening to. Equally be sure he was talking in a foreign language, I am quite sure Dave has told you all of this he did a good, but only half of the job."Said James looking quite sure of what he had said.

Jason listened in surprise, he decided then he was not a sleuth he had been suspicious of James, now he remembered why James had got the job for Cooperate Developments Ltd; as their new CEO he had brains, talked little, but did a lot! Jason for the time being was satisfied; with what his staff had been doing, but his PA, had just advised he could see Juan who had just returned her call at his office, immediately.

When he entered Juan's office, Juan had another detective with him, Perry Olsen who he introduced as someone who had been doing field work on the Drug squad for years. Jason immediately launched into an explanation of what he was going to do.

"Cooperate Developments Ltd; will hire a team of security agents to quietly guard; all affected Staff, this protection will include all of the company executives and all their families and the head of the security firm will be instructed to speak to Juan before they start their duties." said Jason.

Juan and his associate nodded their approval, so Jason left immediately. Jason had returned to his office and ordered his plan be put into place, but he advised his PA; Rita he wanted to interview the Security Firms Manager once he had been selected, himself? He left for the day feeling a little better, but still shaken by the phone call from the previous evening, he had a distinct feeling that voice would be calling again real soon.

That night Jason and Jean called on both of their sets of parents, and told them what was happening; and how there had been threats issued. As could be expected this was a real shock to their parent! The idea of having guards posted at all times was a novel idea, but they realized there was nothing else Jason could do? The parents were asked to warn all of the siblings, what was happening, and men were being posted to guard them all as well? The guards would be told to be very discreet; and to keep themselves inconspicuous, and if in any way there should be a problem with the guards, they would be changed? Jason finally told their parents, that he was handling the security arrangements himself, if there should be problems, they should put an urgent person to person call though to him through his PA.

The next morning Jason confirmed with his PA; the security firm's manager was calling on him at 11.00 am ready to put a program into place. James had vetted and selected the firm he considered the best, and would be present at the meeting. Jean had decided to spend the day with her Mother, so Jason left home with as much confidence as he could muster, under the circumstances.

The meeting at 11.00am with James and the new security manager, was progressing well until Jason said he may take his wife and Son away overseas for a period of time? James immediate reaction was that the media; would see that as running away. Jason was very quick and blunt, you are the CEO here not me I am only a consultant now, why must I be shackled to Sydney?

At this the security manager cut in and said, you are correct as far as the importation of the Drugs is concerned, James has that problem not you? But you are wrong as far as the target for these criminals is concerned; your Son and Wife are the main ones that are in danger? If you run they will persecute Cooperate Developments Ltd; unmercifully they will have won and you will be disgraced beyond redemption, there must be a really strong security with your Wife and Son at all times, but we will make sure they are unseen?

The next meeting was with Juan at Police headquarters, and again the assistant was there as well. Jason confirmed everything he had done, and advised there was now a security team attached to the Cooperate Developments Ltd; investment group, which would deal with the Aussie Feds. Arrangements had been made for James, to bring the new security manager in, to discuss the drug problem and all security systems that would be in place?

Juan confirmed that Jean and Jnr; would be the main targets of any attack by the drug syndicate, but they must not leave and go overseas, he also confirmed the Aussie Feds would be moving in on Cooperate Developments Ltd; within days, to pick up their sales manager, but they would be as discreet as possible. Finally he warned that the security needed to be tightly in place before they moved, the Aussie Feds he said had no doubt Jason and his family would be targeted immediately. It was ironic, but any security reaction, against Jason and Cooperate Developments Ltd; would confirm the sales manager's guilt!

That night there was a panicked call to Jason, one of the executives had been attacked by two men, but the attackers had been thwarted by the guards. The attackers had escaped, it seemed they hadn't realized there was guards posted and had escaped because the guards were to slow to react, it seems they had been surprised and their quarries had managed to escape. The Executive and his family were now at home terrified, even knowing the guards were there didn't mollify them.

It was that day, the first media interest was roused, at this stage it wasn't strong just a mention of the Aussie Feds; meetings with Jason Andrew's. There was speculation about what was going on, but nothing firm was stated! Jason knew there would be at most two days before the story broke; in spite of his promise to stay, he decided to take a one week holiday? He warned James and his PA; he would be away for a week! He also asked

James to hire a media manager, who would in future handle all contact, with the press and electronic media. Finally he had Dave into his office to report on progress; it looked as if the Latino would be going down for the count, with the Aussie Feds any day.

Dave said that his digging around; had put their sales manager in the worst possible light! We are getting close to beating the Aussie Feds, and springing the trap! Jason was told by Dave, but the Latino was only a mule and a foolish one at that! He had been caught with $1,000,000 in cash, and trying to launder the money, this is how the Aussie Feds had locked him into a net. The fool had incriminating evidence left at his parent's home! He had the badge of a retired Aussie Feds officer he had stolen, while visiting that officer as a friend. He also had a number of fake driver's licenses, under different names; all of this evidence was in his bedroom at his parent's home.

When Jason went home that night he and Jean packed immediately, then Jason went to hire a rental car! They drove all night before booking into a motel, on the border with Queensland, a NSW town; all the time being as discreet as possible. They paid cash for everything, and only Jean went into the reception to book in! They never said anything about little Jnr; luckily he was normally a very quiet child, and it was a two bedroom motel, it was small but comfortable just what the family needed, the flamboyancy of big business had really palled for them both?

The next day Jason contacted his PA; on his personal mobile, and told her he were fine, and that all hell would break out within a few days. He was right on the third day; the media was in full blast, print and electronic it was as if Cooperate Developments Ltd; and Jason were drug importers of the worst kind, and that's why Jason had enjoyed so much business success, drug money linked to Jason Andrews they claimed.

The Australian broke the news in bold print on the front page! Jason Andrews in Major Drug Bust! Not enough profit in wrecking companies! Cooperate Developments Ltd; subsidiary import's 100 kg of Cocaine from Mexico! The Aussie Feds have confirmed that they have picked up one of the Cooperate Developments Ltd; 'Managers' on Drug import charges, the Sydney Morning Herald and the Melbourne Age trumpeted. That man with the golden touch has done it again; Andrew's not content with wrecking companies, now wrecking human lives, the talk show hosts were speculating, and advising what they would do in Jason's place! The home of Jason, Jean and Jnr; was shown on the TV news besieged by reporters, it was another media debacle, but 'what a way to make a living' said Jean as she and Jason watched it all unfold on the telly. "They look like what they are a bunch of voracious parasites trying to devour every, and anything they can find, trying to destroy Cooperate Developments Ltd; and Jason Andrews one minute then eulogizing them the next." In spite of themselves, Jason and Jean seemed to have been hypnotized by watching the media in its frantic efforts to destroy especially Jason; but in reality Cooperate Developments Ltd; as well.

The following day Jason was still in the headlines, but now he was reported as being in hiding from the Aussie Feds. The cartoonist's, had a field day in one Jason was shown as a rock star, surrounded by fans wanting to buy Cocaine. A mafia like figure was in the background saying, that's the best salesman we have ever had! The other group had Jason hiding behind a big rock, with a periscope looking over the top at a crowd of people milling around on the other side. In one hand he has a mobile phone and is saying what you want another delivery, but we just sent you 100kgs have you sold it already ok we will send another 100kgs? It's a bit tough just now those bloody cops are after us! And so it went on for the rest of the week, there was a different headline every day, but suddenly Jason and Cooperate Developments Ltd; were off the front page at last they had found something else to write about, they were back to the old perennial, the war in Iraqi and the 'American President' were in the headlines again.

The family decided to move on up to Queensland, and not buy the papers or switch on the T/V; this way at least they wouldn't know what rubbish was being promoted through the media. All too quickly the week was up and Jason felt they must return to Sydney, so they did, but booked into a major hotel rather than going home. This way Jason knew the media at least would be kept outside, and they could stay inside for a month if need be. A conference room was arranged for Jason to meet with any staff or genuine callers, who may need to see him, and all calls were diverted to the new media consultant Cooperate Developments Ltd; had hired.

Any Aussie Feds calls that could quote a special number, was put through to Jason immediately, it was all so bazaar, as if a real drug lord was in town; and trying to keep himself isolated from the media. Jason was now an even bigger media figure of huge interest to the people, just the mention of his name was big news and his activities of any kind attracted the media circus? Jason had more big shocks coming, but at this stage he was already heavily stressed and wanted to have time to think, he was in constant touch with Rita his PA; but never went near the office. James and Dave kept him abreast of all that he needed to know as soon as anything happened if it was important enough.

An urgent call came from his PA; asking Jason to contact Inspector Juan Chase of the Aussie Feds; as soon as possible. When Jason rang them he had a short wait until Juan took his call. When he did, it was to tell Jason they intended to pick up the Sales manager, that day and charge him with the importation of 100 kgs of Cocaine using the Cooperate Developments Ltd; subsidiary as the importer, by stealing the company credentials illegally.

The first charge would be that he had stolen the identity of the company Cooperate Developments Ltd; Investments; the second charge would be that he used that identity, to import 100 kgs of Cocaine into Australia. The third charge would be that he had caused the product to be sold in every state of the Commonwealth of Australia!

Juan stressed that he was ringing Jason out of courtesy only, he would contact the Security Contractor and James, to officially notify them of what they were doing.

Jason then rang the new media consultant; to instruct her how to handle the surge of media attention that would come as soon as the arrest was made public. She was to avoid any reference to Cooperate Developments Ltd; Investments or any of its staff, and Jason himself would only comment on the drugs arrest through the consultant. A request came through from Cooperate Developments Ltd; for a Director-Managers meeting at the Hotel later that day, this was approved by Jason through his PA; and the meeting set for 6.00 pm!

The Directors and Divisional managers were all on time and the meeting was started immediately, with Jason in the Chair as the Managing Director, and James taking the lead as the Chief Executive Officer for the group, with Dave of course as the General Manager.

James very quickly summarized everything that had happened so far, including the arrest of their 'Sales Manager' one Hemi Chavez a Mexican born Australian. Chavez had worked for Cooperate Developments Ltd; for over two years first in the import division and then promoted to become the sales manager of the entire group. The police had confirmed that Chavez was only a mule for the big operators; he had been the front man who had set the deal up, but that he would never have been able to fund such a big amount of 'Cocaine' on his own account.

On his last holidays Chavez had gone to 'Mexico' and set the deal up including the wall tiles, then he came back and arranged to purchase the wall tiles on behalf of Cooperate Developments Ltd; Investments. He had had an import purchase order forged which was easy to get done, and had arranged delivery to a warehouse on behalf of Cooperate Developments Ltd; as soon as the shipment arrived. The name Cooperate Developments Ltd; had avoided any interest from customs, and the tiles had been delivered to the warehouse as arranged. The drugs had been concealed in the tiles and been taken out before the tiles were transferred to the construction division. The 'Cocaine' when it has been received by the gang had been broken up and was sold on the streets at full street price. The street value at up to $400.00 per gram gave the criminals an income, which was estimated to be well in excess of AU$25,000,000 quite a haul for a bunch of criminals.

James, went on to explain the threats that Jason had received and what had been done, the security agents were now all in place and every person at this meeting, was under guard 24 hours per day. Further the company now had a media consultant, whose full time job was to check the allegations being made by the media. Anything being claimed against Cooperate Developments Ltd; and Jason was to be thoroughly checked, and they would repudiate everything that was wrong? Counter claims through the electronic media, via paid advertisements attacking the media, just as brutally as Cooperate Developments Ltd; was being recorded of Jason were being attacked, especially on the Chavez drugs issue. As far as possible, the outlets used to attack the media, was to be any International Media outlets that weren't involved in the character assassination of Jason and Cooperate Developments Ltd;? The budget for this campaign was substantial Cooperate Developments Ltd; Investments and Jason had decided that they would smear the media just as dramatically as they were being smeared, the intent was to prove that Cooperate Developments Ltd; was now too big to be treated so badly, time would tell which side would give up first. Jason had committed personally to the funding of half the cost, of all the money used to attack his favorite enemy, the much hated media or in his own words Satan's Eyes.

The meeting was closed with James very obviously having taken the lead, and Jason only acting as what he was the Chairman of Directors, he was very pleased at how the meeting had gone. This was now going to be a battle with big money involved, but nobody cared Jason especially, who knew he could in one deal make a very large sum of money so why should he be intimidated by a lot of media and criminal thugs. Jason loved to do battle this was a different battleground, than he was used to but it was still just another battle, and he was a real warrior now, and he knew what to do. The first thing was he would close up the house, and move into this Hotel permanently, in this way his family would be easier to guard.

CHAPTER 9

A new Start:

Jason' realized now he had allowed several problems to beat him, the major one his marriage was on the way to being healed, Jean was feeling safe in the hotel and their marriage had returned to the physical union it had once been. Jason and Jean, had had a full marriage from the start, now that former intimacy had returned. Both of their families came to visit at the hotel, as often and whenever they wanted to, the question of religion was now not an issue. Jean now understood and accepted, she couldn't force Jason into a Catholic relationship, he just wasn't a believer in her faith and never would be? Jason Jnr; had been christened into the church, only his Mother went to mass and took communion etc; the boy would be exempted from church dogma until he was old enough, to make up his own mind what he wanted in the way of spiritual guidance. His mother would talk to the priest and attend confession, but she wasn't to try and influence the children in any way until they made their own minds what they wanted. Finally the priest wasn't to come to their home; he was Jean's mentor not the Jason Andrew's family priest, Jean was to meet him only at the church he wasn't to be invited to their home.

Jason had made up his mind about what he was going to do now, he would fix up the meat losses and he now knew how to do that. Strangely he had had a dream and realized when he awoke it was the perfect answer to the tariff problem in America and great for Cooperate Developments Ltd. As soon as the meat losses were fixed he was going to sell his 25% share of Cooperate Developments Ltd; Investments and retire; from any business activity involving the company. Because his shares would be worth $3-4 billion dollars, he had plans that he wanted to use his fortune for, Charity mainly, in something that to him would be worthwhile.

He was going to go after the criminals that had dared to threaten him and everything he stood for, to do this he was going to set up someone to be his partner to work with him, someone who could teach him the idiosyncrasies of the criminal world preferably a retired detective with a background dealing with drug criminals, he was determined to find out who was behind the drug syndicate and to have them jailed. He would have real financial muscle, and he was going to use it attacking drug peddlers, and doing his bit by doing what the Aussie Feds couldn't do?

He now decided to have James come in so, he could outline how they were going to fix the Meat Losses, and turn those losses into profit. Then he would have Dave come in and he would offer to employ Dave personally to be his front man, this would allow him to be the planner, he would just sit back and plan just as he did with his corporate bids, that had been so successful. This was no different than setting up a business; he would just put the deals in place, and let others run them while he planned the next moves.

He arranged for his old mobile number to be reconnected, he wanted that voice to be able to get through to him, now the chips were down he was ready to play the game. He rang his PA; and asked her to arrange for James to come to see him the next morning at 11.00 am; in the hotel conference room, and the day after that he asked her to have Dave come and see him at the same time, also in the hotel. Everything was ready now he had had his mobile changed and he was ready, so he went up to his hotel suite and waited. That evening as he expected his mobile rang and it was that voice again!

I told you not to cause us any problems didn't I said the voice, now you will have to pay, send me $5M or one of those most close to you, will die.

You can get stuffed said Jason, your man is in jail now and he will stay there for life if you do any harm to any of my people. Further we are coming after you, you fuckin idiot, did you really think you could blackmail me, for a paltry $5M. Bugger the Aussie Feds they are bloody useless, if necessary I will spend $50M to track you barsted's down, I don't care what area of the world you and your fuckin mates are in we will find you. Now kill one of mine if you dare, but the Aussie Feds are nothing to what I can do, so fuck you? If you think the paltry profits you made out of that 'Cocaine' is big money, I will teach you what real money is that shitty 'Cocaine' money is chicken shit to me.

"Well that's your choice, yes I am only the messenger and have no power, but let me tell you that you have just condemned at least four people in your organization, and yourself to death. There is no use abusing me I am just the messenger and you were lucky last time, the gang didn't know you had set up guards, but they know now and it won't work next time believe me? Anyhow I have done my job and delivered the message, once again they don't care if you do go to the idiots in the Aussie Feds, they couldn't find their noses if they were on fire?" The phone clicked at the other end of the line, that must be a landline thought Jason must get that traced if we can in the morning, he went home that night full of confidence, but first he rang the Security firm to warn them he wanted double guards, and then he rang Inspector Jean Chase and explained what he had done. To be quite honest he was beginning to lose confidence in the Aussie Feds they seemed to be doing nothing, just as James had said, they were waiting for the company to do their work for them. After that he went home and had a great meal! By then his wife was ready for bed and Jnr; was asleep, they had great sex just like on their honeymoon life was great again, he was gradually settling down to the life of a happily married man, if only the media would desist. The thought of those Satanic Eyes watching everything he and Cooperate Developments Ltd; did was beginning to be totally frustrating, all he could do was hope that other news would at least take him and Cooperate Developments Ltd; out of the headlines, surely they could find others to persecute?

The next morning he rang Juan and asked if he could trace the phone call from the voice, then he sat and waited for James to arrive.

James was as punctilious as ever and eager to get any news, so Jason filled him in with what he had done, a look of admiration entered James eyes, which strengthened Jason for the discussion ahead.

"Now James," Jason said, "here is how we are going to fix our meat losses we will turn losses into profits. You are to send our buyers out and we want to buy up at least a dozen export meat firms with American orders, they will all be suffering losses; but unlike us they haven't the resources to hold out and keep their businesses functioning properly. They will all be suffering, from these new American Tariffs, as we would be ourselves if we were in their position. They will sell cheap to Cooperate Developments Ltd; believe me! Then we will cancel all of the orders they hold, and close the companies down, but first we will transfer all of their stock to our own companies. This will mean the Americans can sue but by then we will have sent the companies into voluntary liquidation, so all they can sue will be the liquidators, but because we will have taken out all of the assets, there will be nothing left. Cooperate Developments Ltd; and myself won't be involved but we will then have the stock to sell that isn't committed to sell at the pre tariff price, so we can sell all of that stock at post tariff in this way we will cancel out our losses and still make an average small profit, say an average of 10% over the lot. The Americans will squeal like hell but who cares that's not our problem, they will get our committed stock at the pre tariff price, but will have to pay full price for the stock we will be buying. Have no fear even the smaller Kiwi companies' will be happy to sell to Cooperate Developments Ltd; then, they have all been hard hit as well and unless saved may go broke. They have a couple of giant meat companies over there, but they won't have the versatility to act because they are Cooperatives. The Americans cannot leverage the companies we will have bought out because you are to buy them off the liquidator into a nominee company, and take them into our assets off balance sheet, that is all fair and above board. The Americans will have to buy at the right price, and it will all be fair and straight forward just as they would do themselves in a similar position? By selling the stock we have bought cheap at full price off the companies we have bought indirectly for Cooperate Developments Ltd; we will be earning our losses back. We can sell to their client's make our losses back and make profits, from the buyout of those companies, which by then Cooperate Developments Ltd; will then own.

Again James had the look of admiration, that's brilliant he smiled all of our losses back plus the takeovers. This will mean Cooperate Developments Ltd; Investments will be the biggest meat operator in Australia, and we will have beaten the American tariffs bravo that's brilliant. We will have this all completed in a month!

Now said Jason, I have one final message for you my friend, it is my intention to sell out my shares in Cooperate Developments Ltd; Investments I am going to retire it's time to move on my friend, the pressure has been hard and for the sake of my family I want out!

James smiled, as soon as these meat changes are completed, your Cooperate Developments Ltd; Investment shares will go up a dollar at least, if not a bit more it will be a smart time to sell. Actually my broker has orders to buy Cooperate Developments Ltd; as many as he can get, we have managed to buy over 50 million shares at about 25 cents discount on market price, but I am the opposite to you a buyer not a seller. You have built a great company Jason, and I am proud to be a holder of the shares, your sell out will leave me as the biggest single shareholder in Cooperate Developments Ltd; Investments but unlike you my shares are bought on borrowed and margined money. I owe my banks a hell of a lot of money but it will be worth it Cooperate Developments Ltd; has a long way to go yet, before it reaches its true market value, up at least 25% is my guess.

Jason was surprised, that is good news to know that someone is going to be with Cooperate Developments Ltd; or is with them as I move on, now let me tell you another secret. My shares as you know will fetch from 3.5 to 4.5 billion US dollars all of that money is of no use to me, so most of it will go to charity. A bequest of maybe $500,000 will go to my Son the same to my wife, about $1M will go to our family's overall, and I will put $10M aside for myself, the rest will go to charity. As for myself, I want to work as a consultant to business, this will allow me to do the work I love, but not be in the firing line making money. I want my main purpose in life to be with my family, not just my presence but my mind as well, it will be nicer of course if we can have some more children let's just wait and see, but we are both very hopeful?

James had a look of amazement on his face, that's a hell of a lot of money to give away are you sure, that's what you want, it's not just a whim of the present because of being so sick of the pressure?

"Yes I am sure you know all of my shares have been acquired by capital growth, there is nothing owing on them, the banks can get stuffed. Tell me what would happen if all that money was left for my family, it would ruin them all and there would be nothing but heart break I know that. That money could do a lot of good if it is used properly, my wife is a Catholic, and she thinks I know nothing about her religion, but she is wrong they do no more than sit on enormous unused assets. I have studied the Catholics and they are a faith that after 2000 years are still financial imbeciles, they couldn't even run their own bank, but sent it broke. They have huge assets but no cash, why is that! It's because they have a lot of old men, who graduated from being priests, but have never really experienced life in the raw, they don't know what to do with money never have? Their idea is to encourage the wealthy to leave them their estates when they die, that's all they do, oh they once used to collect old bones they had dug up and sell them to the pilgrims. Some of the stories I have read are hilarious, of priests gathering up any old bones and selling them to the peasants to pray over and hasten their path through Purgatory, poor buggers. I am going to set up a charity with a deed of development. All of my money will be donated to that charity, and Jason Andrews will have no influence at all, I stress that under the deed I will be able to do nothing. I knows the media will be screaming tax dodge and it will be, but who cares they can all go to that favorite Aussie place buggery and take their Satan's Eyes with them for all I care? The charity will do only one thing, any church or group of churches be they Catholics, Muslims, Main Line religions including Born Again Christians, any can apply for a donation? This donation must be matched dollar for dollar with their own money, and it must be for any type of work, to benefit the poor. Their own dollar contribution must come from any asset they sell, but they must have owned that asset for at least ten years. The idea is to force some of these old fellas, to sell some of their heirlooms and turn them into something good for their flock, by doing that they will get the said dollar for dollar from the charity. So yes I am sure of what my money needs to be used for?" said Jason.

"I think what you want to do is really great, and we will all applaud you for doing that, but what are you going to do with your time, you cannot sit around just playing with your wife and children, what else will you do," asked James?

"How much does Cooperate Developments Ltd; pay me for consulting work," asked Jason?

"I think it's about $15,000 dollars per day, or something like that, but then you get 25% of CDL profits as well," replied James?

"Well that will be the rate $15,000 per day or part day will be my rate, that's enough for me;" Jason smiled at the look of incredulity on James face.

"But you could get $100,000 a day all day every day, the charity is fine and I understand that. All you need to do hang out your shingle, and public companies would flock to buy your service Cooperate Developments Ltd; would be at the head of the queue and happy to pay that per day."

"That's true but it's why the small companies can't afford me, no I don't want to work for companies like Cooperate Developments Ltd; my intent is to work with the small Fella's. Oh and I have one final intent, and that is to learn a new profession that will be catching corporate crooks, that will be the real job for me it will be really great," Jason said with a laugh.

As James was preparing to leave he said to Jason, "you have shown me a new man today, and it's one that will earn our total respect. What you are going to do is something better than you have ever done before, and anything we can do in the future to help, would be to my mind a privilege. I should tell you that in view of what you have told me today, it will be my hope to get your job as Chairman and Managing Director of the Cooperate Developments Ltd; Investment group of companies."

The next day Dave was scheduled to see Jason at the same time as he had seen James 11.00 am and like James he was right on time. Jason explained what he intended to do; the same as he had done for James, but he wanted to go further than what he wanted to explain to James, Dave had always been personally very close personally to Jason and his family.

Dave for his part was very surprised the same as James had been, but he was different in that he had only a limited view of what his future with Cooperate Developments Ltd; would be with Jason gone! Jason had been his mentor for years, so for him to be losing his mentor was a blow that he had to get used to, and that wouldn't be easy.

Jason then went on to explain that he wanted Dave to transfer from Cooperate Developments Ltd; to working for him personally with his new endeavors. That job would be as the front man for Jason in his crusade of working for small companies, and setting out a program to catch corporate crooks. These would be the type of crooks, such as those that had invaded his and his family's privacy so casually, this was the work he wanted to follow and which he wanted Dave to work with him doing, Dave was to set things up and Jason would do all of the background work.

Jason had also explained that he had set up products they could sell on a commission basis, mainly from NZ but they could also develop the Australian market as well. Their area of work to start with would be in China and in America, but for the present he didn't explain in depth what their full agenda would be, he was content to let that be done at a future date, but he didn't realize how far away that date was going to be.

Dave of course was delighted, and left Jason looking like a man who had just been retrieved from disaster!

The next day the arrest of one Hemi Chavez was in the headlines! The involvement of a Cooperate Developments Ltd; company with the importation of 100 kgs of Cocaine was such important news, that the story covered the full front page of the Australian with the others, almost the same. The electronic media went overboard with some of the silliest comments being made; it was amazing they were not being cautioned by their editors. But their victims were only Cooperate Developments Ltd; Investments and Jason Andrews and they were fair game so anything was allowed.

As usual the cartoonists were featured in the attack, the Australian showed Cooperate Developments Ltd; in the shape of a pirate boat, and Jason was depicted as the captain a very nasty looking character. The sides of the boat were bulging with a full load of Cocaine, and Jason the captain was singing here we go me hearties we be off to Australia, and we be taking solace to those poor buggers down under. The Sydney Morning Herald and the Melbourne Age showed Jason on Wall St. roistering loudly with a group of befuddled looking Americans. He was shouting look we Aussies are catching up to you lot, we are leveraging 'Cocaine' wholesale and making more money than 'Wall St' ever dreamed possible, $400.00 per gram and we have 100 kgs hows that for an easy buck and psst there lots more in Mexico where this last lot cane from.

Then the International Media news on Foxtel came out with a lead story, which was highlighted all over the world. Australia Icon Company slandered by a foolish press and free to air T/V. A major Australian Company has been slandered by the Australian media, when it was linked to criminals that had stolen its identity, and the criminals then used that identity to import drugs into Sydney Australia. The Company has released a report to the international media, denying the claims of the local media, and ridiculing them (the media down under) as just stupid. The Chairman of the Group Mr. Jason Andrews, has persistently been attacked by that media, because of his record of buying Companies, restructuring them keeping some parts and selling the rest. This is a genuine business function in the civilized world, but apparently not in Australia as Cooperate Developments Ltd; Investments and Jason Andrews are again the victims of their constant critics. The company finds it strange to think even the most foolish media, cannot see that drugs as a business, isn't profitable enough for them to waste their time with. The company employs directly 100,000 people in Australia; and another 200,000 indirectly! Because one of those employees in a management position of trust betrays his employers, does that mean the whole company should suffer? The company wants the world to know, that just because the media is stupid, Australians are not; and it's time for that media to finally grow up. Mr. Andrews has built Cooperate Developments Ltd; from nothing, but it is now owned by 10,000 shareholders and is considered to be an Iconic Australian Company with major interests in, Retail Stores 2000, and Child Care centers 800 all franchised and operating Nationwide. As well the company owns a Meat Export Company that is the largest in the country, and recently took control of the Countries major Airline. Mr Andrews still owns 25% of CDL; but is considering selling out? He feels betrayed by an idiotic media that would be best employed on an Island in the Pacific, with only coconuts and monkeys to which they could preach their gospel of stupidity.

The effect was immediate, from that day the media was muzzled by their owners, only real facts were divulged, and Cooperate Developments Ltd; started to get some positive media comments. But as far as Jason Andrew's was concerned it was too late he hated the media with intense venom, to him they were really the eyes of Satan and he would never forgive them.

In the end he had won but at what cost, now he was setting up to go after those criminals, a new period of his life was opening and once he got out he would never again be there for the media to victimize, well so he thought anyhow, but there was a long way to go before they would ever forget him?

CHAPTER 10

Murder:

The media circus had almost vanished, the major papers and big city electronic services had died down dramatically; obviously the most aggressive parasites had been muzzled at long last. But Jason had decided that he with his little family was going to stay on living at the hotel. Jason shares were being sold down progressively, there was no attempt to sell them quickly, that would have dropped the price too far, Jason had set a minimum price at which he would sell per share. The Charity had been set up with a full set of governing rules, just as Jason had directed the lawyers to facilitate, it was a tax haven that's true, but the only beneficiary was the charity.

Cooperate Developments Ltd; had a new 'Managing Chairman,' James, had applied for and won the job he wanted, and he had continued on using the same agenda; the company had operated to with Jason at the helm. Dave had resigned his job as the GM of the Cooperate Developments Ltd; group and was now working with and for Jason on a personal basis. They had an office within the hotel, so they didn't need any receptionist or other staff, the idea was they were going to be small lean and mean, although living in a 5 star hotel wasn't exactly the image of lean and mean, but who cared the tax dept; and GST; paid for 40% of the account anyhow.

The only work they were going to do for the near future; was to scheme how to catch the real criminals behind Hemi Chavez. Jason had compromised his consultant's rate; he was charging $25,000 per day and restricting his services, to companies with a maximum staff of 200 people. He was being besieged by clients most only wanting one or two day's motivational lectures and personal talks with their staff, but he was only taking bookings for six months into the future.

The first job Dave had was to visit Chavez in the Silvercity jail, at Silvercity to see if any information could be gleaned, from him. At the jail Dave had found he needed to make an appointment to visit Chavez, so at the appointed time he arrived early, because he was getting to see Chavez for only 60 minutes, he wanted to be sure he was there on time, to make the most of the opportunity and get as much information as possible, but he was well aware of how prone Chavez was to bullshit he had learned belatedly of the man's reputation for dishonesty, and wasn't impressed but he had a job to do and he was going to do it to the best of his ability?

Chavez was as cocky as ever, but it was obvious he was concealing his true feelings, he soon seemed to relax and tried to be as friendly as his, he thought, ex boss would like him to be, and gradually managed to show a suitable remorse.

Dave greeted Hemi cordially, but came straight to the point, "we want to know more about how you got into this mess, more to the point we want to see the real criminals in jail, and you released and back at work. We know you are just the fellow; who has been set up to take the heat if things went wrong, now they have gone wrong and you will be in jail for bloody years, unless we work together to try and get you out of this dump, but in the end it's all up to you not Cooperate Developments Ltd."

Hemi's eyes went moist with emotion as he responded; "you mean you would help me in spite of what I did he asked? That makes it harder none of the gang have bothered with me, they have left me to face the music, what can I do to help myself. The Aussie Feds have promised me I will get about 20 years at least, so the future indeed looks bleak." said Hemi with tears in his eyes?

Well Dave started, "we aren't the Aussie Feds and we won't be working with them, but I have been put on your case by the company. Our Directors are not being altruistic they want the ones who branded Cooperate Developments Ltd; as drug runners to pay the penalty, and I have told our Directors you are a minor cog in the organization. They have also threatened all of our senior executives and their families, so my job is to bring them to justice. Oh and they tried to blackmail Jason Andrews the real boss for $5M, they sure are a cheeky pack of barsted's, and really need to be checked, the Directors are furious with you, but more specifically with your bosses."

"Ok what can I do?" Asked Hemi, "it's pretty hopeless from here there's nothing I can do, if there was it would have been done before now."

"Well let me say again we are not working with the Aussie Feds we are being funded by Cooperate Developments Ltd; to see if we can do something without them, and if we can find the culprits; we will deal with them the same way as they deal with others, do you understand me properly," asked Jason?

"Well it's pretty clear you want me to work with you, and you will arrange to catch them without using the Aussie Feds, if you can find them is that correct," asked Hemi?"

"Yes that's it precisely, you probably don't know the leaders, but you may be able to give me some leads, it's not me who will do the field work, we will use licensed private investigators. We will if we succeed, work to get you down to about 3-5 years jail time, we have the best criminal lawyers in the country working for us, and they have said if we can break the gang, that's what they guarantee to get you down too, but we cannot guarantee getting you off altogether, you will do real time that's for sure we cannot stop that. It will depend in the future how honest you are with us just how much help you get, it's all up to you nobody else, personally I suggest you do the right thing, because they will drop you if they think you are feeding us bullshit?"

For the first time Hemi started to smile, "these fellows are smart he said, the boss lives in China and he cannot be linked to the gang members, even though he is the boss. I don't know his real name, but I do know he left to live in China about six months ago; his wife and daughter have shifted to the USA and are living there. I know where he lived here up in Darlinghurst, but the actual address I don't remember so I will draw you a map." Which he did immediately! Now Hemi asked, "are you sure the Aussie Feds aren't involved, because if they are it won't be safe for me, even if they have to get at me in here. It's not that they fear the Aussie Feds, just the opposite but we have been sworn to keep our silence no matter what goes wrong. I am being paid even though my career with them is over, but if at any time we break ranks, we will be punished and that means death, so I have trusted you with my life.

"Hemi" said Dave, "you are a brave but foolish man, to get mixed up with people such as these who are really at the heavy criminal level. But my instructions are to help you, if you will help us, obviously we don't know where these people have contacts, even here in this prison, so be very careful what we have spoken about, don't trust anyone in here. Now here is a code that is between you and myself, just to be sure you aren't at risk by me coming here I will send various people, to see you in my place. Each one who comes will give you a new code, so the old one never gets used twice? We really do want to see you safe Hemi! Cooperate Developments

Ltd; and Jason Andrews are very honorable people, respect them and they will give you some real help, they are paying me to straighten this out, don't forget that?"

"Well it could be easier just to give any messages you have to my sister Miriam she can be trusted to bring them to me any time there is a need," Hemi said.

Dave left the prison, but he had reassured Hemi that his now full time job, was to catch the drug cartel bosses. It was hard not to feel sorry for Hemi, he was only a young man who unless he was very lucky, would spend the best part of his life behind bars. As the warder led him away it was as if he was descending back into hell, he probably was but truthfully he had done the damage to himself? Dave felt that he may never see Hemi again, instinctively he felt drawn to that foolish young man, he would work hard to track down the real culprits, but in the end he could only do the best he could.

Meantime Juan had been in touch with Jason and confirmed the phone call from the voice, could be a good lead but they would move carefully. We want to catch the leaders not their flunkies we don't care what you do, but at present we are just watching, he then gave Jason the address of the voice with name and details.

The voice was that of a small time crook Garry Evans, who did donkey work for anybody who would pay him a few bucks; he had probably got ambitious and tried to blackmail Jason on his own account. The real threat was still there, but not from the voice, he didn't have the muscle to do the heavy work. It could be a good lead to follow, but Juan was saying, "this Evan's was small fry hardly worth the effort of following him up; certainly the Aussie Feds wouldn't be doing anything."

Jason was really annoyed at Juan's attitude but passed the information on to Dave, who had that information plus what he had got from Hemi, which he was going to follow up on. The instructions he had from Jason were that he had an open budget, all Jason cared about was results, the costs were irrelevant and as far as Cooperate Developments Ltd; and Jason was concerned the sky was the limit, costs were not a problem? Dave had rented a small office in one of the suburbs of Sydney, (Burwood) ostensibly he was a private investigator who had a few wealthy clients, for whom he provided small services. In fact he was working for Jason Andrews, the former high flying financial guru now retired and living at the most expensive hotel in the Sydney city center.

Dave had also appointed two private investigators to do any hands on work, but they weren't to divulge who they were working for, if they did they would both lose a well paid easy job. Their first job was to get close to Garry Evans and to find out what he knew, and who he had been briefed by when he had first rang Jason. While they were looking after that Dave had traced the house in Darlinghurst that Hemi had drawn the map of, and found it had recently been sold for a price well below apparent real value. The house was standing in a select position just a five minute drive from the city center; it was a very large palatial property the land on which it stood would be worth several million dollars. The house although it could only be seen from the road was obviously an architect designed dream home of immense size, with an Olympic sized swimming pool and on the grounds a double tennis court. The trees and palms had obviously been brought in from the Putty National Park and transplanted when they were fully gown, with the manicured lawns the effect was fabulous, by far the most sumptuous home in the inner city area.

This picture of tranquility naturally raised strong suspicion's, who was the new owner and why had he been able to buy the place so cheap, who was the previous owner, and why had he sold so suddenly and so far under the real value? It was obviously a home that had had a lot of tax free dollars spent on it, which meant it was listed on the government valuation way below real value, otherwise the sale would have been stopped the state tax was high on such a property, but it was obviously improperly listed.

The two investigators returned to report on Garry Evans who for a few dollars, confirmed he had done some work, in return for a few grams of Cocaine. The rumor was there had been a big shipment of Cocaine arrived, and the market had been flooded with cheaper Cocaine; for about eight months. Garry had been a runner delivering to clients, and selling the odd few grams himself, but he had been sacked recently for none payment of his account, and he was being hassled that unless he paid soon he would be dealt with harshly. Garry was a dead beat that would, unless he was very lucky be found dead in a gutter one morning, he did confirm the gang's headquarters where somewhere in Darlinghurst, but that the boss had sold his luxury home and gone to live in China. It seemed strange to the investigators that such a high ranking criminal, could be fingered by such low level pawns like Evan's and Chavez, he must have they said graduated through the ranks quickly and in the early days not been careful about his identity, but now having reached the pinnacle in the Australian drug world, he needed to be far more aloof from the everyday small time crooks that worked for his gang.

Dave then sent one of his investigators to find out, who now owned that house in Darlinghurst, who the previous owner had been, and what the new owner was doing because he was probably still in charge of the Australian operations of the gang? It looked as if it wouldn't be hard to trace the ownership back and so begin to find the genesis of the gang, if indeed it was started in Australia which Jason doubted.

The other investigator he sent up to Darlinghurst to check out the house, and get the registration numbers of any cars, that he could spot at the house, and looked as if they were good enough to be owned by gangsters flush with cash, and silly enough to flaunt their wealth a common undoing of many gangsters who were of low intellect, unlike the leaders who were as cunning as rats?

Dave had co-opted the help of a man at the motor registration office, who could give him the details of vehicle that he wanted traced, in return for the odd reward. It was easy to get the property data from the lands and survey dept! Dave and Jason had set up an effective surveillance operation with a team of operators, to do all of the legwork. None of the cars in the area were of any interest, but Dave had filed them away just in case, they were linked at some time in the future.

Jason had been very busy too! He had got the names of some hard cases; who wouldn't hesitate to do special jobs when called on to do so, they didn't know Jason, but he knew them. At this point Jason was trying to be a tough guy just like his business image, he soon found being a tough criminal was not his vocation, nor would he ever have the unscrupulous character to be a real criminal.

Dave was now sent to set them up and brief them, that they were going to do was what the Aussie Feds, seemed unable to deal with satisfactorily. They were going to work with drug dealers, who had so much money they were immune they had crooked lawyers, and could do whatever they wanted, that was abhorrent to normal society! This investigative team wouldn't be interested in the small fry they were just the mugs, the Aussie Feds could deal with them! What they could be suddenly required for was any special job, and that included getting rid of, any problem people, although Jason soon found he had no stomach for giving such orders? There would be dealers who may be found, that belonged to the drug cartel, and who were too hard to pin drug charges on, but who were proved by Jason's team as being guilty with drug dealing and importation? Jason had decided they must work to take those they could out of operation by handing them over to the Aussie Feds, even though they were finding them quite useless!

Dave got an urgent call from Inspector Juan, Hemi had been attacked in Jail by one of the dangerous criminals, the intent had been to kill Hemi, but he had been too quick and strong when he was attacked, he had reversed the situation and the attacker was dead, he had died instantly from a lucky knife blow straight through the heart. Hemi was seriously injured but would survive, he was in hospital with knife wounds to the lower left chest, luckily the knife had missed the heart. A decision was still being made whether Hemi was to be charged with murder, or just with the possession of a dangerous weapon?

Dave had thought immediately that perhaps the drug cartel was on to him, and the attack on Hemi was a warning, but he wasn't worried the whole executive team was still closely guarded, and very hard to attack. In a way Dave found it amusing, money was going up against money, but Dave knew that if necessary Jason could get more money than any drug dealers could. Dave had finally understood what Jason was doing, he was setting up to take the money back off the druggies, to him it was just another business deal Jason would be fair, but unscrupulous even if he was too soft hearted?

When the news of what had happened got through to Jason, he felt as cold as ice just as when the heat was on with a business takeover, all he could think of was never mind when the time comes we will take all of them barsted's out, that's a promise they will all be in jail for a very long time? He was wrong when the time came most would be dead?

Dave went the next day to see Hemi's sister, she was very upset but real cool! My God this one is like her brother he thought, she will work with us to the very end now, and when we get them she will dance on their graves, but at the same time he was unconvinced she could be trusted, like Hemi she had a reckless streak that could end her in trouble some day?

Hemi was alright she assured Dave, but now realized what a fool he had been, he had got bugger all money, and now they had tried to kill him. Miriam the sister was only 22 YOA; but for sure she would be in there now; getting Dave all of the information she could get, even at risk to herself she could now be a real dangerous bitch, the big question was who too?

The man who had been killed was in for murder, and he had been a really dangerous individual! Hemi hadn't conformed to the prisoners rules, it was as yet difficult to know why he had been attacked, but it was thought the prisoner hierarchy, had decided he was expendable? They had stuffed up with his execution the wrong one had died, only time would tell if there would be another try, but Hemi would never be taken lightly again. He would now become one of the leaders in the jail, he had been attacked with the intent to kill, instead he had killed his attacker, and he would now be a hero to certain low level crim's? These were the ones who were not accepted by nor who accepted the present leaders!

The report came back to Dave about the new owner of the Luxury home in Darlinghurst; he was the apparent owner of a security business, and had a lot of hard cases working for him. He had a front man who acted as the owner operating out of Sydney! The firm provided security bouncers for clubs and hotels all over the city of Sydney as well as in Melbourne and Brisbane. The network was extensive and in a perfect position to peddle drugs, time would tell just how they operated. The fellow who had left and gone to China was the real Australian leader, and the one who now owned the house was the number two in the gang? At present he was the acting head in Australia and New Zealand, and a very dangerous individual, but the links were through the real leader in China; and from him through to the USA?

The number one man had sent his wife and daughter to live in the USA, and he had established residence in Shanghai with extensive investments in Dubai. Dave reported everything back to Jason, and was told to come in the next day for his instructions, but first he was to find the leader's wife and daughter in the USA through the Australian immigration dept? Jason gave Dave the name of a friendly official who for a fee would find the start of their journey, and give him the name of an official in the American immigration dept. who would trace where they were in America at present. Dave would pay no fees, Jason had all of that under control because he had known some of the officials for several years, and he had never used them for illegal purposes, only when he was tracing activities of officials working for companies they at Cooperate Developments Ltd; were to trying to taking over.

CHAPTER 11

Following the trail.

The next day Dave came in for his brief and to report on the Daughter and wife, they were in Chicago at a hotel and waiting for the husband (leader) to visit. Apparently he was very busy in Shanghai working on building projects, many of which he owned outright others for which he represented American owners. The wife and daughter didn't like China and had refused to live there; they had only lived in China for a short time but hated the place, that's why they were in the States.

Jason now issued Dave's work schedule, they had to follow up and trace how the drugs were being sold in Australia, and they had to find the new source. That was to be done by the two investigators and the two hard cases, but they were all to work alone. They were to draw no attention to themselves and they were to drink only lightly, one was to work Brisbane one Melbourne and two were to work in Sydney. They were to report back in eight days to Dave, and he was to dismiss anyone who didn't have a full verbal report.

Dave was booked to fly immediately to Chicago, to check out the drug leader's family; and while he was there he was to set up the right connections, if he could find them then he was to be back in a week.

Jason was in his own mind firmly setting out his goals! First he wanted to trace the drug gang's leaders, and then before he had his team take any action against them, he wanted to find out their method of sales and distribution of their evil product. Then he was determined first to make them pay back the cash he was spending, they would pay the costs for their own destruction. At this early stage he had no idea how it would be done, he thought it probably wasn't much different than a corporate takeover, but he didn't allow for the danger inherent in what he was aspiring to do. First comes the need to find the target, and then comes the strategy! This was no different than his previous work, but in this work he had to completely destroy that target, and see the leaders in Jail? Jason wasn't interested in the mugs such as Hemi Chavez, he was after the leaders and he was determined to get, and have them charged, Chavez was just a small cog in a huge wheel.

When Dave got back from America he went straight to Jason's hotel office to meet with him, and report back on what he had discovered in the States. First he had found the leaders wife and daughter, both were having a great time and enjoying sexual adventures that fairly sizzled. The daughter was 18 YOA extremely promiscuous and had a change of sexual mate about once a month. Her current love was an Italian Stud who was enjoying a temporary lavish life style, and had been in residence with the girl for about three weeks, so he was due to be replaced? The mother was dallying with another woman, and had discovered her preferences for the Lesbian life style! They were living in Las Vegas at present and living the life style of the idle wealthy, this was starting to attract attention of all the parasites that are so prevalent in Las Vegas. Dave, had set up a connection with people who would keep a professional eye on the pair, he had also set up the right contacts if they needed investigative work done. Dave was due to meet with his team later that day, they had been sent to do the work finding out how the drub syndicate worked, and just how many countries they were selling drugs in at the present time? Another meeting was arranged for the next day with Jason, and Dave would bring a full report on drugs sale methods in the Eastern States of Australia. The next day as arranged Dave was back, this time with a very pleased look on his face, the firm that was dealing with the drug sales had security contracts all over Australia, and the teams were set up in units. Each unit had a team of guards; all except one at each sales point had no knowledge of the real job, which was selling drugs. The gang was associated with groups in America and England as well as some connections in Europe. The one guard who was part of the drug team, did all of the selling for his group and he was the boss of his group. The security firm's team and the drug team were two separate companies, as far as the security guards knew they had a boss, but it would be naïve to think they didn't know what was happening. They probably didn't know how the system worked, but they would be stupid if they didn't know what was going on at the different venues. The three states operated under the one security umbrella and the manager of each club gets a cash kick back that was for having given written contract agreements to the security teams? But they would like the innocent guards, have to be stupid not to know what was going on, every night of every day, and seven days a week?

Jason by this time had tracked down where the leader was living in Shanghai China! Dave was told he was booked to go there in two days time! While he was away he was to send his teams out again, but this time two were to go to both Melbourne and Sydney, there would be none sent to Brisbane. Finally before he left he was to meet with Hemi's sister and find out what was happening with Hemi, how he was recovering, and what information she might have, and try to evaluate if Hemi and his sister could be trusted?

Dave met with Miriam (Hemi's Sister) that day; she wasn't taking the whole thing very well just at present, she was asking to be able to do more to help her brother, who had been warned that next time he would die for sure. The gang had abandoned Hemi for his meeting with Dave; as far as they were concerned he was a dead man, apparently the orders had come from the top man in China. Dave left the next day for China, and Miriam had been put on Dave's staff, she was to move amongst the woman, who hung around the clubs but wouldn't start till Dave got back. Jason had been very busy building up a full dossier on the drug gang and its leadership! He had also set out an operating strategy for the security teams; it was exactly as he would have done before executing a business strategy, but now he was operating internationally.

Dave arrived back from China, once again full of enthusiasm, I have he said; seen the leader and he sure is a suave looking fella! He is just the sort you would expect to be sitting back and protecting himself, while the mugs take the fall, he is investing in Shanghai and the Chinese think he is an influential western man, which he is, isn't he? I suppose! He must have sold a lot of drugs because he is investing hundreds of millions of dollars, he is almost at your level Jason, Dave said with a smile. But his is crooked money he isn't using any skill he is investing in high rise buildings, crikey you should see some of them he owns outright. Be assured this man has a worldwide drug business, and he doesn't care a fig about anybody, not even his wife and daughter. I haven't set up a watch on him; he is too dangerous for me to deal with, only you Jason could deal with this fellow in fact I don't want to have anything to do with such a character, he would think quicker than me when he is asleep!

Jason smiled at his friends assessment, what he appreciated about Dave was, he had never been afraid to say when he couldn't deal with a situation, this was an invaluable trait in any man who was in a trusted position. "That's fine Dave," Jason said, "it's still the same though, the whole team has to be destroyed not just him. What must happen; is we will set everything up so that the entire gang is rooted out at the same time. We also want to trace all hidden assets, so that we can hand all of that information to the Aussie Feds at the same time as we destroy his drug businesses. In this way all of his assets can be claimed, on behalf of the state. Now what we want your investigators to do is start tracing all real assets held in the leaders or other associate names? Any person who may be acting as nominees for him, we need to get the lot Dave! Now the hard case two are to be kept working in Sydney, and they are too slowly ingratiate themselves with the guards not the drug sellers, we need to be sure our own men don't get compromised. You will now bring Hemi's sister in, but she is to not to be known by our own men for a while, she is to be our spy you need to set it up, but keep her safe at the same time, we don't need her to be caught?

Dave left with a happy feeling he liked this job better than working for Cooperate Developments Ltd; he liked the feeling of excitement that was constant, he rang Miriam and arranged to meet her the following evening. He told her that if she had a steady boyfriend she trusted to bring him too? He met with his own team and set them to work as Jason had requested, then he took a little break, the first day off in two months.

Jason was puzzled he was sure that they were not doing as well as it appeared, all of his senses were finely honed from the constant twists and turns in the corporate world, his intuition was now telling him they had missed something. The trace had just been far too easy to follow; his instincts were telling him very clearly there was something else. He decided it was something he had to figure out, and to do that he had to sit back and think it was important there should be no more interruptions.

Inspector Juan had rung him that day and asked how his work was going! Jason had told him (Juan) nothing, just that he now knew who the drug gang leader was, and that he had worked out the gang's modus operandi of selling drugs, here and in America. Juan asked if he was going to tell them what he knew, and went very silent when Jason said a very firm no way, they would only stuff up the work he had done? Juan protested loudly, but Jason could not be changed; he flatly refused any thought of Aussie Feds cooperation, at this stage he felt James was right and the police were only sitting back waiting for him.

After Jason had hung up on Juan, he suddenly realized what his intuition was telling him, there was no way they had the gang leader, the man they had was high up, but he was only a front man the leaders were still well hidden. This came as a surprise, but he knew he was right, in matters like this he trusted his instincts implicitly, and his guess was the real bosses were in the USA or somewhere in Europe. This organization is just too big he realized to have been born in Australia; he and Dave had a lot of work yet to be done, so far they had found only the tip of the ice berg and it would be a long time until they found the ones he wanted, it was more likely to be an American crime syndicate than anything that could ever have been started in Australia!

Dave's meeting with Miriam the next evening was quite interesting, Hemi she said had recovered but was now extremely defiant. His spirits were low, and if they tried to kill him again they would have to use several men, he was too big and agile to be treated lightly especially now. He was training constantly and doing heavy gym work, he was determined that if he must die then he would take at least two with him. Miriam said she had no boy friend she would trust with her brother's life, if the gang found out she was working with anyone who wanted to destroy the gang, Hemi would certainly die.

Dave told her she was to be their inspector, they wanted their own people being watched, money he said corrupts then suddenly stopped talking. He had realized too late what he was saying! Tears came flooding into Miriam's eyes, she knew so well her brother had caused his own problems, and she was crying for him as any sister would, and Dave's words lacked any empathy for the family pain. He promised himself he would be more sensitive in future, Miriam left with a determined look on her face, she would be a top employee Dave could see that and was well pleased, but she had the same traits as her foolish brother and he would have to be careful and watch her closely?

The investigators came in and reported that the Leader had been selling down the property he owned in Australia, he had owned quite a large port folio, but had sold several properties over the last 12 months. The money was being transferred via the currency markets, he had a large currency account and he was trading the money via another account into Chinese currency. The other account belonged to an associate who had an account in China, the account in Australia had lost large sums of money to the Chinese account, and it was obviously just a ploy to avoid Australian Taxes.

Dave's, two men were going well ingratiating themselves into two different groups, both had been employed as guards and were very happy with their now two jobs, one for Dave the other for the drug gangs?

Jason was at a loss, he knew now the drug gang was a lot harder to penetrate than he had thought, how he wandered do we progress from here, he decided to call Dave in for a strategy meeting.

Dave when he arrived; was just as perplexed as Jason and had made no helpful comments, all he really had to say was, well we have our team in place now it's up to you as it always has been you are the only one who can lead us from here!

CHAPTER 12

Security breaches.

The next day the phone went and it was James, after the usual pleasantries he said! "Jason we have a disaster here, a mother of one of our executives has been shot dead, as she got out of her car at the local shopping center. I am investigating the matter right now, wait until we have more information I will call you back, but her security man failed to keep her safe, Jason was devastated what the hell must he do now?"

It was only about two hours later when James rang back, it seems we had another man who was working for the same drug ring as Hemi, it was likely they executed his mother to show they could do whatever they wanted to do, and we need to be very careful? I got that information from Inspector Juan Chase; he seems to be saying that you Jason have bought this on us, because you are refusing to work with the Aussie Feds.

Jason's, reaction was only one that was possible from a man who felt very sure of himself, "that James he said is a sad indictment of our society; the Aussie Feds can do little or maybe nothing so they blame me for not supporting, their poor performance, but why on earth is it my fault? Cooperate Developments Ltd; is spending a fortune on trying to run a business and keep their executives safe, meanwhile the Aussie Feds cannot even keep the people in the jails safe, it's not worth my while to react to such nonsense. What are the Aussie Feds doing to break this drug ring that's far more important than casting aspersion's on me, James please don't ring me with such nonsense because you know as well as I do it is nonsense don't you?"

"Yes that's true and you are right that's sure, but you need to know what is going on this is high level Aussie Feds I am talking about here, and the need to respond as only a friend is important. The important thing here is the murder of an innocent woman, and the fact that another one of our managers has been found as corrupted. The other question is whether or not any more of our own team, has been compromised by these drug cartels, you know if we keep losing managers we will be in trouble very soon," James named the latest manager who had been found, and only then did Jason feel the total shock, "I cannot believe it he said in exasperation, what the hell was he thinking of the bloody fool!"

Jason had received such a shock he was over whelmed, this was long a time employee and his mother had been a personal friend for at least 20 years. Oh well he finally sighed that just shows that these criminals have corrupted even the best, and I have another grudge against these inhuman thugs.

Dave rang later in the day and Jason told him to come in for a conversation, one that could not be had over the phone!

After Dave had arrived and Jason had explained what had happened, Dave was as amazed as Jason had been. "So where do we go from here boss, it was too good to be true that we were making such good progress, how do we find the real leaders and where do we go from here?" Dave asked.

"We have to penetrate even deeper into that gang, and not let them know who is attacking their organization. If we can get deep enough to put the structure at real risk, we may get the dragon to show itself, while we try to destroy their organization at least here in Australia and NZ. It really is terrible situation I thought this only happened on T/V; and overseas not here down under imagine they have even polluted little NZ. The trick will be to make it so the leader we have found cannot come back to Australia, they will send someone else, but that someone will have to be at top level. The leader we now know of is obviously aware he is at risk here, that's why he left. We have to attack as quickly as we can, so that they have to send someone else! You need to arrange a time when we can have a full gang working say a Saturday night! The idea will be to have all of the teams working and have them all picked up with a raid in the three States, which will rob them of their retail outlets. The clubs and hotels can be charged with allowing drug sales on the premises, and their licenses will be under threat. The sales men will all be caught with drugs for sale, and they will all finish up with Hemi? Now I want you to have the teams getting this all together, and we need Miriam to be watching very closely that our people are genuine? If she sees even one of them do anything even a little suspicious then we will have to abort, but if they are real we want to run with the Aussie Feds within the next two weeks. Dave you are to work hard to get this all together and get Aussie Feds the blame and or credit for the whole raid. After you leave today I will speak to them, and set the raid up with them. But I will tell them as little as possible, let's just say we don't even trust the Aussie Feds we trust nobody Dave only ourselves?" Jason said.

As soon as Dave had left, Jason rang Inspector Juan Chase, and arranged a meeting within the hour at their office, and then he rang for a cab and was taken to the Aussie Feds head office.

As soon as Jason had arrived Juan and his helper entered the room, they both listened as Jason outlined what he wanted to do; they agreed to be ready for the raid when they were advised of the time? Jason left and went back to the hotel he was a little nervous, but he had watched both of the men carefully, and felt they weren't involved with the drug cartels. They had said it would take at least two weeks to set up such a large bust, but he could see they were keen on the idea of getting so many of the drug dealers at the same time. And to get them in the three eastern states would be wonderful for their careers?

Dave had called in all of his operatives but not Miriam, without telling them the extent of the proposed bust, he asked for the full schedules and names of every spot the drug dealers worked at. He also wanted their names, and told his team there was a bust coming, but not who was doing it, the idea was to let them think it was a private bust, and the Aussie Feds weren't involved. He figured this way the bust if it got out and the gang was warned it would be arrogantly ignored, and in no time just set up again, the gangs would be being naïve, but that was not what Jason wanted he wanted the bust to work? There was no way they would get any of the gang leaders this way, but it would hurt them quite considerably and that was a start instead of just talking, there was going to be some real action.

Miriam was then asked to come into the office as soon as she could! When she arrived she was told she had to be especially watchful, over the next two weeks and to move among the clubs, she had an expense account to fly to and observe Brisbane and Melbourne as well. She was to be back in Sydney with a full report in two weeks time. Dave himself left the next day to fly to Chicago, then to Shanghai he had let Jason know he would be back in ten days, but would contact him if he needed help, if he did it would only be because it was urgent? Now the time was coming up Dave didn't really savor this part of the job, he knew he had to spy on the leaders and he was uneasy.

When Dave arrived back in Chicago it was obvious the daughter was looking for a new man, so he decided to find her one, he arranged through an associate of his own, to have a young Italian arrive on the scene and sweep the young miss of her feet. Then it was arranged that the young lovers would elope, for a two weeks jaunt on the French Riviera, but they would tell no one she would pretend she had been taken by force.

Unknown to the young miss a note was sent to her mother, demanding a ransom fee of USD10 million payable within two days or she would be killed. The intent was to see what her father would do, when he was notified his daughter had been kidnapped. Dave for his part was booked into the hotel and prepared to watch and listen with interest. He had had the suite bugged, and had gambled the young couple wouldn't hear about the kidnap claim, where they were on the Riviera?

Dave was prepared to bet the father would refuse to come to Chicago, he would send some of his goons to try find the girl, while he sat in Shanghai and watched as the kidnap unfolded. Dave was wrong, the father was there within 24 hours and strongly berating his wife, for not taking proper care of the girl. Dave sat transfixed as he listened to the drama unfold in the suite, there was a panic as the father arranged to get the money immediately, he spoke to someone on the phone, a local call, and arranged to get the money delivered. Then he set up a team of men to follow the kidnappers, when they arrived to pick up the money. There was to be no violence until the girl was back home, but then the kidnappers were to be killed immediately, and the bodies left for the police to find.

Dave then left a note under the door at about 3.00 am; then he sat and listened until the note was discovered. Meantime he did a trace on that phone call, and had come up with a name and address. He also did a trace on the call arranging the killing of the kidnappers and got another name and address, good he thought so what do I do now? He moved out of the hotel and booked into another close by, but now he changed his name and again waited on his listening device. It wasn't long in coming! The same number was called and the instructions issued on how to deliver the money, then the other number was called to the kill team again, with the pickup details. Dave was amazed they didn't question how easily the trail was left to follow the kidnappers, surely they would realize it was a scam, but they didn't just carried on as instructed.

The young couple would soon be back and the scam would be out in the open, the gangsters would be buzzing around like flies, trying to find out the purpose of it all. It wouldn't take long to realize the intent had been to get the leader to America, and then the hunt would be on for real. Dave booked a flight to Boston then another under a different name back to LAX, from where he was booked to fly to China. But from LAX he would be one of many hundreds who flew to Australia every day, he cancelled his flight to Shanghai, and booked a flight to Sydney under his real name, then flew back to LAX under an assumed name again. Let them try to trace me now he thought, as he finished booking the complex route he was taking. Then he sat back again and listened to the drama as it unfolded next door. First there came the report that the money hadn't been picked up. Then the call that there wasn't anybody remotely resembling the kidnappers around, where the money was supposed to be picked up. Then came the sounds of anguish as the mother was crying for the lost girl, at this point it was time for Dave to leave, only Jason could handle the upset from here, he would know what to do, but for Dave it was time to go home? Dave wasn't a gang land type it was way too complicated for him, he just wanted to get home now and do his own work?

As soon as Dave arrived back in Sydney he felt safer, and immediately rang Jason for a meeting. After he had given Jason a full report, including the phone numbers and names in Chicago, he went back to his home for a well earned rest.

Meantime Jason spoke to friends in Chicago, and had the information Dave left with him followed through! It appeared as if all of the contacts Jason had been given where members of the Mafia group in Chicago, now Jason knew they were getting to the real leaders, it was time to be very careful that none of his people were traceable, these mafia people would kill without thinking, that was their trade mark.

Jason was well satisfied with how things were going, the news of his retirement and donation of almost four billion dollars to charity had stopped the media cold, he was no longer news. His private work now was started and beginning to bring him in an income, the news of his work and the fees he charged were mentioned, but then forgotten! He was yesterday's man and no longer of interest of any in the media! Jean was proud of how he had dealt with the whole problem and wanted to go back to their home, but Jason wasn't ready yet he needed more time to assess just how safe it was.

CHAPTER 13

A police raid.

After he had finished setting up the police raid he would think through whether or not it was yet safe at the house. Jean was now getting very impatient, hotel life had palled, and she wanted the freedom of being in a house. Jason had been thinking about Jean's wants, and decided they could give the house back they had been living in, it was owned by Cooperate Developments Ltd; and they could do with it whatever they decided. He told Jean she could go out and buy a simple house in a nice neighborhood, and pay for it in her maiden name. Then she could buy a small car and put that also in her maiden name! She could buy all of the furniture she wanted and buy it at different shops, again all in her maiden name. In this way maybe they could stay inconspicuous for as long as possible, and hopefully say after 12 months he would be completely forgotten. Then they could buy a far nicer home without worry of media attention ever again! Well that was his dream, but would it ever come true, only time would tell? Meantime what she was doing would keep Jean occupied for at least two months by then it should be over, and the Aussie Feds crackdown on the drug syndicate would have been completed; that was what he planned but he didn't know if it would work.

Meantime Jason had been in touch with his contacts in America, and discovered that the leader's daughter had come home, with a beautiful French Riviera golden tan, but already with a new boyfriend. The latest lover was French and she had met him on the Riviera, and given the Italian stud she had gone there with the flick, just as if she was changing into a new dress. The Italian didn't care either, he just went off with another wealthy girl to play with, this was the French Riviera everyone exchanged playmates, as far as the men were concerned it was as easy as changing their underwear. When the daughter walked in so casually her parents, usually so compliant to her many wants were enraged. How the hell they asked can you be so unthinking as to just leave and say nothing! For her part she couldn't have cared less, she simply told the Frenchman to come back in a few days, then went to her room and stayed in bed for the next two days, recovering from her adventures.

The leader wasn't so silly as to not know something had happened, but he guessed it right, somebody from Australia or maybe NZ was tracing his contacts and they had found the mafia. He was convinced that someone was the Aussie Feds; so he could do nothing except send a warning through to his man in Australia. Just be very careful he had warned because the Feds are up to something, we don't know what the hell is going on, but keep a sharp watch on any move made by them. Had Dave known all of his moves on leaving America were unnecessary, he would have been delighted, but pleased at having erred on the side of caution. All of those flights had worn him out and he got home totally jet lagged.

Dave, had his reports in from his men in the field, that all was well and he had the lists of names and the timetables of the working spots, and when the times the drugs were usually being heavily sold. They advised that the sales men constantly refilled their pockets with new supplies, but the hiding spots were also pin pointed in their very comprehensive reports. Miriam came in after the men had gone and confirmed the all clear, she had had two of her sisters help her do the job, all were keen to help their wayward brother. Their parents were distraught especially their mother, who was a nurses aid she was distraught for her only Son, even though he had bought such shame on the entire family. His eldest sister and her husband had disowned Hemi, but had yielded to their mother's insistence that they keep that news away from Hemi.

The time for the Aussie Feds raid was getting very close, the reports in their entirety had been sanitized and passed on, and the Aussie Feds would never be able to find Dave's team, no matter how hard they tried. It didn't really matter if they did, but Jason had no trust for the Aussie Feds security, and preferred they know nothing. The time had arrived; the Aussie Feds teams hadn't even been told what was happening. The leaks by crooked cops would spoil the whole raid, and the entire operation would be a waste of time. Just an hour before the raids in the three cities were to be started the teams were first told to hand in their mobile phones, then they were briefed and the raids were finally underway.

Inspector Juan Chase had been preparing for the coming bust very carefully, from the day it had first been proposed by Jason Andrews, even though he was cynical that it would actually happen. How he wondered had the Cooperate Developments Ltd; team could never have dreamed of such an attack? His Aussie Feds team could never have been able to coordinate a plan of this scale in the three states at the same time. They had received a report from a car dealer, about a Mexican with a lot of cash, some of which he had used to pay for a new Mercedes Benz car. They had raided the man's home and caught two men with cash of over $1,000,000 in their home; this had been the start of the trace to Hemi Chavez and his drug connections. The two men had been Mexican's; and from information in the flat the Aussie Feds had been able to trace Chavez, but they had been unable to connect him to the money and drugs. In fact drugs had not been involved, the money was claimed to be gambling money, but the suspects had been unable to prove where the money had been won from. One of the two men imprisoned had given a statement, indicating that Chavez was actually the leader, and was a major drug dealer; who had imported the Cocaine from Mexico. He had also told the Aussie Feds how Chavez had bought the drugs into Australia, but he didn't know the name of the company; Chavez had boasted he had several companies he could use. In return the man had been released from prison on bail, and the police hadn't tried to stop him going back to Mexico. In the meantime there was nothing done about Chavez, the police just sat back and watched him. Chavez had weekly visited the other man who was still in jail, and had shown little concern that the police knew about him, he just carried on as if nothing untoward had happened. The police then traced connections Chavez had among the Bikie Gangs, by simply bugging his mobile phone, and they found his connections were substantial. They had kept a trace on Chavez for over 18 months and found it was true he did have managerial control in several companies, but the big one was Cooperate Developments Ltd. When Chavez had finally been picked up in his possession was found, the identity badge of a NZ Inspector of Drugs, which was stolen, and also three NSW driving licenses although his own license had been suspended for several years, by the courts.

Juan had promised Jason he would be given progress reports from the field and that promise was kept by Juan himself. All of the raids were a stunning success, over 1,000 busts were made that night, all of the salesmen had drugs on them plus their stashes were all found, it was an amazing police coup. There was no leak that a private firm was behind the information that the Aussie Feds were working with, Juan was promoted to Commander for the good work, and his helper was promoted to Inspector. Jason was getting some strong support from the Aussie Feds now, but only Commander Juan and the new Inspector Ian Jones knew that Jason even existed; it was indeed a fait accompli.

The two in Dave's team who were working as guards, were able to report the devastation to the gangs drug business, the Jailing of so many key men was a disaster, the surrogate leader went to China to meet with his boss. Dave's, men was able to get one of the leaders team to work with them, it was a counter espionage situation, Jason's team was even penetrating now at top level, Jason's was using his money to really get into the inner workings of the drug organization. The whole system was working, because they were a very small team and not the Aussie Feds! It was amusing because the Aussie Feds were being blamed, but the gangs were not able to find anything, only Juan and Ian knew anything, and they were enjoying their success they wouldn't be talking. Jason, now met with Dave and warned him they were to get no bigger, he now had five men and Miriam, he didn't want to get any bigger because being to big would leave open the chance for mistakes and that would ruin the whole system. Exposure now would be so dangerous, and Jason didn't want any more risk!

Jason had donated all of his shares in Cooperate Developments Ltd; to the charity that he had set up, but he had in the end kept $50,000,000 by value in cash, and put them into what he called a drug busting account, which was earning interest of $5,000,000 per year. This was the money he was using to finance his drug busting efforts. He had kept $10,000,000 for himself and Jean, and set up a reserve account for their son and any other children they may have. In total the Charity had received just over USD4 Billion, and now had their own independent Board of Trustees. There was no way that Jason could ever have access to any of the money, it was no longer his, the Australian tax laws forbade him access in any way, and the charitable income if any would be tax free. Jason was now of no interest to the media; there had been a time of surprise when the charity was first announced, but it was now over, and finally he was being left in peace.

There had been a lot of media attention to the mass arrests of the drug salesmen, it was as if the Aussie Feds had done well, but as far as the media was concerned it was about time, they did something, if they had known the truth that it was Jason who had engineered the bust, it would have been a political drama?

The number two leader was due back in Australia! Jason was looking forward to what Dave could get from him about the Chinese meeting; and what they were going to do to fix up the damage done by the Aussie Feds raid. Jason felt they would think the Aussie Feds had been able to plant a Judas in their organization; and they would be setting out to find, and trap that person. Dave; was also wandering what the gang would do now, and he was waiting for the return of their Judas who was in his pay, so that he would have inside information.

It was only a few days later that Dave received a phone call, from his contact inside the drug team, he wanted a meeting as soon as possible! Dave agreed and the time was set for the next day, at a local Chinese restaurant. Both men would be alone, and Dave was to bring the money that was due to be paid to his contact, if the money wasn't paid there would be no information provided. Thank goodness we have nobody like this on our team Jason was thinking, but we will have to be very careful and selective, the fact that most of Dave's team had been allowed to earn two lots of wages would, he hoped keep the team satisfied. But he and Dave would have to develop security measures such as were used when working on a corporate takeover, on that type of work it was very stringent and nobody was taken for granted, because the stakes were so high, higher than the drug gangs would ever be?

The two men met as arranged and the information provided was very revealing! The leader was back in China, and he was convinced the Aussie Feds, were very skillfully penetrating their organization. He believed the debacle in Chicago within his family had been created by the Aussie Feds and they had also been able to plant a Judas in the American gang's ranks as well. The Americans had demanded the Australian Leader find the Judas immediately, and kill him there was to be no mercy. The drug sales had to be set up again unless a new method when one could be found; but there was now a serious problem. The gang was committed to their suppliers to take another batch of 'Cocaine' this supply was due to arrive within a few days, and was another 100 kgs. If the supply was intercepted by the Aussie Feds it would cripple the gang in Australia, and they would be forced to retreat to their roots in America. Dave's, contact could not, or had not, confirmed how the drugs would arrive! Dave felt the man knew, but didn't want to completely destroy the gang, which after all was his main employer, unless the offer from Jason was far higher than at present. He showed no fear of being found out as a Judas, quite the opposite he hated the Americans'.

Dave and Jason met and decided not to pass the information on to the Aussie Feds, they didn't want to put their contact at risk, rather they decided to keep it to themselves, and see what they could do by themselves. Dave and Jason, realized it may be dangerous for their team in the field, they decided to keep them in place, but they would be told not to take any position selling drugs, if they were offered such a job Dave was very careful to inform them how dangerous it could be. The leaders were looking for an Aussie Feds plant, and they didn't want to be mistaken for that, they weren't Aussie Feds plants never had been? Dave also met with Miriam and told her to be careful, and if she was frightened she could pull out. Miriam wasn't at all frightened as she rightly said all I am doing is going to clubs and hotels, so why should my brother's problems stop me from doing whatever I want too? The contact Dave had didn't know what they were doing, but he did know there was a concern that executives and their families Cooperate Developments Ltd; were in real danger, of that he as yet knew nothing, but he would try to get abreast of that if he could. He warned Dave that execution orders came from the Mafia in Chicago and were carried out by hit men sent by them, they didn't trust the Australians with such dangerous work and never would, but they may have a local Australian hit man who only they knew about, none had any idea on that type of work, because the local leaders had refused to be involved unless their own families was at risk.

Dave met with Jason, and both of them decided they had done a lot of work, but now it was time to take a break to let things cool down. Jason, was going to keep monitoring the situation but he would do nothing, for the time being.

Everything seemed to be going well, until an urgent call came from James at Cooperate Developments Ltd; another of their Executives had been compromised and had been shot dead. Jason was devastated, "my goodness he said it seems Cooperate Developments Ltd; has been heavily infiltrated by this gang of criminals, how many more of their team are compromised? James, you had better start a search before you have more staff being executed, what is going to happen next, I dread to think now who else is involved obviously Hemi was just one of a team? We will try to find out for you who else they have at Cooperate Developments Ltd; we have been harboring these criminals for a long time it seems?" Jason had said.

"OK I will work on it from my side, if you can snoop out some help for me it will be good, we don't want any more of our people being executed, better to find them first and fire them, it could be safer for them," said James.

Jason contacted Dave, immediately with a request for help from Hemi, and Miriam was sent to ask her brother, if he knew anything that would help. Miriam was back within three days naming another three of the Cooperate Developments Ltd; team who had all been in the gang far longer than he had been, one in fact who had recruited Hemi! Miriam asked

Dave to be very careful because Hemi's life could be lost if the gang got such strong evidence against him. The first attempt to kill Rene had not been the gang after all, but if they got evidence he was squealing from Jail, they would move immediately and he would die for sure. Hemi stressed that the execution of those who in any way squealed was immediate and would be done by gang members in Jail.

Dave reported back to Jason, and was assured that there would be no sudden sackings at Cooperate Developments Ltd; in fact the information would not be passed on to James at this stage. The death count over the last 12 months was now three, Jason was feeling very depressed, he felt that so far he had failed, and now he knew that in some way the Mafia in Chicago was involved he thought of giving up, then decided he had to carry on, but he needed something else to do for a while. He decided he would increase work with his consultancy clients, for which he had many bookings waiting for him to ring back and set up a time. Jason met with Dave, and told him to lay off the team for two months on full wages, they were to circulate among the clubs etc; with one each in Brisbane and Melbourne, and again two in Sydney. Two of them were employed as guards anyhow, the other two were encouraged to try and get jobs as guards as well? The idea would be to penetrate as deep as they could into the gang but keep away from selling drugs! Miriam was told she was not to be employed by the gang, but was to circulate only in her home town of Sydney. There would be going to times she would be asked to do work for Jason, setting up his appointments etc; in fact she would probably be in the office full time very soon.

Dave, wasn't getting any break he was going to work with Jason, but behind the scenes neither he nor Miriam would be doing anything up front, full anonymity was to be kept for future drug bust needs? Jason was concerned they were not getting to the leaders; and he had to work out a strategy that rectified that problem. He knew now the problem was in Chicago, but he didn't really want to go that far, in fact without a structure he couldn't go that far. The point was they weren't vigilantes, but they did want to revenge the killings that had so far been perpetrated in their own ranks.

CHAPTER 14

Changes are coming:

It was time for Jason to do some work and make some money! He wanted to pay the costs of Dave and the team out of his income, and keep the money he had put aside for a fighting fund for any problems that may arise. He felt the $50 million plus interest he had saved from the sale of his shares, was an emergency fund that was to be used only if they got into trouble. Jason truly believed that before the battle was over with the drug gang, he would be spending all of that money, but if he was winning the fight he would spend it all gladly.

Now he wanted to start work and make some money from his skills as a businessman, Miriam was to handle the bookings etc; and Dave was to be his research assistant.

Miriam, was bought into Dave's private office for training and the two of them worked there, totally engrossed in what they were doing, setting up a small operation for Dave was fun, and for Miriam a new type of job.

Dave had found Miriam, was semi trained and he congratulated her on her work because it was clean and neatly presented "you are here to do the entire bookings etc; for Jason and keep an account on the payments that are due, and when they are received neither him nor me, are any good at that sort of work. When you get a phone inquiry from a prospective client asking for Mr. Andrews to do a job for them, you are to get sketched written details of what they want done, and how many days they think it will take. You must tell them the fee is $25,000 per day or part day payable in thirty days! Finally they must be told that you will ring them back when you find out if Mr. Andrews will accept the job, and that you will let them know by phone when you hear from him, you will also let them know when he is free to actually do their job if he accepts," Dave had been careful to instruct Miriam clearly.

"Every inquiry, I will take your phone instructions and then report the sketched details, back to Jason to find out if he actually wants the job? Every job he decides he will actually do I want you to ring them and be able to give me a report, on what they want Jason to do in full, and then I will research the job for him?"

The first client was a manufacturing plant, one that was producing precast concrete products, but was having difficulty with the sales prices, because of very strong competition from a lot of small mum and dad plants with no overheads. Jason was booked for two days at $25,000 per day.

Jason's advice was very clear he asked their manager, "What lines do you produce that sells the best, and who is your closest opposition that would be in the same position as you are?"

Having been shown the products they were most successful with and why, he was then told the history of their opposition.

Now asked Jason, "is your opposition in a position to sell to you, or maybe they want to merge, but tell me first are their best selling lines the same as yours?"

The answer was "no their lines are different and like us they dominate the market, with their main lines."

Now asked Jason, "What percentage of your sales are products that you dominate in and what is theirs?"

The answer was that his client's dominant sales were 50% of their total and the opposition is also 50% of their total.

"Well" said Jason, "the answer is surely that you buy the opposition out, what is your business worth at present and what would it be worth if you had their sales, and could cut out producing all of the lines that don't sell well?"

The answer was the value of the business would more than double!

"Well then" said Jason, "you need to make them an offer, because they want to sell just as you do, because they have the same problems as you, but here is what you do. Make them an offer subject to the value of the stock they have and the money that is owing to them. And you offer to pay in a period of time say six months, and you issue a promissory note that you will pay, how do you get on with your bank?"

Q/ how they asked do you know they want to sell. A/ because they like your firm is in the same trouble. But the only way out for both firms is either sell or merge.

The bank wasn't a problem, they would lend money on the stock and debtors, and if they knew the trade would double they would back that too, in other words the Bank would guarantee the promissory note.

"OK" said Jason, "so you make the offer and pay them the value of the stock and debtors up front, since your turnover is double your profit should now increase by 150%. You will have a successful takeover or merger, which ever they prefer and believe me they will want to deal."

Q/ and how they asked do we pay them out. A/ well the stock and debtors will all come in within 60 days the balance is covered by the promissory note and if your assessment is right, your company will be worth twice as much with the enhanced flow, so you said your bank will back you. Naturally his clients were delighted.

The second day was to be a motivational talk split up into four, one and a half hour breaks.

Jason started the first session off by explaining the agenda for the day. Session one was to be on finance, two was production, three was sales, and four was management.

Jason had started by saying, "Finance is the most boring area of business, but sadly for me it is my area of work! Many years ago when I started my career I would have chosen any other area of work, but nobody would have employed me now everybody would give me a job, so one never knows what way life will go.

Jason went on to show he was very well versed in how to motivate all of the staff in the work place, everyone present learned a lot that day. He had the ability to be very interesting, and kept his listeners wide awake all day as they sat back and listened to his, often very amusing anecdotes on the variables of business.

"What do you do if your business is going broke?" he asked at one stage.

You close it was the general comment.

"No, you sell your business to somebody else who is doing well, after you have bought them out!" Jason replied.

"What you do if your company has lost a vital contract to a competitor, he asked.

You cut back your costs and consolidate they answered.

"No you offer a high price to your competitor to buy them out, if they accept you borrow against their contract from your own bank. Effectively you are buying them out with their own business! If they don't agree then you increase the offer, or offer a merger.

"What do you do with a manager who isn't doing well at his job?" he asked.

"Fire him," they replied.

"No you send him to the human resources people, and then place him in a job he can handle. A good company only sacks staff if it's unavoidable?" Jason said.

The whole day was spent in interaction with his listeners they loved it, and they really did learn.

The next client was a group of mushroom farms growing cultivated mushrooms.

"What is it you want me to do," was Jason's question.

"We are a group of twenty farms, how do we integrate our activities so that we can cut overall costs?" was the Query.

"It appears your business structure is too big and unwieldy as it is," was Jason's answer.

The best thing that can be done is to form the group into a farmers' cooperative, in this way the tax costs are spread to being paid on dividends only. The work can also be also be spread with different farms doing different tasks, so as the mushrooms are produced uniformly as the market needs are met?

There was barely a day's work involved, but the clients were well pleased at the result of the advice he gave them.

At Cooperate Developments Ltd; things had been quiet for a while and James had produced good profits, but of course there had been no takeovers, only Jason who was no longer with Cooperate Developments Ltd; was the master in that field. The company had performed very well with Capital and Trading profits, at a very high level considering there were no special profits, being made.

The day at the head office had started as usual with nothing special expected, when two men dressed in business suits walked in and asked to see three of the top executives, of the company, they were quite ordinary looking blokes and the receptionist took little notice of them she had no reason to question them their executives often had visitors from other companies. They introduced themselves by saying they were on a special assignment from a well known company in Sydney, so that no suspicions were aroused. The receptionist; had tried to contact the three men but in the end gave up, she told the men waiting that only two of the men they had asked for were available, and they would be out in a few minutes. The two men smiled and thanked the receptionist, then just stood quietly waiting for the two men to arrive. The girl remembered later the two men had accents, but didn't sound American. The Executives walked out to the reception area, both of them walked forward smiling and held out their hands in a greeting. Instead the two strangers asked if they were the two men they were waiting for, and when they were assured yes they were the ones, the two men casually pulled out pistols and shot the two men through the heart. They fired twice into the same heart area, and then casually walked out of the office, followed by the hysterical screams of the staff who had just watched in horror. It was a traumatic shock for the girls in reception; suddenly the two senior men were lying on the floor dead?

At the time this happened Jason was enjoying the work he had been doing which was a nice change, from working to try and undermine the drug gangs, but then he got an urgent call from James at Cooperate Developments Ltd; "Jason we have had another two of our managers shot and killed, you and I need to meet if you have time please. I really don't know what to do, this is beyond my experience apparently they were linked to the drug gang the same as the others were?" said a very upset James.

James came to the hotel to meet with Jason, later the same day to discuss the drug gang's deep penetration of the Cooperate Developments Ltd; management staff. "Things have really got bad at Cooperate Developments Ltd; the total of our staff now found to have been involved is four, and now three of them have been executed? Add in the lady shot down and we have four deaths and one in Jail! Where is this going to end, are there more of our managers involved? I am completely lost and none of the Directors have any idea's either, the total staff at Cooperate Developments Ltd; are unable to comprehend what has happened!" said James.

Jason now felt a little guilty had not having told James of the knowledge, he had that there was still another one manager involved. James he said, "I must now tell you the truth there is still another one on the staff, perhaps you have got to let him go before he gets killed as well as the others. I am so sorry for not telling you, but we didn't want to get involved, Dave and I didn't know they would kill those men just like that."

"That's fine I know you would have a good reason for keeping the information to yourself, no one would have thought they would kill so casually, but what do we do now with the last one do you think," asked James with a grimace on his face.

Jason replied, "James you must be getting short of managers by now, but for His and the Company's sake its probably better to let him go now, but tell him why so he can try and protect himself. This is developing into a real mess, they are probably linking them all with Hemi Chavez, and it seems they have missed with trying to kill him. One minute we are told it's not the drug gang that tried to kill him, next it was them! It's hard to know what the hell is going on the Aussie Feds don't know anything, what is the Cooperate Developments Ltd; security doing? It seems their much vaunted security team is not achieving much, there has been four killed now that were being protected by them, what do they have to say for themselves?"

"Not much they are looking silly and are not at all happy," James said, "these people just walked into our office and shot the two of their clients, then casually walked away. Then they got into a car and drove away as if nothing had happened, it was so professional it's hard to believe this could happen in Sydney. Killings like this only happen on T/V in New York or Chicago not here, well not until now anyhow the problem is, now how do we protect the families? I will have our agent release a media statement, but we aren't of much interest to the media anymore since you left and vanished! We will name the one who has left the company ostensibly because he was asked for when the gunmen came, so is too frightened for his life and feels he had best leave the country, since Cooperative Developments Ltd cannot protect its staff?"

"I will call on Commander Juan Chase," Jason said, "and see if he has anything for us, he is probably still basking in his last success, but we never know he may know something of interest, they haven't been much use have they all talk and no action, you were so right when you said the Aussie Feds sit back and leave it to the victims, at least that's all they have done so far," Jason had suddenly gone quiet because he realized suddenly that James didn't know it was he and Dave who had initiated the Aussie Feds success in its recent drug raid?

James, left Jason but he was deep in thought he had a big business to run, now he was seriously short of managers! The Directors were asking questions they were a useless bunch of barsted's if ever there was one. How the hell did Jason put up with them for so long, James was sick of their whinging and asking silly questions, no wonder Jason had quit if he had Jason's money he would quit too? All they ever wanted to know was how much the Directors fees were going to be this year, and whining because there were no more takeovers with big profits, which gave them extra big bonuses every now and again. All they ever wanted to know was when Jason was coming back, and why James didn't move for a takeover bid, like Jason would do, they couldn't accept that Jason's work was lost to them now, and he wouldn't be back.

As soon as James had left Jason had rung Juan, "can you help the Cooperate Developments Ltd; crew he asked, James has just left me he is a deeply worried man, and he needs some help what have you got?"

"To be honest we are just as much in the dark as you are," answered Juan, "I don't know why they have taken those two men out, but they must have a reason. Surely it's not because of our successful raid, because that was just an Aussie Feds job it had nothing to do with CDL. Hemi Chavez is still very much alive, it would be more logical to kill him, but maybe he has got them bluffed. I hear he is the big man at Silvercity Prison now days, typical Latino bullshit I think! Anyhow Jason if we get anything you should know we will give you a call, but don't sit waiting, this is going to be a slow hard slog, believe me."

"Yes while you slog and go nowhere Cooperate Developments Ltd; is losing a lot of its executives, let's face it Juan even your successful raid only came because of Cooperate Developments Ltd; efforts, I don't think the Aussie Feds is any use at all," this statement greeted by the loud objection from Juan.

Next Jason rang Dave, "we need to have a meeting right away here he said, and tell Miriam to cancel my engagements until further notice, we have big trouble in the ranks. Two more of the Cooperate Developments Ltd; managers have been shot and killed, things look bad, the drug gang is on the attack right now they are killing to create fear in their ranks. And they are using the Cooperate Developments Ltd; staff as their target because the company is so well known. Can you come to the hotel as soon as possible please Dave?"

Dave arrived within the hour, Jason had special secured parking in the hotel car park, which Dave always used when he called on Jason. To the hotel staff Jason was known as Mr. Jones, a business man from NZ who they rarely saw, but who came and went through a private entrance, and lived in the Penthouse. Any visitors for the Penthouse came and went in the same way with total privacy! The manager had met Jason once in the dark, but Jason had a hat on so he couldn't be recognized. Jean who wasn't known much even by the media made all of the arrangement's to lease the Penthouse, and the accounts were paid through an account in NZ that Jason had, which was in the name of Jason Jones.

Dave was just as stunned as Jason was, the two men killed were personal friends, he had known them for years. "My God this gang is deadly, they kill it seems indiscriminately, these are Mafia style executions what the hell do we do now?" Dave asked.

Recently a friend of mine was talking to the father of Chavez, and without knowing the father said, "oh we the family, all know Hemi is innocent the Aussie Feds have nothing against him. All of the imports were brought in by Cooperate Developments Ltd; nothing is in his name and his accounts have no money in them, if he had drug money his accounts would have lots of money in them. This of course is wrong his money would be hidden off shore, he would have nothing here," said Dave. To top that off he told his father that others had bought products in from China, also in the name of Cooperate Developments Ltd; so none of them have bought in any products only Cooperate Developments Ltd; had done this. "We need to be very careful with this bloke and his sister. We could be walking into a trap ourselves, that would be an even worse disaster, we need to think about this but we will work out a trap to test the both of them?" said Jason in a subdued voice. "I have been told by the Aussie Feds that it is not unusual for drug dealers to have no money, they keep it off shore to buy more drugs and invest, so no notice is taken of that defense."

Dave went back to his own office, but he said nothing to Miriam yet except that she was to cancel any more work that she had for Jason except the jobs that he had accepted those ones he would be doing but they would wait on instructions from Jason, before any more work was taken.

James had told the man Jason had named, that his life was in danger and the company had no choice but to ask for his resignation, he had been named as a co conspirator with Chavez and the three men who had been already killed. James had said, "You would be best if you vanish because you are the last one left that we know of at Cooperate Developments Ltd; and we don't to want to see you killed as well."

The man vowed his innocence as could be expected, but he resigned on the spot and left the premises immediately, he left through the back entrance looking as pale as a ghost.

Jason then had to tell Jean what had happened, she as could be expected was soon paralyzed with fear, all she could think of was Jason and Jnr; her fear was back, but this time worse, where can we go to live now she had asked?

Jason felt that he needed to get more closely involved than he was, he wanted to go out into the field and learn how to be an investigator on his own behalf. His only problem was being so well known, what if he tried to disguise himself? He could perhaps travel with Dave and let Dave do all of the legwork while he Jason, gave the instructions! Somehow Jason knew he had to get closer to the action, Dave was a good honest man, but he couldn't think well or quickly enough to do the job by himself? Jason kept thinking of different ideas in his mind, but had none that seemed to satisfy him. He was a businessman his thinking was like a businessman, he had to learn to think like a crook, and to learn to do that he had to mix with either cops or crooks. He decided he had to stop sitting in the background, and move into the front line with Dave and the team. Jason, was a man who could be more easily disguised now that he had aged a little, but it would be dangerous for everybody, if it ever came out that Jason Andrew's was playing at being a detective. Like it or not Jason had to be on most occasions a back room worker, even if he was the brains behind the whole operation. He decided he would get more involved with his main team, but wear a disguise at all times while in the field? Jason had to remind himself how he had got into chasing crooks, and remembered it was trying to protect his family nothing more, now it was harder than ever with four people killed, and one in Jail he needed to be more active. Jason was well aware the people so brutally killed, except the mother, had by being involved with the drug world put themselves and their own families at risk, but that didn't make the murders any easier to bare, his determination to find the killers was heightened, and he was prepared to work as hard as he could for vengeance, he only wished he knew more how to be effective in the quest to bring these brutes to justice. When Dave arrived the following evening, Jason briefed him on changes that they were going to put in operation, as quickly as possible. The two hard cases and Miriam were to be left out in the field, so they could be used when needed. The two Investigators Dave and Jason would work together with, but Jason would just be one of the team, he would be disguised and would say little except sit and listen at meetings. He explained to Dave that they both had to learn now to be Investigators, so they would learn on the job, but they wouldn't admit that to the two men they would be learning off. It was up to Dave to keep in touch with his contact in the drug gang, this was easy so long as he was paid he would do whatever he could, here was man with no sense of loyalty one who could never be allowed to know too much, because if he did he would sell the information immediately, as soon as he could with no sense of remorse.

That evening Jean was excited, "I have found a home that will be just what we want, it's small and in an unpretentious area nobody will even notice us, and we could move into it in six weeks time. Here is a video of the area and the house; can you look at it now please dear, the agent has put it on standby for me, but only if my husband agrees? Oh and here is a list of the other householders all of them are just simple working class people such as our own families are, and there is a local preschool that Jnr; can go to." After looking at the video and agreeing with Jean it was just what they needed, a simple three bedroom house in a typical working class area. They agreed to buy the house in Jeans maiden name, and he would arrange it to look as if she had come into an inheritance, and was buying a house for the family? Jason didn't reveal to Jean he had already set up a private trust account for Jean and Jnr; in such a way that the money couldn't be traced. Jnr; was now almost two years old and Jason knew that what he was doing was dangerous; he wanted his Wife and Son to be safe if something happened to him.

A week after they had agreed to buy the house Jean wanted; she suddenly had the hotel serve them up a celebration dinner. When Jason got home that night his Wife was vivacious and coy just as she had been when they had first been married, he had forgotten it was also the way she announced the coming birth of Jnr. After a terrific evening with the drinks and meal served up by the hotel in the Penthouse, Jean announced to Jason's delight she was pregnant again!

Wow Jason said with a great smile and congratulations to his wife, "we will have a pigeon pair and the boy is the eldest! How about that first a Jason Jnr; now a Jean Jnr; what could possibly be better, it is like all of my dreams have come true, I have always wanted to have a boy and a girl, more children than that actually but that's a great start, Darling?

"Is that not a bit premature how do we know we are going to get a girl?" Jean laughed out loud.

"That's true, but I can feel it in my inner being, we are going to have a girl next you can mark my words its Jean Jnr; on the way," Jason said with a sincere smile.

But the celebration was premature; they would never again celebrate in such a fashion, Jean announcing the birth of a child as a real disaster struck the next day.

CHAPTER 15

A new man a new life:

The next morning Jason had left the hotel early to go to a meeting, and left his car in a parking garage for about five hours, it was quite a normal procedure for him but one he would regret for over eight months of severe pain mental and physical. When he returned to the parking station and just as he started his car, it burst into a flame that completely enveloped it! He had just locked himself into the safety belt and it took him a few vital seconds to release the belt, and then finally jump out of the burning car, then of course he had to get away from the vehicle because he expected it to explode. His clothes were burning strongly and he could feel the flames searing his body just like barbecued meat he was thinking, when suddenly there were several people around him trying to put out the flames. One of them finally found a fire extinguisher unit and sprayed him with foam, but the damage had been done he had severe burns to 80% of his body. Most of the burns were second degree, but the burns to his face and upper torso were first degree, he was really in a critical condition. He was rushed to the burns unit of the nearest Hospital which was only a ten minute drive away, but the doctors there as soon as they saw agreed him with each other, he had only a 5% chance to come out of surgery alive. But of course they had to try and save him they had no idea who the patient was until some hours later; it was of no matter who it was they were there, to do their best for the victim of this deliberate fire.

Jean had been notified at the hotel and she had rushed to the hospital without thinking to notify anyone else, she was in a state of hysterical shock! But as she sat waiting for news of her husband, she had finally thought to notify others, first she rang both families and then she notified James and Dave. They all realized that it had been a Mafia hit another attack on Cooperate Developments Ltd; and its staff but there was no inkling how Jason had been set up, of course he was supposed to have been killed the car had been set up to explode if they had succeeded he would have died immediately, although at this stage it seemed as though they had burned him to death anyhow. In no time the hospital was swarming with mostly media, as genuine visitors and family were jostled aside unmercifully by those media hound's looking to make a buck? Jason Andrew's was back in the news, but now it was a sympathetic media, none would dare be critical! This man had donated over 4 Billion dollars to charity; those who dared to criticize him now as he lay dying would indeed be foolish. The Murdoch media had a life time story of the man, who had he chosen could have been among the wealthiest men in Australia. They gave a life time report on the man who had risen from among the poorest suburbs of Sydney, Blacktown, but who in the end had given all of his money except for $60 Million away? The public was agog they knew of Jason Andrew's, but they had never realized he had given most of his wealth away. Who would do such a thing they wandered, surely he was either a saint or an idiot, most women went for saint and most men thought he must be some sort of idiot. The Sydney Morning Herald and the Age in Melbourne had a scoop; they had a huge photo of Jean on their front pages, with huge lettering proclaiming, "New business genius on the way." Mrs. Andrew's has one new Jason growing up and another just six months away. Jean looked as if she was ready to faint, but she was being hounded, now she was the top media event of the moment, she suddenly realized just how tough it had been for Jason and why he had hated the media?

The hospital released a medical report, Jason Andrews on point of death, burns too serious for him to survive, but he was still alive. Mr. Andrew's is in the "Intensive Care Unit" he has spoken to his wife and his parents, but he is too weak to have other visitors. Doctors give him only a 5% chance to survive Cooperate Developments Ltd; toll getting higher every day, private security fails in attempts to safe guard their executives. The top news the next day was how Cooperate Developments Ltd; and Jason as the former Managing Director of that company, had been persecuted by the drug gangs in Sydney. There followed the story of the stealing of the companies identity by the Cooperate Developments Ltd; Sales Manager Hemi Chavez who was now in Jail for importing 100 kgs of Cocaine. Then the threat to all Cooperate Developments Ltd; executives so that a full security team; had been employed full time to guard the Execs;

and their families at a huge cost to the company, but how that strategy had totally failed.

The report went on to detail how three executives, had been executed by the drug gang, as well as one of the mothers of another member of the Cooperate Developments Ltd; team. Then the details of how Jason and his family had been living in seclusion fully guarded, but they had got him anyhow. Then followed a lurid report by some insensitive parasite, of how Jason's execution would make it four of the Cooperate Developments Ltd; team who had fallen to the gang, in the last six months in spite of the security. Finally that reporter asked of what use is the Aussie Feds, they have been unable to do anything and were looking increasingly useless, just as the private security team was totally useless? The entire media was asking if Australia had become part of a large network of drug and gangland criminals, and whether the effect was worse than the fear of terrorism, because the Govt; had at least concentrated affectively on terrorism, while drug related crime was out of control.

The daily bulletins the hospital was issuing about Jason were all extremely bad, but in fact he had at least started to come in and out of consciousness, Jean had immediately asked the hospital to keep issuing none committal reports. Only family were allowed in to see him, this on the assumption he wouldn't recover, and therefore they would be able to pray over him, and say their goodbyes. His injuries were extremely severe, the burns on his body were severe enough, but the burns on his face meant he would always be severely scared, if he lived and his chance of living was still set at only 5% if that. But Jean hung on she spent all of her waking hours by Jason's bedside, she did nothing but pray and ask her God to save her husband who she loved so dearly, she just wouldn't give up in spite of all medical reports that her husband must die, his injuries were far too severe for him to survive. One day when he was awake and aware of what was happening around him, and he was alone with Jean; he had told her that now was the time for Jason Andrew's to die. Jean had been devastated, but had no time to talk back to him as he again drifted back into unconsciousness for the rest of the visit. The next time he woke when she was with him, he relieved Jean's mind by telling her she was to speak to the doctors with Dave. The time had come and he wanted to die so he could be born again incognito, and he gave her a name that he would be using, it was the one he had used in NZ for over 15 years again his instincts had served him well. He asked that Dave should be with her until he again woke up, then he would tell Dave what he wanted him to do, he told Jean he would recover, and she need not worry anymore.

Jean had rung Dave, and they both waited for Jason to wake up, and when he did they were both pleased with how much more lucid, he had become. After speaking lovingly to Jean, Jason said to Dave, I want you to find a Plastic Surgeon and he is to fix up my body and my face, when I am improved enough. My face is to be a new image I need to be born again with a new image. We need for Jason Andrew's to die and be cremated as quickly as possible, this will be until we catch these bloody drug dealers, let the barsted's think they got me. Then he told Dave the same name as he had told Jean, Jason Jones, and he instructed Dave to set up a background for the new man, he was to be a Kiwi. Jason gave Dave the contacts he needed to talk too, but he wasn't to say who the new Passport, Drivers License, Birth Certificate, were for, just a client was all he was to say. Jason told him how much the job would cost; and he was to pay in cash. Having given the instructions Jason just went back to sleep peacefully, now with much less pain and obviously less worried. Jason's, burns were horrific, but slowly he began to stay conscious for longer periods, and much too the doctors surprise the prognosis had slowly changed he was now obviously going to survive his painful ordeal, but as far as they were concerned it was a miracle that rarely occurred. Your husband has a very strong will hasn't he? This was the comment from one of the senior doctors, made to Jean. Jason began to stay conscious for longer periods, but the pain was so severe that he wanted to stay unconscious. Nature has its own way of protecting the badly injured; he hadn't been expected to live so now he had to face the agony. The pain he underwent for the next three months, had him swearing the time would come when he would exact vengeance on the one who had ordered him killed, and the one who had set the bomb, but time would eventually heal the anger? The Aussie Feds had confirmed the bomb had not gone off properly, only the fire had been lit at extreme heat the actual murder attempt had failed. Had the bomb detonated Jason would have been blown to pieces and killed immediately, only the intense heat had been generated and Jason had managed to survive. The doctors were now able to say Jason would live, but the media had been informed of the death of Mr. Jason Andrew's and his cremation! The usual eulogies had been provided by the media, those who had once denounced him so loudly were now espousing his high moral character. The International media gave the world a fair assessment, noting how he had founded a major Australian Company and was indeed a business genius? All without exception praised his contribution to charity, and gave the details of how the charity functioned, exempting none from the right to claim contributions for assistance on the basis of a dollar of their own money, would be matched by a dollar from the charity.

Dave had made all of the arrangements as Jason had instructed him, and had also arranged for Jason to be transferred to a private hospital, under his new name. And so Mr. Jason Jones, a New Zealand citizen arrived a new resident in Australia! Their new patient had come as far as the new hospital knew, especially to be treated by their resident Plastic Surgeon, a doctor of world renown for treating burn victims. He was a private patient and was paying his own medical and hospital accounts, via a credit card as they were due. Everything had been set up by Dave and money had been deposited in Jason's New Zealand bank, to cover all of Jason's Jones needs. Everything had been done as meticulously as the Aussie Feds would have done had they been setting up a new identity, under their witness protection program.

The hospital Mr. Jones now lived at was very small having only 80 beds, and was owned by a group of Plastic Surgeons, who specialized in treating burn victims. The hospitals proud boast was, they would make their patients all look like new, all burn scars would be removed we never fail they claimed on their advertising pamphlets! The hospital and the surgeons were also known to be very discrete, about the progress of their private foreign patients such as Jason Jones. Jean and Jnr; had shifted into the new house, but a nurse had been employed to allow her to visit the hospital every day for several hours. Jean was now becoming very advanced in her pregnancy, and was due at any time to give birth, this time her Mother would be with her in the delivery ward obviously Jason could not be there at all except in his thoughts. Jason Jones was now awake during the day most of the time, but still had strong pain killing drugs fed to him intravenously, even so he suffered a lot from the burn pains. Jason was notified when Jean went into labor and thus into hospital, this time the baby a little girl Jean Jnr; was born within two hours of the first labor pains and with no difficulty. Jean of course was radiant and Jason could smile inwardly at the memory of his claim, it will be a little girl and it will be named Jean Jnr. It was almost two weeks before she bought little Jean to see her daddy, he was very happy, but couldn't show it the pain was still so great. Jason Jnr; had not been to the hospital to see Jason, both parents felt it would be too much of a shock for him to see his father so heavily bandaged. Slowly Jason began to improve, but it would be some time before he would be ready for the several operations, he would have to undergo before he had all of the repairs completed to his face and body burns.

In the meantime Dave had let the investigators finish up for the time being, and kept on the two who were working as bouncers with the Drug gangs. Miriam was kept on as a casual, she was handy doing office chores, and was kept fairly busy doing work for Dave. She also visited Hemi weekly and reporting back about what he was doing. Of course none of the team had known their real employer was Jason, so that to them his death was another gang triumph over Cooperate Developments Ltd; they thought Dave was really working for Cooperate Developments Ltd; so that their own work as well was indirectly for the big business conglomerate that was in a battle with the drug lords. Hemi was sending messages through Miriam; and it was him who confirmed that Jason had been killed by the drug gang. There was a feeling that perhaps they still needed to get rid of James, but when they did Cooperate Developments Ltd; would be open to a takeover bid, because the shares would drop sharply in value on the share market. The decision had been made to take the company over by the manipulation of its share price; they expected to buy the company at only 50% of its real value. When they had full control of Cooperate Developments Ltd; through nominee buyers they would then use it as a vehicle for the importation of drugs. Jason when he heard what the drug gang was going to try and do was fascinated, they must be going to bring drugs in by the tonnes was his first comment, how silly to even think of turning a major listed company into a drug unit? The New Zealand division in particular was thought of, as a safe destination from China or Mexico, then the drugs could be transshipped to anywhere in the world. The gang bosses had decided on New Zealand, because that country was considered as a safe country to export goods to and from, especially by Australia and America authorities. The routes being considered were from the drug supplier countries to New Zealand, and then from there to the drug users. Cooperate Developments Ltd; as a major meat exporting company; would buy out a major meat company in New Zealand, no matter what the cost would be. The intent was then to use frozen meat packaged in New Zealand to re export drugs to off shore countries, because the frozen products would obscure the smell of drugs, and dogs would be unable to smell out the frozen drugs. Meat would be so attractive to the dogs they would be pointing at every carton, and eventually the inspectors would get sick of the dogs making mistakes, and would become lazy. The cartooned meat being exported was to be Bull, and Boar meat which has a heavy smell and would further distract the dogs as they tried to sniff for drugs. It was going to be a perfect scam but first the drugs had to be gotten into NZ or Australia, both countries have long coastlines and NZ in particular with its small population would be more exposed to the drug lords than Australia. It would be at this point when drugs could start to be exported worldwide from New Zealand; a small country in the South Pacific which no one has ever heard of in the big drug infested world. All the drug lords wanted was a safe route to bring huge amounts of Cocaine and Heroin into the USA, nobody gave a thought to NZ and what damage could be done to their economy, frankly they didn't care they would think they were doing the country a favor; buying all the type of meat that very few would buy, it was after all only suitable for animal food.

The Plastic Surgeon had told Jason, that he was now strong enough for the first of the three operations, which would have to be performed. All together the operations would take over three months, but the final dressings could not be removed for about four months. "You are doing well, but it's time now to move on and fix all of those scars, when we are finished you will be like a new man, even your wife may not recognize you will that be a problem?" he asked.

Jason had asked the Doctor, "what will I look like when the job is complete?"

"Your face structure will be the same, but unfortunately we cannot guarantee that you will look the same as you did before?" the doctor had replied.

"Yes but can you guarantee I will look different?" asked Jason with a smile.

"Why if that's what you want yes we can shape your face to look good, but in your own words different. It will take longer because we will have to study your bone structure, and then decide how the operation should proceed. It may cost you substantially more can you afford that?" he asked with a smile.

"The cost isn't a problem doctor, but I don't want the barsted's that tried to kill me to be able to have another go. It wouldn't be safe for me out there if you don't change my face. It's important to us all that's me and my family should be able to live a worry free life," replied Jason.

"Ok if that what you want we will work out a new face for you, it will be a challenge but we don't want you back again now do we?" the Doctor replied with a conspiratory smile.

"You wouldn't get me back," Jason said with a laugh, "they won't miss me twice be assured that if there is a next time they won't miss, these American Hit Men don't usually fail I was very lucky, that's why you have to make me look very different. It seems that even in Australia and NZ we aren't safe anymore from them."

When he told Jean when she arrived that day for her visit, she said with a laugh, "Gosh am I getting a new husband, the only one who will complain is Jason Jnr; he will kick up a fuss for a few days then he will forget, but it is for the best we both know that. Who else will know the new Jason Jones not too many we hope?"

"I haven't decided that yet, let's talk about that later, obviously our families and a few business connections, but no more," replied Jason Jones. As the time for the operation approached, Jason began to wander just how long it would take, and just how much pain he would have to accept.

The doctor (Plastic Surgeon) had been to talk about the operation on the day before it was to be done; he had said it should take about four to five hours, because there was a lot of work to be completed. There would be another doctor who would help, because the sustained concentration would make the job too arduous for any doctor to perform alone. They would work in hour shifts as would the whole medical team!

The next doctor to visit was the anesthetist, who was very friendly and sat and talked to Jason, "have you ever had an operation in your life before?" he asked kindly.

"Yes once but your work is not unfamiliar to me, your job is to put me to sleep, and then keep my breathing and temperature balanced during the operation. When the doctors are finished it's your job to wake me up again, in short during the entire operation my life is in your hands is that right?" Jason said with a laugh.

"That's it exactly you are well versed, so I have no need to guess if you know the procedures you have explained my job exactly. So I will meet you in the morning at the operating room, you don't need luck you have the best team in Australia looking after you including me, so I will say bon voyage until the morning good night for now?"

Jason had several visitors that night to wish him well on the morrow, his Parents, Jean and Dave, but prompt at the end of visiting hours they were all asked to leave. It was explained to them all, the nurses had to do a pre op immediately, and then they had to put him to sleep all ready for an early 7.00 am start the following morning.

They all left, Jean was the last as she stayed to hug her husband and wish him as pain free a journey as could be possible, then she left sniffling softly.

The pre op was painful as the bandages were removed, but soon he was bathed and ready for the ordeal in the morning.

As he lay and reflected on the things that had happened his thoughts were changing these drug lords had in many ways done him a favor, he would have a new life, and he had had time to start thinking about a new business, one he couldn't pursue as Jason Andrew's. He was certain of what he intended to do and he would use his time of convalescence to work things out properly, but he and Dave would be very busy, the business was only possible because of his connections in NZ and to a lesser extent Australia. He didn't want to do too much in Australia too quickly some smart Alec would work out the connection. They may link him to Jason Andrews, and then if they did there would be a real uproar.

He was taken to the operating room at 6.30 am and was the first there, the operating team and the anesthetist were all there sharp on time, and it was time to go to sleep under the doctors expert hands.

It seemed as if nothing had happened and time had stood still, when Jason was suddenly opening his eyes with the feel of a hose in his nose, another attached to his arm, "what the hell happened," he said as a peal of relieved laughter issued from Jeans mouth? "It's over" she said "the first ones over Darling, only two to go, how do you feel?"

Dave was there too looking very relieved his mentor had made it!

"OK I guess, but the pain is still there! I hope it's not going to be as bad as this the next two times, anyhow that's one down and two to go, wish to hell they could do the next two together tomorrow and get it all over and done with?"

The surgeon came to see Jason later in the day, and was impressed with how well Jason had stood up to the pain, once the anesthetic had worn off. "The results are excellent Mr. Jones you are a strong man, and your body took it all very well. The anesthetist had a bit of a problem you didn't want to go to sleep, but he managed to get you there, then it was all plain sailing for him as well, congratulations, we can now look forward to the other two ops with full confidence that you can take it. It is always a bit of a concern when a patient comes out of the first op the pain is excruciating we know that?"

"Why thank you doctor," replied Jason, "but that's only the first one we still have another two to go, and I can only hope it goes just as well!"

Dave came in that evening and was very impressed, gosh you are the hero of the hospital, they told me the first operation is a great success.

Even Jason was smiling under the great swathe of bandages that still hid his face from the world.

Dave he said, "I want you to keep our boys ready for when I am better, then we are going after those barsted's big time. They want to buy Cooperate Developments Ltd; do they? But then they will be operating on my turf, so we will teach them a lesson. They can think about it as they rot in jail we will take their rotten money of them, and give it all away. The one thing that I do know is that when we have caught those barsted's and I can take back my identity, now we will see what can happen when they are on my turf!" unfortunately he was forgetting in his own words Satan's Eyes they would never let him have peace, not in Australia anyhow.

The look on Dave's face was incredulous as he thought about what Jason was saying! "So the sacrifice of your identity is only temporary, you just want to trap them and then take their money as well, good on you boss we all believe you are just the man to do what you say?"

The month between the first and second operation went so slowly; Jason felt as if he would go mad, but the time finally came around again.

As before Jason was prepared for the next morning, but this time he had no visits from the doctors, but of course had a lot of visitors wishing him well again, none knew except Dave and Jean that he was having a change done to his appearance, not yet, they wanted to see first how it all worked out then all who needed to know would be surprised. He received his pre op; the same as the first time and was delivered to the operating room at 6.30 am as he had been for the first operation. The medical team arrived right on time 7.00 am and without any waste of time, Jason was under the anesthetic and the operation was under way. This time all expected him to be as stoic as he had been the for first operation, so there was no surprise when he came out of the anesthetic this time sounding strong and confident.

The third operation was the same with no messing about, the doctors were very confident this was the last operation that would be needed, and all would go as well as the first two had done. The team was on time as before and now Jason went to sleep like a baby, which was a good omen for the doctors, they were all delighted in fact the entire team were brimming with confidence that this was the last operation for Mr. Jones, and he would soon be going home they all thought to NZ. He had been an excellent patient and everyone at that small specialist hospital was wishing him well, but they would all miss him he had been in residence for almost six months, they all felt close to him and his few visitors. This time when Jason awoke Jean was there and excited! The usual tubes were firmly in place, but it was quite clear the doctors felt they had completed the job. Later in the day the two surgeons who had done the three operations, came in to see Jason; they were very complimentary. You are they said a very easy patient to work with, and the results are extremely good, we both think you will be very happy when the bandages are removed in about 30-40 days, then you will all see the new man we have built. The days dragged by from then on, Jason was excited he wanted to get out and for the first time for a long time he would be a free man, no media driving him crazy, no drug gangs making it so dangerous that he had to live in a fortress like penthouse. He was excited at the thought of being just nobody living in a nowhere house, with his wife and two children with no fancy company car. Jason, wanted to be just an everyday Joe even if it was only for a very short time, he knew he had to get back to work and catch those crooks, but for a time he was going to rest? When he came out of hospital he was going to set up his new business and he would brief Dave on what they would be doing.

Dave came in and said the drug gang was back in operation, but the technique had been changed somewhat, and now they were much more cautious about who they hired. Their own two men who were working for the gang as bouncers were well entrenched by now, because they were considered to be old trustees and could be left to do their jobs without much supervision. Miriam was bringing in reports from the Jail and Hemi was sending dire warnings, the gang was serious about the attack on the share prices of Cooperate Developments Ltd; and they would be moving within two months. Hemi didn't know how it all worked but the attack was serious, and would be managed by a lead team of agents, they would front up at the market and begin to offer for all shares in Cooperate Developments Ltd; at a guaranteed price which would be paid at full value, at time of settlement.

If on settlement the price was $8.00 per share that's what they would pay, if it was $35.00 that was what they would pay, but the bid would give a guarantee of cash to 100% of the share holders of Cooperate Developments Ltd; shares and options.

There were four banks in place, because the takeout would need about twelve billion in loans, and two billion in cash and the funds were all available, guaranteed through an American Investment Bank.

Jason, was delighted it will be my pleasure to clean them out he said, but James will have to be bought into our confidence, we will need him to lead the switch our friends will lose at least two billion on this market attack, and the Cooperate Developments Ltd; shareholders will make a motza.

Jason was so excited about the share market play that was coming up, his progress was faster than expected; it was thirty days when the doctors said it was time. The bandages were to be removed the next day! Jean was coming in to the hospital she wanted to be the first one to see her husband's new face, it was to be a day of high excitement.

The big moments had arrived; the nurse had the wet tray so she could soak the bandages gently off Jason's face. The lead doctor had come in to assure himself there would be no damage, as the bandages were removed; he also was keen to see how his work had turned out.

"You will have quite severe bruising, but that will soon go away," he said as Jason's face began to appear.

Jean was radiant and as Jason's new face began to emerge her excitement was contagious, everyone in the room started to join her enthusiasm.

Then quite suddenly the bandages were all off and everyone even Jean had become silent.

Jason became perturbed I must look like a monster he thought, but then the nurse bought him a mirror so he could see for himself. When he looked into the self reflection in the mirror his first reaction was who is that, it's not me surely, he was looking at a new man one he didn't recognize at all. The next thing he automatically did; was turn to the doctor and thank him for a job very well done. Finally he turned to look at Jean who seemed to have been lost for words, well my Dear he asked what do you think of my new look?

"It's amazing," she said, "even me as your wife wouldn't recognize you, if I didn't know it was you, it will be interesting to go and see your parents; they won't know you either. But honestly you look great, and the media will never harass you again, not even if you told them who you are they would simply say rubbish. Like you I just want to congratulate the doctor for his work its wonderful she said as she turned to the Doctors and offered her hand in thanks."

All of the body bandages had been removed for some time; those burns hadn't been as serious as the head burns. Jason's hair was just a stubble, but looked as if it wouldn't be long and the hair would be needing a cut, the bruises were very obvious and looked as if they would vanish simultaneously with a haircut. Those were the only things now to wait for, and then Jason would be perfectly normal, in every way.

The doctor smiled as he left and said, "Jason tomorrow you can go home, first we must do final tests to assure ourselves you are internally well, then we will have finished. The nurses will get blood and urine samples today and the Lab will complete your test, then he said turning to Jean you will be welcome to take your husband home, how long has it been?"

"Just over eight months," replied Jean with a happy smile, "it will be great to be a complete family again, but our son will think I have bought home a new man she said with a laugh."

After everyone had left the room husband and wife hugged each other, it was indeed a wonderful happy day for them both.

The next morning Jason was discharged at 11.00 am; it had been a long hard journey, but again he had beaten the odds and survived. Jnr; was with the nurse and when Jason walked in the door, he immediately went to pick his son up, but the boy let out a cry for his mother. Jean started to soothe the boy down, and was saying daddy is home; here just talk to daddy for a little while, but Jnr; would have none of that; this wasn't his daddy it was a stranger and he wasn't going near that man. The nurse with a smile said, "You have to give him a while to get used to the situation he is almost three years old, if you just let him get used to Jason again he will be fine by tomorrow I guarantee that."

As the nurse had predicted by the evening on the next day Jnr; was happy to play with Jason, but it took a few more days before he would call this new man 'daddy.'

After another week the bruises were starting to vanish, and at the end of a month they were all gone; and Jason had had a haircut, finally he felt all mended, a new man indeed.

CHAPTER 16

CDL Takeover.

The next three weeks were like a dream to someone like Jason, who for years had not been able to move from his home without, being tailed by the media looking for a story. It had been over eight months from the day of the fire, but it felt like years; Jason couldn't believe he was now able to move around freely. In his inner mind he felt it would be justice, if because of that freedom; he was the one ultimately able to smash the drug ring, and put the leaders on trial for the four murders; and the near fatal attack on himself. He had however no idea of just how big the drug organization was, it was in reality one of the biggest crime gangs in the western world, excluding China and the Asian world none could match them.

Dave came to a meeting with Jason and like Jean was surprised at the now full change in Jason's image, "Struth no one would be able to indentify you now, you will be able to move around as you like, this is really great, how ironic it will be if that attempt to kill you ended in their arrests," he laughed loudly at his own thoughts. Jason could only smile at the conjunction of thoughts between himself and his friend.

The next night there was a small homecoming for Jason, only the two families, plus Dave and James were invited, it was to be small and not at all expensive, there was no intent to show any sign of money for the neighbors to speculate about. James was asked to come in a rental car, not his company limousine!

As they arrived they all commented on the new image of Jason, and little Jnr; proudly introduced his new daddy to them all. Jason's and Jean's parents of course had seen the new man and so had Dave, only James was new to the image of Jason Jones. But they all enjoyed listening to Jnr; introducing his new daddy; only James was shocked! "My goodness even the Cooperate Developments Ltd; shareholders wouldn't know you now?" he laughed.

During the night Jason told the visitors he didn't think there was any more danger to any of them, because the big fish; the gang had wanted to close down Jason Andrews was dead, and so the security guards would be cancelled all would be free at last. "This is for me a great time of celebration, as once more freedom is achieved over the forces of evil, let us all raise our glasses and drink to that?" he said. The last thing Jason did as the guests were leaving; was to arrange a meeting with James and Dave for a week's time, there are some business moves to be made he said as they left. The following week the three men Jason, James and Dave met in Dave's office in Burwood and it was quite an interesting meeting. Jason outlined how the drug gang wanted to buy all of the shares of Cooperate Developments Ltd; for their own purposes. The strategy was to own a major Australian Company, but to use it as a drug courier business; using the export frozen meat division. Jason proposed to buy 500 million options at 10c exercisable when the shares hit a certain rate and the call couldn't be made unless the shares dropped in value by 50% of the price on the day the options were purchased. The shares were currently trading at $25.00 so the options couldn't be called on unless the price dropped to $12.50. The options would stay off balance sheet until a call was made, James had to agree to the terms as Managing Director of Cooperate Developments Ltd; but there was a side agreement that any profits Jason made would go to his charity. The Cooperate Developments Ltd; shares were tightly held so an on market bid would be expensive, only amateurs would consider such a dangerous move, but they were Drug dealers not business people? These men were looking at moving hundreds of tonnes of Cocaine to the world; they had become blind to the business dangers, they were only aware of the billions to be made in Drugs. Dave and Jason didn't reveal they had a contact within the drug gang leadership, this was of course how they had got all of the information on the gang strategy, but it was really all being manipulated through the Mafia in Chicago, the Australian leader was just a pawn. Jason was putting up the $50 Million he had put aside from the sale of his shares, and this money was being used legally; it had been designated as money for the attack on drugs gangs from the time he had started selling his shares.

The only problem Jason had was he had to now have a front man buying the shares, but it had to be someone with the influence with the banks, because there were other moves in the pipeline. The only one who could do this was James, and he couldn't be expected to do the Job without a fee. Finally Jason and James agreed on a fee of 10% of the net profit would be paid to James on full and final settlement.

The next move was the dangerous one Cooperate Developments Ltd; had in hidden accounts over $600 million that had been accumulated by Jason in a hush account over many years. What was intended was that at the right time Cooperate Developments Ltd; would announce a special profit of $600 million, but that money would be paid only to shareholders who had held their shares for over two years? The money coming out had to be announced as a special profit therefore would attract a $180 million tax bill; this would leave a dividend to all shareholders including Jason's already sold shares because the current owners were not eligible. The strategy was to announce the special profit when the Gang had started their attack on the Cooperate Developments Ltd; shares and suddenly the share price will shoot up. This is why the guarantees were foolish; the gang would be in a noose they couldn't get out of, the Mafia in Chicago would be heavily compromised?

This will cost them a lot more money, but when they had almost completed the takeover at the increased price, the options would be announced; this would cost them another couple of billion dollars if not more to complete their buyout. But more strategically the share price would now plummet, and their losses would be astronomical, if they continued with the takeover. Jason's guess was that they would cut and run and keep their losses down to about USD2 billion. The Gang leaders wouldn't be able to hold out as the sharks started to circle, they would be forced to sell as their bankers bayed for blood, and blood is what they would get.

Jason estimated the Gang losses would be close to six billion dollars, but all payable in cash, they would be in a trap, but they could if they stopped keep it down to only USD2 billion. The only way out was to get big drug volumes onto the markets, but that's when the last trap would be sprung, the Aussie Feds would be provided with evidence which Dave's teams would supply, Jason was hoping for a fait accompli.

James was very enthusiastic, but asked Jason for a week to go through the details, speak to the banks etc; if the banks were in then so was he?

In the meantime Dave reported that his team was ready to meet their real boss, and he had set up a meeting for the following day. Present would be the two hard cases, the two investigators who were being bought back on board, and Miriam. At the meeting Jason was introduced as a NZ business man, who had been caught and robbed of a lot of money by the drug gang's leader. He was now looking for vengeance! Jason went out of his way to be very friendly to them all, but he stressed that at all times they all had to be very careful. He was paying them well he said, but that was because of the risks involved when dealing with the Drug Lords. None of them were to take any unnecessary risks, there was a job to be done, and when completed there would be bonuses for all, out of the money the drug lords would pay?

The information from Dave's team was that the drug strategy had been changed, the teams still had their contacts with the various liquor outlets, but the drug salesmen were not part of the security teams. The fact the drug gang still had their contacts with the liquor outlets were enough to warn Jason that the local Aussie Feds force must be involved somehow. Every week the salesmen were being changed, so that the security team members never knew who would be selling drugs, until they started work each night, and even then they rarely knew. The drugs sales people could be male or female, and only the manager of each venue knew what was going on. The person selling would be circulating and approaching known addicts, and then passing among the crowd; as they moved from one to the other. The guards were never changed, but there were new sales people every night, and the sales team only repeated a venue about once in every sixty nights. This of course meant the drug teams in Sydney for example were sixty strong, and the security or guard teams were well over a thousand strong. The Melbourne numbers were much the same, and Brisbane had about 60% as many as each of the other two cities.

The investigators were now being hindered as they were kept in their teams and not moved about! Miriam had been bought in off working in the field and was doing only office work; but she was working with the team to glean any information they may bring in to the office. Dave was going to China with Jason, and he had been set up with a duplicate Australian New Zealand passport and a NZ drivers license.

While he had been off being treated for his burns he had been planning a new business, and since he had been home convalescing Jason had been putting in place the new business plan, but it was only because of his prominent position in NZ that he was able to seize the opportunity. He had arranged contracts to sell various products for NZ producers on a cost plus basis, which meant he would sell at their price and any extra he could get he would keep as his commissions. It was only because of his business reputation in NZ that his proposals had been accepted, he was well known having traded in NZ for many years as Jason Jones and now those advantages were coming in very handy. Jason had all of the information about China and Chicago, and was going to China in order to connect with the gang leader, but also to start his new business. Jason intended to pose as a business man in the meat industry from New Zealand; and he had genuine stocks of frozen meat he was selling to China. He was also selling heifers (young cows) to Chinese farm groups, also from New Zealand. He had for sale canned Tuna from Fiji, and had full crops of fruit for canning and jam which he wanted processed in either China or Fiji. The fruit and jam would come from and go back to both Australia and New Zealand. Dave was to be the man in the field, so that his work was actually being processed daily by Jason. Neither men realized what a great business they were starting up and just how profitable it would be, even Jason hadn't realized what he was getting into, when he finally did catch on he was delighted. But initially all he had been after was a way to get in touch with international drug cheats! The two men left for China immediately, and both were to stay at the same hotel as the drug gang leader, there was no doubt that as fellow Anzac's they would soon Pal up with the drug Lord and their team, as fellow business men from down under. Jason had never been to China, and his first reaction on arriving was my God, there are more people here than ants in Jean's kitchen, how the hell do these people live like this we in Australia would surely die if we had to live like this? Dave had been several times as a tourist, and once while working for Jason; so he found Jason's reaction as quite funny.

The hotel was quite another world, a world which was only for the wealthy Chinese and foreign business people, it was reputedly the only five star hotel; in Shanghai at that time. Jason was well used to five star hotels, he had lived in the penthouse of one in Sydney for several months, but this he found as unbelievable. Of course some of the services would never be offered in a Sydney hotel, there would be a public outrage, Jason could imagine the media reaction to such immoral behavior but in Shanghai anything one wanted was available at any time. When one of the hotel male attendants offered beautiful girls, and Jason declined because he was a married man, the attendant shook his head in dismay. What he asked has that got to do with beautiful girls, you don't have to marry them here in China, you only have them for the night and you can have a different one every night. When Jason still declined and went alone to his suite, he left a very bewildered attendant, what he asked is wrong with Chinese girls, they are very beautiful?

The next morning at breakfast, the Australians could be easily seen among the crowd. They sat separated and were quite noisy, but neither drunk nor were drug affected. Jason and Dave sat alone and Jason briefed Dave what he wanted done, the job was to set themselves up as genuine Kiwi traders selling frozen meat, live cattle, and canned tuna. They were also buying building materials and other general merchandise for transfer to Australia, New Zealand and Fiji, with Dave doing the field work, and

Jason the negotiating with the Govt; and the banks. This was a genuine trading situation, Jason had set the infrastructure up completely including arranging freight both ways, veterinary services for the live cattle, and everything had been carefully planned and was ready to be executed. After a few days Jason and Dave had been acknowledged by the drug leader, and gradually they all got to at least nodding at each; then one day they spoke, just a friendly greeting then finally they introduced themselves.

Jason said they were New Zealanders who both lived in Sydney Australia, he then revealed the type of business they were doing in China, knowing well they would be checked out immediately, but aware their credentials were all in place. The leader professed he was there investing in China, with a permanent residency, and they were all Australians originally from Sydney. Jason said he and Dave were there only for as long as it took to set up the sales, especially live cattle and frozen meat, which Jason could see drew a flicker of interest; but no comment from the leader. The two men parted promising to introduce each other to their respective colleagues at some time in the future, but Jason could see this leader's character was one of extreme caution. Dave and he, would have to be well investigated; before there would be any closer contact than they had achieved so far, Jason realized a lot of the caution was because these were not the real bosses, for that he had to get far deeper. Jason was determined he wouldn't push themselves on the Aussies, they would just wait and if need be leave and come back, several times to assuage any suspicions.

Dave, had done quite well he had sold the 2,000 heifers for delivery in six months, and was now in firm conversation with buyers of frozen beef from either Australia or New Zealand. He had found the Chinese keen to do reciprocal trade and he had prices to buy, glazed roof tiles, kitchens, bathrooms, wall tiles and earth moving equipment etc. The fruit canning proposal was easy; the Chinese quoted an acceptable price, and freight to and from China was also approved. Meantime Jason had been working to set up the export and import documents, as well as arranging the Chinese bank that would work with the New Zealand bank, to facilitate the payments based on the bills of lading. This meant confirmations of product delivered to the wharf and bonded, so that the letters of credit at the banks could be paid out. This had been the secret of Jason's idea; the Chinese could pay for their purchases by selling products in exchange for what they were buying. In this way all countries trade ministries were happy, payment in fact was made internally and the buy and sell of the products were balanced out equally, this meant little money actually changed hands. The only cash payments that had to be made was the commissions payable to Trade Attack Systems were the scheme facilitators, operated by Jason and Dave the developers, everyone was happy and none cared about the commissions since all were getting the net price they wanted for their own products. With their very low costs, Trade Attack Systems could do very well on only a 3% profit margin, but they were earning more, much to Jason's surprise.

There was three members in the Leaders team; and Dave and Jason; they all began to acknowledge each other quite freely, whenever they should see each other, either in the dining room or just passing by. Gradually but surely an initial friendliness was developing, Jason had expected nothing for the time being, he was convinced the next trip would break the ice. Dave was enjoying his job and didn't care how long or often they stayed, he wasn't married and thought the Chinese girls quite wonderful. Quite suddenly the Chinese confirmed the purchase of 250,000 tonnes of frozen meat, plus the 2,000 heifers. Then Dave agreed to the price on the materials they wanted to buy, so everyone was happy, and it was time to leave. The products sold were worth about $200 million, and they had bought approximately the same amount from their hosts, so both the Chinese and the Kiwi's were very happy. The buy sell value was just over USD400M a fantastic result for a new business.

On the day before they were due to leave, Jason sent a complimentary drink across to the Australians after the meal, and bid them farewell from across the room. The Leader came across and asked what they were doing, and was told they had completed their business for now, and would be going home to New Zealand on the morrow. Jason said, "This has been a very profitable trip, but we must now await the stock from New Zealand arriving in China; and then the Chinese stock arriving in New Zealand. When the banks settle we will see what we have to sell, but the next sales will probably be to the USA not here, so farewell for now we leave early in the morning!" Jason could see the Leaders curiosity was well piqued, and the next trip there would be far more inter group conversation. For now Jason was satisfied this was no different than a corporate raid. At first it may take a year even several years before the trap was sprung, but when it did the flood gates usually opened wide? The arrival back in Sydney via New Zealand was achieved by two very weary men, both glad to be home. They had stayed in New Zealand, to finish up the business agreements and assure themselves; the transfers were in place ready to be finished, and then confirmed the bank transfers of the letters of credit. The cattle ship was the hard one to check, the boat had to have the NZ Govt Vet approve it; for the transport of cattle. After the meat delivery had been checked; it was just a matter of time for the Chinese products to arrive at the docks, and the job was complete? Under the agreements negotiated by Jason, TAS was entitled to its commissions as soon as the bills of lading were approved which meant the products were in the bond stores. They had to be paid by electronic bank transfer not by a delayed letter of credit.

It was a great welcome home for Jason! Jean was waiting at the airport with little Jnr; and both were excited as Jason emerged from customs with no problems at all, the first trip away with no media harassment was complete. They both had a week off work, and then a meeting was arranged in Dave's office with all of the staff. There wasn't anything of great value to report from the team, the drugs were still flowing freely and the Aussie Feds as usual; seemed not to be doing anything. Miriam reported privately, the gang was still moving forward with its plans to take over Cooperate Developments Ltd; and the offer would be released within a month. The gangs offer would be 100% cash, for all of the issued shares and options of CDL; and all of its subsidiaries, and a prominent American Broker would be the agent representing, the private American money fund.

Jason had forgotten to put in place a trap for Hemi to fall into! He did so now by giving Miriam some false information, and that was that the police; were getting ready to raid the security gangs in the three States again, and there were plain clothes Aussie Feds operating at all of the gangs contracted night spots! Both Dave and Jason believed that Hemi was acting as a double agent, he was feeding information to someone fairly low in the gang's management level, who was in turn supplying Hemi with low level information that he was passing back through Miriam. They had deduced this by analyzing and confirming the information they were getting was low level, and what the gangs would be quite happy to pass around. Dave and Jason, wanted to confirm several suspicions they had, the attempt to kill Hemi was a local vendetta, created by Hemi while he was staking out authority, which some other crim's; objected to in the Jail hierarchy. Hemi was quite influential in the gang leadership, he had money invested of shore from his drug forays, his whole family believed he was innocent, and if let out on bail he would flee to Mexico or China. The belief was the whole Chavez family Miriam included, would do anything they could to get him out of Jail so they could all run and leave Australia. Jason and Dave were both convinced; Hemi could be used to very good effect; for their own purposes when the business battle started. "He will possibly cost his comrades a hell of a lot of money by the time this game is played out!" said Jason.

There was now an urgency to first go to America and then back to China! Jason wanted to see if they could trace the source of the money that was being used to buy Cooperate Developments Ltd. They now had more products to sell in Shanghai! The only product they had failed to sell in China was the canned Tuna fish, there was no interest there for that product, but Dave felt he could sell the fish in either New York or Las Vegas?

When they arrived in New York, Jason went searching to borrow $500 million, which he wanted for a private investor in New Zealand. Dave went searching the food and beverage brokers to sell NZ wine and the Tuna from Fiji! As he had expected the tuna fish sold quickly, the wine would sell, but the price was unacceptable, too expensive.

Jason had been to all of the financiers on Wall St; but the interest rates offered were unacceptable, he didn't visit the agents representing the drug lord. His real intent was to go back to Shanghai and let it slip, he had not been able to borrow USD500 million and see if the leader would make them a connection. It was all a part of the trap Jason was working on, that he hoped would work but it was long odds.

They had to make a quick trip to Las Vegas for Dave, where he finally got his price for 100,000 cases of wine of a mixed variety and vintage, they left America for Shanghai both feeling very pleased with their work.

Back in Shanghai this time they were greeted cordially by the leader, on their first morning back he actually came over to their table and sat down at Jason's invitation, to enjoy a glass of Australian wine. Dave made a joke; by saying he was going to undercut the Australian price; with a better quality NZ wine, this was good for a friendly laugh with the leader, who seemed after breaking the ice to be quite a convivial character,.

It was obvious the leader was very curious, so Dave said, "I have another 2,000 heifers to sell and 200,000 cases of second grade meat, but we are asking for a slightly higher price this time, you know what the Chinese are like they will haggle for days over the price hike, but in the end they will buy we hope?"

The leader laughed, and politely commiserated; when Jason moaned about not being able to borrow USD500 million in New York; because the interest rates were too high for the Kiwi's, even though top rate real estate security was being offered. But he didn't offer any connection States side!

The leader went back to his own table after welcoming Jason and Dave back, and suggesting they enjoy a Chinese banquet one evening all of them together; Dave and Jason both accepted with thanks, and professed themselves keen to meet their Australian compatriots. Later when they were back in their suite Jason said nothing because they both believed their rooms would be bugged, and everything they said would be noted down for the leader's attention. They had agreed on the way back to Shanghai what to expect, and they were ready!

Dave said that banquet will be nice, I get sick of talking through an interpreter all day, then the girls are all sign language to, but they know well what the wide eye men want, they are just the same as the Chinese men they all wanted sex. Dave and Jason laughed heartily hoping it was all being heard! From then on when the two wanted to say something private, they passed each other a note; or sometimes a few simple signs were sufficient.

Dave suddenly said by way of talk, "This frozen meat sells well we could sell all we can get, but it is hard to find the top price they will pay, they set up a squawk about the new price list, it was as if their world had caved in. But the Friesian heifers they never even blinked, they like the New Zealand livestock better than the Australian ones. Ours have their calves and can be milked about a month earlier than the Aussie heifers, and they are cheaper to transport here. It was good getting rid of that Fijian tuna fish in New York, and the American's paid a top price as well, this trip should get us sales of about USD250 million; maybe a bit more, with the back sales to the Chinese and the Americans we should top over USD500 million this trip. I hope to finalize the canning agreement any day soon that will be a nice commission as well. Both countries have large crops that could economically be picked and freighted, both ways, with all up costs at least 20% cheaper than competitive processing; would be in either Australia or New Zealand. This was a very smart move by you to use your connections to sell produce away from home, and buy products be way of the customers paying for what they buy, it's the old barter system and the Chinese love that, they are even prepared to pay a little more this way, mind I suppose they charge us a little more for what we buy, but there is no way we can beat these Chinese when it comes to barter. Did you realize when we first came away from home what sales we could achieve, it's been amazing and yet quite easy and a hell of a lot more profitable than what we were doing before," Dave said with a smile.

Yes replied Jason with an impish grin, "We should have been doing his years ago, there's no problem's its all legal, and we are making much more money than before. Those coppers can have their bloody mutts smell our frozen meat all day; the bloody things only get frozen noses. We watched them checking out the last load when it left for the States! It was so funny, the bloody mutts refused to work in the end, they had frozen noses, and it was bloody hard not to laugh out loud. This is especially so because we had no drugs concealed in the meat anyhow, it's just annoying having to stand and watch I feel like a criminal when they put their bloody mutts on us don't you?"

Both men winked at each other, and burst out laughing!

And so the deliberate misinformation continued, if ever there was an example of a corporate scam this was one at top level. Both men knew they were really inviting, the leader and his Chicago bosses' into a takeover disaster; and both were enjoying the game immensely.

The next morning the Leader came to their table and was so friendly, because Jason knew they were taking the bait, they would now be convinced they wanted to be in the meat industry and the buyout of Cooperate Developments Ltd; was a great move. The leader wanted to confirm; a banquet had been arranged for that evening, he expressed pleasure when both Jason and Dave accepted the invitation, and they had thanked him. It will be good they said to enjoy some home friendship, even if it was with Aussies because there doesn't seem to be any Kiwi's around? Dave said as the Leader (George Savarkis) left them, "it seems to be a good idea to meet all of our fellow compatriots from down under?"

The banquet that night was a ten courses affair of the quality only the Chinese can provide, the food was really top class; and the wine the finest Australian blends. The waitresses were extremely beautiful, but the men all seemed to be sated with female wiles, so the women weren't much commented on, even Dave seemed ambivalent as to any sexual needs?

The talk between the two parties started off being a little restrained, but as the meal progressed there was a noticeable thawing on both sides. Jason started off by saying how pleased he and Dave were; that they had decided to include China in their itinerary, while Dave waffled on about the girls, a conscious decision to confirm Jason as the brains and boss of the outfit.

They had just come from Las Vegas Dave said, but the girls here were far more attractive. Jason laughed and said, "Obviously my partner likes Chinese girls, although I don't know what is wrong with Kiwi's and Aussie's myself, I prefer them by a long way especially the wogs!" This bought a huge laugh from everyone, but the comment had only been made to break the ice, which it did very successfully.

"What precisely do you two do?" asked the Leader, "You seem to travel a lot and my Govt friends here are very impressed with you both. They like your program whatever that is they won't say, but they are pleased with the products. I have heard about the Heifers which they say are superior to the Australian product, is that true or is it just Chinese hopes?"

"I think with the heifers it's not so much that they are superior animals, but they are bred younger in NZ so the calves are born earlier, therefore they produce milk quicker, that impresses the Chinese greatly and it's right really they get milk thirty days quicker," Dave said. "Our Frozen meat is a little more expensive, but we have a special arrangement here with a group of meat processors, and that works out well for both of our countries. There is a direct transfer of products we want to buy here for NZ, so everybody is happy"

"And how do you sell, on contract or do you buy and sell?" asked the leader.

Jason replied, "No we are commission agents, our deal is easy we get a price from the suppliers, and anything we receive over and above that price is ours, it's very simple really. All we do is make the sales and buy what we need for buyers back home and that's Dave's job, then we arrange the banks that's my job. Finally we just check the bills of lading, and see that the Chinese and the Australian and New Zealand banks are ready to settle. Oh we have also to arrange the bills of lading, and ensure all Govt documents are in place. There isn't much money changes hands though, because our sales to back home are almost equal to what we sell overseas, only our commissions are payable normally. We are really buying and selling on both sides of the ditch!"

This drew a laugh because all Australians and Kiwi's knew what that comment meant, the Tasman Sea between the two countries it's a pretty big ditch!

Having answered in depth the questions about themselves, Jason felt it was right to ask what their hosts, were doing in China, which he did.

"Oh we are developers, and we are building several of these high rise blocks you can see going up in the foreground. John over here is our Projects Manager, Theo is our Architect and we all represent the American investors, who will squeal like hell if we don't make significant profits for them," George the leader said with a smile.

Jason and Dave had earlier learned the leaders name, Jason was wandering, what his name would be with the American Investors, when they had to face a USD2 billion loss on the proposed takeover of Cooperate Developments Ltd. Jason had heard the American Investors in this case the American Mafia did not take well to losses by any of their partners, such losing partners had the habit of vanishing without ever being found. To awaken his determination Jason only had to remember the pain he had gone through when they tried to murder him, and the four dead people attached in some way to Cooperate Developments Ltd. This always allayed any misgivings he had and confirmed his determination to create havoc within this gang reinforced. He knew he would never forget nor forgive the murdering barsted's in Chicago for as long as he lived, and he knew now these blokes were only pawns doing their masters biding. They were probably locked in so tight that if they did anything their masters didn't like, they would pay with their own lives.

In true corporate sensationalism the collapse of their bid would hit the headlines, and the method by which it had collapsed, would hit the world media. Jason knew the real finance would be from American banks, with the deposits etc being drug money, but those deposits would be disguised as capital appreciation. Jason knew that the media would initiate a real trace of funds, and it was at this point the drug syndicate in Australia and NZ could collapse, he had planned all this so carefully. It was almost like the taste of a true corporate takeover, only it was better after all those Criminal American barsted's had tried to murder him, only one year ago and vengeance would soon be his. Well at least that was what he hoped, but it wasn't going to be so simple, there was a long hard road ahead!

They all had a wonderful evening, George was the perfect host his attention to detail was unique he missed nothing, and his two guests were treated as honored friends, Dave especially loved it unlike Jason he wasn't thinking of vengeance?

The evening ended with all toasting each other; and reminiscing about their home countries Australia and New Zealand, it was almost gallant in its ending.

The next morning the two parties, at their respective tables looked a little disheveled, but the new friendship between them seemed to have been well cemented, and there was an air of community obvious now; that wasn't there before.

Dave was having a hard time keeping up with the banquets, that were such a big part of his business discussions, with the different organizations he was trying to sell his products too almost every day. He was putting on so much weight, even Jason was commenting on how fat he was becoming! But that was the system the Chinese always wanted to eat before talk, and Dave loved their food so he had a real problem, he vowed that next trip back home he was going on an exercise and diet regime. Jason had less of a problem with food, Bankers and Govt; officials were less prone to hospitality, but more focused on possible cash sling backs which Jason wasn't offering. This was creating some difficulty, but so far Jason had got what he wanted without having to resort to such tactics, this policy wasn't creating any special friends though, and he would probably have to change his approach soon.

Gradually Jason and Dave were becoming used to the Chinese environment, but it wasn't easy Dave's job could entail days just talking about what were to him trivialities, but which his interpreter assured him had to be done. Jason was getting sick of seeing unsmiling stony faced officials, his interpreter told him that this would be the norm; until he understood the Chinese protocol, and scattered some money around? His friendliest interpreter told him the that on their first trip, he had only got away with it because they would give him a chance to learn, but now the learning period was over, and he had better conform to what in China was just natural, and not considered a bribe. If he didn't then his mate could sell everything, but they would never get the documents he needed, or the bank support that was vital to any firm of importers and exporters. There is the interpreter told Jason, two essentials for doing good business in China, one was a healthy appetite, the other cash to grease the wheels of Govt; and Bankers, which was all Govt; anyhow. After all the Interpreter said with a laugh, "you don't pay for it; all you do is add their money onto your prices, whats the problem anyhow, they all know the prices will go up to cover their fees you think of it as graft we don't, we just see it as a normal method of trade relations?"

"Oh it's not that, but back home this is discretional and it's not so open, how do we offer money here when we have to use an interpreter?" Jason asked.

"Oh just tell me I will tell them then you deliver the money, and just give it to them it's all very open and just normal, shall I tell them you will be bringing them money?" he asked with a smile.

"Why sure," Jason said with a relieved feeling! After the interpreter had told the men at the next meeting, money was coming it was all smiles again, and once again the documents that had been blocked up, suddenly started to come through almost immediately.

Dave for his part found the little discounts they had been asking for, in other words the objections to prices suddenly stopped, and there were hearty smiles again all around.

Great progress was again being made with the drugs team, and most evenings they had coffee and drinks; together with George playing host. It was obvious he wanted information, but of course couldn't ask openly.

When they left each evening Jason and Dave made it a practice, to finish the day in their own lounge room; ostensibly going over the day's work, but in reality sowing seeds for George to think about.

For example Dave may say, the prices are right provided the special ingredients are right, or the quality of the last shipment was terrific, they want that quality as much as they can get and as often if not more often. The word drug was never uttered, but the innuendos were all there, and there were very liberal expressions about huge profits from various products. These comments were easy because they were correct!

Jason would say for example, that canned fruit going to Australia will be a great new line, when does the first shipment arrive and how long will they take to process a whole boat load? There was a shipload due, but the innuendos about massive profits were only there to inflame the Leader (Georges) imagination. He would be thinking about drugs, but that was up to him to think nothing was ever said about drugs, by either Jason or Dave? If the drug leader was listening in to their conversation and taking his own interpretation out that was his fault, neither Jason or Dave's, they were just talking business, and that wasn't about drug business even if there were lots of innuendo's.

Once Jason had liberally greased the palms as we in the west would say, all of the problems vanished and business started to move very smoothly again, just as it had on the first visit. It was truly amazing and within days all of Jason's work had been completed, and prices had been approved so that they were once again ready to go home.

Jason decided this time it was up to him, so he invited the drug team to a banquet evening paid for by him, and once again it was a wonderful evening. He would have loved to ask George, when the takeover offer for Cooperate Developments Ltd; would hit the stock exchange in Sydney, but of course couldn't. He did satisfy himself by telling them all openly, that it had been a wonderfully profitable trip, and hoping the Kiwi's and the Aussies had lots more products to sell. All of the Aussies John, Theo and George Savarkis wished them a safe voyage and looked forward to seeing them back in China quite soon.

They left the next morning very well pleased with the trip, and the seeds they had sown for the forth coming battle for Cooperate Developments Ltd; Jason was convinced that before they left Australia again, the offer would be in and James would be at the head of a massive battle for the control of Cooperate Developments Ltd.

Arriving back in NZ they had soon completed their documents, and all of the bills of lading had been reported from China as being in place. The final sales figure from China to Australia and New Zealand was close to USD300 million and the sales, to China was just over USD300 million so just over USD600 million, plus another USD100 million in New York and Las Vegas.

Dave had to find sales for American products, equal to what he had sold in the USA, but that wouldn't be hard both Australia and NZ were tariff free countries with the Americans. They needed to try and find products to sell in Fiji as well, but that would not be easy. Finally Jason suggested getting uniforms made in Fiji for sale in America, New Zealand or Australia. We can buy Chinese material and send it to Fiji, this way he said we can even it all out.

Dave agreed, but in his own mind was asking himself what the hell is the boss on about now, buy from China, send to Fiji for processing then sell where ever, why the hell doesn't he think like the rest of us? How the bloody hell; am I supposed to keep up with his mental gymnastics?

The arrival back in Sydney was the same enthusiastic reception as after the first trip, little Jnr; was now three years of age, and Jean Jnr; was at the airport as well to greet their Daddy home. Jean was radiant and very happy that Jason was home again, but managed to ask, "How long will you be home for this time Darling?"

"Well let's see shall we," replied Jason with a smile, "it will be interesting to see what is going to happen, but we both expect the attempt to buy Cooperate Developments Ltd; will hit the markets soon."

Jean gave a big grin and looked at her husband, this was she knew where he excelled, buying out companies but this time he was going to be on the defensive, would he be the boy wonder in this different role, but she thought he may have his biggest win ever.

It was during their weeks break that James rang and said, "Mate there are rumbles on the market now, the media have got the scent of a takeover attempt on Cooperate Developments Ltd. There won't be any blood for a while, but it's on very soon, can we meet when you start work again?"

Two days later the media had it, a straight buyout for the old Jason Andrew's company Cooperate Developments Ltd; they trumpeted. American cash box fund, on the attack Cooperate Developments Ltd; vulnerable too many assets with the market price for the shares to low, Jason Andrews would turn in his grave. Even that was stupid, since the same media had been aware Jason had been cremated; but they were renowned for stupidity, this was just another example of media naiveté?] James as arranged had come for the meeting and both men were ecstatic, my goodness was his first comment when he arrived at Jason's home was, "there will be blood on the streets this time for sure, these Yanks will wish they never heard of Cooperate Developments Ltd; by the time this is over."

When Jason described how he and Dave had fed them misinformation, James couldn't stop laughing! "That is all a stroke of genius, but never mind the battle lines are drawn now so the fight begins are you ready."

"Of course I am this is what I love doing, this will be our biggest coup yet your shares will double in price by time this fight is over, mark my words but they must not find me, if they do some smart barsted will put it all together, no sorry mate you are all alone this time."

James was the biggest shareholder in Cooperate Developments Ltd; but leveraged at 90% he figured by time the fight was over his leverage would be down to about 40%, and since he had such a large block he would be a very wealthy man, they were finally in play at last he couldn't wait for the full fight to start.

Jason broke into his daydreams and asked, "Do they have a holding in Cooperate Developments Ltd; and have they asked for the current financials?"

"No they have no holding at all, and they haven't asked for anything, but of course they will after they have proved to the exchange any offer they make is financed, because they are foreigners!" James replied with a laugh, "these barsted's are locked in and the minimum they can lose is USD2 billion."

"These guys have more money than brains," said Jason; "In fact they are bloody crazy. They think because they can sell drugs and build skyscrapers in China, they are business geniuses. It will be my pleasure to show them how to lose at least two, maybe even five billion dollars it depends how stupid they really are." Now it was Jason's turn to laugh, he was going to pay them back, for all of that time he had been wrapped up in bandages?"

The next day the media was at full blast, the Yanks want our Icon company they trumpeted, quite forgetting how often they had attacked Cooperate Developments Ltd; in the past. Cash offer for 100% of the shares, with 51% being the minimum level of acceptance.

The cartoonists at the Australian were at it again, but now it was James fighting back an American attack, and he was wielding a sword with which he was going to cut those American predators down to size? The Sydney morning herald and the Age in Melbourne, had the Yanks coming back as they did during the WW11, but this time they were on the attack led by General Mc Arthur and Cooperate Developments Ltd; was the Aussie under attack. The American commander was shouting this is just all good fun, but these bloody Aussies better surrender, because we will take them anyhow?

It was all great fun now as far as Jason was concerned; he now bought the hidden funds into play!

The next day it was announced the Americans now had their 51% plus acceptances on the market, so the game was on and the play would quickly develop, the Americans hadn't tasted blood yet, they didn't know it but the blood was going to be their own.

The evening news announced a special dividend to Cooperate Developments Ltd; to all two year aged shareholders of over $4.00 cash per share. Then the market went crazy!

As Jason had predicted the share price on market almost doubled, and the Americans were in a trap already, with the other plays from Cooperate Developments Ltd; still to come.

On the day after Jason and Dave were back in Shanghai, the special options were exercised on market, and the American's were in even worse trouble immediately, it would be a real blood bath if they continued with their bid, even the media could see the future and marveled that even from the grave Jason Andrews had still left a trap.

Jason and Dave were back at the hotel, but strangely there was no greetings and bonhomie this time. The leader looked very stressed; and his two mates looked positively sick they greeted Dave and Jason with a great show of friendliness, but it was obvious there was something upsetting them all badly especially their leader, he looked real sickly?

The next day the options were released in Sydney, and the next morning the drug team didn't even show for breakfast.

Back in Sydney the media was going really berserk, the ghost of Jason Andrews they all trumpeted, the American's are in an ambush General Mc Arthur should have stayed in the Philippines where there is no Cooperate Developments Ltd; it is far safer there.

Meantime Jason and Dave were just going about their business, and boasting they were going to top their last sales, to be over USD800 million all up this time. They also let on their sales in America would soon go up substantially, with the new meat system that the dogs couldn't smell because their noses got frozen.

Dave in jest said maybe the bloody mutts noses will fall off, but if that happened they might find another way to examine frozen meat, to which Jason dutifully let out a laugh of derision.

The fourth day after Dave and Jason had arrived back, the drug trio had vanished!

When Jason enquired about them at reception, he was told they had suddenly had an urgent call from the States, and had all left unexpectedly?

There was no doubt what the emergency was, but the pair never said a word, they continued on making business remarks as if nothing was happening, but of course they knew the lines between Sydney and Chicago would be red hot. The American drug gang had made a play in Australia and it was back firing, the Mafia didn't like to be made to look foolish, there would be a terrific panic at present in both Sydney and Chicago. They had made a play for 100% of an iconic Australian Company, and it was all going wrong even the Chicago Mafia would have trouble to fund this one, and the more they tried to bluff their way through the bigger the losses. If they cut and run now they would only lose just over USD2 billion, these figure were now proved up and the media was quoting the situation, because it was so obvious. The question being asked was, "will they run or will they play has Jason Andrews got them from the grave?"

Jason just sat back and smiled to himself, 'James would be getting the credit or abuse from the media, either they would brand him a crook or a genius,' it didn't matter all those who had known Jason would be wandering if the old fella was still calling the shots. Perhaps they speculated he was defending his company from the grave, many were spooked but all thought it could be true.

James was enjoying his first taste of fame, he was the new genius and most were now trying to trace his background, which was impeccable anyhow?

Meanwhile in China Dave and Jason had progressed well, this time Dave had 200,000 cases of NZ wine and another 100,000 cases of Australian wine to sell. This as well as frozen meat but only 1,000 heifers this time, the season was near an end in New Zealand for them, they would in future have to find Australian heifers to sell in China. The wine was proving hard for Dave to sell, so remembering the lessons of the previous visit Jason through the same interpreter, spread some extra money around and again all of the problems were immediately solved.

The fruit for canning had arrived in Shanghai from both Australia and New Zealand, and would soon be canned, and ready to be returned to their country of origin. Jason had arranged for fabrics to be sent to Fiji, which would then be processed and sent to Australia and New Zealand, for sales in the retail shops. They were producing simple lines like bed clothes, to get into dresses etc was too dangerous, that was an industry neither of them understood.

Almost all of the work in China was done, now they were getting ready to fly out to New York, and then down to Las Vegas. This time Jason got serious about raising loans for New Zealand clients, and he did get the loans they wanted, at the right interest rates.

Dave, had got good sales of Leather products and wine, he sold 200,000 cases at a better price than he had got off the Chinese, but it didn't matter since he didn't even have the wine arranged yet, but he was confident he could fill the orders. He also sold the canned fruit the Chinese were canning so the entire shipment would be diverted to the USA instead of back home.

Down in Las Vegas Dave sold more wine and some lamb carcasses that were cryovac packed therefore did not have to be frozen, but the Americans would only accept new season New Zealand lamb. They got a surprise order for New Zealand pine lumber from Chicago, a sample order of just 50,000 tonnes! Dave was very enthusiastic about the lumber sales; there were large volumes of that product in NZ for sale.

Dave wanted to go to Chicago, but Jason decided against that, he had decided it might be too dangerous; they might run into their drug friends; he thought that wouldn't be very smart at this time.

And so once again it was back to New Zealand to settle the bills of lading then on home to Sydney Australia.

This time there was nobody to meet them at the airport, the two children were down with the flu; and Jean was feeling a little down. The media was upsetting her with their constant reference to a Jason type defense at Cooperate Developments Ltd; and she was worried for their privacy. When Jason got home Jean broke down, oh my God she wailed can you get away with this play? The media are saying only you could set up a play like this, what is going to happen she sobbed?

"No its ok" Jason said, "James will deal with it somehow!"

"That's fine, but the media are going crazy, they say the Americans could lose up to USD five billion, and there will be hell to play in the USA; but they are trapped with no way out. James has admitted the play was there from when you sold out, and donated everything to charity. He also said the charity was the main beneficiary, and that you had planned it that way before you were killed, you had known there would be a play for Cooperate Developments Ltd; because they had been too successful.? Is that true asked a wide eyed Jean did you really see that type of attempt to come?"

"Well yes it was if you think about it the move once they had killed, me was to try to get Cooperate Developments Ltd; thinking it would be exposed, instead they have run into a trap. But it's a trap detonated by themselves not me, and yes they could lose up to five billion American dollars which at the current exchange rate will be six billion Aussie dollars. This will probably be the biggest loss on a stock market play in Australian history, and it serves them right remember they tried to kill me, so why should I be sorry for them? But to be honest that defensive play was there to protect the company, why not if there are buyers out there they will have to pay the real value, we don't want another Jason Andrews to break my work up do we?" he laughed.

"No I don't think you should be sorry, I am just worried they may find you now the hounds are baying so loud, do you really think James can pull the whole program off?" Jean said with a tremor in her voice.

"Yes I do think James can deal with it, he is a very capable man and will field the hounds with a relish, I could never muster; to my own heavy cost," Jason said with a confident smile.

Later in the day they met with the male staff in Dave's office! All of them wanted to discuss the Cooperate Developments Ltd; attempted takeover by the Americans.

Jason was very none committal, just said the takeover would fail and never had a chance from the start, it was just a matter of time; until the Americans realized they couldn't win, but as usual the media was giving the public a big dose of misinformation?

There was no essential information received from the team, but the penetration by the two hard heads was getting deeper, because both had been approached to sell drugs. They had refused, on the grounds that drugs were too dangerous for them; as they had been instructed to do.

The two security men had little to report, but had themselves been offered security jobs; which they had accepted and also were now slowly penetrating the gang as well.

They had left the office to just continue as they were doing, all getting paid on the two jobs which was a happy situation for them. Dave and Jason were doing so well they didn't care about a few dollars out of what they were making.

Miriam was asked to come in and report, but her information was old now, Hemi had sent word that the takeover was ready to start and the Americans were convinced of success. Miriam had said her brother was doing quite well, but becoming depressed which was his own fault anyhow. Even their parents no longer believed his claims of his innocence, they now realized he wasn't the victim as he said, but in her Fathers words he was just a crook. Miriam, was now the full time office girl, who looked after any queries when her bosses were away, on their sales trips and she liked her job.

The final meeting was with James, but that wasn't easy all of his and Cooperate Developments Ltd; lines would be tapped! That wasn't a problem Jason knew that James, quiet as he was, could handle the job really well! Jason in the end decided not to contact James, it could only lead to a disaster if they did; and James would know why he, Jason was keeping away.

The next day the media featured an interview with James on their lead pages! James had told the press that he wasn't the architect of the Cooperate Developments Ltd; defense Jason was. He explained how when he was appointed in to the Cooperate Developments Ltd; Managing Directors job Jason had explained the hidden defense that he had put in place. The options were in the name of Jason's Charity; they also got the special dividend that Jason's shares qualified for, even though he had sold them, they were bonus income, of the special dividend which also went to the charity.

The media were asking if there were any other locked in traps set by Jason, but of course James refused to answer such questions. He countered by asking if they wanted him to get the sack, because his share holders would surely turn against him, if he answered such a leading query.

Jason felt proud of James, he had handled the media like a pro; and never faltered!

Jean was really happy again as she realized that James could indeed handle the media, and seemed to be comfortable with them.

Jason and Dave settled down to their new business as importers and exporters, working from Dave's Burwood office and Miriam loved her work.

The next trip the Kiwi's had colored lamb skins, frozen meat, dried milk and pine lumber for sale! They were developing Australia and now had frozen meat, canned fruit and beef skins salted but untreated and 2,000 heifers from Aussie.

They had over USD800 million worth of product to sell who the hell thought Jason, wanted to be bothered with pushing drugs, just for a while he forgot his vendetta against drug merchants. The next day James managed to get a message through to Dave's office sealed and only for Jason's attention. The note merely said hello and things are going fine. James would see them when they were once again in Australia!

The itinerary this time was Shanghai, New York, Chicago, Las Vegas and Los Angeles a car trip down to San Diego and finally Mexico City. Then they would be coming home through Honolulu, Auckland and finally Sydney! Jean had been invited to come, but decided it would be too much work with such young children. When the children were older she would travel, but because they were trying for more children, that may be a fair while away.

CHAPTER 17

New teams.

Miriam, had as requested made the bookings all open tickets and all business class, Jason couldn't be persuaded to travel first class; in spite of the success they were enjoying. We are business men he declared, not just traveling on the company account; business class is good enough for us? With a laugh he said if Dave complains to me we will be transferred to economy class, and he is getting so fat he won't fit in the seats so you tell him that.

This time when they left Jean looked so sad that Jason promised that the next time home they would go away for a month's holiday, up in the Northern Territory. They would have a really nice trip and drive up slowly. At this Jean brightened up and looked happy when they left. Little Jnr; seemed a bit upset, and Jean Jnr; put her tiny arms up for a cuddle from Daddy.

The trip to Shanghai was as usual uneventful, and the trip to the hotel the same, but when they went to breakfast, the next morning, the Leader was absent but his two mates John and Theo were there, both looking very sullen. Jason went over to greet the two and asked after their leader! Oh he is in America they chorused he won't be back for at least three months; you may see him in Australia next time you are home. Some of his plans at home have gone awry, and he needs to be there for a while to fix them up. Then he will be back they said, without any conviction.

Dave and Jason continued on with their usual prattle, but they didn't think there was much of a strategy needed now. The die had been caste it was only time now, then they would see what the drug lords in Chicago would do, the Leader unless he could come up with an answer may vanish for good? The Takeover was in trouble big time, and nobody failed that badly when working for the mafia. Jason remembered James Hoffa the President of the Teamsters Union, he had vanished after he had made a mess; and his body had never been found? That also had been the Chicago Mob; mistakes weren't tolerated, not at the leader's level.

This time Jason and his friendly interpreter, met the Govt and Bankers reps early; and spread the goodwill, this to make Dave's job easier.

Dave, came in full of enthusiasm that evening, he had strong interest from the buyers in everything he had to sell in China except the colored lamb skins, but he would sell them in the USA.

Jason was just as successful! 'Crikey' he said, "we will only be here about two weeks this time; it easier now that we are spreading the wealth around. But the American stretch will be a lot harder; we need to develop over there, so we are going a round trip; just to feel out the opportunities and get information."

Jason now wanted to explain to Dave and it didn't matter who was listening. "The aim he said is to do four trips a year, but next time around we will be bringing three new men, just to train them. This life is fine for you unmarried men, but Jean is starting to get upset so the next trip will be my last, except on supervision trips. We will want you to do Europe and the UK with a different partner, and we will put a new pair on China and the USA, how does that sound? Oh and we will only have unmarried men it's too hard for the families of married men. Believe me I know!"

"Sounds great to me, it's getting a bit heavy with these Chinese and their bloody banquets; look how fat I am getting!" Dave said with a laugh.

Right on time as Jason had predicted it was only two weeks and they were ready to leave, so bidding farewell to the remaining two members of the drug gang they were off.

In New York things went quite well, but it was far harder than China! After a lot of work Dave achieved his sales target and Jason was finished, so it was off to Las Vegas, with the same result. They had been in Las Vegas for two days, when they got a phone call from a stranger requesting a meeting; as soon as possible and giving no details of what the caller wanted to discuss, when asked if he was a buyer he had been very firm in saying no he wasn't. A meeting had been arranged for the next morning straight after breakfast!

They had just finished breakfast when two men approached their table, and introduced themselves as the ones; who wanted to meet with the two Australians. Dave and Jason had no idea who they were or what they wanted, but Jason had guessed they may be Mafia soldiers.

Having introduced themselves and without invitation the two men sat down! "We know you are both New Zealanders trading mainly through NZ, but also selling Australian products is that right?" One asked

Dave and Jason agreed they were, but said yes they were Kiwi's but living in Australia then waited for further explanation from their visitors, which was soon forthcoming.

We are here they said on behalf of others to ask what you know of the Australian Share Market?

'Well quite a bit', said Jason, "once upon a time I was a trader; but gave the game up for better fields, we are now making ten times the amount we could make as share traders, why do you ask?"

"We have some problems over there have you ever heard of Cooperate Developments Ltd; in your travels over in Australia?" the stranger asked.

"Yes of course we have, that is a major Australian and New Zealand company; again why do you ask?"

"We wandered since you have local knowledge, as you have said you do have; can you could do some work for us down there in Australia?" the same man asked.

"Not really we are so busy with our own business, we are traveling most of the time; any time at home is rest time and we would be loath to work then. This constant travel is hard work and we just look forward to a break, but what has this to do with Cooperate Developments Ltd; they never commission us to sell their products, if they did we might be able to help but they don't so that's that," Jason said very firmly.

"Maybe that could be changed if what we want you to do for us down there works," said the Mafia spokesman.

"Well what the hell are you doing," said a Jason, "who was obviously getting bored with the conversation, which to him was only going around in circles."

"We are buying out Cooperate Developments Ltd;" said the leader of the two.

"You are what?" Asked an incredulous Jason, "gosh that's a big job that company is an Iconic Australian company, how the hell do you even start to buy them out?"

"That's what we want you to tell us, we had heard about you both and checked you out, and you he said pointing at Jason, have a reputation down under that very few enjoy. Now will you take the job we want to offer you? It's very important to my bosses and they would make it well worth your while!"

"No not really, we have a big job with our own affairs; we just don't have the time to work for your firm as well, nobody could pay us enough," sorry said Jason.

"What about if we make it an offer you can't refuse?" the man persisted, "my bosses may just be able to make you think again?"

"I doubt that," replied Jason, "not because we don't want to, but because our time won't allow us to do anything else."

"Well we can make you a very lucrative offer," the man said again!

"Can you match the commissions we are earning working for ourselves, I don't think so we have a very profitable business, and we don't need anybody else."

"Ok then name your price we will pay whatever you ask for," again the man persisted.

"You haven't even told me what you want done yet, so how the hell do I give you a price?"

"We want you to complete our takeover bid for Cooperate Developments Ltd; our own people have failed and we need an expert, you have been named as an expert, so what do you say how much would you charge?" he asked again.

"You are talking about Cooperate Developments Ltd; are you?" Jason asked? "No I don't think that's a job we would want, if your people have failed why do you think we could succeed, that's a big ask how much did your team offer, and how was the offer expressed?"

"Why a 100% cash offer for 100% of the shares, with a minimum 51%, but there was a trap in the infrastructure of Cooperate Developments Ltd; left by its previous Managing Director, and we are now in a trap. But our people never take in shareholders outside our own group that's why the offer is for 100%!"

"You mean your people have fallen into one of Jason Andrews financial traps; I wouldn't touch anything he was involved with even if he did sell out. Who in the hell led you Americans into that company, that's an Australian Icon, and won't easily be taken out let me assure you of that." Jason said with a smile.

"Well that's too late now, we want to know how to get out of this bloody mess and it needs an Australian, not one of our people. We have messed up big time!" he said.

'But was it an American that got your team in, if so make him get you out? Jason said cryptically, "no that's a dangerous job and I have no intention of playing with Cooperate Developments Ltd; that was Jason Andrews's baby and there is no knowing what traps he has set."

"No it wasn't an American it was an Australian that got us in, he claimed he knew so much and yet he has made a mess, believe me my bosses are very angry with him and he will have to pay back every dollar, ""Well let me tell you said Jason, no sane Aussie would try for any company that Jason Andrews had played with, and Cooperate Developments Ltd; is a crazy play. You say an Aussie made the running, well I know all of the Aussie operators and none would dare take on Cooperate Developments Ltd; only because of Jason Andrews even though he is dead."

"Look let me have my bosses make you an offer the man said, you will find them very generous!"

'Yes I believe you' replied Jason, "but no that job is too dangerous, they would I am sure be generous, but if I failed they would be equally hard in their retribution, it doesn't take much of a guess to know you two are Mafia soldiers, and I don't want to get involved with them no thanks? Our work is just as lucrative, but a damn sight less dangerous! Our sales will be up to around the USD1B per two month trip soon, and we don't have to play any silly games, just do our work and keep moving around? It's a real free and easy life why should we take a risk by working for the Mafia in Chicago?"

At this stage Dave spoke up, but only to say that that was the play that was going on when we were in Sydney last, the media were going crazy, but you were off with Jean and the Kids? I read it but it was of no interest to us so I took no notice!

The two men then stood up but said they would be back that evening!

Jason asked, "Why we aren't going to change our minds, it's just too dangerous and we don't want a bar of the Mafia, that isn't going to change today or ever."

'Besides' cut in Dave again, "we are leaving for Los Angeles later tonight so we won't be around for any meetings."

"That's ok we can meet you there as well that's not a problem, but we do have someone who may be able to change your mind in our favor. This is someone you got to knew in Shanghai and he needs your help real bad," the mafia man said with a smirk?

"Ok then it's better to meet in Los Angeles because we still have commitments, and they aren't going away too easily, said Jason with a puzzled look. After the two men had left Dave and Jason still being cautious asked each other who it was from Shanghai that needed their help," but neither guessed.

They had only been in Los Angeles for one day, and the same mafia man rang again asking for a meeting in the evening, and that they were bringing a guest.

"Well today is not suitable let's make it tomorrow after breakfast, and we will put any meetings we have back a couple of hours. Who is this man you are bringing, and how well do we know him, you say he is an Australian and he works for the Mafia in Chicago. Why don't you just tell us who it is, we may not even want to meet with him whoever he is?" Jason asked.

"Oh you will meet him all right, and he certainly wants to meet you and Dave." The voice on the phone said.

When Jason told Dave the meeting was on for the next day, as he had done Dave asked who is this mysterious figure, but he wrote on a piece of paper. It's George the Leader who has gone missing from his team in Shanghai.

Jason gave Dave a wink and a note, 'that's the only person it could be; we know no one else from Shanghai do we? If we did it must be a phantom because there is nobody that I can think of right now, can you think of anybody?'

And so it was going to happen, 'George' the drug gang leader from Australia, was asking to meet them, he must indeed be in serious trouble.

Dave and Jason had just finished their breakfast, when the Mafia soldier who had done all of the talking on the last occasion, walked in with George Savarkis their Shanghai Leader.

The two Kiwis acted suitably startled, what the hell are you up to asked Jason, although he knew well what the answer would be? Dave just sat with his mouth wide open!

"Well you see I was the architect of the plan to take over Cooperate Developments Ltd; and now it is all falling apart and we stand to lose a great bunch of money, unless you can help me," George said in a pleading voice.

"Struth Mate why did you pick that company, that was Jason Andrew's Baby you have; from what I have now heard, walked into a bunch of traps. Jason was killed but he is striking back from the grave, but how can we help, we will look at something for a fellow Australian, but it won't be easy Andrews really knew the game well." Jason said. "We know you are an expert on corporate affairs, and I don't know how to get out of this disaster, I need you to help me if you can?" George was pleading and it seemed as if Jason had achieved his goal all he had to do was wait and George would be dead, the trouble was he now knew the real killers were in Chicago.

"Well I don't really know what the play is, I know the media was braying away when we were home, but my two children and my wife were after me to spend time with them, tell me what the of your bid is. Have you played by all of the stock market rules, over there and what is your bid all about, I suppose the Mafia in Chicago is backing your play?"

"Yes they are funding the play and the full cash offer was made last week, with a 60% acceptance to make the deal irrevocable. We have reached that?" George said with a grimace.

"That's big cash need what was Cooperate Developments Ltd; valued at when you made your bid?"

"Oh it was moving between $15-16 per share, but there were traps we didn't know about. They had a hidden cash box which they bought out, and paid a cash dividend of $4.00 per share, which was bad enough the price jumped to $32.00 per share overnight and no sellers. Then they presented 500 million options that Andrews had paid up to 10%, and they were locked in at $20.00 each, if there was a takeover bid." it's a bloody nightmare.

"Hm yes Jason Andrews had no peer when it came to corporate strategies, how much are you in the can for if we can't get you off?" Jason asked.

Up to USD 2 billion George nearly cried, in his anguish," Hm just like I did when you tried to murder me Jason was thinking!

"And what are your backers going to do if you lose that much of their money?" Jason asked looking at the Mafia Soldier.

"It's not for me to answer questions like that, I suppose it would depend on George coming up with a way to pay them off, but it's a hell of a lot of money. What do you think a creditor for that much money would do, frankly I wouldn't like to be in George's shoes, he may just finish up dead, I really don't know?" the Mafia spokesperson said.

"Well we are going back to New Zealand and then on to Sydney, how do I contact you Jason asked. Are you going back to Shanghai or what?"

"Yes I will be going back, they will give me time to get out of this mess, but only you can help me Jason Andrews has reached out from the grave and caught me? It was me that put him in his grave now he just may put me in my own grave! This was said with very sincere melancholy," as if he knew what the Mafia would do.

"And if your bid had succeeded who would have been the winners you or the Mafia," but that's a silly question isn't it the Mafia of course?

'That night the notes were going between Jason and Dave flat out, if you wanted to is there anything that could be done?' Dave had asked.

'Not that I know of replied Jason, the trap is pretty watertight believe me! But I didn't have the heart to say Jason Andrews has got you mate, so there's nothing anyone can do, but who knows I will sleep on the problem. Just maybe there is an answer we aren't killers, but let's see what can be done? It's strange now that the goal has been achieved there is no pleasure in success, let's just say we aren't meant to be killers, but hell when they almost cooked me it was like this time would never come, what would it be like if we had the real killers in a vice?'

Jason canceled the trips to San Diego and Mexico, to be left for the next time, and they boarded a plane straight back to New Zealand, and then finally back to Sydney for a rest but he had forgotten that holiday with Jean and the children; and that certainly would be no time of rest.

Jean and Jnr; were at the airport excited, because they were going away for a month's holiday. Daddy had promised last time he was home, so Jean had shared the promise with Jnr; little Jean was still too small to say anything but goo, goo and da, da.

'Jason, quickly arranged meetings at Dave's office, but the team reports were still the same. Their operatives were penetrating ever deeper and Jason now had a team that was well entrenched within the drug fringes, as well as an informant at top level.' The problem now was whether it was all wasted, they had the way through to the top and perhaps it was time to withdraw and close the team down, but it was really only a small cost and the Chicago Mafia was the real target anyhow, so Jason decided they would continue. The new business was going so well that Jason decided to continue on as a drug busting organization, but in the back of his mind he was still curious what to do with Chavez and his sister Miriam. 'Miriam was called in to report on Hemi, he was soon coming up for trial on charges of importing 100ks of Cocaine, and he could no longer fool even himself that he was innocent. Miriam was crying she knew her brother had bought everything on himself, but their Mother was still insisting they try and help him?'

Jason in spite of everything decided they would pay his own lawyers to represent Chavez, but told Miriam as nicely as he could that he didn't really need any more information, except to know how her brother was getting on personally?.

Jason now had no problem to call James and ask for a meeting, because now he was working for the drug team, James came that night and couldn't believe what Jason was telling him. "Looks like you are in the box seat that's sure so where do we go from here now?" James said with an amused laugh.

"Well you treat me as a negotiator for the buyers, and I will treat you as the target, let's have some fun out of all this shall we?" Jason said with a smile.

On the following morning Jason rang James at Cooperate Developments Ltd; and requested a meeting on behalf of the Americans, and then he rang the brokers dealing for George, to ask for a meeting on behalf of George.

The brokers were well aware the bid was in trouble, they just wanted to know what Jason was going to do. Jason admitted he had only a couple of days before, been in Los Angeles and approached by George, to see if there was a way out and that he had told George there was little if any hope.

"Well there is nothing that can be done we have told George that, you are only wasting your time this Australian company, he wanted to take over is no easy target and he should have been more careful. There is nothing you can do how did he find you? Are you an expert on Australian Companies because I am, and I am telling you not to waste your time and mine as well actually?" He was an arrogant young know all and Jason almost told him to shut up, but he restrained himself.

"To be honest," Jason said. "I will be checking just how good the advice was you gave your client, so I wouldn't be too cocky if I were you there's nothing worse than bad advice in a big deal such as this. Because if you have stuffed up it will be your balls on the line not George's, so far I think you may be going for a ride not George, but we will see but be sure we will check out your work real close because, I have a feeling you may have messed up?"

The broker changed immediately, "no we advised the job thoroughly George just would not listen, I warned him it was a dangerous play for a firm like Cooperate Developments Ltd."

"And did you have George sign the advice documents, before he went into the Americans, and arranged the money because if you didn't then you are in the shit?" asked Jason in a real friendly tone.

By this time the broker was really groveling, "no I didn't get George to sign he wasn't here, and he wanted speed so we did the documents quickly, and made the offer immediately."

"Well you know as well as I do, you cannot represent a client unless he has signed up to you, in this case I think you are the buyer not George. I suggest you see your lawyers immediately, because I will be reporting to George you are the buyer not he, are you insured?" Jason asked.

"Yes we are insured, but we would never have made a play; for anything Jason Andrews had set up that would be a fool's play." said a now much chastised young agent.

"Did you tell George that, or did you just think of the huge commissions, you were going to earn I am sorry for you, but for sure you are in real trouble?" Jason asked.

Then Jason met with James and explained the broker's problems, which made it the Insurance company problem! James though it was a hell of a good joke, in common with most people there was no love for the insurance underwriters and seeing them go for a ride was good for James sense of humor.

"So there is no way out one way or the other, it's either the insurance company or the Drug team; good Lord may we never have to tangle with you." James laughed as he thought to himself, 'my goodness this man has made me not only rich, but famous he really is a bloody genius.'

CHAPTER 18

Off the hook

"That's fine Jason said, you just keep dealing with the parasitic media, I hate them barsted's believe me we have to congratulate you on how well you seem to be able to handle them, my wife loves watching you deal with them."

Later Jason rang Dave and told him what had happened; he was as usual full of admiration for Jason's abilities, and like James had no use for insurance companies either.

After that Jason rang George who was still in Chicago and told him that he probably wasn't the buyer of Cooperate Developments Ltd; and he explained why, It's really easy Jason explained all you have to do is ask for the signed contract of the agreement between you and your brokers, they have none so they are stuffed, if the deal had worked they could have taken the deal off you anyhow, so now you can stick it to them just as soon as you are ready, but my job is finished thank goodness for that. 'Jason also warned George, that he would probably have to come to Australia, to clean up the total mess, so he would need to be sure it was safe for him here?'

George was almost hysterical with excitement, "you have saved my life he said, the Mafia here were giving me three months to pay them out in full. If I didn't they haven't said what would happen, but we can both guess can't we? Ok I will now go back to Shanghai, but we can talk later when you are in Shanghai, thank you so much I will never forget this I wasn't ready to die yet, and it was just so hard waking every day and wondering what would happen?"

When he arrived home, it was to announce that the next day they were all going up to the Northern Territory; and he promised they would have a full month.

Jean, of course was ecstatic, and little Jnr; was running around yelling hooray we are going on holiday, he didn't really know what holiday meant, but he thought he did.

They left the next morning with the car fully loaded, and with lots of home baked cookies; within 30 minutes Jnr wanted to go home, 'this is so boring' he declared; as his mother tried to get him to go to sleep. Then after that he took to asking every five minutes, 'are we there yet?' Jason by the time they got to Brisbane Jason was totally pissed off.

The next stage of the journey was Townsville, and by then Jason was a nervous wreck, why he asked did we ever decide to drive, it would have been far better to have just flown to Darwin, this bloody kid is driving me nuts! Jean just kept silent and said nothing, she also was wandering why they had decided to Drive to Darwin, it was just as well little Jean couldn't talk she was thinking, but it was too late now; it looked as if Jnr; was going to ruin his parent's holiday.

The night in Townsville then the last leg to Darwin, and it was pure torture for Jason and Jean, when they finally pulled into their booked motel in Darwin, both parents were totally distraught. Jean was in tears and Jason had lost his temper completely, and Jnr; why he kept right on asking, 'how long are we staying here?' he asked, and 'I want to go home because I don't like holidays.'

The next three weeks though were idyllic as they went sightseeing, but they dare not go too far out of Darwin because Jnr; would start his nagging again, 'when are we going home?' He would whine incessantly.

It was coming to the end of their holiday, but Jason couldn't face the trip home with Jnr; whining all of the way, so he booked the car onto the rail and they flew home. It had been a memorable holiday, one both Jason and Jean vowed they would never try again, imagine they commiserated with each other if Jean could talk as well; both of them whining all the way to Darwin, Jason loved his Son but oh dear no more holidays in the car.

They were back for another three weeks and then Jason and Dave would be off again, but this time they had three new men travelling with them. Jason had explained to Jean he wouldn't be going away so often from the time their new men were trained, they were teaching three men, one would work with Dave and the other two would be working in the area that Jason and Dave had developed. Jason said I may go on one more teaching trip, but no more after that he said I will be staying home to run the Sydney office. The problem is this new business is growing so fast, that as soon as I make a change its old and we have to change again, so don't be surprised at other changes still coming.

Jean of course was ecstatic and Jnr; copied his mum's excitement, one more maybe two trips and their isolation without a daddy & husband was over.

The media had caught hold of the story that the broker, hadn't set up his contract with the Americans properly, so sadly for him he was the buyer of Cooperate Developments Ltd; not his clients. The Insurance Company was really kicking up a fuss but there was nothing that could be done, the Americans were off the hook! The Insurance Company had to pay, but they did so with a very bad grace, Jason thought they had done quite well at least they didn't go bankrupt he told James!

Jason of course as the recognized representative of the Americans could call on James anytime and they were certain his office wasn't bugged. Just to be sure Jason had a note with him telling James, 'not to talk openly, as they never knew where his clients had managed to plant bugs.'

James told Jason he had reached a settlement with the Insurance Company, the company shares had bounced up to a top price of $35.00 and now everybody had accepted the change, but it wouldn't affect the profit the shareholders would earn off the aborted takeover. As any man who had just made a huge profit because of another man's skill should, 'James made a note for Jason thanking him personally for making him a wealthy man.'

Jason's comment was, 'you took the risks and you won congratulations!'

Dave was told to have one last meeting at his office with the staff, Jason wasn't coming he would be interviewing the three men Dave had accepted, to accompany them on their next trip.

Dave reported the next day that, 'everything was moving smoothly with the team they were just infiltrating as they were meant to do'. The meeting with Miriam was fine, 'she had a full grasp of her job now; and was quite capable to deal with any office problems.' The trap that had been set for Hemi hadn't worked, 'apparently he was genuine at least, but who knows what the future was for him a big stretch in Jail probably.' He had disgraced himself and apart from his family none were really sympathetic.

Jason had approved the three trainees, so Miriam had made all of the bookings; they were due to leave in two days time, going first to Shanghai. It seemed strange travelling with such a big team, but by the time they got to the hotel in Shanghai they were quite comfortable together.

As was natural George greeted Jason with enthusiasm at breakfast, and asked if he could talk privately to him, after they had all finished breakfast.

It was agreed the two of them would meet in one of the hotels private rooms, after Dave and the new team were settled into the start of their day. Two of the men were going with Dave and one was waiting on Jason, they were going to change every day, so the new men could be conversant with both jobs.

After that was all settled Jason came down to the lobby; to meet with George.

"First let me say how much I appreciate what you did for me, it was pretty rocky going with the chiefs back in Chicago; I have never felt so frightened in my life. They want me to offer you a place working for them, but I took the liberty of saying it was doubtful that you would even give that a thought, the offer is there if I was wrong. We have heard from Australia the proposal to purchase Cooperate Developments Ltd; has foundered and there is to be an Insurance Company payout, if I have any objections they gave me seven days to reply."

"The Chicago mob are delighted naturally, they think you are a genius and I agree, but you would be too smart to stick your neck out like I have, am I right?" Asked George.

"Yes you are right, there is no way I would even consider working for or with them, once one is in it would be hard to get out, as I am sure you know. Your expression of thanks is appreciated, but for me it was just business you will be getting an account for services rendered. Don't take me wrong; but that work is part of what I do for a living, I only refused to do the job for that Mafia soldier; because I don't want to even get close to them. This isn't the first time that offers from gang connections have come in, I have nothing against them except; there's no way it's safe being in bed with them," Jason said.

"Yes I know what you mean, but it's too late for me to be so meticulous, I should have thought of that a long time ago, it's too late to get of their boat now? I know far too much to ever again be free in the sense that you mean, as you have so succinctly put it, once having been in bed with the Mafia there is no divorce," George smiled in a sad way.

"Now there is one thing we have to get clear before we go further," said Jason, "you mentioned having had Jason Andrews killed when last we met. Let me tell you something George, Jason Andrews was my mentor and a close friend; it was him that taught me the twists and turns of the world of finance. So in a way it was him that saved your life, it was because of him I was able to figure out how to get you out of that mess? When you said what you did, I had to wonder what Jason would have wanted me to do, and it seemed he was telling me to do the job. It didn't matter what the cost we have our Integrity and it was time to be magnanimous, so I spent the time and energy to save your hide. I just want one thing in return, whatever you are into I don't care, but it wasn't to let you go on killing decent people you were helped, promise me there will be no more killings ordered by you," Jason said.

"I can only be humbled by what you have just said, but let me tell you that there has never been anybody killed on my orders, but yes I have been the executioner on several occasions. I can promise you that is the truth, and if you want to have revenge then you can rely on me for help. This was an example of having me as the scapegoat, but it was really my Mafia Masters; looking for the means to import Cocaine into New Zealand, Australia and the USA. I am not an expert on financial affairs but they believed they could help me through, but when it all backfired then suddenly we in Shanghai were alone. The Chicago Don's really cut up rough, and many of the soldiers were at risk, as well as all of us in Shanghai. We are drug dealers, and our other function is washing the drug money for the Chicago Mafia! You can well imagine this is dangerous work and I wanted out, because there is work that my own money could now fund, but when I told them in Chicago; it was time for me to retire they laughed? The only time you retire they said, was when we bury you and it doesn't have to be from natural causes, so there it is," said George.

"This is good said Jason, because that's what I really wanted to know! I figured you might have been the executioner, but it's the Judge we want; of course being an Aussie helped, but let's be honest this all looks more like work done by the American Mafia not Aussies. You know Dave and I got into this import export work, by accident we were really wanting to work in America, but a friend said why not try China now here we are. I was approached to sell drugs, and Dave and I have often joked about selling Cocaine, but I am the father of two Children and a beautiful wife so it's not worth the bother. Much to our surprise we feel our sales will grow past USD four billion per year with a very small staff, and we don't believe we could make as much peddling drugs. When you are on to a good thing stick to it, isn't that how the old saying goes?" Jason said with a laugh.

"Yes it is" laughed George, "Oh and let me tell you my two associates would like to get out too, but we all know too much so that's not possible for them either!"

Jason and George left their meeting both feeling good about their very open discussion, and Jason vowing he was now going to go after the person who had decided, so many Australians must die. He had achieved everything he wanted, 'he had a new and flourishing business, the drug saga was now well understood and he knew where his real enemies were, as a parent he needed to continue his crusade against drugs, and he had a new and happy life with no media in it watching everything he did and adjudicating on him, but always pronouncing him as bad seed.'

The next few days were momentous for Jason, he was pleased to find they had chosen well their new staff, but he had changed his mind again and decided Dave was to be the manager. He sat down with Dave outside of the hotel and explained the conversation with George, but still truncating his words, 'some things he kept private for himself only.'

'Dave was happy to accept his new job he would always be travelling!' Jason had decided they would be selling in 'Shanghai, USA, UK, Germany, France, Italy, Spain and Japan' as commission agents. There was to be two teams one would develop the countries they were already working in plus the UK, another would be doing the other countries. If the program worked as it was doing so far they would just add another team. Jason would stay home and work with the office, but they would still be after busting the drug gang. Jason would run the office but he would develop the means to attack the Mafia in their own country. In spite of the accommodation with George none but Dave and Jason would know what was going on, Jason hadn't divulged any of the plans to George etc; he was putting in place when he had talked to him.

The training program was going splendidly, the three new men proved very adept; at picking up what the teams would be doing. The trainees like Dave were older single men, who wouldn't have to be worrying about wives and children back home. They all had nobody back in New Zealand or Australia, who were always asking why Daddy was away all of the time; Jason had really had enough of being away from home and not seeing his family most of the time, he had decided there was no need for him to travel again, and they would hire another man as soon as they arrived back home.

The trip was just as successful as the three previous ones had been; the Chinese buyers and sellers were now quite used to Dave and Jason. The arrangements were made for Dave in future to spread the goodwill around that was the magic that opened all doors? In the USA it was a lot harder, but the progress was still very good! The trip finished with just over USD850 million in cross sales, so Jason was very comfortable that he had set up a great new business!

Another man was hired, and briefed on what the job was all about by Jason, the teams were to do one trip every three months. There would be seven weeks away, two weeks doing local work, and four weeks break every three month term, it meant four trips per team per year. Team number one would be the one doing the area Dave and Jason had done, plus the UK, and they would leave six weeks before the second team.

Team number two would be doing all of the new area except the UK, and Jason would be responsible to get products to sell, within the two countries. Getting products those countries A&NZ wanted to buy was up to the teams, they must always go to New Zealand on their way back to Sydney. Having thought his way through all of that planning, Jason then realized he was wrong Dave was a salesman, and he was very capable at that type of work, but a salesman was not normally a good buyer. He Jason would have to put on a buyer as well so that the sales teams would have the products to sell. The buyer would only have to travel to Australia and NZ it would be quite a nice comfortable job, but still best for a single older man.

Before he left Shanghai this time, Jason met with George and arranged personal call numbers, this was so that each could contact the other; at any time it was needed. 'It wasn't stated, but George was left in no doubt that Jason wanted revenge, on he who had judged his friend, and that if George betrayed him he would have not only the Mafia to worry about.'

Jason had all of the good intentions of staying home a lot more, but it wasn't to be for a while yet! There was still the strong urge within him, to get revenge on the Mafia, but he didn't want George or even Dave to know what he was up to or know what he was going to be doing yet. Mainly because he didn't know himself. Miriam and Jean had a secret mobile number and only they could contact him at all times.

After the two teams had left Jason spent some time with Miriam at the office, and then suddenly announced he would be away for a month. Jean was disappointed, but realized it was only a month this time, so she was content her husband would soon be home.

This time Jason booked into the hotel, George's wife and daughter stayed at, he was looking to get leads on the Mafia without involving George. From what he had been reported by Dave on the first trip, the two woman were rather a shame to themselves; so Jason had decided to see if he could get a Mafia connection, just by watching them. Jason was convinced although he hadn't said so; George's family were hostages to the mafia just to be sure they were in complete control.

Once again in didn't take long to understand which guests were George's family! They were shameless in their behavior, the wife with her Lesbian friend, and the daughter flaunting a young stud, who Jason assumed had not yet reached the use by date.

It was about two days before any nasty Mafia looking soldiers; appeared on the scene and there was no doubt they were chastising the women. Probably now that George was back in the good graces of the Mafia Dons they were starting to look after his interests, the two women protested vigorously, but their protestations were ignored. It seemed they were getting a warning behave or else, Jason figured the threat had been they would be sent to Shanghai. Whatever it was the two women started to be more cautious in their philandering, it seemed obvious they had no lust for China, and it didn't matter where in China.

Jason had decided it was time to become friendly as in Aussie to Aussie away from home; that always opened doors easily. The next day at breakfast Jason introduced himself to the women, he simply said he had recognized their accents, and they were obviously from Sydney.

The two women were delighted and invited him to join them, and a delightful interlude it was, until Jason announced he had work to do; and bid them both good bye.

Jason had noticed one of the Mafia soldiers were watching, so he figured there would be some type of confrontation. He was happy to wait until he was told to buzz off, and then he would be the women's hero and tell the soldier to go to buggery, a place well known to Australians of all age groups, and after all both of them were Australians.

The approach wasn't long in coming; the soldier first spoke to the women, and then came to speak to Jason!

The approach in Jason's mind was very amateurish, the man simply walked up to him and said, "Look stranger just keep away from those two women; if you want to stay healthy?"

"What are you talking about?" Asked Jason in feigned astonishment!

"Didn't you hear what I just told you," the man said; now belligerently," I said keep away from those two women and we don't intend to say it twice?"

"There's no reason why I should!" Jason responded, "Unless they tell me to that is who are you to them anyhow asked Jason? To me they are just two of my own country women, and if there's no law against it I will talk to them; whenever and where ever we please."

"That could be quite dangerous for you, something serious may happen to you and maybe them as well; it's not quite right to be accosting females by themselves here in America," now said in a very threatening manner.

Jason could see this fellow wasn't very bright so he just asked, "is that what your boss said or are you threatening me, because if you are, you are the one who should be worried not me?"

This seemed to puzzle the soldier," who the hell are you then he asked; I am just doing a job and my orders are to keep those two females behaving themselves?"

"If that's the case and you are being ignored by me, its best you take me to see your boss isn't it said Jason with a grin?"

"Yeah I guess so!" replied a totally bewildered man, "come on then and my boss will tell you to keep away, just the same as I have tried to do?"

It was only a short distance to the boss's office, where he sat with an equally dumb looking bunch of men over whom he seemed to be presiding as some sort of senior dumbster.

"This guy here has refused to listen to me, when I told him to keep away from those to dames you told me to guard, now he wants you to tell him why he isn't allowed to talk to dem boss so here he is?"

By this time Jason was smiling in a friendly manner and simply asked this boss! "Your man told me to buzz off and I wasn't to talk with two fellow Australian's, my question was why should I unless they told me not him, who is he anyhow he and even you mean nothing to me?"

"To be honest," the boss of the Dummies said, "we have to look after the interests of the husband and father; who works for us in China. Those two girls have been naughty, so we have been keeping an eye on them for him; that's all we need to tell you our intentions are quite above board? Let me tell you myself then keep away from those two even if they are Australian's," said the boss with a sardonic grin.

"And what happens if I don't asked an amused Jason," who was smiling just as sardonically at this big boss.

"Well why don't we just wait and see," said the boss man, with some malice in his voice now, "but it won't be good for your health let me guarantee that Aussie, I quite like Australians but not bloody cheeky ones."

"Oh well its bad luck I suppose, but it's quite obvious, those two women are being intimidated by you blokes. That's not quite fair now is it? If you are so worried about their man, then send them back to Australia that will fix it all! As for me I am happily married and don't need their problems, but there is no reason for you to bully them now is there, you blokes are just bullies? As for being cheeky, that's bullshit I am just sticking up for a couple of distressed Australian females nothing more?"

"Ok mate that's it you have had your say now buzz off," said a suddenly bumptious boss man.

Jason left rather amused at the situation in regards to the two females, he went straight back to the hotel and spying the two sitting in the dining room at lunch, joined them. "It seems the Mafia has a vested interest in your husband he said speaking to the mother, they are trying to ensure you two girls stay pure and true to him, well that's what they told me. When I told them I was a family man and only interested in the fact that you are both Australians, they told me to buzz of not sure what that means probably bugger off in our language?" Jason said.

The two females started to laugh, "you can't talk to them like that they are the Mafia in Chicago and they run this town and a few others beside, do you want to get yourself killed?"

"No not particularly but I am not used to being told who I can or cannot talk to, how long have you lived like this?"

"Not long really, my husband got himself into trouble with them and now they are monitoring us like a couple of criminals, it's a sick joke really they the Mafia being so high and mighty over our morals, yet they would kill us without hesitation, we want to go home to Sydney, but we are not allowed we are hostages for my husband, can you believe that?"

Having heard Dave's opinion from when he had first sussed them out, Jason did believe it but he smiled and commiserated with them, and invited them both to dinner that evening, which they happily accepted.

CHAPTER 19

Setting up in the USA.

That night the Wife was very open about their situation,' and confirmed most of what George had told him, that really he was just a stooge for the Mafia and they would never release him alive, because he knew too much about their organization?' They were trying to find a third party country like New Zealand through which to import drugs, 'they had tried Australia but a stupid mistake had been made so they were sent to China?'

The two women had been sent to Chicago to be hostages, but life had now turned sour because of the stupid monitoring and now they also were being controlled. 'It seems the wife was angry because her husband was in China doing whatever he pleased with the women there, but she was supposed to be a hermit, and she was very angry. The Daughter, well she just liked men and she was getting frustrated, she was looking at Jason speculatively but he declined the obvious invitation.'

The point as far as Jason was concerned he wanted to get a connection locally with the Mafia, but he wasn't sure how to go about it, so he confided to the two women what he wanted and why? "They murdered one of my best friends in Australia he said and I want to get revenge, how do I get into that organization without being one of them?"

The women were keen to help but didn't know how, they suggested lunch the next day at a place they knew wouldn't be bugged, 'they weren't bugged themselves yet but soon would be with Jason around.' Jenny the wife wrote out an address and they agreed on a time that they would meet the following day.

Jason arrived early so he could look the place over and the two women arrived right on time.

The two girls seemed to be excited at the prospect of working against the Mafia, and cared little about the risk, "if we are caught they will kill you not us they both laughed."

Jason cared little for their silly joke, and just sat and listened to their idea, but agreed 'he was the one taking the risk and they would only be chastised if they were all caught!'

Maria the daughter apparently had a Mafia soldier boy friend that was rising in the ranks, 'but she had given him the bums rush in spite of his strong objections and connections.' He had she said with a laugh, a strong propensity to boasting in bed after sex. An act for which he was not much good at which is why he had been sacked. Maria proposed to reinstate him and have her room bugged, it would be a bore for her but one the Mafia would allow since Gino was one of their own.

Jason could give Maria questions and after sex she would get Gino to rabbit on, as she called his post sex habit and she would ask the questions, while he was at the height of his self aggrandizement.

Jenny who had no inclinations towards men other than her husband anyhow, 'had no trouble with the Mafia because of being friendly with Jason; they would probably ignore Jason once Maria was back with Gino.'

Jason thought it was a great idea, 'but at that time hadn't realized he would be listening to Gino and Maria copulating.'

The next day at breakfast Maria appeared with a man of Italian appearance, surreptitiously she had cast a look at Jason across the other side of the room and smiled, it was clear she was saying this is Gino!

Jason returned the smile and wandered just when that little vixen Maria was going to start the recorded pillow talk messages they were after.

After breakfast Jenny came across to Jason, and told him to write out a list of queries for Maria to ask Gino over the next few nights, copies of which would be kept for Jason daily. Jenny also suggested they should not upset the Mafia soldiers who were ordered to keep an eye on her, Maria would she felt get Jason all of the information he wanted.

It would be best Jason felt to start by asking very innocuous questions, and letting them become more revealing as time went by. He wanted Gino to become comfortable with Maria asking him questions, the more important or revealing ones would be fed to him slowly. They could then wait and see just how much Gino would divulge; it surely depended on how gullible he was, 'but maybe the sexual interlude would lower his defenses,' by Maria's comments Gino was very prone to pillow talk after sex so Jason was quite happy to wait and see what came out of their joint strategy.

Jason that morning wrote out a set of questions then numbered them in order of importance; he then met Jenny and asked her if she could memorize what he had written. It was important that no pieces of paper were left lying around, if Gino should suspect anything he may get very angry and who knows what may happen if he did?

Jenny thought she could memorize his writing and so Jason left her to study what he had written, and when she was comfortable he destroyed it in front of her.

Jenny made an arrangement to meet at a private place with Jason each afternoon, and bring her girl friend with her this would allay the Mafia suspicions, and she could deliver a tape of Maria and Gino in bed. If the tape had no real information she would ignore him at the breakfast, but if the tape was worthwhile she would smile at him while eating, and later deliver the tape.

Jason knew he was getting into an area he was new to didn't really understand, but he had to make a start and this was a start. Ideally what he wanted was a Judas in the Mafia camp, but this was hard to achieve maybe by listening to Gino they could find such a person. If they did there would be no risk to anybody but the Judas and he wouldn't betray himself if he was well paid.

The biggest problem was ahead unlike Australia where the Aussie Feds were fairly clean especially the Fed's; America was well violated by crooked cops right up to the top? There was no way he could just pass on his messages as he did in the successful drug raids in the Eastern States back home. Here he had to find his way first to the Mafia gangsters, and then avoid the police gangsters here in Chicago, before he could create a successful raid. Jason had no interest in murdering the people, who had tried to kill him, what he wanted was to see them in Jail; as murderers for a very long time, the thought of being a murderer himself was sickening to even contemplate for Jason. But eventually he came to understand these Mafia types knew only one way, and that was death for anyone that got in their way they had failed to kill him once, they wouldn't fail the next time.

It was three days before Jenny smiled at Jason at breakfast so he knew the girls had something, and as arranged he met with Jenny and her friend at the appointed place. When they were all together Jason asked, "How do you know this place is safe?" Jenny laughed and said, "Because the owner is my brother, he has been here for a long time and is a naturalized American now, he and I have always been very close and he would never do anything to hurt me or mine. The Mafia know he is my bother and they don't bother me if we are here or with him and his family at his home, mind he lives in Beverly Hills so they have no reason to track him?"

The tape when it started startled Jason he hadn't expected to hear Maria and Tino making love, he felt they could have cut that rubbish out, he got a sneaking feeling that' Maria might be an exhibitionist and into kinky sex.' Gino had obviously improved his sexual performance, Maria seemed to be enjoying herself immensely, but after the sex they started to talk.

"Wow" said Maria, "you have been practicing where did you learn all of that it was good?"

"Yes well you told me to get the hell out and don't come back without learning how to fuck, so I did and here I am."

"Yeah, I will have to call you my lover boy now wont I, lover boy? Anyhow how are those bloody morons you work with, still fuckin morons I bet?"

"Well they are not so bright, but they make money and that's what I care about, who gives a stuff about them I don't, but so long as they know how to bring in the bread well I'll be their man. But if ever someone looks after me better I'll be off have no fear of that, I am going to look after Gino not those clowns."

Quite a dialogue followed, until Maria suddenly asked," well who is the bloody boss anyhow, they pester me and my mother all of the time they are all bloody dim wits?"

"Yeah you have never met the boss his name is Jacko, but he sits in the background and just gives out orders, he isn't one of the top dogs though we never see them, but we know who they are " said Gino with a laugh.

"So Jacko is the boss is he, because I want to know who is pushing us around all of the time, mum and I want to go and tell him to get stuffed. We are so sick of his bullshit, we had an Aussie speak to us the other day and one of the goons told him to bugger off, not that he cared he thought they were just clowns? My father worked for them in Australia, don't know why he was doing very well by himself, then they come along with a line of bullshit and look at us now? Dad's in smelly bloody China, Mum and I are here just bloody hostages, we can't do anything and it gets worse every day. I just wish we were back in Sydney at least then we were our own bosses, here everybody is our boss even you?"

"I'm not your boss, shit that would have to be the worse job in the world, you would tell me to get fucked every day, no thanks," laughed Gino.

"Suddenly Maria said I would stick to you if you had a different job, but they fuck my Father and us around and then to have you, as one of them would be way too much." sighed Maria.

"Well I am low grade in the mob but I know the way around, it's a matter whether they would let me out and then if I could find another job, but I'll try darling now what say we do that again," he chuckled.

"I thought you had blown your stack," Maria laughed, "but I'm ready lover boy, let's do it the more the better?"

Jason was quick to see that he might be able to get a Judas into the Chicago Mafia, 'Gino was only low grade but he was a start,' and he may guide Jason to higher levels time would tell.

The next day he smiled at Jenny at breakfast and she smiled back, so it was another meeting that afternoon at her brother's restaurant.

When the women arrived Jason came straight to the point, "I want to meet with Gino somewhere private but not here, I intend to offer him a job without him trying to get out of the Mafia. Just tell Maria to arrange a meeting with just Gino and me, you girls are not to be involved because when Maria gets sick of him again, we don't want that to mess up our understanding with him. I want Maria tonight to ask Gino, how and why he got into the Mafia, does he have any blood debts or anything like that he has to pay?"

The next day using the same system Jason received another tape which had the same sexual starting point, which Jason put on fast forward until he was able to hear Maria ask Gino. "How did you get into the Mafia anyhow surely you could have found better than that, so why do you stay with them they are only a mob of brutes?"

"I got involved when I was a kid," Gino said with a laugh, " I was young and stupid and now am trained for nothing else no one will employ me, if I could get a decent job you don't realize how quickly I would get out. Who knows one day someone may offer me a job and I will take it real quick! I have seen some terrible things happen with the Gang, but it's just a matter of time you wait and see! I have no debts with the gang, but I have learned a lot, who knows maybe they won't let me go, but I don't think so I am not high enough up the ladder yet to be that important. The only problem is I do have an uncle who is very high in the hierarchy he may object to me wanting to get out, especially after we had so much trouble with your father."

"What are you talking about trouble with my father, he won't cause any trouble while they have Mum and I locked up here? He told us when he was here recently he was in trouble, and they may kill him if he couldn't get out of what he had caused. They didn't bother to admit it was them who have forced him to do everything; we even left Australia because he got into trouble because of them? I hate them!"

Jason listening to the tape couldn't decide if Maria was just a very smart young woman or one who was trying to embroil him, Jason into their family problems. One thing he did know was he wasn't silly enough to get trapped unless they had a better reason for his support than he had heard so far.

Suddenly Jason heard Maria say, "I know a man an Australian who could offer you a job, he was trapped by the Mafia once too and he wants to get back what they cheated him for. I don't know if he would employ you but he may do if I ask him, that's why I have been asking you these questions, I think you could still stay with the gang and work for him too, what do you think of that idea? It would have to be fast though Maria continued he is going home in a couple of day's time, oh how I wish I was going home," Maria sighed!

"We'll see if he would give me a chance, I can meet him tomorrow night if he wants to interview me, does he pay well?" Gino asked.

"I don't know all I know is he is looking around and I thought you may be able to help him! What I do know he is a world import export agent, so he must have more brains than us don't you think? Another thing I know, sorry I forgot, he isn't a drug dealer of that I am very sure," said Maria.

"How do you know that I suppose you are going to say women's intuition," Gino laughed?

"My father went into drugs now he is in a bloody mess, because of the bloody Mafia, your bloody boss that's right? I can smell a drug dealer a mile away the same with you, I know you don't take drugs if it wasn't for that we wouldn't be together now."

"Yeah ok just set me up with this Aussie and I will bring you home a joint tomorrow then," Gino laughed out loud. "Of course I don't take drugs, but I know a lot of bloody idiots that do and I can't stand them."

'It s time for me to start really planning what and how we are going to deal with this problem of drugs,' Jason was thinking. My intent when I started all of this was simply to find the Australian drug lord, and then to punish them? 'Now it looks like we will have to set up to take on this Mafia in Chicago, and who the hell knows where that's going to lead me, South America or Mexico to take on the drug lords worldwide, so let me think about this and understand what we are doing myself.'

I am an expert financier, but it was my dream to give the money away and get out of that, we have done all of that and more.' I am a new man and we, my family and I, are free?' Satan's eyes (The Australian media) have lost their trace of me, we don't want for them to find me again, so we must be careful, but the job cannot be done from 'New Zealand or Australia,' that just too far away. Dave and I have found a new business and it is a worldwide one with huge profits, not as good as the one we had before stripping companies, but good never the less and no shareholders. If we decide to join a war against the drug cartels we could be small operators that no one knows about, and while the Americans spend billions trying to stop these drug cartels, we could spend millions and do a better job? So what must we do to be effective, and stay below the radar of the Govts and the drug cartels?

First we have to accept that we live too far away and my anonymity could be lost at any time, so we must relocate to live in America or England, but Jean must choose. Dave will have to become the General Manager of our new business, but I shall be the front man he must operate in the field alone? It will be up to me to head an effective private attack force against the Cartels; none must ever know except Dave, but he can be trusted with my life. As far as all except Dave will know I shall be the head of an import export business, with our head office and our trading base in New Zealand. It will be up to me to set up a team doing just the opposite to the drug cartels, and that team must gradually penetrate deep into the Mafia and the Cartel's. We will attack the Mafia and the Cartels, but we will stay hidden somebody must be out front , who the hell is that going to be it, guess we need a drug fighter over here to work with us how else can we move forward?

My job shall be to set up the teams in 'Chicago, New York, Las Angeles, Mexico City, and Beijing,' but first I must find a leader over here, so there will be three of us in the know, Dave Myself and our new gang buster if we can find one?

That night Australian time, Jason rang Jean and asked her if she would be able to make the move he wanted, when she agreed enthusiastically he gave her the option of where? He suggested the UK or the USA, somewhere North of San Diego, or the American Midwest, in America or North of London in the UK. They would buy a house and set up quite nicely, because no one would be watching them as a family. Jason had already told Jean the weakness in their privacy was her, she was after all known as Mrs. Jean Andrews, now Jones, it would only take a snoopy media hound to put it all together and all hell would break loose. He hadn't meant to frighten Jean, but what he had said was true!

Jean said she was happy to shift,' but wanted time to make up her mind where she wanted to live!' After a week she decided on Phoenix Arizona because the climate was the closest to Australia, when Sydney was in the middle of a heat wave which after all was quite often.

Jason asked Jean to put the house in the hands of an estate agent and leave it under management, then pack what she wanted and privately book seats for herself the two children and their Nurse to Los Angeles airport and he would meet them there. He told her she didn't need a Visa, because Australians could stay for three months, without one, and by the time that period was up he would have proved their eligibility for a green card. Jean promised to start immediately doing what Jason had asked her to do, and suggested she would be in L/A within two weeks?

Jason then rang Miriam and told her he wanted to be based in America, and would like to set her up in NZ would she go to live over there? Miriam was delighted she said she would be happy to shift and so would her family, because Hemi had bought so much shame on them all?

Finally he rang Dave because much as he would have preferred no one to know he knew Dave was indispensable and Jason needed him badly as a back up at all times? Jason told Dave they had things to discuss and he wanted him to fly to Chicago as soon as he could without upsetting what he was doing?

Gino was delighted with this arrangement 'he quickly agreed to his monthly bonus and that he would and could report on all drug movements within his own gang clan.'

Jason paid him in cash immediately for the first month which delighted Gino even more.

There was to be no intermediary, and they would meet monthly so that Gino could give Jason a report, and if he had information he needed to get through urgently he had a special number only for emergencies.

Next Jason wanted a man in Mexico which was a lot harder because he didn't speak Spanish, so he had to leave it for a few days while he tried to work that problem out. In the meantime he needed Maria to keep nagging at Gino to see if he would talk about his new job! After a week Maria reported that Gino had stopped talking about his work altogether, Jason was delighted.

After a few days Jason began to wander what other boyfriends Maria had who could be of use to him, so he asked if she had had a Spanish speaking Mafioso preferably one who lived in Mexico? To his great surprise she did have, her only comment was if I haven't got what you need then I will get you one that's easy, what other language do you need? I don't care for Mexicans though they are smelly little buggers so you will have to be quick a week at the most!

Within two days Jason had a Mexican crook sent by Maria, and again to Jason's surprise this one was very presentable too, he wanted to get back to Mexico to live and like Gino was willing to work within his group to get information, just as Gino was doing.

The big problem this time was how did he get the information to Jason? After a day Jason had worked out a private code that could convey simple messages and one that was important, if he got an important one Jason would fly to Mexico and the two men would meet, at a pre arranged rendezvous.

The pay arrangements were also soon worked out, with a delighted Mexican getting his first pay off this silly Gringo with too much money.

CHAPTER 20

Jean memories:

The time since our marriage had been to say the least dramatic, first we had had problems mainly because of me being a Catholic and wanting my own way in most things. Jason and I both had different points of view, but this was exactly as the Priest and my Family had warned, everything they had said came true and it was hard on both of us. We managed to work our way through our personal problems, or we were well on the way, when a really big problem hit the both of us Cocaine.

The drama started with the Cocaine being imported by a rogue management level staff member and the trouble seemed to grow rapidly from there. That was a terrible time for us all, but the only thing it did for us personally was it bought the two of us back together, with all religious differences forgotten. As I watched Jason dealing with the problems, my heart and love went out to him as I realized how hard he was affected, and how determined he was that he was going to fight back.

We booked into a five star hotel and took the Penthouse Suite for about six months, it was great for a little while, but then the novelty wore off and it became like a fancy jail to me. Jason like myself seemed to be locked in, but for the sake of Jason Jnr it seemed the right thing to do, when we finally shifted into a house it was just wonderful, to a limited extent we were able to come and go as we pleased.

The day I got the notice that Jason had been in a car fire, is the most traumatic I have ever experienced, at that time we didn't realize it was an assassination attempt, we thought it was an accident. When the doctors told me the burns were so severe that there was little hope he would survive, it was as if it was my time to die too. My love for Jason had become the strongest emotion in my life without him there was nothing, of course I wasn't being rational Jnr; was still there for me. When they told me the burns to his head were 85% it was so devastating, but in my inner consciousness I refused to believe he would die. Then when Dave came to the hospital and told me it had been a murder attempt, ordered by the Mafia in the Chicago, it was such a shock I thought Dave was wrong, no one would do such a thing to my husband, no it must be a mistake. Gradually it sunk in that what Dave had said was true, but by the time it did the doctors had changed their minds and was saying there was now a chance Jason would live. Then a week after that it became definite and they were sure he would survive.

I will never forget the day Jason awoke and gave Dave certain instructions, my heart skipped a beat as it dawned on me that maybe we would get some privacy out of this traumatic experience.

I hired a nurse to look after Jnr while I spent every day nearly all day at the hospital, she became just like one of the family and is now a permanent fixture with us in Scottsdale Arizona. But at the time she first came it was just one great tine of stress, that is until being told Jason was so tough that he would survive, my 'Daring Beautiful Husband' was going to live.

Eventually it was possible to spend most of the days with him, his body which wasn't so badly burnt was soon out of bandages, but his head was heavily swathed in bandages. I was told he would need three operations by a top medical team before he would be right, but that he would make a full recovery.

The time while we were waiting for the operations to be done was probably the best time ever for us, we sat and talked for hours, but very little was said about business because we had both had enough of business, and I was glad he had given his shares away to the Charity. We did talk in length about how the drugs had become such a sad part of our life, I say sad because it was obvious that Jason was determined to hit back and I feared what would happen.

We reminisced about the wonderful times we had had on our honeymoon and when we were courting it was all so wonderful that sometimes I forgot his bandages, and began to think we were back on our honeymoon. My Darling Jason used to just touch me, he said it was to reassure himself it was all real and we would soon be normal, at times like that for me it was like being in a paradise of my own, I just wanted to touch him and know he was still all mine.

I dreamed about him and Jnr; every night, but they were all such happy dreams for me it was a disappointment to wake up and suddenly realize my man was still in hospital.

It was nice when I walked into the hospital every morning all of the staff knew me and they used to say, "Your brave husband is still winning the fight," and the women used to smile and say "you have got a good one there such is your luck any time you wanna swap let us know," it was all good natured encouragement and we both needed it especially at the start, later it was good for laughs.

Jason had told me of his new business plans, but he said it would only be a small business and mostly Dave would do the work, and it sounded great no more big corporations with the media hanging around. We used to hug all of the time; Jason said it made him feel strong for the coming ordeals on the operating table. When the time came for the first operation my heart was all a flutter as in my mind I pictured him on the OP table. Then when he came out with such good reports, I felt so proud of him once again, he was beating those rotters who had tried to kill him. But there were two more to go and although Jason was confident I worried about my man having to face it all twice more, but it was encouraging to hear the head doctor say the worst was over, the rest would be easy. That evening when we were alone, I threw myself into his arms and sobbed for at least a half an hour, the hope that it was going to succeed was getting so close to reality my emotions spilled over like a dam had burst. We had such a wonderful but frustrating half hour; he was still swathed in bandages so we couldn't kiss each other.

The finally came the big day, the bandages at last came off and there he was, gosh he was better than new, and I laughed until once again the tears came and the dam burst again, but my man was beautiful all over again even if he did have a new face it was lovely beyond my dreams. When we got home the next day Jnr didn't think so he wouldn't go near his dad and little Jean was too small to know the difference. It only took Jnr two days and he accepted his dad was home and he forgot the change.

When Jason started his new business and started the foundations of his Drug Attack Team it was terrible, instead of being away for a short time the trips got longer and longer, and I could see Jason was getting stressed again. He told me the business was going better than he had planned and he had to change things again because the main thing was to catch the drug lords from Australia. Then he realized the main quarry was in Chicago so it was all mixed up again, I missed Jason so very much, that I spent most of my time on the verge of tears.

One evening Jason rang and asked if we would be able to live in London or America my choice where it would be, I jumped at the chance to be close to my man that's all that mattered to me, we were gone and in the USA within a month, I prayed God to give us a new life. The constant fear of being recognized in Sydney had been driving me crazy, this would indeed be a new life, with my Husband and we could settle down to have the six children we both wanted.

CHAPTER 21

War on the Drug Gang's

The organization that Jason was setting up was becoming substantial, it was expensive but because the import export business was doing so well it didn't really matter what the costs where. By merging the 'Drug Attack Systems' (DAS) with the very profitable 'Trade Business Systems,' (TBS) there was a tax advantage. 'The Drug Attack Systems' in Australia was starting to penetrate deeply into the gang there, but under strict orders they were not allowed to become drug pushers, or to do anything illegal their jobs were information based; nothing else unless requested. It was an easy well paid job that Jason had thought about disbanding, but changed his mind when he had decided they might set up an international drug busting unit. The big problem was that he had no experience and didn't really know what he was doing, he knew what he wanted but he didn't know how to do it, this was a real problem. What Jason did have in abundance was patience and money, a very strong combination, when used judiciously and wisely, and coupled with natural intelligence.

The American Gino in Chicago, and Pablo in Mexico were expected to do the same, penetrate deeply for the purposes of information only, they were different than Australia in that they were already gang affiliated, and had now joined the overall 'Drug Attack Systems' ranks funded by the business group. This was a good start but then Jason didn't really know what to do with the information when he got it, he decided he needed to hire a retired detective, one who could run and coordinate the total drug operations in Australia as well as the USA; but who and how was he to find such a person?

The 'Drug Attack Systems' structure was growing and was as private as Jason could make it. Because he didn't really trust Miriam, Jason had decided to set up the 'Drug Attack Systems' office in the USA, and he had already applied for a business green card. Jason, was completely funded from New Zealand and drew his income from there so he had no problems with U.S. Immigration, his business was actually spending a lot of money in America. As well his business was exporting and importing to and from the USA; so the Americans were glad to have him and his family living in their country and under his own umbrella, he could have bought quite a few NZs to America to work as far as their immigration dept; was concerned.

Jean and the children had arrived and the family had bought a very nice home in Phoenix Arizona, which is not an airlines hub city but Jason had to accept that, and he would have to put up with changing flights in exchange for living in a city they both liked. When Jason had met his family, and their Australian Nurse at the LAX airport, it had been an exciting reunion with the two little ones running to their daddy as soon as they saw him waiting for them. Jean Jnr; was now toddling and talking a little, she was 18 months old and her big brother was a grown up four year old, asking more questions than ever, 'how long will we stay here was his first question?' Jason hoped he wasn't going to ask that every five minutes. Jean and the nurse were looking harassed and Jason didn't have to think hard to know why, he only had to remember their last ruined holiday in Darwin. He only had to think of having Jnr; for the minimum 13 hour flight from Sydney to LAX to wince at the thought, he hugged his wife tightly as his way of saying Darling I understand, but he couldn't hug the Nurse.

Jason had had agents looking for homes in Phoenix, but they stayed in a quality hotel suite until they could choose and pay for one, which Jason had figured would be at least two months, but in the end he beat the system simply by paying in cash for the home, and moving in immediately under a contract of consummation. The family loved their new home town Scarsdale, which wasn't the same as their little suburban location in Sydney had been. Neither child asked about going home much to their parent's relief. The Nurse a fifty five year old widow, was called Nan by all in the family and who really loved the children, all hoped another baby would soon be on the way, but Jean wasn't making any comments yet? Jean was just so glad to leave Australia where she was haunted by the fear they would be found out by the media, she had lived there in dread that one day there would be a knock on the door and there would be reporters asking for Jason Andrews, insisting he was alive and still cheating the public.

Dave had finished the first trip as GM and now had two teams operating independently, while he secured products to sell until his buyer started with now more products coming from Australia than NZ, but as he had predicted he seemed to be always in an airplane, he now joked that his home address was Qantas 747 c/- Boeing of Where-ever.

Jason could see how hard the job was going to be so he relented and instructed Miriam to book Dave always first class, which he knew would ease the stress of so much flying, but the reps were all to fly business class. None of the reps were supplied cars rather they had rentals arranged at every airport at which they landed, this included Wellington and Sydney.

Jason had set up a small office in the city of Phoenix, and Miriam had been relocated to Wellington in NZ, but because the Chavez parents expected Hemi to be in Jail for many years, they and the youngest sister decided to stay in Sydney?

Some new recruits in 'Chicago and Mexico' were in place, and Jason had worked out how to pay Pablo in Mexico without a problem. Jason was now looking to hire an ex detective from New York or Los Angeles who could be trusted, and would work with the team in the field and he planned to increase the staff to three in Chicago, two in Los Angeles and another two in New York as well as one more in Mexico, he was setting up a gang busters team that he wanted to penetrate deep into the gangs and feed in information. Unlike Australia where the 'Drug Attack Systems' team all worked as a unit, in America and Mexico he didn't want the gang to know each other, only his ex detective would know the inner workings, so that he could manage the team but Jason was being very cautious neither his Detective or Dave would know each other. Neither 'Trade Business Systems' (TBS) or the 'Drug Attack Systems' would know they were linked only Jason would know that and he intended to set up as a simple office manager who didn't care if he got no customers? This had been the original intent but he soon realized this didn't work he had to have integrated team work, and to keep this all separate soon became unworkable. Jason was the head of everything he was after all the founder, but he had wanted the structure to show as if he had two customers 'DAS' and 'TBS,' both totally legal and independent. It wasn't that he wanted to conceal anything he just wanted his 'Drug Attack Systems' teams to be as safe as possible; but he soon found it was more than he could reasonably achieve.

Jason asked Gino if he knew any ex detectives he could hire, and he had promised he would get a name of somebody, not necessarily retired but young and smart with at least fifteen years in an American police force, but he warned Jason he may have to take the pension entitlements over, which Jason confirmed wasn't a problem. Then he sat back and waited until Gino rang him which he finally did. He wanted an appointment for a Chicago detective who was interested to leave the force to enter private practice, but would consider taking on a management contract to manage a private team, exactly what Jason wanted. Gino seemed to be as enthusiastic as Jason was, about the possibility that his detective friend may join the 'Drug Attack Systems' team; and he was just as happy about the future of the team, once it was underway properly.

The Detective Mrs. Carol Watson and Jason met as arranged by Gino and the two of them had an immediate rapport and understanding of each other's needs, Jason had been surprised when Gino had told him the detective was a women, but was more than happy because he had always trusted females more than males in positions of trust.

Carol was 45 YOA and had been a detective for 18 years, she had achieved the rank of Commander, but had grown tired of the harassment from her male colleagues, and had been moving towards setting up in private practice, when Gino had spoken to her. She had started as a cadet in New York at 16 YOA was married and had two children, both at university. Her husband was a Detective as well but outranked her, and worked in a different area of crime specialty which was homicide. Carol had auburn hair styled in to shoulder length, stood about 165 mts, weight 110 lbs, brown eyes and light complexion. She had the appearance, of someone who was fit and would stay that way for several years to come. She had told Jason she knew Gino well and had mentored him for years, but as a Mafia member she had to be careful, Gino had gone to school with her Son, they were both 24 YOA and were close friends. Carol had known Gino since he was ten YOA; and knew he was wasted working for the Mafia, but she was resigned to the fact he was locked in for life. She realized had he wasn't real Mafia material and would probably never rise above being a soldier, but as she said who wanted to in that outfit?

Jason explained what he was trying to set up, and explained he had the private financial resources to back up his dreams. He also explained he had been attacked in Australia by the Chicago Mafia, but had escaped with his life whereas four of his colleagues had died, which was why he had set up a drug buster account, and he had a business with sound profits also dedicated to the same cause, drug war?

It was obvious they could work well together if they could reach a contract agreement. The negotiations were simple, Jason made an offer Carol countered with a terms request and it was over, Carol would start for 'DAS' in 60 days from the signing of a formal contract. The contract itself was very simple; Carol would manage the 'Australian, Mexican and American' areas of the 'Drug Attack Systems' and would travel as needed to the three countries, but appoint a new manager in 'New Zealand' to manage the Australasian office in Auckland, and work under her guidance. She would work with Jason in the American office which would be based in Phoenix, and she and her family would shift to that city as soon as possible. If they were successful Jason wanted to expand to the UK; and she would be expected to run that division too. Jason stressed they were not going to be a big conglomerate! He wanted 2 operatives in New York, Chicago 3, Mexico 2, Los Angeles 2, and one in Las Vegas and an administrative office in Phoenix operating as the central office of a private detective agency. The time would come when they had two operatives in London as well, but that was in the future. The point was their operatives were mainly just feeding back information about the activities of their own gangs, for this they were to be well paid on a fixed monthly stipend.

A private hire Jet Plane would be at Carol's disposal so she could move anywhere quickly in the continental USA; and Mexico as needed, and she would fly to 'Australia and NZ;' through LAX on NZ Airlines, business class always. Rental cars and 4 star hotel accommodations would be provided at every location except Phoenix Arizona.

The wages etc; were easily settled, Jason could well afford to be generous in all terms of remuneration provided he was getting the tools he needed for attacking the gangs. Carol undertook to find all of the staff needed, for Jason to check out and approve, to ensure he was satisfied with the crooks Carol wanted to hire. And finally Carol understood Jason didn't want any killing, unless the criminals killed each other. The goal of 'DAS' was to put criminals in Jail not kill them, but he was quite happy for the criminals to kill each other!

The first trade report from Dave came in and once again was very impressive with total cross sales, up to USD900 million for the trip and that was just on the Chinese, American side of the business. The teams would separate the next time out into the number one team doing China the UK and America. The number two team would do the Europe and Japan area and would leave six weeks after the number one team had left. The first sales to Europe and Japan would be on the next agenda, with Dave helping as much as he could to get that division underway, he would stay with number two team until they had started to settle down. If and when the sales went as well for the number two team as it had done for the number one team, then a final third team would be added. The sales goal within 12 months was projected at USD12 billion split up evenly between the three teams, the problem was going to keep up; with enough product to sell. Probably an extra man would have to be added to the team as an extra stock procurer quite quickly.

The optimum staff that Jason was looking at was 'TBS' twelve and 'DAS' eighteen a total of thirty includes Jason. Because all of the team members were well paid the wages bill was quite high, but 'TDS' was earning from its sales ten times the total amount of all costs. Jason was delighted with the prospects of the two groups for the future, and already had told Carol there was nothing reasonable that he wouldn't pay, in this his personal fight against organized crime, except disruption to his family.

Another report had come in from Dave that his sales from Group one was USD900 million for the last finished trip so he was sure that group would achieve at least USD3 Billion over the next twelve months. Group two had achieved sales of USD400 million for the first trip, so they had an all up sales for the two TDS groups of USD1.3 billion for the three month period. Dave had told Jason he had to employ a second procurement agent to ensure they had enough products to sell; and he also said that it would only be three months before the third team was needed. He told Jason finally that they would exceed USD1.6 billion in the next quarter's sales period mostly from new sales by group two. Jason now sent word to Dave that he was to be relieved of his responsibility with his 'DAS' team in Australia, because he had appointed a Chicago detective as the GM, for the entire 'DAS' group worldwide just as he Dave was the GM for 'TDS' worldwide. Dave was delighted, he had sent a message thank goodness it was such a worry because it was too much and if I tried to do that work as well here in Australia it would meant complete failure for me. There is no way for me to do what you had set me to do plus that, you would have had a call from me any day soon, asking you to drop me out of that work thank goodness you saw the need first and I didn't have to start whining, thanks boss?

Carol was progressing well and had sent several men from the three states that Jason wanted to develop his 'DAS' program into. 'New York, Los Angeles and Chicago' and after a month they were fully staffed. To consolidate that Carol wanted a group meeting to be held in San Francisco and all of the new team members including from 'Australia' were flown there for a bonding session and conference. He had finally fully understood that a team approach was better than his insistence on privacy, and since it was to be done that way he had wanted to set up a bonding program, even if his team were all crooks. The one thing they all had in common was they all hated the purveyors of drugs, especially the hard drugs such as 'Heroin and Cocaine,' these were all family men, crooks yes druggies no. Carol had been very careful with her choices.

It was quite a gathering all of the wives had been bought to San Francisco as well, but weren't allowed to attend the conference for their own security reasons.

Dave, had also been invited as the GM of 'TDS' and to Jason's delight he and Carol got along very well!

Carol was the main speaker for the 'DAS' group and she laid out carefully what the team's goals would be! 'DAS' she started is a private group dedicated and funded by one man, Jason Jones, for the battle against Drug Gangs anywhere in the world, eventually but at this stage America, Australia and NZ. She then introduced Dave who was the GM of a company owned by Jason that was intended to be a worldwide Import export business, which from profits was funding everything. Carol stressed however that Jason had the resources to fund the groups alone, from private funds if necessary, because Jason didn't want it thought that if 'TDS' should fail then 'DAS' would fail as well. This wasn't so because the reserve fund of USD50 million Jason had dedicated to the drug war was still earning enough in interest to fund 'DAS' if necessary. She explained that Jason and Dave's work were dedicated to four people in Australia that had been murdered by the Chicago Mafia, and were being revenged by the work of these two New Zealander's. Dave and Jason got a simple ovation from these crime hardened men, they were all men who had been involved in some way in crime, but all were united by their hatred of the 'Drug Gangs,' because unlike the 'TDS' team of all single men, the 'DAS' team were mainly married with children and feared that some day they would have to face in their own homes the scourge of drugs.

Carol, then continued setting out the values that Jason wanted pursued! His first dislike was murder if they created situations where the gangs murdered each other then well and good, but he wanted his own team to if possible work without guns. But he accepted that it may be Impossible to do so, they could carry guns but 'DAS' wouldn't pay for them. Unless a women should be directly involved they and their children may not to be harmed. The men were expected to try and develop situations where drugs coming into or from the countries in which they were working, full information could be got back to Carol and from there she would deal with what she would do maybe to intercept them somewhere along the way. She explained drugs could be redirected to another opposition gang, or if there was no alternative the police may advised of the coming importation route. There was to be two main aims one was to cause dissension between the gangs, and the other to stop the drugs being sold on the streets. There was a final acknowledgement, that the police as well as the gangs weren't trusted and all must understand they were a private anti drug gang, but they were to do nothing illegal within the structure of 'DAS', what they may do in their other jobs was not to be overlapped with 'DAS' work which was really just the supply of information. The conference finished with a general feeling of bonhomie amongst them all and after enjoying a week's holiday at Jason's expense all returned home with the promise of the conference being an annual event, next years would be on the ski fields of NZ.

Now that all was in place and both of the GMs were in full control Jason and Jean had a well earned holiday, they first went to Las Vegas and then to New York, both places Jean had never been to but to which they went with Jason not doing any work. Everything was now structured and only Dave and Carol had access to Jason, but they had that privilege 24/7 although the reality was they very rarely contacted him, only when they weren't sure what he wanted.

When he got back to Phoenix he was pleased to hear their first drug bust was coming up and a delivery from Mexico had been reported bound for a New York none mafia gang, which Carol had arranged to have stolen by a drug team working against the Mafia in Chicago. The hit was for over 400 kgs of Cocaine and would be the first of several hits that would be redirected from none mafia gangs against the Mafia. Carol was excited with the prospect of creating a serious problem for the Chicago Dons, it won't be long she insisted before the none aligned Mafia gangs, started to object and they will hit back in some way against the Mafia controlled gangs. The Mexican agents were keeping Carol well informed of drug flows out of Mexico and the teams in 'Chicago and New York' were moving very quietly to do their disrupting work.

Carol was certain it would only be a month and their first success would develop; and she predicted a police raid on 'Chicago.' After that she was aiming for the same in 'Los Angeles and New York,' the trick was to play the gangs of against each other, while keeping 'DAS' well away from the action, all they were doing was passing information. The 'Mexican' operatives were top class they were the key in finding out where the orders were being directed, but again from different suppliers, so the 'DAS' activities couldn't be traced. It was all exciting stuff and was the start of the war against the drug lords of 'America,' who in reality were the ones who controlled the drug supply and sales down under.

In the meantime Carol was off to 'Australia and NZ' to meet with Dave, and then to stir up some action over there, while she was away she had asked Jason to set up the office in Phoenix. Jason was keeping himself busy studying the Chicago and the Sydney stock markets wandering if he should take a plunge to create more funds for his two attack teams. He decided not to move at this stage because he really didn't need the money, the 'TDS' teams were going well and the last trips had as projected yielded over USD1.6 billion in sales which was right up to budget.

Dave, had intimated he may soon put a third team in place one operating out of Europe, because he believed the 'UK, France and Japan' sales would catch up to the 'Chinese American' sales quite quickly. He was proposing a team for Europe excluding 'France and the UK,' but including 'Russia' and that would be the last team, that would cover all important markets and give them consolidated sales of over USD12 billion per year. Dave had suggested he thought they could reach those sales volumes within 12 months.

Jason had agreed to Dave's suggestion that they would cover the world with three teams, and wandered if he should find Europeans to do the work in Europe. Jason thought that first he should see how best to find suitable staff in 'Australia or NZ,' if he couldn't then by all means he could use staff from somewhere in Europe. He suggested it would be a nuisance for the local staff to have to cover the administration chores, that had to be done after each trip but also the European staff would be harder to settle into the products, both being sold and also being bought for the overall trade needs. Dave had agreed to meet with Carol in NZ to settle her into her office there. Then he would accompany her to Sydney to meet with the team, but more importantly to familiarize Carol on Australian drug bust conditions such as the Aussie Feds connections although he wouldn't introduce Carol to them yet.

Jason now set about to staff the office in Phoenix which was quite easy, because they wouldn't have the administration of the 'TDS' as Miriam had in NZ; in the end only two staff was needed in Phoenix.

Carol, contacted Jason from NZ to tell him the first drug redirect was being done within seven days, that was the 'Chicago job and both New York and LA' were in line for redirects over the next month, finally after all of the planning and spending a lot of money the first fruits were finally going to show on the vine's.

The first inter gang bust happened just 'South of San Diego,' the truck carrying the 'Cocaine' was intercepted and the drugs removed from his cargo, then the switch was made to the new gang and payment received. At this point nobody knew which gang had initiated the bust or the switch, it was just a highly organized raid, and it would take very few such raids for the gang wars to break out. Then the two hits on deliveries to 'LA and New York' were just as successful, but 'LA' was a lot more dangerous than the other busts they were fairly close to the Mexican border, and could react far more quickly. Having now completed three busts and sold the products the unexpected problem came up, Jason hadn't thought out what to do with the drug money he had now received. There was over USD600, 000 in the cash cache even after the raiding teams had been paid, this was an unexpected problem Jason just waited and did nothing he was though, concerned about having so much money lying around in his office safe at his home.

There was a buzz now starting to emanate from the Mafia gangs in the three states! What the hell was going on their Don's wanted to know, their lieutenants were instructed to find out quickly and fix up the problem before they got serious, so far it was but an itch on an elephant, but there can only be so many itches on any elephant before it starts to get annoyed.

The same problems had re'occured twice more in each state, and now the itch was a major pain and the elephant was definitely rumbling, what the hell is going on the Don's asked their Capotes. These under bosses were just as confused, none of their soldiers were reporting anything unusual as far as they knew the streets were real quiet, and yet the busts were real so far the Mafia in Chicago had been hit three times, it had better not happen again they insisted, because if it did then someone must die, and it wouldn't be the lieutenants it would be among the soldiers.

So the soldiers in fear for themselves started to snoop around but found nothing, they hadn't realized this was a new attack gang and they weren't selling the product, they were passing it all on to Mafia gang opposition.

All of the local gang lords went into an enclave to try and work out what was happening, so far no blood had been spilt, but it would happen soon if these busts weren't stopped and quickly.

Because of the breadth and depth of the 'Drug Attack Systems' penetration they were creating confusion, and the Don's were getting jumpy this was a new challenge and they didn't like it, they could feel it, real trouble was on the way.

In the meantime Carol was getting the inside information of how the Don's were reacting, all of the 'Cocaine' that was ready for delivery across the 'Mexican' border, and who would buy the product when they captured it. The beauty of the whole system was no matter what happened, the drug gangs aligned and unaligned to the Mafia would never cooperate; they were independents and worked alone it was only the Mafia that were so organized and dangerous because only they had such an extensive network nationwide from which to draw information.

The others had networks too but were not as effective as the Mafia, they were by comparison next to nothing because of their lack of an integrated organization, this was the only reason the whole scheme could work, that was the overall hatred or jealousy of the Mafia.

The next loads coming through were not touched, but the ones after that the whole diversion happened and the busts were just as prolific, the three states and all mafia busts.

This time the Don's were really upset so again a enclave was set up, this time in Chicago and again they had not a clue of what was happening, but they insisted for the future trips they would have gunmen hidden in the cargoes of the trucks, and they would pistol whip the raiders and bring them into the head Mafia office in Chicago.

That failed too the raiders pulled out the mafia gunmen and pistol whipped them then sent them home with a message of defiance, but they accidentally on purpose let slip that they belonged to one of the Mafia gangs, but didn't name which one. Carol was delighted what a stroke of genius she exclaimed, that was better than what I had planned for them, this will set up suspicion among the Don's themselves, what a wonderful scoop?

Just so they wouldn't stretch their luck too far, Carol now asked the teams to give her some leads from other sources, and almost immediately links came in from a Chinese source, via several major airlines. Jason, was staggered but Carol of course had suspicions because of her police background, she was so happy that she told Jason, "this is what I have dreamed about being able to hit back at those barsted's you will never know just how it feels, to stand by and know they have so much corruption right up to the top, when you first outlined to me what you wanted I just couldn't believe how lucky it all was for me. But you don't know how many detectives are like me, the trouble is the police organization is so big it only takes a few to stuff it up for us all. You have hit the right spot because there are just as many unhappy criminals they will do anything, but most of them hate drugs, they fear that someday their own evil will come back to them and they will pay so heavily for their sins. Oh by the way she said we have a lead on drugs coming into New Zealand they are using Cooperate Developments Ltd again and sending the stuff into the capital by boat in a load of building supplies. We won't interfere with the load until we pick up the dealers after they are taken out of the bond stores, then we will follow it through what do you think of that?"

"I think that's wonderful, but perhaps we should in that situation let the Aussie Feds do the donkey work, I think you should meet with the team in Sydney and then decide how to deal with it, Australia is corrupt, we have no doubt of that but perhaps they can be forced to act. Try to think of it as small town stuff down under and also have Dave with you until you are well set up, tell him that if he feels its right he must introduce you to Commander Juan Chase. After that you will have control of the full structure we have set up including the method of selling to the addicts. I will ring Dave and tell him to arrange his travel to blend in with yours, and he is to do things we cannot talk about or discuss over the phone but you will convey to him personally. I will also stress to Dave these are his last chores for 'DAS' because I know he is so stretched, they are setting up in Russia right now, so he will be glad to have 'DAS' right off his plate?"Jason replied to Carol.

Jason rang Dave almost immediately to pass on that message, he was in Moscow fast asleep when his call got through.

Meanwhile things were heating up in the 'USA deliveries from Mexico' had been allowed through unmolested, but now an attack on airline sources had been completed with again the same three main areas losing their full deliveries. Then Carol ordered her team's to stop for a while, but to now attack the 'Las Vegas' Mafia supplies and leave the others alone for three months or even more, she wanted to let the simmering anger manifest into fighting by the Don's at which point retaliation would be ordered. She asked that the same hint be dropped again accidentally when they raided the 'Vegas' supplies, because they also had a Don on their control board.

Carol, waited for two raids to be completed on the 'Vegas' drug supply, then she ordered a two month moratorium, as she said let the Don's stew on what we have done so far. Then while things were quiet at home Carol flew out on a direct flight to Sydney, then on to 'Auckland NZ.'

She met with Dave in 'Wellington', and they spent two days together with Dave as the chauffeur. Carol, took over the office control from Dave, but only the 'Drug Attack Systems' work and the two GMs discussed the need to separate the two offices. Dave explained how they had Hemi Chavez who had been the sales manager of one of the Cooperate Developments Ltd companies but had been caught and was now in Jail. He was feeding back information through Miriam his sister who worked in the office in Wellington, but neither Dave nor Jason trusted them. Miriam was being used to feed back misinformation through Hemi and they still weren't sure of them, but they both weren't trusted. Dave also gave an over view of how Jason had saved the Mafia head man who was in Shanghai. He was under a death threat until Jason had saved him, because he had led the Mafia into a takeover bid that threatened to lose them up to USD5 billion. Dave gave Carol an opinion that Jason was a financial genius, who could afford to just sit and wait while his teams penetrated deeply into the Mafia; and then he would get his revenge for the close friends of his, the Mafia had had killed. Just for his own pleasure and to bring home the point, Dave told Carol that Jason had given away over USD4 billion to charity, then he realized he had spoken out of turn and was immediately highly distressed. He immediately asked Carol to please not repeat his foolish remark because it would blow Jason's cover, but stressed Jason was only hiding from his own fame; it was the perpetual life in the media he had most hated.

Carol had guaranteed she would honor that confidence, but as an ace detective it didn't take her long to follow up who had donated so much to charity, and how he had died. It was only a few days until Carol knew everything about her new boss, and found that she had nothing but admiration for him, Jason's secret would be safe with Carol, but it helped when she was setting out to praise her boss to know who he really was.

In the meantime Dave was in a state of self contempt he had let Jason, Jean, everybody down and there was nothing he could do to take back his foolish words, he had no doubt what so ever that by now Carol would know just who Jason really was. Dave felt sick with remorse, and he knew he couldn't even ring Jason to warn him, if he did then the whole secret may come out and Jason could be hounded again. Dave quite forgot that in Australia Jason had been a big fish in a small pond, but in America he would be a small fish in a big pond, so he wouldn't be of much interest to the American media. But the trouble that Dave had gone too with his own silly remark now Jason's anonymity could be compromised. The only way that Dave could contact Jason to warn of his slip up was by old fashioned snail mail, so he wrote him a letter with such regrets expressed from the depth of his heart.

Meanwhile the drug supply of 250 kgs had arrived into the port of Wellington and Carol had a trace on the shipment, and sure enough as soon as the material cleared customs a truck with the insignia of Cooperate Developments Ltd emblazoned on its sides picked the load, and started the trip to Auckland, about a nine hour drive.

When it arrived in Auckland the load was left at a warehouse and no one came near for over a week! But one day three men arrived and spent several hours locked inside, obviously extracting the drugs from the full cargo of building materials. From there they drove their van to a point below the Harbor Bridge in Freemans Bay, where they met a high powered speed boat to which they passed two heavy bags obviously the 'Cocaine.' By this time it was midnight and the boat left immediately obviously it was going to cross the Tasman headed for the East Coast of Australia. When she realized what they intended Carol had swum out to the boat in the twilight and fastened a tracking device, 'a number of which she always carried with her, to its hull' in this way she could have the boat tracked all the way to its destination.

She then drove out to Whenuapai airport and hired a private jet to take her immediately to the 'Bankstown airport in Sydney' where she had two of her team waiting for her to help trace the speed boat and find where it was headed for, most likely the Gold Coast. They had another light plane ready to take them to the nearest airport, once they felt they knew the landing point of the speed boat.

Carol was with her team in 'Bankstown within three hours' and had a special clearance through customs quite quickly, then the three of them started tracking the boat which should take about six hours at least to arrive from NZ. The Aussies thought that the Gold Coast was the most likely spot, but on reflection Carol who had studied the map was opting for somewhere on the south coast probably around about Kiama or nearby.

As the signal got stronger the course did appear south so they all got on the plane; and landed on a private strip about a 30 minute drive from Kiama. In the end Carol was right it was Kiama so now they had to take the car that was standing by, and find out where the boat would land. That all proved to be remarkably easy, they were even able to spot the car that was going to make the pickup, which was just a little south of the Kiama beach and was easy to spot.

So far they had followed the drugs from 'Wellington, Auckland and Kiama now where was it going to in Sydney' from here, it was going to be more difficult to track without being noticed. Two more rentals were acquired and they were going to keep taking turns doing the tracking over the three hour trip to 'Kings Cross,' which would be somewhere near the drugs destination.

Carol took the first leg as far as Wollongong, then car two took over until Sutherland, at which point car three took over until Paddington; and then they all converged together to see the car go into a hotel garage at Kings Cross? It was a simple matter to find out what site they were staying in and the trace was complete!

Now the decision had to be made, did they have the Aussie Feds pick up the culprits or did they allow the Gang to distribute the drugs, the next day. Carol decided it was best for the police to do the job, and she had the contact number of Commander Chase for after hour's calls, she used that number to request a bust immediately. Juan Chase agreed he would have a team on the spot within 60 minutes, after he had called in his men and taken their mobile phones.

The three operatives just sat and watched as the police arrived just like a swat team on T/V; much to Carol's amusement, within another thirty minutes the team was being escorted out, handcuffed and into the Aussie Feds paddy wagons. They finished off a grand night with a few drinks in one of the Kings Cross all night joints, and celebrated another hit against the Mafia in Chicago, now there really would be trouble back in the USA?

Carol couldn't help her feeling of high hopes, as she contemplated what was still in store for the hated Mafia when she got home.

The next morning the headlines were ablaze Aussie Feds does it again, Commander Chase has led a raid on some of drug land's top criminals and catches a big trophy, and photos of four drug lords were pictured. Carol couldn't help herself; she rang Jason and told him to check the Aussie news on the internet.

When Jason and Jean connected to the news in Australia it was as if their plans were all coming true, the men that had been caught in the net where all big shots in the Drug business. None of them were little fish like Chavez had been, and amusingly they were all being held for trial in the same jail as Chavez. It would be interesting to be able to listen in to their discussions as they all congregated together in the dining room, and in the exercise yards. Jason immediately sent back by SMS a simple two word message, great work.

The furore that broke over the drug bust in the media was reminiscent of the previous howl that had been set up, when Chavez and the 1,000 little blokes had been jailed, but this time the police were able to say they had got some of the big operators, and this really down played the importance of Chavez, it proved conclusively he was only a little fish.

The media went after James big time, but he unlike Jason relished the lime light when the media interviewed him he really sparkled. He accused the men that had been caught as being mere flunkies for American gangsters, and reveled in the fact they had been caught, when Jason viewed the interview he worried that his friend may get a death judgment from Chicago such as had been set up against himself.

Dave took the opportunity to ring and congratulate Carol, he said that finally they were going to see some justice, but only when the leaders in the States where behind bars will Jason be satisfied. Carol before she left had a meeting with her full team, and then went to NZ to interview the new team that had been set up over there, this was on her way back to Phoenix.

When Carol got back home, she had by now relocated her whole family to Phoenix also in Scarsdale, and her husband now had a transfer also to Phoenix. Jason had met her and asked for a private meeting at a park bench in a park in the hope they weren't bugged, because he had received Dave's letter and naturally was very upset.

CHAPTER 22

A professional war on Drug's:

When Jason started to talk about how he had had a letter from Dave, with his self recriminations at his foolish talk Carol was quick to agree yes Dave had been foolish, but she would honor that mistake and never mention the information she now had, ever again. She agreed that because she was a detective it was natural for her to follow through on everything she got, therefore she now knew everything about Jason Andrews, but she swore herself to secrecy. She told Jason that she much preferred to know who she worked for, and now she knew it all, but she had the highest respect for Jason and what he was doing and had done. Carol said that not many men would given away as much as Jason had to charity, then she suggested the matter need never be discussed again. This was of course much to Jason's satisfaction!

Jason sent an SMS to Dave just saying problem fixed; never to be discussed again regards Jason Jones's.

Tension had lifted to fever pitch within the Mafia in Chicago, they had been busted three times in San Diego once from China now the hit in New Zealand, the Don was really hopping mad, he was certain one of the other Mafia gangs were after setting him up. Several loads of 'Cocaine' had now come through, but they were still trying to find out where their other deliveries were, they had lost now 2,000 kgs of Cocaine and 1,500 kgs of Heroin and it was hitting them hard.

'New York and LA were on the warpath having each lost 1,000 kgs,' and 'Vegas had lost 300 kgs,' what the hell was going on, but they all blamed it on their own colleagues, none dreamed an upstart such as 'Drug Attack

Systems' would be harassing them. The black money in Jason safe was now over USD2 million, and he had decided to use the money promoting benefits for his own team members, for himself he had no use for such rotten money.

It had been four months since there had been a bust on the Mexico drug imports, so Carol decided to hit them just once more, but she had decided to arrange the hit on the Mexican side of the border, this came off beautifully so once again she had to pass the drugs on to one of the unaligned gangs which she did, and passed the cash on to Jason.

They immediately did busts on the 'Chinese supply's including Vegas' and again they had drugs to pass on, but by now Jason had asked how they could get the drugs sent to honest police.

The reports coming in now from the team members was that a war would soon break out among the Mafia aligned drug gangs, because 'Chicago believed that New York was sabotaging them and wanting to take over in Chicago, LA was blaming Vegas and Vegas was blaming Chicago,' it won't be long now Carol reported.

The following week there were two Mafia Capotes executed in New York, and then there was the same in Chicago, so the fight was on. Now Carol released a report to the media from an insider that explained to the public, that the Mafia gangs were stealing off each other, and blood would soon be running in the streets unless the police acted.

Then Carol released a report to the 'LA police blaming New York for the busts,' this information was claimed to be from an anonymous source.

The media announced the Don's were going to meet in 'Chicago to try and stop their inner conflict' and that meant no more stealing from each other.

While they were together in the enclave, Carol and her team had busted them again, but this time let the 'New York delivery gets through'. When this information hit the Don's at their meeting place, it was like a bomb had exploded in their midst. The meeting broke up immediately with expressions of anger especially from 'Chicago, their Don was really confused' and had castigated his under boss mercilessly, in front of everybody the anger was such that none could see it was all; a trap and they were walking right into it, anger had broken down the walls of common sense.

Carol told her teams that it was time to lay low and let the dogs bark at each other, but they had to keep up the harassment so the Mafia cohorts could be made to make foolish mistakes, as the anger and suspicion grew to mammoth proportions.

The team members reported back to Carol that the cancer was spreading and there was no surgeon smart enough to cut it out, they were all making terrible blunders and accusing each other. Carol laughed after all they only had to sit back and think, and they would realize it was all one big nasty trap, and the cost of falling into that trap would be enormous in blood and money.

The next action wasn't unexpected another two of the New York Mafia Lieutenants were gunned down first then there was a hit in 'Chicago, and finally hits in both Vegas and L/A' it was happening; the war had been declared it was hard to say where it would go where they were at now.

But Jason had become sickened by the increasing killings, even though they were killing each other.

Carol got a report that said a hit had been put out for the New York Don, because he was considered to be the Don who started, and was now perpetuating the troubles.

Jason had been given a copy of the report, and was very emotional he knew it was him who had started it all, but then he remembered no it wasn't it was them who had victimized his friends then even given out a hit order on him, so when all of these memories floated back he changed his mind and joined in the jubilation. Jean when he told her what was happening here in America was awed, she looked at her husband and said the Lord God has blessed you beyond human comprehension, a reaction that of course left Jason shaking his head in wonder. What he asked himself has God got to do with it all, but then he was an agnostic and would never understand as far as his wife was concerned, she pitied him his lack of faith and inability to confess and be free.

The family had now been living in Phoenix for a little over a year, so Jason and Jean decided it was time for them to take a trip home. Their nurse also was feeling a little home sick! When Jnr; was told he was going back to see his grandparents, he was as could be expected excited, but Jeannie was also now able to run around waving her little arms around cheering. Dave was in Shanghai so Jason decided to take his family home via Shanghai and meet Dave, as well as renew his acquaintances there. When they arrived at their hotel Dave was waiting for them in high dudgeon, he had been encouraging his team on, the Chinese had the team a little intimidated, and Dave had had to spread a little more encouragement and goodwill among his customers, much to Jason's amusement.

Next morning at breakfast the Australian team where all there, and Jason had gone over to their table it was as if he was a long lost friend, they were so happy to see him. That evening they all joined into a 10 course banquet, with Jean also in attendance a great time was had by all, but Dave was off the next morning to France and then on to Germany, so they broke up early because he had to give Jason a report.

Dave was very excited about how 'TDS was developing' sales were going ever higher, they were steady in China and growing quickly in the USA. England was also going well as was all of Europe but Moscow was a little slower than the rest of Europe. Japan was the only real disappointment, sales in that country were quite slow and Dave was going there when his team was next there, to see if anything could be done. Dave's expectation on sales at that point, was a little over the USD12 billion for their second year in business, and even Jason gasped with delight, "Gosh he said that is a great effort young man, we are all proud of you!"

Jason then went on to describe to Dave how well Carol was doing with the 'Drug Attack Systems' and how there was terrific progress in that field of endeavor as well. Nothing was said about Dave's slip while talking to Carol that was forgotten.

The females quickly decided they didn't like Shanghai too smelly they declared, and the children seemed to agree with the women as well, poo they both chorused, there are so many people Daddy where did they all come from?

So the next day having bid goodbye to his friends Jason and his entourage were on their way back to Australia.

Their flight was via Wellington NZ, where they were stopping for two days then back to Sydney at last. Jason went into the office in Wellington and met with Miriam and her now staff of five others, but they had little to say for themselves except hi Boss, so then it was the final flight home. Jean had wanted to do a tour of NZ and Jason had promised they would on their way home to Phoenix.

The greetings in Australia were tumultuous to say the least, but it was in private Jason didn't know what sharp eyed media hack could be around, and may recognize Jean, so they had a private gathering at Jason's parents home. Jeans Parents and siblings were there but they were not fitting in well with the Andrew crew sadly for Jean, but she said oh well they never fit in together with themselves, looks like it's still all the same?

Mrs. Johnson the children's Nanny had time off to spend with her own grown up children and now grandchild, she stayed with them for three weeks, but then started to pine for Jnr; and Jeannie and couldn't wait to come home as she called her situation with the Jones's family.

The family had a grand time at home, Jason and Jean took them to Taranga Zoo and the slippery dip park at Luna Park, as well as up to the blue mountains, a month passed so quickly it was almost time to go home before they knew what had happened. Jason's family were all so close and had a great time together at a farewell party which was usual for them. Jean had a great time with Jason's family, she was now beginning to realize the difference between her own and Jason's family. When they went to say goodbye to her Family they hardly raised a comment, which for Jean was sad, she so wished they could be happy just like the Andrew's but that wasn't to be, so it was just a bleak goodbye, and then Jean cried all of the way to the airport.

Jason had spent so much time concentrating on revenge that now it was being realized, it was like an anti climax there is no triumph in such a victory, he felt it pulled himself down to the same level as the victims of his efforts. As in his mind he enumerated what had been done and what was to follow, he almost cringed at the thought of it all. There were four gang leaders in Australia in Jail, and they now had a trace on the NZ connection, this all through the efforts of Carol. There had been two high ranking Mafioso executed in New York and another four soldiers gunned down, this was a total of six dead. A contract had been taken out against the New York Don this would soon lead to inter gang warfare; all up Jason was concerned about what he had unleashed? It seemed to him he was as bad as the one who had first judged the Cooperate Developments Ltd staff and himself in Australia, and from what he could see many more would die; in the near future.

As he had promised Jean they had a fortnight in the Nth Island of NZ flying to The Bay of Island's, Rotorua, Taupo, and then Wellington before flying back to LAX then Phoenix, it took them all a week to recover from the jetlag, but the children were full of life within two days.

He called Carol into a meeting as soon as he arrived back in Phoenix, but when he spoke of his concerns, he was reminded of the death and destruction spread by the Mafia and other drug gangs, and that what he Jason had done was a gift to all decent parents who feared for their kids.

Jason asked what he was supposed to do with the USD2.5 million dollars, he had in cash that he didn't know what to do with, as far as he was concerned he didn't want the money so what should he do?

Carol laughed and said, "Hey boss why don't you open a clinic in Chicago for drug addicts who want to give up drugs, there are plenty of such medical clinics but they keep failing from lack of money. Many honest doctors donate time to this work each week, but they lack the necessary fund for rehab drugs?"

Jason was delighted, "give me some phone numbers he asked and Jean and I will fly to Chicago and arrange to support these clinics, this way we can spend the drug money and if that's not enough we will donate extra, that is such a wonderful idea, thank you so much."

Carol smiled, "that's why you have the Midas touch, it's because you give money away as fast as you make it, nobody here in the USA would give away what you have, and even the master of Microsoft doesn't match you in that you gave away 95% of your fortune, but he and his wife are wonderful people too, they also give away billions to charity?"

When Jason told Jean what they were going to do the next week she was thrilled, "that is such a wonderful idea, it will be really something to support those drug clinics," she said as she hugged her husband happily. Then with a smile she announced they were going to have their third child, her doctor had confirmed earlier in the day, that she was two months pregnant. Both Jean and Jason danced around the room in a frenzy of delight, 'another little Jean? Jason proclaimed loudly' as he twirled his wife around the room.

Jason rang two of the numbers that Carol had given him, and after speaking to the owner's of the clinics had made appointments to visit them both. The next week on the Wednesday he and Jean went to Chicago and then went to the first clinic in Evanston. When he arrived, the owner, a doctor came out and invited them into his office.

As Jason began to explain what they wanted to do the doctors eyes started to mist over, you don't know how hard I have prayed for such help he said, and revealed he was a Catholic, much to Jean's delight.

They got into a serious discussion about the work that was being done in the clinic, and their new friend revealed his clinic that had over fifty beds, and he had several doctors donating time, but the shortage of drugs meant he could only keep ten beds filled at a time. His dream was to have the clinic full and he could get more doctors to donate time, but he didn't get enough donations to buy the drugs the clinic needed. After they had talked for a while, the 'Doctor Hannah' had offered them a tour of the facility, and then Jason and Jean could see just how a drug clinic worked. It was divided into cubicles just big enough for a single bed and hand basin for the nurses, who were exhorted with signs up everywhere, about the importance of washing their hands after touching any patient. In the examples they looked at the patients undergoing treatment were curled up in the beds, with Nurses keeping a constant watch on them. They were being given drugs, but over a period of three days the dosages were gradually reduced, and then they were sent home. The only patients who were accepted into the program were those who had full family support and who were genuinely interested in getting off drug dependence.

Having had a good look around Hannah was asked, how much money he needed to keep his clinic open full time with all beds filled. His answer was USD20, 000 per week just over USD1 million per year. Jason smiled and wrote out a cheque immediately for USD500,000 and promised that every six months, he and Jean would donate the same amount to his work, that would be provided that when they came to give him the money he could show them how well his work was doing.

It was decided that the clinic would become part of an aid program that Jason had been planning, he had discussed the idea with Jean and she was totally committed to it. They had agreed that that all profits made from TDS the company Dave was running, would be committed to financing a chain of drug clinics in the USA, Australia and New Zealand. The trip to Chicago was meant only to be a preliminary investigation to work out how they should be run. Obviously each clinic would be run by a doctor founder, and they would be given an annual grant equal to 50% of the running cost of their clinic. A board of Trustees would be set up of mostly doctors running their own clinics, but Jason and he hoped Carol and Dave would also be board members. On Jason's estimates he thought they would be easily able to fund 250 clinics in the USA, 35 in Australia and 15 in NZ a total of at least 300 clinics in total.

They had decided to wait and see the procedure for the next patient coming in for treatment that afternoon, and it was a really sad performance to watch. The patient was bought in and was given a final examination by the doctor, before his parents were interviewed. Then the parents were interviewed and asked to give an assurance that first they agreed to the treatment, then that they would look after their Son and bring him back for the next two weeks daily treatment. The patient was then taken into the cubicle and given half an hour to settle down before the first medical treatment was given. Once the treatment had been given the patient was left to sleep for about 2 hours and then he was wakened up and given another dose of the medication, but he was told there would be no more for another 24 hours no matter how hard he pleaded for another fix.

The next clinic they called on in Chicago was in Lincolnwood and in much the same position and needed the same amount of money. Again the Jones family agreed to donate the shortfall and keep on funding them provided they could show the results that justified the money, and again Jason handed over a cashable cheque for $500,000 and again there was a very relieved doctor. Jason had told him there may be a Charity being set up to help fund clinics such as this one but it was only in the early stages of conception, he still had to finish the development work to see just how effective these clinics were, and how much help was given to drug addicts. It was natural for the doctor to offer to give any help he could to demonstrate his work, and arrangements were made for future interrogative work which would assist Jason and other trustees to properly evaluate what they were achieving. But then Jason realized the problem, how was he supposed to pay himself the money back, he had given good money but he had bad money to take back. Oh well he would have to ask Carol what to do because he didn't have a clue? Jason was beginning to wonder where it would all end, now he had to try and get his money back and yet he had done nothing wrong as far as he could see, but what was that Jean kept saying maybe it wasn't illegal to seek revenge, but her God said vengeance is mine, so maybe it was against her Gods laws.

Jason was beginning to see he had set in motion a force beyond himself, it was not something he wanted, but certainly was something he was responsible for and it was all about vengeance, bloody hell he was thinking this is all to bloody hard. All he had wanted was for the one who had ordered the death of all of those Australians including himself to go to jail, he was beginning to feel that he was no better than any Mafia Don who sat in judgment and ordered death to others so easily, what was he to do? All the way back to Phoenix he was absorbed in his own thoughts, while Jean was so happy with what they had done that day, and the wonderful feeling of another little Andrews growing within her womb, she was at peace with the world. The only cloud on Jean's horizon was being unhappy over her family back home in Blacktown. That night when they got home there was such a welcome from their two children, that Jason's mind was put to rest for a while, he hoped and Jean prayed that their little ones would never have to go to the type of clinics they had visited that day.

Jason rang Carol the next day and asked if he could meet with her again in that same park and she agreed to come immediately.

When Jason explained the problems, and how he had given away $1,000,000 in Chicago the previous day, but how was he to get his money back now, there had never been any dirty money in his accounts before, so what should he do now. He had over two million of dirty money in his safe, it would be ironic if he got pinched for money laundering and jailed then what?

Carol agreed to think the problem through and she would come up with an answer within 48 hours, so on that note they parted, Carol to work on the problem, and Jason to work on his conscience!

Jason got home and decided to share his thoughts with Jean, he felt that this was a family problem because any decision he made was going to affect their family, but he was careful not to frighten her after all she was pregnant again and that was what was most important, not his dreams of vengeance that now seemed to becoming a little too hard for him to understand. The mounting death toll was starting to worry Jason, even though the criminals were dying at their own hands, there could be no doubt who had loaded their guns Jason Andrews. There was one big thing he couldn't be comfortable with, and that was the drugs being sold very cheap to other drug gangs, that in a sense made him the biggest drug dealer of them all, and that he could no longer abide. He understood it was dangerous to hand the drugs over to the police, because the products could just finish back on the streets and maybe cause good cops to go bad, he now understood how badly money corrupts.

Finally he made up his mind any drugs they got in future had to be destroyed, the money he had spent that day would have to be reimbursed by 'Trade Business Systems' and the future commitment would have to be honored by them on behalf of 'Drug Attack Systems.' Now he had satisfied all of that in his own mind he decided not to worry Jean because of the new baby, but rang Carol and told her he had fixed the problem, but that they should meet as soon as possible same place.

Carol said she was free and maybe they should deal with Jason's needs straight away, after all he Jason was the funder and founder of the whole network so why not deal with it immediately?

When Carol heard what Jason wanted to do he was in full agreement, "I had been wandering about that myself, but figured that since you were donating the money to charity, it was up to you now you have given the instruction, the stuff will all be destroyed but secretly, maybe just you and myself could do that job if you like? I am sure it would give us both a strong feeling of satisfaction when we dump it in the water somewhere, but we will have to be careful we don't turn the fish into druggies," at which they both laughed.

Jason could now reassure Carol he was satisfied, that what they were doing was a good thing if the criminals disagreed and killed each other well too bad, but if they could be caught and sent to jail so much the better. Carol began to explain to Jason the way criminals think, first it didn't matter how much money they got they would spend it all and would be waiting for pay day. She explained she had chosen crim's with children and a strong marriage because this was the only way to get though to them, I have she said worked with this type of people for over twenty years, and I believe my judgment in choosing the team we have is sound. They are all men that have been known to me for years, and they have one thing in common and that is a strong fear of drugs, they all fear that some day if they deal in drugs the Lord will take vengeance on them through their children, that is why they can be controlled. Basically they are good men, but unfortunately have very few brains, but they have an easy job with us and won't want to mess it up for themselves.

Things were very quiet in Australia and NZ, the loss of the last shipment had left the market low on Cocaine, but it didn't take long for another source to spring up. 'The big advantage for the Drug Attack Systems was they knew immediately that the market was being sourced again, but they decided to do nothing for a while, as Jason was now asking if we can trace all this so easily, whats wrong with the Aussie Feds there must be something?'

Meanwhile from Jail Hemi Chavez was complaining as loud as he could, he claimed he had been only looking to help a friend who was in jail, who had been caught with a lot of cash money, and he was trying to launder the money through an associate, but it wouldn't work because the associate didn't know it was drug money he thought it was gambling money. Then another person who was in Jail had ratted on him and that's how the Aussie Feds had got through to him! He was now claiming again he was innocent, and in fact had been set up by the police, this was now a problem that had to be straightened out, Jason rung Dave and through their now competent private code asked how much Chavez knew about the organization which of course meant how much did Miriam know.

Because it couldn't really be discussed enough even through a code, Carol would have to be sent to find out what Hemi and his sister was up to. Jason arranged for Dave and Carol to meet in Sydney, when Dave was back there, or as soon as possible, then they were to decide what to do. The alternatives Jason gave Carol could either to ignore Hemi, and leave Miriam in NZ and cut out her travel allowance. Meet with Chavez in jail and find out the substance of his claims, if there was any substance then take the right steps to see he got a fair go, but 'not to believe he wasn't in the drugs haul that went through Cooperate Developments Ltd that crime was an immutable fact' but what others at Cooperate Developments Ltd; was in it with him all except one was dead so he would be hard pushed to prove his innocence now. Even if they could find the one who was still alive, he was hardly going to testify for Hemi why should he, and put his own life at risk?

As arranged Dave met with Carol in Wellington first, and they also met with Miriam to try and work out what she knew and by extension, her brother would know. Hemi didn't really know what was going on, except they were telling the police what was happening, except they could be the ones who had advised the police. He didn't know how much but he knew they at 'DAS; had been involved in saving the Americans, from their aborted takeover of Cooperate Developments Ltd but that didn't matter in any way because that was public knowledge freely available to all'.

Their meeting with Miriam was quite low key, Carol was introduced as a detective from New York who was trying to locate all sources of Mafia drugs worldwide, on behalf of the Chicago Police Dept. Someone who would report back to his superiors that yes or no, the Mafia was still getting drugs through Australia and NZ.

In this way any penetration by the local police in Australia, would be put down to cooperation between a police division in America, to the Aussie Feds. Even Miriam had been misinformed, because all of the information that had been fed to her for quite a while, didn't have any specific information because of Jason's feeling that Miriam was now corrupted by her brother Hemi.

Because of Dave's heavy work schedule, it was decided that he would give a letter of introduction to Carol, and she would visit Hemi alone. Ostensibly this was because of Dave wanting to help the 'American Police in their war against criminals,' but in this case drug dealers in particular.

Carol had a description of Hemi, who had a Latin Mother and apparently a Black Father! He himself was about 1.9 meters tall; dark skinned had been over weight but would now be trimmed down from working out in the prisoner's gymnasium. His Mother had married a Latin man, and they had three daughters all Latin in appearance, but devoted to their half brother the Mother excessively so, but his stepfather tending towards being far more conservative about his recalcitrant stepson. Hemi had the gift of talk but if listened to carefully, little of what he said made sense to an intelligent listener, and if he was let talk freely he had the tendency to tell all about everything. Carol arrived back in America with a strange story from Hemi about how he had been led astray by an old man for whom he had worked as a secondary job in Sydney. To get the full story Carol had had to visit Hemi three times over a period of two weeks listening, to a strange and garbled explanation of how he got into trouble, she gave a cut down version to Jason for him to decide if they should try to help Chavez?

When Chavez was 16 YOA he had met a sixty two year old man who had taken Hemi under his wing and first employed him in a medical surgery as an assistant when he was 23 YOA. From there he had progressed to being mentored by that man and had begun to learn quite a bit about business technique. But the years had gone by and Hemi had begun to his see his friend's health was failing and he was needed more and more to take over as the business front man. He had done this on a casual basis in charge of some AUD500 million worth of real estate in Australia and NZ and he found himself totally responsible for several companies, with gross assets worth over $700 million. His mentor had become severely ill with heart problems and left him alone and gone to live with a woman friend; but left Hemi poorly prepared to take over the business and he was soon in trouble. This time of problems had been so hard that Hemi had gone astray, and had got mixed up with a motor bike group with whom he had soon compromised himself, by borrowing money from the gang in his own name. Because of the money some AUD39, 000 which had to be repaid, pressure had been put on him too help the gang by arranging the importation of drugs, mainly Cocaine from Mexico? This he had done through one of his mentors companies, which had come through successfully and eased the pressure on him with his bikie gang member friends. It was at this time the stock market started to fail and Real Estate contracts of sale, worth AUD350 million had failed because of banks tightening up and values dropping by 30-40%, so the companies all four of them were in financial distress in common with a lot of other middle range companies. At this time his mentor had had heart three heart attacks, and again finished up in hospital, but this time the hospital had pronounced him too ill to recover and he had only six months to live. Meanwhile Hemi had been working for several years for Cooperate Developments Ltd and had got mixed up with some of the senior staff who had worked with him to again import Cocaine, from Mexico. This time a larger amount 100 kgs had been bought in through 'Cooperate Developments Ltd and they had helped him, but when he got caught the Company executives had run for cover and had given information to the police that led to the leaders being traced. From this lead the American connection had also been traced, which is why the vendetta had been set in place and the executives all except one, had been executed. Jason Andrews had been executed on orders from Chicago because he was to be gotten out of the way before his company was taken over, there had been a fear in 'Chicago that he would thwart the takeover, which he had done anyway from the grave?'

Having heard Hemi's story Carol had decided to try and interview the man who had mentored him, to try and verify what he had been told that perhaps there had been unfortunate circumstances, and that Hemi had been unlucky with his activities.

The man had been interviewed and confirmed he had been given a prognosis of only six months to live, but he had survived and could still get around very slowly. But his memory of events was different than those outlined by Hemi. He hadn't wanted to discuss the debacle in any depth, but he did say that perhaps Hemi was being less than honest with some of his assertions. For example when Hemi had been left alone, the companies had had adequate staff for the running of their administration, and Hemi had not been honest in his claims, because quite a substantial amount of money had been diverted from the companies for his own use. A management contract had been signed and he had been given the right to run the companies, which he had done but strictly for his own advantage, much to the company's cost. When the company had been put under investigation by the Aussie Feds, all of the financial arrangements in Saudi Arabia, America and Australia NZ had failed because of being linked with Drugs. The mentor had lost everything plus his reputation because he was the sole Director of the company that Hemi had used; he therefore was linked with drugs to his great surprise, and his financier's objection. When the mentor had come out of hospital he found his companies were all financially black listed as he was himself, and his whole structure had crumbled because of his 'company identity been used for the importation of Cocaine.' It had all been a disaster which because of his health and age he couldn't even hope to rectify, the direct losses were up to USD160 million and all of the dreams lost to a young man's selfishness. Funds of USD395 million had been approved the money coming from a Middle East country but was all messed up by Hemi and his drug activities. There would be no further investigation instigated against Hemi, but conversely there would be no help given either, because of his betrayal of trust in many other matters that weren't open for discussion. The old man expected to be interviewed by the Aussie Feds, and he would not get involved beyond the stealing of property from one of his sons, an ex NZ Inspector of Police whose identity badge had been used, and the use of an 85 YOA woman relations, private address details in his nefarious schemes.

Carol said she was reporting as she found the Hemi Chavez case and the only comment she had to make was the Aussie Feds had a report on one Hemi Chavez which classified him as a person of a very bad character. They had reports going back from the time he was only fifteen of years old, when he was first convicted for the theft of over $12,000, the proceeds from a cheque he had stolen cashed and he had kept the money. The Aussie Feds had him noted in their report as a person of very bad character, and untrustworthy!

On assimilating the information that Carol had bought back, Jason had decided to cancel any further discussions with Chavez, and Miriam's travel allowance was to be cancelled. She was to be told the reason was that her sponsor had decided that there was no point in continuing their support of her brother, because he had proved to be dishonest in his reports to the American Police. Any reports he had passed on had been of little use to the Aussie Feds and he wouldn't be used anymore. But the legal assistance that had been given would be continued until his trial was finished!

Carol had advised Jason it was now time to continue the war on the Mafia especially Chicago Mob. They were going to once again start disrupting the drug loads, but now keeping the contents of the raids and destroying them immediately by tossing them into water. After each raid she and Jason would dump the drugs in one of the many water systems and destroy them, she wanted Jason to see the drugs destroyed so he could be sure that the job was being done correctly, and Carol's reputation remained beyond reproach.

The first load was ready to be intercepted, and the truck was to be stopped just north of San Diego! Although Jason and Carol were not to be in the team taking control of the truck they would be just far enough away to watch the action as it all happened.

There was one intercept car with the driver plus three passengers, and Jason with Garry watched as the truck was stopped. The car pulled alongside the 18 wheel semi trailer and the driver was signaled to stop, simply by hand signals! When Jason asked Carol why he wasn't stopped via the CB radio which all trucks carry, she laughed and said, "We don't want all of the trucks on the road from here to Los Angeles to know a heist was underway, the Mafia would know within minutes and then there would be a gunfight? We are prepared for that but we don't really want that to happen! The raiders quickly cut the locks and put new ones in place! That's to lock in any riders in the trailer, in they cannot use their radios in those refrigerated trucks, and any person riding shotgun in the driver's cabin will have been disarmed by now.

The truck driver was hustled into the intercept car then blindfolded and a driver from the car took over!

The truck was then driven to a pre- arranged location with gunmen in the car following at as safe distance as needed. The trailer doors were opened up cautiously in anticipation of gunmen within the load, but the original driver had been telling the truth he had no escort, and that he had been going direct to Chicago with the load, he claimed not to know of any drugs on board, which could be quite true?

All the time Jason had been watching the truck hijacking he had been deep in thought, "why he asked don't we just destroy the load, and not have to bother with getting the drugs then destroying them etc?"

"Just because we want to set the Mafia up to fight each other, and in so doing get the one who ordered the murders in Australia, isn't that what you want?" Carol asked. "Oh and also didn't we want to keep ourselves a secret, and not let the gangs know that there is a team setting out to cause problems, by destroying their drug supplies'. If you want to change that system it is far easier just to destroy the drugs and let them try to find us, which I assure you they will and then there will be a real problem, we have been far too successful for them to let us carry on destroying their businesses. Then some of our team members will die, but it's up to you we can make the change right now if you wish!" Carol said with a confident laugh.

"No let us carry on and do the complete job then we can talk tactics later, I understand what you are saying the only part I don't like is danger to our own teams, that is totally unacceptable!" Jason said wistfully.

The men were working in the hijacked truck for about three hours when suddenly a two tonne load capacity van pulled in behind the trailer and the doors of both vehicles opened. It took about 15 minutes for the men to load several cartons into the van and then the car and the van left for their two different destinations? The original truck driver was taken still in the car and let out in a lonely stretch of road still blindfolded, and bound up so it would take at least a half an hour for him to free himself, then find his way to a phone. By the time he was able to send out the warning; both the car and the van would be safe and the load disposed of! The hijacked truck had also been taken to a lonely spot and abandoned, just waiting to be found, and the legal load delivered minus the drugs.

Carol had followed the van to another isolated spot; and she had taken it over with Jason following in the car they had been both been in. The original car was ready to pick up the gang of hijackers and they drove off into the night!

Jason followed Carol to an isolated river, and helped her to dump the Cocaine into the water! There was 20 cartons each weighing about 30 kgs so all told at least 600 kgs that would never get to the market place in Chicago. The van was abandoned over twenty miles away then the car after the plates had been removed, was also abandoned quite a way from any of the other stolen vehicles, the job was complete.

Carol and Jason stayed in an L/a motel just outside Orange County and the next day took turns driving home to Scarsdale Phoenix.

Jason was in a quandary, they had two choices if they continued to steal the illegal drugs and destroy them they would still have secrecy. None of the gangs would believe the drugs were being destroyed and they would fight among themselves. The confusion created would cause a panic among the gangs and 'DAS would go still unknown as the war escalated and got under way'. On the other hand if they revealed they were just another gang, destroying drugs, there would be a full scale search for them and they would be found quite quickly. The big advantage would be ease with which the raids could be carried out, and the drugs destroyed in transit to their illegal destinations.

Carol had calculated that they could safely work on the basis of destroying about 5 tonne of hard drugs a year; and another 5 tonnes of Cannabis? They could do that safely for several years, because the gangs would be so busy fighting they wouldn't step back and realize the truth. On the other hand Carol said that in her opinion if they went the way of just destroying the loads; they should only stay for 6 months then get out before they were all killed.

In the end Jason decided they would stick with what they were doing, and just carry on quietly with the goal to destroy the drugs as they had just done. He also assured Carol he would be happy to destroy the drugs and keep it all quiet and fairly safe, he agreed with her that the drug lords wouldn't be chasing a gang such as theirs, they would be searching for a fairly big drug ring?

Carol received a message from the Mexican operatives asking her to come to Mexico, for a one day trip because they had plans to give her that were too comprehensive and dangerous, to be sent she had best pick them up rather urgently? When she arrived they had information about a big load of drugs going to Florida in a small private seaplane, there would be stuffed on board one tonne of Cannabis and 600 kgs of Cocaine. The load was to be picked up in a two tonne rental van and delivered to a warehouse for the Chicago Mafia, but it would be a very dangerous bust. They had all of the details, time of arrival, pick up point, and the route being taken to drive to Chicago, which of course could be changed at the last minute? There would be a convoy escort for the van all of the way, with ten trigger happy guards five in a car up front and five in another car out back and another five gunmen in the Van. The three vehicles would be in contact only via a modern navigation system, they would not be allowed to make any type of wireless contact at all, for fear of a police intercept. Carol went back to Phoenix with a lot on her mind, this would be a hard bust to perform; the gang had too much at stake this time, and if this cargo should be lost there would be big trouble. She knew that she needed the full resources of the Arizona Police force, and the FBI because the drugs were being transported across state borders. There wasn't much use talking to Jason about what she was to do, until her plan was complete; after all that's what he paid her for to work out the plan, and then go to him for final approval. The first thing she needed was police help, but that negated what she had agreed to with Jason, so she needed police help but then she needed to steal the drugs off them. This would be a fait accompli if she could pull it off! Getting the police help was easy her husband could arrange that, but then it was how would they steal the drugs at great risk only to destroy them? This again needed the help of her husband, they needed the Arizona police to deal with the two cars front and back, while posing as the FBI a team of her own picked crim's they would take the drug vehicle and then destroy the drugs, while pretending they had got away with the lot. Carol having worked out her plan then went home to discuss it with her husband, who fully supported her and Jason as being a gang of drug buster's, He fully supported what they were doing and agreed it would be foolish to let the police have the drugs, but he could also see that the secrecy of the drugs destruction was vital? It had always been vital their own operatives didn't know the drugs were being destroyed; they were after all only crim's and were bound to boast about that, and who would blame them after stealing so much drugs and then destroying them. The most dangerous period would be at the point of taking over the van, there would have to be a warning given that it was the FBI who was stopping them and the police who had the other two vehicles. There would have to be police vehicles swarming around the whole area, and the gunmen would have to be immobilized, handcuffed and put in another van, one that carried Arizona police license plates. But they would be held in a prison in Arizona until they were released on bond, or the police realized they had been fooled and the drugs stolen. Then there would be a real outcry and a nationwide search initiated, this would be the most dangerous part of the raid, they would have to keep a video of the drugs being destroyed for the future if needed. The van that carried the drugs would be taken over away by four men dressed still in FBI style and delivered to Jason and Carol for them to do with whatever they had planned. First Carol got an agreement from her husband to help, provided he was shown the video of the drugs being destroyed. Then she explained her plan to Jason who immediately agreed do whatever he could to help her spring the whole trap. The both knew it was dangerous, and it depended if the 'Chicago Mafia could be made to believe one of the other Mafia groups had stolen their drugs. Carol knew them all and had no doubt they would blame New York, probably in collusion with Las Vegas,' this would start a war with the Dons and Carol with her team would lay low for about three months. During this period Carol would work to prepare for another spate of busts, but also she would spend time in Australia and NZ perfecting their team work there.

The time for the raid was getting close, the same proto cols as Australia was to be followed, but this time with Carols husband arranging the raid by police, and only telling the swat teams at the last minute what was happening. Carol had arranged to get FBI badges on loan, Jason couldn't believe just what was happening, but she reminded him she had the rank of Commander of police, which remained with her for the rest of her life. Her husband was waiting to be promoted to a police commissioner, so as she laughingly said you have some heavies on your side, because what you have done is good. Carol said the key was being so small, the police numbers are so big it was inevitable there would be rogues in all of the forces, including the FBI. Finally it was time and the start of the program to steal drugs were underway, two spotters had been employed to ensure the drugs arrived on schedule and were picked up, everything was just as Carol had been advised they would be. The seaplane had arrived the drugs had been transferred and now the vehicles were on route to Chicago, three of them. First in the convoy was a car with five gunmen in it, then came a two tonne van with another five gunmen in it, finally came the last car with another five gunmen in it, it was a real show of force by the Chicago Mafia. Carol had an unmarked helicopter in which she and Jason rode, its listening device was so sensitive that all of the men could be heard talking in the criminal convoy. All of the fifteen men were obviously high in their Mafia gangs and one could be heard saying, we better get through with this load or there will be real hell to play. There is real bad blood already, goodness only knows what will happen if we lose this lot of drugs. Another said hell they will need an army to stop us this time, the police aren't geared to deal with a team this size, we would sacrifice the lot of them. Yeah that's unless they bring in a swat team said another, then we would be in real trouble, those barsted's are bloody dynamite once they get involved? The helicopter had to land for a while then, Carol didn't want the drivers to spot that they were being tracked from the air, no use setting of the fireworks to early? But she had radio contact with her husband who advised they were right on target with a large swat team to take on the criminals in the cars at the right time. His teams were well aware of the size of the group they had to subdue and they knew the FBI were going to take the drugs and store them for evidence to be used at the right time if needed. After all this was supposed to be a Federal Bust! It had been arranged where he drugs were to be destroyed in a furnace, but Carol was to video the burning so the evidence was irrefutable, after the drugs had been burnt copies were to be kept one for Jason one for Carol, but both would store them in their bank vaults for safety if they should ever need them. Carol would show hers to her husband!

The call from the spotters came in, the crim's vehicles were only ten miles from the raid point, so it was time to take off again but now there was no need for secrecy. Once the Swat team attacked the fight would be on, so the helicopter now hung an FBI flag to its antenna and instructions could be bellowed out from the air if needed. At the same time the listening device in the helicopter was on at full volume! The helicopter was almost in place when there was a yell from one of the cars bloody hell, it's the coppers and they have a full swat team with them, what the hell do we do now? Then another spoke up and said yeah, and they also have the FBI with them; bloody hell this is going to be real tough. To add to the drama Carol started speaking into a bull horn and demanding surrender or they would all be annihilated without mercy. Probably motivated by the fear of retribution in Chicago, the criminals in the cars decided to fight, while the van tried to run the blockade. This of course was suicide and within minutes several of the gang members were dead, and the rest wounded. The attack was so quick and methodical it was almost over before it started. The van with the drugs was run down by the FBI; and the vehicle confiscated with its entire cargo! The surviving gangster's were tidied up and all arrested by the police. The FBI left with the drug van, going to their own headquarters, after arranging to meet at Police headquarters the next day. It was a fast but bloody triumph, although none of the police or swat team had been injured. Carol had said to Jason she would love to have given some of the drug load to the police so the criminals could be jailed for long terms, but they both decided that would be stretching their luck a bit too far. In the end they compromised and destroyed only the Cocaine of which there was 600 kgs and took the one tonne of Cannabis to the police station in the van, and left it parked outside. Then Carol rang her husband and told him what they had done, so they had the 'drug bust and the Mafia in Chicago would blame the FBI; for stealing the Cocaine. The crim's would be safe in Jail from the anger of their bosses in Chicago and Las Vegas!' This was a great climax to a very dangerous bust, without the police and swat it would not have worked. Jason had calculated there had been well over one hundred police swarming all over the place, he felt no sorrow for those real bad criminals who wouldn't have hesitated to kill if they could have done so. 'They destroyed the Cocaine, but kept a video of the destruction as Carol's husband had advised them to do, just in case in future they needed evidence to show they weren't drug dealers. When they both got back to Phoenix it was for a well earned rest, they had taken 1.6 tonnes of drugs out of the Chicago Mafia hands.' Only the Arizona media took much notice for the rest of the country it wasn't worth talking about, except for a few lines on the back pages or an added comment on sky news.

Jean was now almost eight months pregnant and the family were including, Mrs. Johnson their Nanny Nurse, was all getting excited and Jason was still predicting another little girl. Jason Jnr; was running around talking about another baby, and Jean Jnr; who was able to talk now and was asking when do baby come mummy? Jason was as excited as a little boy, this baby was number three that was half way to the six both he and

Jean wanted, as for Jean well she was Mum in waiting, and would be glad when the little one had finally arrived, then she sighed we will be half way. In her own moments of privacy she often wondered how mothers with a full quiver of babies, could survive without a nurse. Jean had little work to do around the house, Nanny and Jason did it all; and they would do, until the baby was born.

It was only on rare occasions now that Jason went to the office, Carol controlled everything Jason was so lucky he had been able to employ her, her connections with the police through herself and occasionally her husband went very deep that had been proved with the successful raid that had just been completed. The operators would be reporting in soon about what the Mafia Dons were doing, these reports were being awaited anxiously Jason and Carol wondered what would happen, Jason was feeling as if he was indeed getting revenge in a very big way?

Carol had been planning well in advance, for her it was more the success of her own vendetta against the drug lords, she hated everything they stood for and felt so blessed to have got her job; through which she felt she was achieving something that she could never have done in her old job, what she was doing now meant far more to her than money ever could? I have a lot of work to do here Carol was thinking, but it's also necessary to keep the pressure on in Australia and NZ she was getting tired of the travel, but it was part of the job so she would soon have to fly out once again even though she didn't really want too.

It was the next day the reports from the operatives started to come in, 'the Chicago and Las Vegas Mafia Dons were absolutely devastated it was a huge loss to them both, the street value lost was huge,' and the effect would be felt right through the mafia system, so much so that both Dons may be forced to resign. It had now come in reports that only the Cannabis had been taken by the police and the FBI agents had been just a bunch of crim's after the Cocaine which they had got, so even with their massive precautions the Mafia had still lost. All of the Dons were going to meet and unless the problems could be resolved there would be a war, and a lot of fatalities would follow, 'the Chicago Don was looking for retribution, but New York was telling them to go to blazes'. Because of the impending war Carol had decided to stay at home for the time being, she was still in a position to arrest any malcontents who looked ready to start a fight, or actually started one. She was still a lifetime commander of the American police entitled to make arrests any time she thought she could prove a case; especially when it came to arresting Mafia Dons, she would love that?

There was no information coming out from meetings being held by the Dons, because there had been a blackout on everything being planned at top level. The leaders from all over the country had descended on Chicago, and only top level operatives knew what was being discussed. Carol had warned all of her team to stay clean; she didn't want any more information for at least two months, only their pays would be coming through. Carol's husband through police link's would find out soon enough, what action the Dons were going to introduce this was the best way to go, this was a point of extreme danger for her team, and she didn't want for there to be any sudden executions of her own operatives. Everything was very quiet for at least two weeks, the Dons had left and gone back to their own territories, and all seemed to have settled down, even Carol's husband could get no information it was all so weird. Then an important call came in for Carol, 'the Chicago Don and two of his senior men were dead as well as the Las Vegas Don he also had been executed'. Apparently the two dead Dons had been weakened by the temporary loss of their senior men who were still being held in jail in Arizona, and the 'New York and Los Angeles Dons had put out contracts on all of the men executed'. The three men in Chicago had simply been accosted and shot at close range by gunmen, and at exactly the same time the 'Don in LA had been executed in the same way'. The murders had been simple and clean in the usual Mafia fashion and Carol didn't think there would be any arrests; it had all been too professionally done. She had immediately asked for and arranged a meeting in Australia to check how the team was doing over there.

Jason was quite pleased after all he had achieved his objective, the execution of the Australians and assault on himself had been revenged, but he just couldn't get used to the idea that he had caused so much death. It was only a few days later that Jean gave birth to a healthy baby girl, and for a while his attention was distracted from the work just completed. Mother and child were healthy and in great condition, and little Jean was so very excited she had a little sister, Jnr; wasn't so sure he had wanted a brother, and he insisted on driving Nanny Crazy asking why the baby was a girl.

Jason had rung Dave to ask him to come to Phoenix when he could get a chance, even though his schedule was busy. Dave had told Jason they were running out of supplies so where could they go for more, he had thought perhaps Indonesia. His three teams were all performing well and they would be a little over USD12 billion in sales for the year, but he expected that to be about the limit from Australia and NZ. Jason had asked if they could hold sales at that level without Indonesia; and Dave had admitted they could with a small annual growth maybe 7-8%. Jason had said he didn't feel very inclined to keep growing as they had been doing, he felt what they was turning over was sufficient. They closed off with Dave agreeing to come to Phoenix within the next two weeks.

Meanwhile in Auckland Carol had met with her office team and everything was in order, then she had flown to Sydney and met with her operatives there, and again everything was in order, they had information for her but she had decided against any action just at that time. She didn't divulge what was going on back in the USA; she realized the Mafia would find other sources for drugs quite quickly. Carol merely told her team to keep up the good work but there would be no more raids for another two months, then she gratefully settled down for her flight back to LAX then home to Phoenix the next day. Carol got back to Phoenix just a few days before Dave arrived, so for Jason it was very convenient because he had decided what he was going to do for the future, mainly it involved 'no more Drug raids in future he intended for DAS; to be strictly for gathering information and passing it on to the police'. He had decided this because he realized it was all getting out of hand! He was well aware he had started the whole vengeful situation, but now too many deaths were being caused, certainly he had attacked the Chicago Mafia successfully but it was now time to stop.

He knew that if the Mafia discovered how they had been duped, they would retaliate in Australia and many of the staff at Cooperate Developments Ltd; would be killed without mercy. After he arrived Dave was allowed a day's rest before the meeting, Carol had arrived two days earlier from her long flight, so she was fit enough to attend just as soon as Dave was.

We all know, started Jason that both of the groups have been very successful at achieving the goals we originally set, up so now it's time to look at a new set of goals. It's shameful to admit that a lot of people have died because of me and my crusade, but I must admit it's not what is my most treasured aim in life, even though I know many of the victims bought their deaths on themselves. To start with the 'DAS work in future will be only an information gathering operation! All future good leads gleaned from what we receive from our operatives; is to be passed on to the police, but only ones that you know can be trusted Carol. It needs to be done in such a way that your identity as the one passing the leads on is kept secret at all times. Now Dave your work has reached the apex of achievement, but again the goals have been met so you are to settle down to a steady growth and the aim shall be 5% per annum, starting from a base of USD12 billion. As you know the profits are huge from this business we set up Dave, but they are of no use to me, so I am going to set up another charity based here in Scottsdale. This definitely is my last effort from now on it's my aim to go into private practice here in Phoenix, having a quiet life doing my own thing, and believe me it won't be making money or chasing drug dealers those days are over. From the time it's all legally set up the charity will own everything, but if you will both accept the responsibility you are both to be the trustees with me still in charge? If not we will have to find others, but the Charity work will be funding drug clinics but not running them, that's doctors work. The clinics will be in "New York, L/A, Chicago, Las Vegas, Auckland in NZ, Sydney and Melbourne in Australia. My Wife and I will be spending a lot of time setting up drug clinics and finding doctors we can back.

Both of you your jobs will be the same, but you report back to the Trustees, you will be self employed contractors. In other words all profits left over after all costs from both businesses are paid will go to the Charity. The Charity will be there to support drug clinics that need financial help, those that can prove their work is really helping addicts. The starting money for the Charity will be the USD50 million, that I kept for the work against drug dealers Dave, but we never had to use it so we will pass it over to this new Charity. This money plus the profits you are making about USD500 million per year but let's say USD300 million will allow quite a lot of support for drug clinics every year, this will be a worthwhile work for everybody, but it will only work if you can control those crim's working for you Carol? Jason said looking at her. I will of course be here to work as a consultant for TDS Dave, and I will charge 60% of my usual fee or USD15, 000 per day.

What would be nice is if you could set up a detective agency as a front Carol and have some private investigators on call to do work for you, then we could have an office together. It wouldn't matter if you get no work and none for me actually. But you need an office to run "DAS" information, and it would be nice to share a receptionist in an office together Carol wouldn't it?

Carol was quiet for a minute as she absorbed Jason words, "First she said it will be great to share an office with you Jason, and let me give you my congratulations, you have helped rid this world of some human scum, who were fouling the air they breathed but I know how hard it's been for you. My husband feels the same way and he sent his congratulations with me today. I think your moves are correct, this way what we will be doing will be completely legal, and my husband and me both have the right connections to use the information properly, keeping trace that drugs aren't stolen by crooked cops. Now one thing before you quit let's do one raid where the police are using our information and just watch your plan in action. I would just love to do that and we will have my husband along just for fun, and it would be nice for you to meet him. As far as being a trustee is concerned, yes it would be my privilege to work in such a needy environment.

"I would love that, to meet your husband just as soon as you set it up I will be ready, and thank you for joining me in running the Charitable trust" Jason replied.

Dave had been sitting with a melancholy look on his face, but now it was his turn to comment. "It's been a long road boss and you have mentored me for almost twenty years, I hope it's in me to do what you want me to do. TDS is after all a USD12 billion a year business, with a huge profit can I really run it that's the big question? But let's just say I will give it my best shot. It's not so easy to go out in the weather when there's always been a shelter, but let's have a go. Like Carol I would like you to do a trip with me and you can see what has developed from what we originally set up it's amazing, you are welcome to come also Carol a world trip paid for by TDS. Bring your husband have a holiday, I know Jean won't come she has a new baby girl to look after. Now again the trustee situation Jason, I think maybe someday but not yet it would be just too much for me to deal with. When I can find my feet and get used to having no backstop to run to when we have a need could be different, but no its not yet. Look James at CDL is still always asking for you and he's a top operator, so yes it's a trepiditous time for me.

Well said Jason with a laugh, "the advice will still be there, but it will cost $15,000 a day that's the big difference, you can tell James the same but he will have to come here because I am staying home with my family from now on. No more business deals for me just Jean and the children and a small consultancy business."But yes first let us do one last bust together Carol, then let's do a world trip with Dave just to watch his team in operation. We will all go first class and charge it all up to him, watcha reckon bout that mate.

Written by Vincent Havelund

❀

Introduction:

Short Stories (# 8)

1973 (# 1)

The Council;

What have Politicians and Beauracrats got in common? They all have intellects below the norm and are overpaid for their low intellect.

There are two officious looking characters out in the office to see you Mr. Stephens; can you come out as soon as possible please? A disaster was about to engulf a very successful company. The fight was to last for two years cost a lot of money and losses of time and from the start, and create a good income for a local lawyer. A company with a multimillion dollar turnover was soon to lose its' way, and baffle the Directors into making bad decisions.

The two characters when Vince entered the office, handed him a Court Order to close the factory down within thirty days. When Vince asked what was wrong and why the Council had decided to close the factory down, the answer was given with very superior airs. This company said the superior one is breaking the terms of it's' license, in that you are selling products to retail clients and only have manufacturing rights.

"Well why have we not been warned, of the Council intention to take this matter to Court? We would have opposed this application, and there would have been litigation to stop this action, now we will have to apply to have this set aside. This is silly and a waste of time and money for us; can we not discuss this with the Council properly?" Vince Asked politely.

"No you can't do anything we have this Court Order there to close you down and I intend to see that order is enforced. You have deliberately done the wrong thing now the position is that I representing the Council have the right to close you down." 'This was said with such a superior air that

Vinces' anger became uncontrollable'. "Now listen you arrogant clown don't tell me that you have the power of life and death over this company, you are just a public servant now get out. You will hear from our lawyer as we apply for a set aside, how the hell you know what we can or cannot do. You are just a clown for the Council let me repeat now, get out!" Vince snarled angrily.

Vince was a Junior Partner out of three Directors and he had the right to answer the way he did, the letter he was given did order the company to close down. He was aware that the lack of being given a notice to desist left the Council out of order, and the chance of a set aside was strong.

A lawyer was retained to apply for a set aside and he was told clearly what was wanted, but each week all he seemed to get was remanded for seven days. He insisted on payment each Friday before the Court sitting at 10.00am and he demanded the money in cash not cheques.

This procedure was continued for three months in spite of complaints of the three Directors. Finally one of the Directors said, "Vince we want to fire the lawyer you are to deal with the Court please."

Why is that Vince asked? You know I am not a lawyer my training is as an Accountant that is my work, not dealing with legal problems. What if the case is lost because I am not good enough?

During the time while the Court action was being followed we had the constant harassment by Council. One week the Council Health Inspectors came and gave the company a list of supposed wrongs. As soon as those problems had been fixed, then the Federal Inspector came and left another list of complaints. Then when those problems were fixed then the Health Dept Inspectors came and left another list, which had to be corrected.

To make it so irritating the factory was new the equipment was all new, and the factory was such that the last inspector had to crawl under the enclosed machines and search hard with a torch to find fault.

One month after the Health Dept Inspector had been, and the problems fixed the Council Inspector was back with a torch to have another inspection. This time in anger Vince wanted to know what the hell was going on the response was, "look for me it's just following instructions, but let me tell you, they want you to kick one of the inspectors out then, you will lose the set aside request. My advice is just do what we ask, there can't be much now its real; hard to find any faults, but I don't want to lose my job. Get that lawyer of yours to hurry this case through, that's what you must do believe me.

Vince realized the inspector was right but at no stage had he thought to take over from the lawyer, because the lawyer was not doing anything effective. Then when he was asked to take the case over he realized that maybe his fellow Directors were right. Maybe the lawyer was really working with the Council, and waiting for the company to fold.

Reluctantly, Vince agreed to take over and do his best, but he was very clear this is the first time for me to do something like this, don't blame me if we fail? The other two agreed so it was left to them to sack the lawyer, and Vince would face the Court the following week.

When the time came to attend the Court the Magistrate asked for the Lawyer who represented the company.

We don't have a lawyer anymore your honor I am the Public Officer and a Director of the company, the Directors have requested that you accept me to speak for the company please.

That's accepted now gentlemen are you ready to proceed please. Vince was very quick to say yes you're Honor; the Council Lawyer seemed hesitant but agreed yes they were ready.

Well it's about time this case has been a nuisance every week asking for a remand.

When both parties had presented their arguments the Judge said without preamble, the Court finds for the Defendant, the Court order to close this company is set aside as requested. Thank you gentlemen and thank goodness that's over.

1975: (# 2)

The compo lawyer.

What have we got when three male lawyers are together in the one room? Two full brains.

It was the day we were due in Court with the claim by the Compensation Dept; for not having a compensation policy paid up for the company's staff. Vince was appearing for the Directors and he knew exactly what at happened and why. In fact Vince had taken over the company a week after the accident in contra for an unpaid bill; this wasn't a company in which he managed the accounts. At the time of the accident two men had been killed on the way to work, when they collided with a car. The two men were on a motor bike, and under Australian Compensation Laws should have been insured. The case was listed for 10.00 am Company the defendant versus the Compensation Board as the plaintiff etc; and Vince was there for the Defendant. Suddenly a little fellow came up to him obviously a lawyer with his satchel tucked under his arm, "You Stephens? He asked, and do you have a lawyer to represent you in this very serious case?" a real nasty little fellow very full of his own importance.

"Yes I am Mr. Stephens and no I don't have a lawyer, don't need one! Why do you ask anyhow young man?" said in a lofty tone one to match the lawyer's arrogance.

"Well you don't really, but you would be wise to because you will be up against me in the court. I will really take you to the cleaners for this lack of company responsibility," said our little man.

"OK fella lets just leave it shall we, because you are really making me nervous now. It's obvious you must be a great lawyer else you wouldn't accost me like this, but that's ok let me try to defend our company, and thank you for the warning!" Vince said with a very big smile.

"That's ok just wanted you to know, that you need experience for this it's a very serious case; and I intend to sue you for a lot of money. That's my next step you know, because you have two deaths in this case its very serious. Today I will prove negligence then I will prove you owe us a lot of money, because I have to pay these cases out you know," said our friend who was so puffed up with how important he was.

"Oh it's such a shame! Yes this will cost a lot of money, but it's doubtful you can prove negligence as you say, let's just wait and see first shall we?" smiled Vince.

The case is called and the two parties enter ready for this big battle. The Judge asks are you ready to proceed gentlemen, both mumble yes and so the fights away. The Lawyer is looking like a cock rooster as he puts his case to the judge. Then Vince stands, gives his written explanation and then sits down.

'The Judge responds by saying Mr. Stephens your case is strong, but you need advice, this case is adjourned until 2.00 and you are to go now to see the Court Magistrate he will advise you. You will both report back here at 2.00 pm'!

The magistrate gives the advice and the two, report back as ordered. Vince stands and asks for a two week adjournment as he had been advised. The Judge agrees and supports the request.

As they leave the Court the little lawyer comes to Vince and says, "You are a real smart Alec, but it's no use against me, I will fix you good next time, I will to teach you a lesson black man".

"Ok little man, you are the dumbest lawyer who ever spoke to me, can you not see what a fool you are making of yourself? You couldn't intimidate me even in a nightmare now for goodness sake run away, and play marbles with the little kids please?" Vince replies pompously.

'I am gonna fix you raved the little man as he stalked off angrily, smart Alec black man you wait till next time in court, I will fix you up real good'.

The day before they are due back in court the phone rings, it's the little lawyer bloke and he says quietly in what is meant to be an intimidatory voice. "It's me, your opponent, I want to warn you we will have two Barristers with me in court tomorrow, we are going to get you smart Alec black man."

"Yes it will be hard to sleep tonight as the thought of facing you again tomorrow, permeates my dreams. Gee you don't need to be so cruel! Do you really need two Barristers? Gee now I won't sleep at all tonight this isn't fair you know?" Vince said trying hard to suppress his mirth.

The next day in Court our little hero is there, and he has two other blokes with him, but they don't come near Vince. The little bloke is waving his hands and pointing at Vince angrily, while his two companions nod their heads wisely.

The case is called and the three acting for the Plaintiff introduced themselves. They then announce their intent to take witness evidence from Vince in the Court.

Vince has already placed his statement to the Court and the Plaintiff and Judge have copies, he has done exactly as advised by the magistrate.

Vince is sworn into the witness box and is ready to proceed. The questions flow and Vince answers all of them clearly and concisely without effort.

After about ten minutes the Judge interrupts by banging down his gavel, "You are now just repeating yourself lawyer, Mr. Stephens has answered all of your questions have you no new ones please? 'No your Honor is the reply there are no more questions, thank you says the Barrister'. Thank you. Stand down Mr. Stephens' case dismissed. I find for the Defendant case closed.

1985 (# 3)

Trucking Sydney Melbourne & return:

That overnight run between Sydney and Melbourne in a semi trailer, down the Hume Highway is a bloody nightmare; just ask Vince if this is true.

An order had been received to supply Pine roof battens to a major firm in Melbourne, but they had to be delivered! Vince had tried to get a competitive price to have them delivered, but gave up and decided to take the load himself on one of his own semi trailers? He was going to be one of the drivers and the other was one of his usual drivers based at one of the timber mills in Richmond NSW. The truck a Volvo N12 with a normal full length trailer, was meant for interstate work but was used for heavy loads between Newcastle and Wollongong and back, to and from one of his three mills? There was no interest in a back load from Melbourne, the time spent waiting to get loaded and then having to unload in Sydney, was not profitable for one of the company trucks?

The load was picked up by the other driver from the Mill at Wyong NSW; about one hundred kilometers North of Sydney. Vince had joined truck and driver on its way through at Liverpool a Suburb of Sydney! Until one actually drives the Hume Highway overnight in one of those road goliaths, one has no understanding of how tough that trip is? Well before they arrived in Melbourne, Vince was regretting his decision to be one of the drivers? With a gross weight of over forty ton those giants of the road are sheer hard work! Vince wandered what it must have been like before power steering, air conditioning and the chattering CB, this trip must have been tough even in his modern all facility truck.

Every little gradient of the road on the way down they had to drop down at least five of the twelve gears, and then when at the top go back up five. If it was a steep hill it was down about seven gears and go to sleep until the truck finally crested the hill, then again up to top gear. There are twelve gears in a road ranger gear box and it's up and down all blasted night and day, no wonder truckers are a crazy bunch. Vince decided this would be his last time ever trip, on the Hume highway to Melbourne return run, in any truck big or small, that's a hard way to make a living too hard for him?

The CB chatters all of the way, which is great else most of them would fall asleep, especially up the hills where the trucks crawl along at about twelve kilometers an hour? The crazy talk sounds silly, but when one is actually driving one of those big brutes, one must go brain dead within one month anyhow? Vince felt brain dead long before they arrived in Melbourne, where much to his horror he found they had to go through most of the suburbs to reach their customers site. The drive from then for Vince was a nightmare, every stop and there were many, it was way down through the gear box and then all the way up to about number seven and then stop again. Then there's another damned stop and it's the same old story, up and down up and down, if he was not brain dead when they hit Melbourne, he was by time they arrived at the destination.

When they arrived at their destination the fork lift was broken down and was being fixed, there was a wait of six hours, but they both went to sleep in the truck cabin? One slept in the sleeper the other on the cab seat, struth it was like sleeping on a railway track with no pillow or anything else? Vince was the owner, but he was the one doing all the complaining, the driver being staff got the bed, and slept like a baby? When he awoke he wanted to know what the hell Vince was whinging about! He had slept all the way through Melbourne and then for six hours at the depot, he thought it was a pretty good trip even if at that stage they had been away over twenty two hours? What the hell he asked are you whinging about boss?

Finally they were unloaded and it was the drivers turn back through Melbourne, but now with an empty truck he whistled all the way, it was he said very easy a great trip! The bunk in the sleeper is fine if the truck is stationary, because there is no noise or bumping. But with an empty truck it just feels like a bucking horse, there is no weight to hold the thing down so it throws the sleeper every where?

Then the driver had worked his quota and wanted to stop and sleep, bugger you said Vince you can sleep like I just did jumping all over the road! So now it's back in the driver's seat and on the way again, but if you go too fast it's easier to hold a bucking bronco? Now the blasted thing is bucking all over the road at speeds between 20 kph and 60 kph, it bucks boy she bucks? But over that speed it floats along as if in a wind tunnel, so you don't want to slow down! There is now hardly any changing of gears she has no weight, so will pull along from almost stop in top gear. Incidentally it was a range rover gear box and Vince is well able to drive clutch less!

The prettiest sight on the way back is the truck stop at Goulburn and then finally into Liverpool. That was the worst drive Vince ever had in his whole life, yet his truck had all the mod cons, the driver thought it was a great trip? Vince has never done the trip again from then on he sent two drivers and stayed home himself; he reckons trucking is too hard for him thanks.

1989: (# 4)

New York PD

Those New York cops are real smart Alecs', again just ask Vince!

Vince was going to a business meeting in Sydney with a leading Australian property owner, his accountant's and legal team had been called; and Vince Stephens was asked if he could attend. He was to be made an offer he would not be able to resist; Vince decided to go out of curiosity nothing more. Why he wandered with some amusement would those George Street geniuses, want to talk to a small time back yarder like me? It was a meeting that would take him all around the world several times, and waste a lot of his hard earned money as he got caught in the recession of 1987-1992. He also got entangled with the New York Police Dept. for a brief period.

It was June 1986 when the phone in Vinces' office rang and an accountant he knew asked Vince if he would come to a meeting in the Sydney office of a leading Law Firm. He and his Partner and a Developer who was known by most of the business community would be present. To Vinces' laughing enquiry of why would you hotshots want me to come to such a meeting, he replied? "You are the only one with the right experience, but also the nerve to take this contract on don't laugh the fee if you succeed will be up to thirty five million US Dollars. This elicited a bigger laugh from Vince yeah sure and Santa Claus is real he said, but ok since we know each other I will come, but if it's all bull you will get a bill for wasting my time. Much to Vinces' surprise the meeting was of interest, after a long and complicated meeting an agreement was reached and all parties left satisfied none had wasted their time. The work that had to be done was the setting up of the thirty four companies owned by the Developer into one holding company, and the raising of three hundred and fifty million US dollars off shore from Australia.

Vince was to pay for all valuations costing two million Aussie dollars and all of his own costs. In the event of success the fee was to be 10% of all money borrowed. Vince had thirty days to accept or decline the offer, and if he accepted a contract would be given guaranteeing that commissions of 10% would automatically be deducted from any loans raised.

The contract was signed in Dec 1986, and the stock market collapsed about six months after. The property market for about eighteen months after, seemed to absorb money being diverted from shares and strengthen, but then also collapsed.

Vince had two years to get the developers chaotic affairs into order then had to travel overseas to raise the loans. One Australian bank and a very large international bank was near collapse, this was why the developer needed to consolidate his affairs overseas. In spite of the developer having his affairs in a mess, his payments on all of his loans were in top class order. The valuations on his properties came to nearly one billion dollars, and he owed only three hundred and fifty million to various banks.

Of all parties at the meeting that day Vince was certain none could see the trap he was walking into. The problem was paying all his costs plus the valuations, at least two and a half million dollars in cash needed. It took valuers almost two years to produce the valuations.

Vince left for America late in 1988 before the property, financial collapse, and had no inkling of the problems ahead. After starting enquiries in Los Angeles then going on to Boston on the East Coast following finance leads, he then arrived in New York just before Xmas 1988.

After negotiations with many of the Wall St firms, Vince got his first solid possible offer, from Americas' biggest Insurance Company that looked very positive. This was in March 1989, but he had to go to Alabama for more talks. These talks resulted in a solid written offer being received, and the instructions to attend a meeting back in New York in three weeks time, for the signing of contracts.

Obviously Vince was jubilant he had the money after less than six months in America, he flew back to New York just in time to attend the meeting. It will be good to be going home, hope the Family are all well he was thinking I must ring them when the contract is signed and it's all ready to be handed back to the developers' advisors. It sure will be good when this whole deal is completed it's now getting boring.

After arriving in New York Vince went to the appointed meeting place for the preliminary meeting, and was exactly on time. Two burly men came up to him and after showing him badges confirming they were New York Detectives, they asked if Vince was the Australian con man who was setting up a scam. You are we believe working with American con men to scam an insurance company.

Vince was very deflated but defiant, I have he said, "All of the legitimate papers here in my brief case to prove this is no scam; we are the ones being scammed! What the hell is going on here he demanded to know? It has cost us a heap of money to do all of this work, and now it's all just a rip off, well I'll go hopping to hell."

The Detective's laughed at the Aussie outburst, after a cursory examination of all documents the Detectives agreed that Vince was indeed being scammed, and only their information had saved him.

Vince returned to his hotel room that night very disappointed but accepting the reality, he was indeed in America where anything can happen. But a scam of that size WOW.

1992: (# 5)

The tax Dept

My friends they turned out to be, a client rang the tax dept; to check me out in 1996 and he was delighted, they gave a top reference and they have never audited our company accounts ever again in spite of my not being a tax licensed agent. _

Good morning Mr. Stephens we are from the investigation branch at the Tax Office, we have to do a full audit of your companies. How many do you have and who does the annual tax returns? Oh and we have to pick up all the account books are they up to date? We will return the books when we are finished if there are no problems, but if there are problems then we will have to meet with you and your accountants.

You are welcome to the books but you will have to sign for them. I have fifteen companies, but they are ones in which my position is as the Public Officer. We don't own shares in any of them except my own administration and that's not a company. I am the Accountant for all of the Companies, but never sat my final qualification exams in New Zealand, that's why you will find me as the Public Officer in all of them. This means the Directors can appoint me to represent their Companies at the Tax Office and in the Equity Court, in the State of Registration.

There you are fellas' the full accounts of the fifteen companies, my private returns and registrations, now if you will sign here you are more than welcome. You will have to have them back within a month or I will come looking for them down at your office. Our accounts are kept strictly up to date on the financials; we don't operate as Accountants we actually advise management at any time we are asked. If we get behind, we would be in trouble if we cannot give correct information, so let me warn you we will be chasing you both in 30 days.

Vince had forgotten the episode until he realized the month accounts couldn't be done, so he rang the tax office and said, to one of the men who had picked up his books, "Where are my account books we need them back today?"

"Yeah sure Mr. Stephens was the reply we were going to ring you later today for a meeting with you next week. The holdup has been because you owe us sixty thousand dollars?" said the voice on the phone.

That's rubbish if we are maybe fifty dollars out then it might be true, but what you are saying is just rubbish. Now young man I will be there in an hour and you will give me my books. Then you and your mate will show me what this rubbish is you are claiming, and we will show you why you are wrong.

As promised Vince was there in an hour and he and his book keeper stalked into that office. Now show me the books he demanded and you better get ready to apologize, because this has almost caused me a heart attack.

Well we are very sorry Mr. Stephens, but we can't help it if you don't keep accurate books now can we said the investigator with a smarmy smile?

Yes well we will soon see about that, now show me why our accounts are wrong, turning to Book Keeper he snarled you had better be right Yvonne.

"Here there is your problem!" said the two investigators looking very happy with themselves. "It's as we say you owe sixty thousand dollars see?"

Looking quickly at what they were pointing at Vince then said, "How can you two be qualified investigators that's wrong look here, what the hell do you two think you are doing?"

The two miscreants looked and sure enough it was very plain, Stephens was right there was a dreadfully easy mistake to see and the tax experts were really out on a limb for bad work.

Now you too smarty's you had better bring out your boss, because there is going to be some very hard words spoken here today, we won't waste any more time with you two incompetents shall we?

Within seconds the boss had come out with his two soldiers, all with big smiles on their faces. Mr. Stephens the Boss started to say, but Vince cut in quickly.

Now you three had better listen to me, I have had heart problems, and suffer from nervous tension. When you two said we owed over sixty thousand dollars, my heart started to palpitate. Now the issue is whether our group should initiate legal proceedings against you three, for total incompetence. What do you three think we should do just in case my heart is now irreparable? Had there been a reasonable mistake well and good, but this is nonsense and we all know that, so what have you to say boss.

I would very much appreciate it if we could overlook this silly mistake Mr. Stephens. Just to show our feelings of stupidity, we will cancel out the five hundred dollars you do owe.

"Well gentlemen let me think about it first, I will check with my cardiologist and he can tell me what to do. Oh what the hell yes we will forget it, but let's hope you two don't treat some other poor bugger like this at some time, we all know what bullies you tax guys can be. Gentlemen it's over, but you remember to put that credit through, as you have promised now boss," Vince said.

"Yes for sure Mr. Stephens consider it done and these two won't make such a silly mistake again, or they will have to retire from this tax office believe me!" he said.

Vincent and his book keeper left and after a wee while she asked, "how is your heart problem boss"?

"What heart problem?" Vince replied, "I said had heart problems and that there were problems, then I said check with my cardiologist I didn't say what we were checking now did we"? Asked Vince with a smile at his book keeper. "Serve those two bullies right don't you agree"?

1957: #6

The Bull and the electric fence;

Ever thought of what it would be like to put your doodle on an electric fence on full bull charge, NO? Well let me tell ya about a big Friesian Bull that accidentally did!

Good morning Mate how are you feeling? We have two Jersey cows coming into season; (Mating) and you need to make sure that damned Friesian Bull doesn't get at them before milking time tonight; they have to go to the Jersey Bull. 'Just to be safe put the electric fence on full bull strength so that big fella can't get at them cows, he can be real dangerous when he knows there are cows ready and he can't get to them'. The cows are in the next paddock but they should be right, find yourself some work to do where you can keep an eye on them.

OK Boss there is some fences to be mended in that paddock so I will do that today, and at the same time keep an eye on the big bloke. He doesn't like us anyhow he blames me when he misses out and the little Jersey gets a go, pity there wasn't one for each of them. The fences stop the Jersey Bull but that big Friesian if he sees cows on heat that's it, he just goes straight through doesn't even feel the barbed wire, but the electric fence usually stops him.

Now down next to the Bull paddock: Good morning Bully Boy how is your mood today? Don't blame me if the cows come in and you miss out, you just aint the right breed for this lot. Anyhow the boss says there is two of the girls' coming into season today so I guess you're going to be real annoyed with me. Never mind the fence is on full strength for you big fella so you had better behave. All of a sudden there's a low growl from Bully boy he is very agitated the boss was right two of the cows are in heat and showing up strong. 'They are jumping on each other's backs and playing at being Lesbians and boy is Bully Boy getting annoyed, he is looking at me and wishing he could kick my butt'.

Wow there he goes he just touched the electricity, boy look at him jump. Now he is pacing up and down that wire and looking at me as if to say, "Mate if only I could get a hold of you it would be a great pleasure to stamp you into the ground; before going down to look after those two females."

'Wow look at those cows boy they sure are hot for the bull sorry about that, but orders are orders and they aint for you fella the little fella gets both of them at milking time'. Look at Jersey Joe way over in those top paddocks, 'he doesn't even know he's got such a nice present tonight if he did he would be kicking up a fuss and wanting them now'.

'Up and down up and down Bully Boy stamps in anger, all the time looking at me in a terrible rage. If looks could kill I would have been dead over an hour ago'.

If he did get through the electric and barbed wire fence there is no way anyone could stop him except those two cows down there in the herd. 'Those females are still going crazy it's as if they are deliberately teasing Bully Boy', but hell they are only cows surely they aint doing that to the poor bugger or are they? 'Crikey look at that he's has his old doodle unsheathed and its hanging down eighteen inches' and swinging from side to side as he walks up and down those wire and electric fences.

Crikey look at those females down there trying to ride the rest of the herd, go for it girls make the big boy swing it higher, he is getting madder and madder by the minute.

Crikey look what's happening now, the entire herd (100 cows) are coming up to the dividing fence to see what bully is going crook about. 'They are standing there over the fence all are shaking their heads as if to say what's wrong with you, you big oaf'? The old cows seem to be saying serves you right, we have to listen to you growling every day!

Wow that was close he nearly hit the electric fence that time, wander what it would be like to get a full shot out of that fence, crikey it would hurt for sure, careful old fella if you aint careful you sure are going to get a shock in your britches, that you won't forget in a hurry?

'Wow there's a go that was less than an inch from the wire; listen to the Big Fella growl, but that aint nothing to what he will have to say if he just swings that thing a little higher'.

Oh now this is tough stuff those two that are in season are right up next to him and still playing around with each other. 'They are really turning on an act for him and the herd I suppose, damned cows they are sillier than ever today'.

'Look at him go and listen to that roar no it's a real bellow now, boy is he mad. He's pacing up and down and looking at me with such anger in his bully eyes, if he could get a hold of me I can see that wish in his eyes'.

'Oh my goodness that done it he hit the electric fence with his doodle, now look at him go his poor old doodle has gone purple, and he is rushing around now as if the world fell on him maybe it'?

'Poor old Bully Boy, he has stopped growling and is trying to fit his massive head under his chest to lick his poor old cooked doodle. His doodle, well that's gone all blue now, wonder if it will still work? Oh well the shows over guess I better get on with this fencing now, but for sure there will be no work done by me in Bully Boys paddock today'!

Pakeha Son in Law,

Bloody Pakehas' ya can't trust the barsted's especially with ya Daughters.

It had been a disastrous day at the surgery; shortage of staff and doctors, inability to service pre operation commitments. Vince's temper was running very short, but having just arrived home the next shock he got was the biggest of the week. The door opened and for once, a usually taciturn (today demur) daughter Maryanne, looped her arms around Vince's neck kissed him and said, "Hi 'Dad how is you?" Three quick thoughts flashed through Vince's agile mind, Mary never jokes the language, she's very excited and she rarely shows her Dad how she really feels, so what the hell is going on here'?

Hm, there's an unpleasant surprise here for me reasoned Vince what's the catch, my Daughter has a surprise for me that's for sure, and it's not going to be to my liking. 'Then the fuss became obvious a large human object, was blocking the view into the family home in Blacktown, and it was standing about three metres behind Maryanne'.

"Dad" Mary chirped with a decided glow in her voice, "This is Mark Craven, Mark this is my Dad." 'Vince managed to step forward, shake Marks hand grunt, hello then escaped into the body of the house, to be met by his beaming wife'.

"What is that object out there with Mary," growled Vince, looks like one of those over height Yankee basketballers only this one's white where the hell did she find it pray tell me, did she steal it from the Zoo?"

"Don't you like him?" asked a badly deflated Wife.

"I didn't say I don't like him, I said I don't like the look of him still I guess with him around me I won't be the ugliest in the family anymore?"

"No you don't, not this time," beamed a reassured Wife, "this one's for real she's got it for real this one and she aint going to let him get away."

'Let him get away, you have gotta be joking if he turns out to be a dead loss, big as he is I will help him on his way and I for sure aint likely to improve his looks believe me," snarled Vince'.

"You can't help yourself can you?" squeaked Wife.

In time even Vince became beguiled by Mark's silver tongue and sound thinking capacity, reassured Vince. 'Mark became a Son in Law in which any father could be proud. At the wedding Vince expressed doubts about anyone taming Maryanne, but he didn't tame her he blended in with her, now that's smart'!

The years were good and soon after a Son was born Nicholas Leslie Craven, when Vince saw how gentle that big guy could be he was astonished. Here was a man who was a better father than Vince had ever been. One day when visiting, little Nick (now three years old) and his father were out deweeding the front driveway edging, Mark was happily pulling weeds and Nick was helping. Vince walked over just as Nick was putting a lump of dirt in his mouth; and looking set for either dinner or a stomach ache. "I don't think that's supposed to be eaten little Fella," said Grandad. Mark just turned to his Son stuck a big finger in the little mouth hoiked out the dirt, admonished again with that big finger, look Daddy said no and continued his work.

This was the first time Vince began to understand his lack as a father, watching Mark perform as a real father was a testing period, but hell it was far too late to change what had been, is an unchangeable truth. The trouble for Vince is the memories keep flooding back, but we know 'one must never look back with regret'.

As the end approaches there is no pleasure in looking forward reminiscing is one of only a few realities left, (pleasures) one cannot look back in regret else one destroys a life of memories, many that are a pleasure to remember." 'In the case of Mark, Mary and Co; the memories Vince has are among the many pleasurable ones.

Their Love for each other has risen above a problem that for many would be a disaster, a mountain many couldn't climb. Like a lot of families a son that is rebellious. Vince is aware of this problem, but it's private and controlled. It's great to watch these two real hands on entrepreneurs, and know that whatever their future they can deal with the problems.

The family has flourished; the work ethic hasn't detracted from the children's well being in any way all except one has flourished. Truthfully this one case is beyond their or any other parents, who are without professional knowledge to deal with this type of difficult problem.

Joshua 18, Caleb 15, Nick 8, Jesse 4, and Vince is starting to see Joshua's problem is really just a adolescent one.

The ugly in Vinces mind only ever referred to Marks size. Vince was envious of Mark's height, but for sure size or not Mark aint ugly now. Vince likes to think that maybe his Daughter helped turn that Drake into a Swan, or is it Goose he can't remember. Vince does know Maryanne Craven and the children are terrific, healthy happy and flourishing and Mark has done so much to create this situation, he is a great Dad.

When Vince heard Mark was going to have his Dad as his best man at the wedding he was deeply impressed. Now that's a wonderful Father and Son relationship. When asked why he had his Father didn't he have any friends? Mark had replied. "Oh yes I have many friends; some since school days but none like my Dad," Vince laughed with admiration. That's not ugly, man that's beautiful._

1957: #8

The Blackbird;

Christchurch NZ has a lot of Blackbirds and they can be really cheeky vicious brutes!

Vince was riding his bike to work at Cross Bros Butchery in Geraldine St; Albans in Christchurch New Zealand. It was 7.25am and he was to start at 7.30 so he was in a hurry, when suddenly he heard a little girl who sounded, terrified screaming. Looking toward the screams Vince could see a Blackbird Pecking at a little girl' who was cowering and screaming loudly! Riding over to the footpath dropping his bike, he then walked up and kicked the bird from behind, allowing the girl to run off into the house whimpering. The bird hopped away defiantly not even trying to fly and looked at Vince, but then decided he was too big to attack so flew off. Vince did not try to follow the girl, he had done what he intended to do now he went to work and arrived a little late.

The suburbs of Christchurch abound with Blackbirds, but this one was extremely aggressive, it was obvious the girl would have been quite injured had Vince not happened along! Vince forgot the incident and continued on to work, which was only about one hundred yards away. He did not even report the matter to the job foreman because he considered the matter insignificant, he was wrong! The only comment that was made was that he had been a few minutes late getting to work that morning. Vince was renowned for arriving a minute before starting time, on that day he was five minutes late.

The next day at work there was a call over the loudspeaker for Vince to come up to the office immediately there was a visitor to see him. Surprised

Vince did as requested and was even more surprised to see two big police men waiting for him. Are you they asked Vincent Stephens of 9 Slater Street St. Albans? And do you ride a bicycle to work in the morning at about 7.30am. All this was asked with Vinces' Boss sitting listening?

The answer to the questions was all yes, so Vince was happy to agree that what they were asking was correct! He then asked why they wanted to know and if there was anything else? He had to get back to work because there were orders to be filled, and the delivery van was waiting for him to complete his part of the work? Having thus explained himself he politely waited for the police reaction!

We are the police said, investigating the claim that you molested a little girl on your way to work yesterday at about 7.25-30am; and we are here to pick you up for investigation. Will you pick up whatever you need and come with us to the St Albans Station?

Pick me up for investigation, it was me that saved that little girl how silly can you be, you should be bringing me a present from her parents? This annoys me the child was being badly attacked by an angry Blackbird which was kicked by me, that saved her! Now you want to pick me up what is this really, because I am a Maori? Why the hell would I want to molest a little girl, couldn't they see the bird's marks on her arms, and I don't have a beak with which to inflict that type of injury. Do you have an arrest warrant or not, to me it seems more like victimization because I am a northerner'.

That will be enough of your cheek Stephens the police Sergeant said, we still need to take you away to consider this report and to have you make out a statement. Turning to Vinces' boss and with a big smile on their faces they said. Sorry Mr. Cross but this man is suspected of assault on a minor, and he is to be interrogated. As you will realize he is a Northern Maori, and we do have a lot of trouble with them types. He may or he may not be back at work tomorrow, it depends on what evidence he can provide to confirm he is innocent of the allegations by this little girls parents'.

Much to Vinces' surprise his boss said this charge if charge it is, is silly, Vince is a highly respected employee here and it will be my pleasure to vouch for his integrity. Let me add he has a very beautiful Wife, at home and believe me has no need to molest girls' either big or small. Now officers' may I suggest you go back to the child's parents' and ask them to check their child's story. Whatever the child says there is no way this man would be interested in molesting her.

The next morning the call came again for Vince to come up to the office! This time the police were accompanied by another well dressed man, who was obviously the child's father.

Bill Cross was sitting in his office padded chair with a big smile on his face. Looking at the stranger and pointing at Vince he said, this is the man who saved your daughter you need to thank him! It is a difficult thing to be accused of such a thing as molesting a little girl, and could have ruined this young man's' reputation, except we know him well.

Yes we know, and that's correct said the man, our Daughter was hysterical and we misunderstood what she was saying. We had a doctor come and sedate her and we know now we wrongly accused you of molestation, my Wife and myself are deeply sorry. He held out his hand to Vince, it was taken and the two shook hands the matter was ended.

The police men then turned to Vince and said you are indeed lucky to have such a boss, a big mistake was almost made. Both of them then shook hands with Vince and left.

Vince only ever had one question, when he wandered did Bill Cross ever see my Wife?